Omnibus edition

SITUATION TRAGEDY
and

MURDER UNPROMPTED

Simon Brett

Back-In-Print Books Ltd

Copyright © Simon Brett 1981, 1982, 2004

The right of Simon Brett to be identified as the Author of the
Work has been asserted by Simon Brett in accordance with the
Copyright, Designs and Patents Act 1988.

Published by Back-In-Print Books Ltd 2004
ISBN 1 903552 42 7
Previously published in Great Britain by
Victor Gollancz under ISBN 0 575 02973 0 and 0 575 03070 4

A CIP catalogue record is available from the British Library.

Printed and bound on demand by
Lightning Source.

Back-In-Print Books Ltd
P O Box 47057
London SW18 1YW
020 8637 0975

www.backinprint.co.uk
info@backinprint.co.uk

When Simon Brett studied at Oxford he became President of the OUDS, appeared in cabarets and directed the Oxford Theatre Group at the Edinburgh Festival Fringe in 1967.

Later he worked as a light entertainment producer for BBC radio and TV before taking up writing full time in 1979.

Simon created the Charles Paris and Mrs Pargeter detective series and, to his fans' relief, he is still writing more. He also made a name as the author of the radio and TV series *After Henry*. The radio series *No Commitments*, the best-selling *How to be a Little Sod* and the novel *Shock to the System*, filmed starring Michael Caine, are other fruits of his imaginative mind. He is married, has three children and lives in a village on the South Downs.

This is a Back-In-Print Book.

- These titles were out of print for some time but Back-In-Print Books has brought them back in to print because of demand from Simon Brett fans.
- This re-print was produced on demand using digital printing technology.
- Paper and print quality are higher than most conventionally printed paperback novels.
- Digital printing may cost somewhat more but ensures that book titles need not go out of print as long as there are readers who want them.

What other titles are available from **BiP** ?

Check out our web site at www.backinprint.co.uk for other titles released by Back-In-Print Books Ltd and news about forthcoming titles.

Do you want any other titles?

If you know of a title which is out of print and you think there might be a reasonable demand please contact us.

Back-In-Print Books Ltd
P O Box 47057
London SW18 1YW
020 8637 0975

www.backinprint.co.uk
info@backinprint.co.uk

SITUATION TRAGEDY

TO THE PEOPLE WHO
TAUGHT ME THE VALUE
OF TELEVISION,
WITH GRATITUDE

"TELEVISION: a medium, so called because it is
neither rare nor well done."

Ernie Kovacs

CHAPTER ONE

THE CAST didn't see the opening titles for West End Television's new situation comedy until just before the Dress Run on the day of the pilot recording in January. Even the Director and Producer hadn't seen the final version till then. The titles were animated and, as every television Cost Planner in the world insists on saying lugubriously at every budget meeting he attends, animation is expensive and takes time. (From the point of view of the cast, the animated titles were a strong encouragement. A pilot show of uncertain future would often be prefaced by a cheap mock-up from Graphics, played over music from disc. The fact that West End Television had invested in animation and had commissioned a special signature tune by none other than Carl Anthony, composer of *Lumpkin!* and other hit musicals, suggested more than tentative confidence in the new project.)

The animation showed cartoon figures of a tweeded Colonel and wispy wife on a golf course. The flags in the holes of the distant greens were Union Jacks. The tweeded Colonel thrashed and puffed bad-temperedly at the ball, while his wispy wife carried his clubs and seemed sweetly to offer unwelcome advice. Carl Anthony's music, though played on steel guitars and synthesisers, had the blimpish overtones of military marches.

Over this pleasing charade, the following words appeared, in varied sizes of type (which had been the subject of earnest discussion between the agents of the various artists involved and the Casting Director who negotiated their contracts):

AURELIA HOWARTH

GEORGE BIRKITT

in

THE STRUTTERS

by

Rod Tisdale

with

BERNARD WALTON

Nick Coxhill *and* Debbi Hartley

These last two, likely to play regular parts in any ensuing series of *The Strutters*, had shrewd agents, who had insisted on their clients being billed at the beginning of the show.

Charles Paris, who would play the regular part of Reg, the golf club barman, in any ensuing series of *The Strutters*, had as his agent one Maurice Skellern, who was so surprised at the prospect of his client being in potentially regular and lucrative employment that he hadn't thought to ask about billing.

Most of the cast were clustered in the audience seats of Studio A at W.E.T. House, watching the titles on the large eidophor screen suspended above them. As the music faded and the screen went blank, Bernard Walton rose to his feet. 'I see,' he commented shortly. 'If I'm wanted, I'll be in my so-called dressing room, Number Three.'

'What's got up his nose?' Charles Paris asked George Birkitt, who was sitting beside him.

'Doesn't like the billing, I imagine.'

'Why? What's wrong with it? He can't surely expect to be above you and Aurelia. It's your show, after all.'

'No, he wouldn't want that. He just probably thinks he should be above the title or have a 'Special Guest Appearance' tag. No doubt he thinks the word "with" is demeaning for someone of his stature.'

'God, it must be awful to have to worry about things like that.'

'Ah well, when you're a Star, it's important. You can't afford to let your status slip.'

'Hmm. I don't think I'll ever have that problem,' said Charles Paris, with his customary accurate assessment of his own position in the theatrical hierarchy. He felt mellow. The price of alcohol was pleasingly subsidised in the West End Television bar. Four glasses of red wine, and a couple of large Bell's to settle them, had slipped down very comfortably. Have to have a pee before the Dress Run starts, he thought lazily.

Once you got used to the pace of television, he found, it was quite pleasant. Once you realised it was just unremittingly slow and that there was lots of hanging around. Of course, it'd be different if you had a big part, if you had to stand around in character all the time they rearranged their cameras, repositioned their sound-booms, and titivated set and costumes. Then you might be affected by the pervading atmosphere of bad temper and barely suppressed panic characteristic of television studios. But when you were playing Reg, the golf club barman, when you had mastered your fourteen lines and two moves during a lazy week of morning rehearsals, and when you had got four glasses of red wine and two large Bell's inside you, you could drift serenely through, unaffected by your environment.

George Birkitt, considering he was about to record his first starring television performance, also seemed commendably relaxed and sensible. He picked up Charles's remark. 'No, heaven forbid. All that star business is just not worth the aggravation.'

'Will you say the same when *The Strutters* is top of the ratings and you can't go into a pub without people saying, "Ooh, look, it's Colonel Strutter"?'

'I'll face that problem when I come to it,' said George with a grin.

'Anyway, there's many a slip, and all that. I've been in too many shows that were going to change the course of theatrical history and then closed after one night, to get too excited about this.'

'Oh, come on, you must have got a frisson when you saw those titles, your name at the top with Aurelia. Must mean something.'

'Not a lot. "Men are led by toys" – I think Napoleon said that.' George Birkitt shrugged non-committally, but there was a gleam of childlike excitement in his eye. Afraid it was too transparent, he changed the subject. 'Perhaps you ought to go and calm Bernard down. He's your friend, isn't he?'

'Hardly,' said Charles, though it was a difficult question to answer. He had known Bernard Walton quite well when the young man had started his theatrical career, and indeed in a production of *She Stoops to Conquer* in Cardiff ('Somewhat leaden-footed' – *Western Mail*) Charles had been the first director to make a feature of the natural stammer which was now such a popular butt of impressionists. But as Bernard Walton's career had shot upwards, he had moved into a rather different league from his former mentor. Charles was quite content that this should be so, since he had never felt a great affinity for the young man, and certainly no affinity for the glamorous, social side of showbusiness in which he now moved. Bernard, however, would occasionally swoop down on Charles with embarrassingly patronising invitations or offers. Charles usually avoided the invitations, feeling, not without justification, that he would only be paraded as evidence of the star's common touch and proof of how loyal he remained to old friends. The moment Charles dreaded was the inevitable one when Bernard became the subject of *This Is Your Life*, and once again wheeled out the old chum from Cardiff to testify to his genuine, unspoiled nature. Gestures like keeping Charles in tow, the charity work he did with handicapped children, fund-raising for the Variety Club and Lords' Taverners (all discreetly leaked to the press by his Publicity Manager), together with comments in the *Sun* about the return of the mini-skirt and descriptions of his favourite pudding in the *TV Times*, ensured that the public was constantly aware of the sheer loveability of Bernard Walton.

On the other hand, though Charles Paris could, and usually did, balk at the social invitations, he never turned down any work that came his way through Bernard. In fact, he hardly ever turned down any work from any source. His was not a career of constant decision, weighing the advantages and disadvantages of one job against another; it was a career of grabbing whatever he was offered quickly, before anyone changed their minds.

And so, when he discovered that Bernard Walton, star of West End Television's hit sit. com., *What'll the Neighbours Say?*, had recommended him for the tiny part of Reg, the golf club barman, in one episode of the series, Charles had had no hesitation in accepting it. He was not then to know, and nor was his magnanimous sponsor, that the success of the minor characters, Colonel and Mrs Strutter (played by George Birkitt and Aurelia Howarth), would be so great that they would be promoted from Bernard's neighbours and sidekicks into the stars of a new spin-off series called *The Strutters*. And that, because of the convenience of the golf club bar for linking scenes (and because the company saw an opportunity to save the expense of a new set), Reg the golf club barman would be a regular character in the new series (if it passed the test of the pilot currently in the studio).

Bernard Walton had condescended to take a guest part, as his old *What'll the Neighbours Say?* character, just for the first episode of the new show, to provide a link for the audience and speed the setting up of the new situation, but he had expected more recognition of his generous gesture. Not just to be dismissed with a 'with'. Nor to be demoted from Dressing Room One, traditionally his on *What'll the Neighbours Say?* recording days, to make way for the recently promoted Aurelia Howarth who, whatever her achievements in a long stage career, had not, to Bernard's way of thinking, anything like his stature in television.

A deeper anxiety, not spoken out loud but hinted at by the cast of *The Strutters*, may also have affected Bernard Walton's state of mind. Though West End Television had an option on dates for a further series of *What'll the Neighbours Say?*, they seemed slow in taking it up. Rumour had it that the company's Director of Programmes, Nigel Frisch, was waiting to see how the public reacted to the spin-off before making a final decision on the parent show.

Which posed a considerable threat to the career of Bernard Walton.

Charles Paris was aware of all this as he talked to George Birkitt about the threatened star. So too was George Birkitt. When Charles had declined the suggestion that he should smooth Bernard's ruffled feathers, saying it was the producer's job, since producers must make themselves useful sometimes, George commented, 'Pity about the dressing room, though. It would have been easier if they'd put me in Number One.'

Responding to Charles's raised eyebrow, he hastened to correct the false impression. 'No, no, I'm not getting big time. I just mean that I could have pretended there was some mistake and done a discreet swap with Bernard. I don't mind having Three. Whereas, Aurelia…By the time you've got that old dear safely installed, it'd be cruelty to move her. And by the time she's got Cocky settled, it'd be impossible.'

Cocky was a singularly revolting, aged Yorkshire terrier belonging to Aurelia Howarth. He was said to have been named after the impresario, C. B. Cochran, one of whose 'Young Ladies' the actress had been.

'Anyway, the dressing rooms aren't our problem,' said Charles. recapturing the Olympian detachment of the slightly drunk.

'Suppose not. Who sorts out who gets which?'

'I think the PA does a list.' It was likely. Production Assistants are responsible for a surprising range of duties in television.

'Ah, the lovely Sadie.' George Birkitt grimaced. 'Well, I wouldn't be surprised if she were deliberately trying to antagonise Bernard. She really seems to enjoy making trouble. Do you know what she said to me this morning?'

'No,' Charles fed obligingly.

'She said, 'Enjoy your brief day of stardom – it's the only one you're likely to get.''

'Charming.'

'Yes, I don't think I've ever met anyone with quite her knack for being gratuitously insulting. I mean, what she said may well be true, but it's not the sort of thing an actor welcomes first thing in the morning on a studio day.'

'No. I think she gets her name from her direct lineage from the Marquis de Sade.'

George Birkitt chuckled politely. There was a pause. He looked at his watch. For the first time he betrayed signs of nervousness. 'If we don't start soon, we're not going to get in a Full Dress Run.'

'What is the time?'

'Nearly five to five. We were meant to start at quarter to. They'll stop at six, however far we've got.'

'Oh, they'll let us finish if –'

'No, they won't. Got to have their forty-five minutes to line the cameras up, and then their hour's meal-break. Union rules. Actually they'll stop on the dot tonight. There's a union meeting at six. In the Carpenter's Shop or somewhere. It was announced over the speakers at lunch – didn't you hear it?'

'No, I...'

'So maybe all our efforts will be in vain. If they call a strike, the show won't get made.'

'That likely?'

'No, I think we'll be all right tonight. But there'll be trouble soon. I've got friends in the know who say all the ITV companies could be out by the summer.'

'What, because the BBC have just got a pay award?'

George Birkitt nodded.

'Yes, of course,' observed Charles Paris sagaciously. 'The BBC went on strike to achieve parity with ITV, so it's only a matter of time before ITV goes on strike to achieve greater disparity from the BBC.'

At this moment the object of their earlier odium, Sadie Wainwright, the PA, appeared on the studio floor from the Production Control. She was tall, blonde and attractive in a thin-lipped way. Her tan seemed to be permanent, as if in homage to her South African origin. She was neatly dressed in beige cord trousers and a flowered shirt. Gold chains clunked round her neck and wrists. She moved purposefully, clutching a pile of white camera cards.

In her wake, hesitant but not daunted, came the trainee PA who was trailing her. At outside rehearsals, where Charles had first registered that she was rather attractive, he had discovered that her name was Jane Lewis. By contrast to Sadie, her skin was almost white, sprinkled with tiny freckles. Her eyes were water-colour blue, but their paleness, together with that of her face, gained distinction from the defiant blackness of her hair, which was centrally parted and cut short.

Sadie made a considerable production of handing out the white cards to the cameramen. 'The Director,' she pronounced, ladling contempt on to the word, 'has changed so many shots in that Sitting Room scene that I've just had to type all these out or you'll never find your way around.'

As she did her tour, she was followed by a tall angular figure in pale green trousers and sympathetically green striped shirt. This was Mort Verdon, the Stage Manager, who was in charge of the outside rehearsals and the organisation of props and a thousand and one other small duties around the studio. One didn't have to see the diamond stud in his ear or hear the swooping drawl of his voice; his every movement had the desired effect of advertising his proud overt gayness.

As he followed behind Sadie, he kept trying to get her attention. 'Sorry, boofle. Sorry, lovely. Quick whisper, eh?'

When she had distributed all her cards, he got his quick whisper. But, though he may have wanted to be discreet, she had no such desire. When she'd heard Mort's request, she snapped, 'No, of course we can't do anything about the dressing rooms at this stage. He'll have to lump it.'

Another fluttering whisper.

'No, the bloody dog has to stay there. Now can we get on with this bloody wake?'

The Floor Manager, a hearty young man called Robin Laughton, who had ambitions to direct, took this as a cue for the start of the dress run. 'Okay, boys and girls, let's have a bit of hush. We are in a Dress Run situation. Can we have all the artistes for –'

'Not yet!' blazed Sadie Wainwright. 'I'm not in the box. You can't start till I'm in the box.'

'But Scott says –' Robin Laughton gestured ineffectually to the earpiece which kept him in direct communication with the director in Production Control.

'Sod Scott! You can't start till I'm in there to do the count-down.'

'Scott says we're pushed for time.'

'And if we are, whose bloody fault is that? What do you expect with directors who don't know what they're doing? Scott Newton – huh. He couldn't direct piss into a pot.'

This colourful invective impressed the studio into silence. The cast stopped muttering in the audience seats. The cameramen disengaged themselves from their cameras. The sound-boom operators hung expectant from their mobile platforms. The assembled throng of scene-shifters, painters, carpenters and men whose only function seemed to be to wear lumberjack checked shirts, suspended their discussion of racing and overtime rates. The dressers stopped bitching and the make-up girls arrested their powder-puffs.

Only one man seemed unaware of the atmosphere. Rod Tisdale, author of many television comedy gems, including *What'll the Neighbours Say?* and *The Strutters*, stepped out of the shadows towards Sadie. He was a man totally without distinguishing features, so ordinary as to be indescribable. The only thing that distinguished him from the archetypal man in the street was the huge amount of money he made from his well-tried writing formula. But since he never spent any of it, even the money was hardly distinctive.

'Sadie,' he said in his toneless voice, 'while there's a lull. I wonder if you could just give a note to Scott. In the Estate Agent's Office scene, I think it'd be better if the Colonel said, "Not in these trousers", rather than "Not in this suit".'

'What?' demanded Sadie scaldingly.

'Should have thought of it before,' Rod Tisdale continued, impervious and without inflection. 'Old rule of comedy – suits aren't funny, trousers are. See what Scott thinks.'

'Suits, trousers – what does it matter?'

'Oh, it matters a lot, Sadie. One's a joke, one isn't.'

'Well, don't bother me with it. Tell your "joke" to little Jane. Maybe she'll write it down in her immaculate shorthand – there must be something she can do.' Sadie turned to leave, but thought of one more parting shot. 'Maybe sometime, Rod, you'll point out the other jokes in this script to me – I was damned if I could see any!'

And she stalked off majestically to the Production Control. The atmosphere relaxed. Charles Paris suddenly was again aware of how much he wanted to do a pee.

But too late. Robin Laughton leapt forward on a cue from his earpiece and cried, 'Okay, we are in a Dress Run situation. We'll take the opening titles as read to save time, and go straight to the Sitting Room scene. Strutters and Removal Men – Okay? And it's only a short scene, so stand by in the Golf Club Bar.'

Oh damn, thought Charles, have to use a bit of self-control.

George Birkitt and Aurelia Howarth took up their opening positions outside the Sitting Room door. On the set the two Removal Men, played by a couple of those character actors who are never out of work, prepared to deliver Rod Tisdale's computerised jokes.

'Okay, bit of hush,' bellowed Robin Laughton. 'This is a Dress Run situation. Good luck, boys and girls. Imagine titles, music, dum-de-dum-de-dum – and cue!'

'Hey, Fred,' said the First Removal Man looking at a cut-glass decanter with a gummed label on it, 'What does F-R-A-G-I-L-E mean?'

But before the Second Removal Man could say, 'I don't know. Chuck it over here and I'll have a look', a new figure bounced on to the studio floor, and, with a cheery cry, ensured that they had to start again.

It was Peter Lipscombe, the show's boyish producer. 'Hello, everyone.' he said. 'Everything okay?'

In spite of their earlier anxiety, they completed the Dress Run in good time. One of the reasons why Rod Tisdale made so much money out of his scripts was that they were always very simple technically. Scott Newton, as a new young director with aspirations, had planned all kinds of clever shots over shoulders, through flower vases and looking down from cranes, but as rehearsals progressed, it had become clear that there was only one way to shoot a Rod Tisdale script, and that was to follow the predictability of the jokes. So the camera script had become a sequence of three linked shots – MCU (Mid-Close-Up) of Character A setting up joke, MCU of Character B delivering pay-off, CU (Close-Up) of reaction from Character A to milk audience laughter. Very little else was needed.

So they finished at five to six, having played their show to the sycophantic laughter of the Producer, the Casting Director (a dramatic ex-actress called Tilly Lake) and the warm-up man, a minor comedian called Charlie Hook, whom Charles Paris remembered, though with little warmth, from a previous pilot he had made for West End Television, *The New Barber and Pole Show*.

Scott Newton bustled out of the Production Control at five to six, with Sadie Wainwright in tow, and Jane Lewis punctiliously following her. 'Right, a few notes,' he said rather feebly.

He didn't look well. The day was proving a strain and he patently wasn't getting the moral support a director can usually count on from his PA. He had only been freelance for about six months, having left a cosy niche in BBC Schools Department for the higher earning potential of the commercial world. Like many others of his age in television, he had recently been divorced, and was finding that the demands of maintenance payments inhibited the glamorous life-style he thought appropriate to a young television director.

The Strutters was his first big show, and he didn't appear to be enjoying it. 'A few notes,' he repeated with even less conviction.

'Okay, boys and girls,' Robin Laughton bellowed, as if testing a famous, but distant, echo. 'We are in a note-giving situation. Could all artists assemble in the Sitting Room set.'

Damn. Charles Paris had been half way out of the studio door on his way to the Gents. Reluctantly, he came back. The pressure on his bladder was almost intolerable.

The cast assembled with indifferent grace in the Sitting Room set. 'Right now, notes,' said Scott Newton slowly.

'Come on, hurry up,' urged Sadie. 'I've got a lot to do. And we'll have to get out of the studio when they start the Line-up at six.'

'Okay, okay, sure. Now, notes. George and Aurelia, in that first scene –'

Peter Lipscombe bounced up again, Tigger-like. 'Hello, everything okay?'

'Yes, yes, fine, thank you, Peter. Just giving a few notes. Er, George and Aurelia, in that –'

'Sorry, love,' interrupted Robin Laughton. 'Can we release cameras and sound? Sound Supervisor just asked me. They've got this union meeting.'

'Yes, sure. Um, George and Aurelia, could you...'

'Oh, I can't wait while you dither around,' snapped Sadie. 'I've got to go and give Telecine all the revised cues. Here are the notes.' She thrust a clipboard at Scott and marched off.

Charles saw his opportunity. What had been an urgent need was now an absolute necessity. 'Just got to nip to the Gents. Be back in a –'

'I'm not surprised, the amount you drink,' Sadie tossed savagely over her shoulder, as she barged out of the studio.

'Okay, Charles,' said Scott Newton, though there was no chance of the actor waiting for permission. 'We'll continue notes in the Control box if we have to move out of here.'

Charles Paris moved swiftly across the studio, trying not to break into the indignity of a run. As he went, he heard Scott continue, 'Now, George and Aurelia –'

'Scott darling,' fluted Aurelia Howarth's cultured elderly voice, 'I am a little worried about Cocky. The poor darling's in the Quick Change Room. I wonder if...'

'Yes, just a –'

'Okay, boys and girls,' bellowed Robin Laughton. 'Six o'clock. We are in a Line-up situation. Clear the studio.'

After the blessed relief of the Gents, Charles splashed water from the basin over his face. Sober up a bit before the next onslaught. It was a long break, an hour and three-quarters, before they were due to start recording. And that would inevitably mean one or two more drinks.

He looked at himself in the mirror. Dressed in the golf club blazer selected by Wardrobe, he looked more respectable than usual. Not in bad nick really for a man of fifty-two. And in work. In work! With the strong possibility of more work. Life felt good.

He walked out of the Gents and started instinctively towards the bar. Sadie Wainwright, in a rare moment of charity, had shown him a quick way up a fire escape on the outside of the building, which avoided waiting for slow lifts. He started up the metal steps, thinking what a flimsy structure it was on the outside of a comparatively modern block. He looked down to the car park some forty feet below.

He was half way up before he remembered the notes. Of course, he must remember that being in work did involve actually doing the job as well as drinking amiably in the bar. He started back down the metal fire escape.

The Production Control box was empty when he got there. All the banks of monitor screens were either blank or showing test cards. There was no one visible through the glass to the left in Vision Control, or to the right in Sound Control. They must be doing the notes elsewhere.

As he turned to go, he heard a voice clearly from one of the speakers. It was a familiar voice, recognisable from its South African twang, and even more recognisable from its tone of contempt.

He only heard two sentences, before the Sound Controller appeared in the box to his right and switched off the sound.

The two sentences were: 'You couldn't kill me. You haven't got it in you.

CHAPTER TWO

'EVERYTHING OKAY, Charles?' asked Peter Lipscombe from his position at the bar.

'Fine, thanks.' Then, feeling that some comment was required, Charles offered the opinion that the recording had gone all right.

The producer confided that he thought it was very exciting, but very exciting. That wasn't exactly the word Charles would have used for the evening but, since the next question was what he would like to drink, he didn't discuss it. The importance of most things diminished when he had a large Bell's in his hand.

Because he had only been in costume above the waist (barmen always being shot with their bottom half obscured by the bar), because he hadn't bothered to remove his make-up, and because he knew the short cut up the fire escape, Charles had managed to be the first of the cast to arrive in the bar. (He didn't pride himself on many abilities, but, in all modesty, had to recognise that he had few rivals in speed of getting to bars after performances.) He sat down with his drink and watched the rest of the actors and crew assemble.

As he did so, he witnessed a transformation of Peter Lipscombe. Whereas during the week of rehearsal the producer had been little in evidence and, when present, unobtrusive and diffident, he was now showing real dynamism in the business of taking people's orders for drinks and putting them through to the barman. Charles wondered whether he had finally answered a question that had puzzled him in all his previous dealings with television comedy. While the director's function, taking rehearsals and organising cameras, was obvious, what on earth was the producer there for? Peter Lipscombe's proficiency as a waiter suggested that at last the function had been explained.

'I think you may have to cope with a success for the first time in your life, Charles.'

The actor looked up to the familiar voice and saw the perfectly groomed figure of his friend Gerald Venables. He had forgotten that the solicitor had asked for a ticket for the recording. Though they had first met at Oxford in the OUDS, for whom Gerald had been an assiduous and commercially successful treasurer, he had never shown much interest in Charles's subsequent theatrical career, except when it involved television. The actor secretly believed that this was because commercial television was the medium whose values were closest to Gerald's own – those being that the sole aim of the arts is to make as much money as possible. The solicitor had certainly followed this tenet in his own show-biz practice, which was one of the reasons why he always walked around looking like the ideal executive in an American Express advertisement. On this occasion he favoured a dark blue double-breasted suit with a nuance of a chalk stripe, a blue-and-red paisley silk tie, and black patent-leather shoes restrained by a redundant strip of metal. The silver hair was trendily coiffed, and the tan would suggest to the uninitiated regular winter use of the sunlamp, but to those who knew Gerald's habits, a recent return from skiing in Verbier.

Charles, now back in his customary sports jacket (described once by a fellow actor as 'a sack with an identity problem'), reflected again on the incongruity of the friendship, as he offered Gerald a drink.

'No, I'm fine, thanks. Just been talking to the Head of Contracts and he bought me one.'

'And you really think this show'll work?'

'Oh, absolutely. It has all the hallmarks of a successful situation comedy.'

'What, you mean total witlessness, exaggerated performances and the perpetuation of harmful prejudices?'

'Now, Charles, you must curb your cynicism. Not only does this offer you more chance of making money than you've ever had in your so-called career, it is also a perfectly adequate, well crafted and well cast little show, which should be good for at least three series.'

'Sorry, I can never judge this sort of comedy. Enumerate its virtues for me, would you?'

'Okay. One, it's a good, simple situation – old fogey from the days of Empire, discipline, National Service, etc. reacting to the slackness of modern life. Two, the script has jokes in the right places and in the right frequency.'

'But they're pretty old ones.'

'That doesn't matter. Audiences like recognition. Old jokes make them feel cosy. Three, it has a very good cast. George Birkitt is a real find. I think that crusty pig-headedness could catch on just like Alf Garnett. The rest of the cast is perfectly adequate…'

'Thank you,' said Charles with some acidity. The word had unfortunate associations for him. One of the high-spots of his theatrical career, his performance of a major Shakespearean role at Colchester, had been hailed in the *Eastern Daily Press* with the sentence, 'Charles Paris provides an adequate Macbeth.'

Gerald continued, unperturbed, 'What is more, the show has a secret ingredient, that little spark of magic which will raise it from the ranks of the commonplace.'

'What's that?'

'It has Aurelia Howarth, my childhood idol. And, though it would have hurt me to admit it at the time, she was not just my idol. The whole country was in love with her – and always has been. Right from those revues back in the Twenties – which, before you make any snide remarks, I was too young to see. But then with all those wonderful movies in the Thirties, and all her work during the war and...and everything. She's absolutely inspired casting. Who thought of her? Was it the producer?'

'I shouldn't think so. Mind you, he's probably capable of buying her a drink.'

'Anyway, as I say, I think you're on to a winner.'

Charles Paris smiled, gratified. 'Well, I hope you're right. And thank you very much for coming to see me.'

'Oh, I didn't come to see you,' said Gerald Venables. 'I only came because I thought you could introduce me to Aurelia Howarth.'

At this moment the object of the solicitor's adoration appeared at the main entrance to the bar. (Charles noticed with satisfaction that nobody else seemed to know about the short cut up the fire escape.)

In describing Aurelia Howarth, it was impossible to avoid the words 'well preserved'. Though she was of the generation who thought it impolite to define a lady's age with too much precision, sheer logic and a knowledge of her theatrical achievements made it impossible for the most gallant admirer to put her birth much later than 1904, which made her at least seventy-five when the pilot of *The Strutters* was recorded. But, with the help of skilled couturiers and a lifetime's practice of make-up, she carried her years gracefully. Even as she entered the bar, encumbered by a huge bouquet under one arm and the odious Cocky under the other, her poise did not desert her. Though she had none of the egocentricity of the prima donna, she could never help making an entrance. Now she paused in the doorway, as if anticipating the applause of recognition. It was not a calculated gesture, just something that was instinctive to her.

She still had the slightness so familiar from early publicity photographs, and still enhanced it by wearing dresses skilfully draped about with diaphanous hangings. These, together with an aureole of pale golden hair (surely not natural, but so subtly coloured as to deny artifice), gave her a blurred outline, as if she was always viewed through soft focus. The skin of her face still had a softness, probably the result of a lifelong application of skin creams, and, though it sagged a little round her eyes and neck, remained commendably taut, but without that synthetic shininess which is the legacy of facelifts.

The eyes retained the pure blue clarity which had been remarked by Sacha Guitry, Jack Buchanan and Noel Coward, and the unfocused, abstracted stare which the pre-war public had found so sexy. They reinforced the aura of charming vagueness, which her manner of speech did nothing to dispel.

She did not have to wait long in the doorway for her appearance to register. Peter Lipscombe gambolled across from the bar, asked, 'Everything okay, Aurelia?' and took her order for a drink. At a slower pace, a very elderly man inched towards her and greeted her effusively.

He was eccentrically dressed in a blue blazer with an elaborate heraldic badge, and what appeared to have been white cricket flannels. His black shoes had the highly polished gloss of a previous generation. An open white flannel shirt revealed a blue, yellow and green cravat, fixed with a pearl-headed pin. The looseness of the cravat accentuated the thinness of a tortoise neck, on which an almost hairless head bobbled uneasily. Face and hands showed the stark contours of the bone beneath, their flesh eroded by the steady wash of age.

'Good Lord, it can't be,' murmured Gerald.

'Can't be what?' asked Charles.

'I think it is, though.'

'Who?'

'It must be.'

'Will you stop being bloody oracular and tell me who it is?'

'Barton Rivers.'

'That's a vaguely familiar name.'

'Aurelia's husband. I thought he must be dead by now. He's nearly ninety, must be. I met him at some charity dinner ten years ago and he seemed so doddery and gaga, I thought he couldn't last long then.'

'They've been married for ever, haven't they?'

'Pretty well. It's always hailed as one of the great show-biz marriages, giving the lie to all those generalisations about show-biz marriages. No, they must have been married in the early Twenties, because I seem to remember they had a son who was old enough to get killed in the war.'

'Barton was an actor, wasn't he?'

'Oh yes, you'll see his face in bit-parts in pre-war British films. Did the revue circuit too. Even wrote a bit, I think. Never as successful as she was, and didn't seem to do anything after the war.'

'Ah.'

'Anyway, come on, what are you hanging about for? Introduce me.'

'Gerald, I can't.'

'Yes, you can.'

When he approached her, he received the full benefit of the misty blue eyes and a throaty, 'Charles, darling.'

'Lovely performance tonight, Aurelia.' It wasn't his usual style, but somehow the old actress's charm seemed to demand it.

'Do call me "Dob", darling,' she cooed. She had always been known as 'Dob' in the business, but Charles wouldn't have dared to use it without her express permission.

Even with it, he had difficulty in bringing himself to say the name. 'Thank you...er...Dob. I'd like, if I may, to introduce you to a friend of mine, who's always been one of your greatest fans.' Charles hated doing things like this. 'Gerald Venables...this is...er...Dob Howarth.'

Gerald took her hand and kissed it gallantly, which was just the sort of thing he would do. Aurelia seemed charmed by the gesture and favoured the solicitor with the beam of her eyes, which still, in spite of her age, remained surprisingly sexy. 'I'm enchanted to think that someone as young as you should remember an old lady like me.'

Gerald glowed predictably, like a schoolboy who had won a prize. Charles tried to work out why he didn't find the exchange as sickening as he did most show-biz sycophancy, and decided it was because Aurelia Howarth was a genuinely warm person.

'But, darlings,' she continued, 'I haven't introduced you to my dear old boy, have I? This is Barton Rivers, my adorable husband...and this is Charles Paris, whom you saw in the show as our barman...and Gerald Venables.'

Charles was impressed by the way she had got the names exactly right. He also felt, through the theatrical hyperbole, a very strong attachment between the old couple.

Barton Rivers grinned hugely, turning his insecure head into even more of a *memento mori*. 'Lovely to meet you, boys. Weather not much good for the Test Match, is it?'

This remark seemed so inapposite at the end of January, that Charles concluded the old boy must now be completely gaga. But then came a wheezing guffaw, which suggested that perhaps the comment had been a joke. Charles chuckled reassuringly.

Gerald was all politeness. Charles often felt in his friend's company that awful childish gaucheness of being with the boy whose manners one's mother has always held up as exemplary.

'I believe, sir,' the solicitor charmed, 'that we met at a Variety Artistes Benevolent Fund dinner about ten years ago.'

Barton Rivers chuckled again. 'Oh yes, must have been a Tuesday. Sun never comes out on Tuesdays.'

This time, surely, there was no doubt that the old boy's mind had gone. But Gerald was not so ill-mannered as to notice any inconsistency. 'Yes, I believe it was,' he went on smoothly. 'I must say, it's a great honour to meet you too, sir.'

'Honour? "What is honour? A word. What is that word, honour? Air",' the old man quoted with sudden lucidity. Charles recognised the line of Falstaff and couldn't help thinking that soon its speaker would die, like its originator, babbling of green fields. But Barton was already off on another tangent. 'Trouble is, though, the Aussies don't know the meaning of the word. All this damned bodyline bowling. You reckon there's a bump on the pitch, do you?'

Gerald replied to this direct question judiciously. 'It wouldn't surprise me at all.'

'Wouldn't surprise you at all, eh?' Barton Rivers guffawed his appreciation. 'Worthy of Noel, young man. Need new young writers with that sort of sharpness. Come and see me after the show one night, young man, and I'll introduce you to Cocky. Hear that, Dob – he said it wouldn't surprise him at all.'

'Yes, darling,' said Aurelia Howarth, and patted her husband's arm with infinite tenderness. She seemed totally unembarrassed by his disconnected chatter.

'Similar thing happened in Paris,' Barton Rivers confided to Gerald. 'No one could be sure, but I knew who was behind it.' He shook his head. 'One bad apple, you know what I mean...'

Gerald nodded wisely.

Charles thought he should say something to Aurelia, to show that he hadn't noticed anything odd about her husband. Maybe something about the dog. He looked without enthusiasm at the little rat body in its shreds of silken fur, and wondered what on earth one says about, or indeed to, a Yorkshire terrier.

The answer was provided by Peter Lipscombe, who arrived at that moment with more drinks. He chucked the little dog under the chin and said, 'Hello, Cocky, everything okay?' Cocky bit his finger.

At this moment Bernard Walton came into the bar. He was with a neat forty-year-old man in a grey suit, and he looked worried. More than worried, he looked as if he was in shock. When Charles recognised the man in the grey suit, he thought perhaps he could guess the reason for the star's discomfiture. It was Nigel Frisch, West End Television's Director of Programmes, the man who was delaying his decision on the future of *What'll the Neighbours Say?*

Nigel Frisch threw his arms round Aurelia and thanked her flamboyantly for her performance. 'Another winner on our hands,' he effused. 'Hello, Barton.'

'Hello, old boy. Keep a straight bat, eh?' Guffaw.

'More news too, Dob darling,' Nigel continued smoothly. 'Sure you've all been in a bit of suspense over the *What'll the Neighbours* situation...'

'Yes,' said Bernard Walton sharply, with uncharacteristic lack of restraint.

'As you know, it's a series that's been really successful for the audience, one that we're very grateful to you for...' Nigel Frisch seemed deliberately to be prolonging the agony, playing Bernard Walton along. He still spoke very casually. 'Obviously it's had its detractors. There are people that feel we've got all the mileage we can out of the situation.' He paused, sadistically. 'I don't know. Haven't really made my final decision yet. But, anyway, what I wanted to say was, we'll certainly be taking up your options for the dates proposed. So even if we don't make the series – and I dare say we will – you'll still get paid.'

Bernard Walton swayed with relief. He still looked pretty tense, but was patently glad of the news. If the company was going to commit itself to the vast outlay involved in contracting him for the next series, then they'd be bound to go ahead with it, he reasoned. 'Oh well, that's nice to hear, Nigel,' he said, recapturing some of his casualness and bonhomie. 'Let me get you a drink to celebrate.'

'I'll have a Perrier water,' said the Director of Programmes.

At that moment George Birkitt and Rod Tisdale arrived in the bar and joined the circle. Having assured Peter Lipscombe (whose finger was still bleeding slightly) that everything was okay, the former, on whom the strains of the day were beginning to tell, ordered a quadruple brandy and the latter a half of lager.

'You pleased, Rod?' asked Nigel Frisch.

'All right,' the writer replied without excitement. 'Sixty-six.'

'I beg your pardon.'

'There were seventy-four jokes in the script. Sixty-six of them got laughs.'

'Ah.'

Charles slipped away from the gushing crowd. His system could only tolerate small doses of show-biz glamour. And Jane Lewis, the Trainee PA, had just come into the bar and was standing on her own.

'Can I get you a drink, Jane?'

'It's Janey.'

'Sorry.'

'Janey. With an E-Y. I decided that'd look better on the roller.'

'Roller?'

'Roller-caption. My credit at the end of the programme. Jane's so ordinary.'

'Oh. Yes. Janey then, would you like a drink?'

'Bacardi coke, please.'

Charles engaged the attention of the barman who wasn't coping with Peter Lipscombe's latest massive order, got the drinks and was encouraged to see that Jane – or rather Janey – was still alone when he returned.

She raised her glass. 'To the success of the show.'

'Hear, hear.' He took a long swallow. He was beginning to feel the effect of the day's drinking. 'How'd you think it went?'

'Part One was about 43 seconds over and Part Two was 1-17 over, but Sadie reckons they'll edit all right. And we're not certain that VTR was stable on one of the Rollback and Mixes.'

'Oh,' said Charles. 'But what about the show itself?'

She looked at him blankly. 'I've said. It was exactly two minutes over in all.'

'Yes.' He paused. 'What do you go on to after this?'

'Next I'm trailing the outside filming on the age-ist series.'

'Age-ist series?'

'Yes. W. E .T.'s just started a new unit for programmes for the elderly. Going to be presented by Ian Reynolds, who's nearly eighty. Phil Middleton – that's the director – said a lot of people would go for someone like Robert Carton as presenter, but he's too boring.'

'Ah.' Janey Lewis was clearly one of those girls who quoted irrelevant conversations verbatim. 'And after that?' Charles asked.

'Don't know. I'd like to get on to another Light Entertainment show, but I don't know. I'd like to get on to the *Wragg and Bowen* show.'

'Ah,' said Charles ambiguously, as if he just might know what she was talking about.

'You've heard, haven't you, that W.E.T.'s just bought *Wragg and Bowen* from the Beeb?'

'Of course,' Charles lied.

'Going to be a huge show, that one. I mean, Wragg and Bowen are definitely the best double act in the country. They're going to be paid ten thousand a week, each.'

'Oh. What's the show going to be like?'

'I don't think that's been worked out yet.'

'Ah.' Their conversation stagnated. Charles was feeling randy with the alcohol and didn't want to leave her. She was a remarkably attractive girl with that black hair and pale skin. Nice shape, too. If only she could talk about something other than television.

But he didn't keep his exclusive hold on her for long. Robin Laughton, the hearty Floor Manager, who appeared now to be in a lager-drinking situation, joined them. Charles found two people talking about television more than he could take, and slipped away to rejoin Gerald.

On his way across, he was accosted by another familiar figure. It was Walter Proud, who had produced Charles's previous, and ill-fated, excursion into West End Television comedy, *The New Barber and Pole Show*. He had lost more hair and there was a wildness in his eyes. 'Hello, Charles, how'd the show go?'

Charles shrugged. 'Those who know about such things seem to think it was okay.'

'Great, great. If you're going over to talk to Nigel Frisch, I'll join you.'

Something rang warning bells for Charles. 'Well, no, I wasn't particularly …What are you working on here?'

'Nothing right now, actually. Got one or two projects sort of around, but, er, nothing right now.' The confession was transparent. Walter Proud was out of work. He'd left his BBC staff job a few years before, and since then had a discontinuous sequence of short contracts with the various commercial companies. 'No, actually, I came down here to see a few chums, see if there was anything going.'

'Any luck?'

'Don't think so. I had a word with a girl who was my PA on something I did here, girl called Sadie Wainwright, but she…No, there doesn't seem to be much around.'

Walter's dismal tone suggested that Sadie had choked him off rather in the same way she had everyone else.

'Oh well, something'll turn up,' said Charles blandly.

'Hope so. Actually, if you are going across to see Nigel Frisch –'

But Charles was saved embarrassment by the arrival of Scott Newton. The young man looked awful. He had no colour, and his face gleamed with a fine sweat. 'Hello, Charles,' he cried, with a sad attempt at conviviality. 'Lovely performance. Can I get you a drink?'

'I think I'd better get you one. You look terrible.'

'No, I'm okay now. Had some sort of bilious bug, don't know, must have been something I ate.'

Charles caught the sour whiff of the young man s breath. He had obviously just been very sick. Something he'd eaten...or, more likely, just the nervous pressures of the day.

'By the way, do you know Walter Proud? You're both BBC renegades, so perhaps you've...'

But no, they hadn't. Charles introduced them.

'You came after the big money too, did you?' asked Walter ironically.

Scott replied in the same tone. 'Bigger, maybe, but not big enough. I seem to have even less since I made the move.'

'If that's the case, then let me buy you a drink.'

'No, no, things aren't that bad.'

They argued a bit, but Walter didn't need much convincing and Scott walked unsteadily to the bar.

'And he's directing you, Charles?' The question was incredulous.

'Yes.'

'God, kids like that get jobs, while people with experience...If I had my way –'

But Charles never found out what would happen if Walter Proud had his way. The door from the fire escape into the bar suddenly burst open to admit Mort Verdon, waving his arms and screaming.

He was making so much noise that everyone was distracted and gathered round him, trying to find out the cause of his agitation.

Charles and Robin Laughton understood at the same moment that it was something he had seen outside on the fire escape, and rushed to the door. Most of the rest of the crowd followed.

It was after half-past ten and dark outside. Charles look down the fire escape, but could see nothing untoward. The car park below was shrouded in darkness.

Then a departing member of West End Television's staff switched on the headlights of his car. A swathe of light cut across the car park.

In the middle of it, at the foot of the fire escape, lay a foreshortened figure in beige cord trousers and a flowered shirt. The light glinted on a gold necklace.

The car's headlights also played on the lower parts of the fire escape. They showed the regular parallels of painted steel and the sudden asymmetry of the railing that had given way.

The car below did not move. Its owner got out to inspect the horror he could half-see ahead.

Charles felt the press of people behind him on the small metal balcony. He looked round at the shocked faces of Robin Laughton, Bernard Walton, Rod Tisdale, George Birkitt, Walter Proud, Scott Newton, Jane Lewis and Aurelia Howarth, and at the grinning incomprehension of Barton Rivers.

There was a long silence as they all looked down at the corpse of Sadie Wainwright, and waited for someone else to be the first to say they were sorry.

Then Peter Lipscombe's cheery face appeared in the doorway. 'Hello,' he said. ''Everything okay?'

CHAPTER THREE

West End Television Ltd,
W.E.T. House,
235–9 Lisson Avenue, London NW1 3PQ.
22nd March, 1979.

Dear Charles,

I'm sure you've already heard from your agent, but I wanted to write personally to say how delighted I am to be able to tell you that *The Strutters* is a 'go proposition'. It's really very exciting news!

I'm sorry it has taken so long for me to be in a position to pass on the news, but the 'powers that be' always take their time deliberating over this sort of thing. However, they have now made up their minds and are backing *The Strutters* all the way. Nigel Frisch really thinks it's one of the most exciting cards he holds, and reckons that with this and the new *Wragg and Bowen* series, W.E.T.'s going to make a very big dent in the BBC's Autumn audience figures!

Many thanks for all your hard work on the pilot, which contributed to make the show such an exciting success. I'm sure you're looking forward to the series as much as we all are – we think it's going to be very exciting! The dates will be within the option period agreed with your agent, with pre-filming probably starting the last week in May, six shows recorded on Tuesday evenings June 12th–July 17th, a couple of weeks' break, and then the remaining six (which, with the pilot, will make a series of thirteen) starting on 3rd August. All sewn up by mid-September.

We at W.E.T. don't believe in changing a winning team, so the casting will all be as for the pilot, and Scott Newton, who did such a splendid job for us then, will again be directing. Rod Tisdale, whose way with a line, as you know, puts him in the Oscar Wilde class, will certainly be writing the first six scripts, though, with the pressure of time, we may bring in other writers for later episodes. But don't worry, we'll keep up the high standards we have set ourselves with that very exciting pilot!

I do hope that everything is OK with you, and that you're going to be able to fit this new very exciting project into your already busy schedule. I very much look forward to seeing you for our preliminary read-through, probably in mid-May, when we hope to assemble as many of the people who worked on the pilot as we can for the start of what I'm sure you'll agree is going to be a very exciting series.

With the warmest good wishes,
Yours sincerely,
Peter
PETER LIPSCOMBE
Producer *The Strutters*

Charles Paris had six reactions after reading the producer's letter.

1. No, he hadn't already heard from his agent, but since his agent was Maurice Skellern, possibly (and this was a bold claim, but one he believed he could substantiate) the least efficient of the breed in existence, that did not surprise him.

2. Yes, it was good news. The Inland Revenue had recently developed an unhealthy interest in his affairs and made the laughable demand that he should supply them with accounts for the last seven years. He felt betrayed by this. How did they know he had earned anything over that period? He certainly hadn't told them. He was left with the unavoidable conclusion that the people who had actually paid him the money must have ratted on him. He reckoned it rather cheapened the magnanimous gesture of paying someone if you then went and told the tax authorities what you'd done.

3. Try as he might, he couldn't find the news as exciting as Peter Lipscombe evidently did. Financially encouraging, yes; good, because being in work was better than being out of work, yes; but he had great difficulty in viewing the prospect of doing fourteen lines and two moves twelve times over with anything approaching excitement.

4. If Peter Lipscombe could seriously describe what Charles had done on the pilot as 'hard work', then he needed his head examined.

5. On the other hand, if Peter Lipscombe dared to refer to Charles's 'already busy schedule', he must be either very ignorant or capable of irony. So perhaps the 'hard work' reference was also a dig.

6. However keen the producer was to assemble everyone who had worked on the pilot, there was one person whose services he would have to forego. And that was the PA, Sadie Wainwright.

The letter made Charles think about her death again. Straight after the pilot he had thought about it quite a lot, and in the eight weeks since it had nagged occasionally at his mind.

Because of his interest in detection and the tendency, that seemed to increase with age, to find himself repeatedly involved in criminal cases, his first instinct was that Sadie Wainwright had been murdered. Falls, he reasoned, are always murders disguised. In detective fiction the next most popular question, after 'Whodunnit?', is 'Did he fall or was he pushed?'

It could have been an accident. On the evening of her death, Charles himself had noticed the rickety nature of the fire escape, and he heard later that the railing that had given way had been eaten through to nothing with rust. On the other hand, Sadie Wainwright, whatever one thought of her character, had seemed to be a supremely efficient woman. Not the sort to make silly mistakes.

Nor, from her surface behaviour, the sort to take her own life.

And, given a theory of murder, one didn't have to look far for people with a motive. Charles knew nothing of her personal circumstances, but it seemed likely that if she behaved at home anything like she did in public, she could well foment considerable resentment in a husband or lover. She had worn a chunky gold wedding ring, but that didn't mean a lot in television; Charles often thought that a broken marriage was one of the qualifications for a job in the medium.

But putting domestic fury, the most common cause of murder, to one side, the studio day had supplied an ample sufficiency of people with reasons to want her out of the way. Indeed, Charles wondered whether there was anyone working on the pilot of *The Strutters* whom she hadn't insulted.

And almost all of them could, in theory, have had the opportunity to get rid of her. He didn't know how many knew of the fire escape short cut. Presumably members of W.E.T. staff were more likely to have the information, but any one of the actors or actresses could have been told, just as he had been.

He had tried many times to reconstruct the events of that evening. He felt fairly confident that Sadie Wainwright had died after he had gone up to the bar. Though he had not actually looked down into the car park, he would surely have noticed the collapsed railing. Anyway, his natural talent for getting to bars quickly had put him ahead of most of the field of suspects.

He remembered that when he reached the bar, the only person present from *The Strutters* recording had been Peter Lipscombe, realising the full potential of his job. That seemed to rule the Producer out of any conjectural list of suspects, but all the others whom Sadie had insulted remained in with a good chance. The fact that Mort Verdon, the discoverer of the body. was the only one who had appeared from the fire escape, did not mean he was the only one who had gone out there. Any murderer worth his salt would have taken the elementary precaution of returning from his crime to the bar via the more conventional lift.

And many of the potential suspects had appeared to be in a highly emotional state. High emotion does not necessarily indicate a recent act of murder, but it can be a pointer.

Bernard Walton had looked unnaturally tense, though that could be put down to anxiety about the future of his series. Walter Proud, too, seemed to be suffering, and admitted a recent altercation with the victim of the 'accident'. And Scott Newton, the young man whose authority his PA had systematically undermined, had been a very late arrival in the bar, and had entered in a terrible nervous state. Any one of those might have had sufficient motive to kill Sadie Wainwright.

But then so might anyone else. That was what really made Charles think the death had been an accident after all. The PA had been so rude to everyone, had antagonised so many people, that it seemed invidious to attribute her death to any one individual. It was more as if the communal will had been so unanimously hostile that an indulgent God had given her a little nudge on the fire escape as a gesture of magnanimous serendipity.

Apparently, an inquest had brought in a verdict of accidental death. No doubt the police had done their customary efficient enquiries. Why should Charles Paris question their findings?

It was all a long time ago, he decided, and he needed a drink. He had been feeling very poor and made firm resolves to cut down his expenditure.

Also, as often happened when he was feeling at his most abject, he had resolved to make contact with his estranged wife, Frances.

But Peter Lipscombe's letter had shifted the mood. Though it didn't contain money, it contained the prospect of money. It gave him the confidence to risk bouncing another cheque on the way to his favourite drinking club, the tatty little Montrose round the back of the Haymarket.

And he could always ring Frances another day.

'First let me say what a pleasure it is to see you all here, and all looking so well. I get that sort of bubbly feeling that everything's going to be okay with *The Strutters*. We've got a wonderful cast, a good team, some terrific scripts, and I think the whole project's going to be jolly exciting.

'Now what I plan to do today – I'm sorry, what Scott and I plan to do today –' the producer inclined his head graciously towards his Director, who acknowledged the gesture with a grin, '– is to have a leisurely read-through of the first five scripts – Number Six will be with us soon – which wonderboy Rod Tisdale has provided for us...'

The wonderboy in question maintained his customary façade of a man on a bus counting the lamp-posts.

'Now this read-through is just so's we get a feeling of the shows – we'll deal with any problems that may come up later. Since we start the filming in a couple of days, I think it's just as well that you should understand the context in which your scenes occur.'

This was a concession that didn't always happen. Charles had frequently been involved in the pre-filming of scenes which were totally meaningless to him as he acted them (and often equally meaningless when he saw the completed product on the screen).

'Now we've got some really exciting locations for the series, so I think the filming should be a lot of fun.'

First time it ever has been, thought Charles sourly. His memories of filming were all of interminable waits, often in vile conditions, usually in the company of huge numbers of people with whom he had nothing in common. But he knew that directors loved it; practically every television director he'd ever met said how much he'd rather be working on film and then started the traditional moan about the demise of the British film industry. He even knew actors who enjoyed it.

'One location in particular, which we are awfully excited to have, is the one we're using for the Strutters' own house exteriors. As you know, that didn't come up in the pilot, but it was pretty well described – a large expensive house with a lot of grounds, conveniently placed on the edge of a golf course. Well, our Location Manager spent a lot of time trying to find just the right place and then – what a stroke of luck – we had the ideal house offered to us, just like that, out of the blue. And offered by someone we all know very well. Yes, good old Bernard, Bernard Walton…he's said we can use his place. Which just happens to fit the bill exactly…'

Peter Lipscombe paused for impressed reaction and got a rather apathetic murmur of appreciation. Like Charles, most of those present had come to distrust Bernard Walton's magnanimous gestures. There was usually an ulterior motive – in this case, no doubt. just to show how big-hearted he was, or to keep a kind of proprietary interest in the series, or to make sure he appeared in any publicity shots that might be taken on his premises or, thought Charles cynically, just to pocket the substantial facility fee which W.E.T. would inevitably pay for the location.

After the producer had said a few more times how exciting everything was, the read-throughs started. At first there was a certain amount of cosy laughter, but this diminished. It wasn't that the scripts got less funny – they maintained unswervingly that level of mediocrity which Peter Lipscombe had hailed as Wildean – but everyone present began to realise the sheer volume of material they had to get through. Five half-hours – even ITV half-hours which read out at twenty minutes (Rod Tisdale's work was always the right length) – was a hell of a lot of reading.

Charles got very bored as he waited for his fourteen lines per episode. However old he got, he never lost the actor's adolescent habit of counting his lines. And, though his realistic view of his status prevented him from aspiring to starring roles, it didn't stop him from finding small parts boring.

He looked around the assembly, wondering idly whether he was in the same room as the murderer of Sadie Wainwright. The little trainee, Janey Lewis, now sat in the PA's chair to the director's right, and clutched the PA's symbol of authority, a stopwatch. So she had benefited directly from Sadie's demise. Another person with a strong motive?

But then they all had strong motives. Or none of them had. Charles decided in a lazy way that he might try to find out a bit more about Sadie's background.

In the meantime, he couldn't help noticing again how attractive Janey Lewis was. She had had her hair cut shorter and more fashionably, and her clothes, too, looked newer and sharper. And there was an indefinable air of increased confidence about her. Maybe this had come with her elevation from trainee status to the full bossing rights of a real PA.

She caught his eye and smiled. Yes, she was attractive. Not mentally, really; conversation with her was like reading a manual of television technique. But physically...And the older Charles got, the less he thought one should dismiss the physical.

At ten to one they finished reading the third script and a folding wall of the conference room in which they sat was pulled back to reveal a lavish buffet and – yippee! – lots of bottles of wine.

Once he was armed with a plate of chicken and Scotch egg and a large glass of red wine, it wasn't difficult to buttonhole the PA. She didn't seem to mind. Charles wondered what else she might not mind. But there was a problem. Had he got the energy to mug up all the vocabulary of television – VTR and MCU and OOV and POV and all that rubbish – which would be essential in this particular seduction? He rather doubted it.

'Hello, Janey, isn't it?'

'Yes.'

'With an E-Y.' He showed off his memory.

'No.'

'What?'

'Janie with an I-E.'

'Oh, but I could have sworn you told me that...'

'Oh yes, I was going to have it with an E-Y, but then I noticed there's a PA at Thames who gets a credit with an E-Y, and I didn't think it looked very good on the screen – you know, a bit ordinary – so I've changed it to I-E.'

'Oh well, at least it sounds the same,' said Charles, and then, with a tiny attempt at humour, added, 'Next thing you'll be spelling it J-A-Y-N-I.''

'That's a thought,' said Janie seriously. 'I'll have to see how it looks written down.'

'Anyway, congratulations. I see you've got the Queen Bee's job now.'

'Yes, I was so lucky. You know, it was because I'd worked on the pilot, I got made up specially.'

'Made up specially?' Charles repeated, looking with mystification at her lightly freckled face which, except for a blur of green about the eyes, seemed remarkably free of cosmetics.

'Made up to PA. A lot of the girls who started as trainees with me still haven't been made up.'

'Ah.'

'Though actually Dinky's got the second PA's job on the big *Wragg and Bowen* show, but I reckon that's not as good as being the only PA, even if it is on a smaller show.'

'Yes, or do I mean no?'

'Anyway, Phil Middleton says he reckons sit com's the best way of learning because you do see the whole thing through, you know, with filming and studio and going right through to the VTR editing.'

Charles agreed randomly.

'The filming's going to be very exciting. Do you know who we've got as cameraman?'

'No?'

'Midge Trumper,' Janie pronounced dramatically.

'Really? Midge Trumper, eh?' said Charles, weighing the name.

'Yes. I mean, and right after *Rainbows Don't Grow On Graves*. I could hardly believe it when I heard.'

'I'm still finding it a bit difficult to take in. Midge Trumper, eh?'

'Yes.'

'Good Lord.'

Charles didn't want to spend the whole of his lunch extolling the virtues of Midge Trumper, whoever he might be, so he asked if Janie would like another drink.

'Hock-A.'

'Hock? I'm not sure. There is a dryish white. I think it's a Muscadet or –'

'No. Hock-A. Hock…A.'

'Hock…A?'

'O…K. Okay. It's how the Japanese say okay.'

'Oh. Okay.'

When he returned with their drinks, he managed to steer the conversation round to Janie's predecessor. 'Quite a hard act you have to follow. Though I must say the atmosphere seems a lot more relaxed without her.'

'Oh, you mean Sadie. Yes, wasn't that terrible. I mean, it's an awful way for me to get a job. I'm not complaining, but it is an awful way to get a job.'

Charles nodded and was rewarded by Janie's continuing, 'Yes, it was awful. Ernie Franklyn Junior says he reckoned anyone could've seen it coming.'

'Really?' said Charles, unwilling to break Janie's flow by asking who the hell Ernie Franklyn Junior was.

'Yes, he reckons she'd been under a lot of pressure.'

'What, at work?'

'No, no, nothing upset her at work. She could manage the job standing on her head. No…' She lowered her voice mysteriously. 'A man.'

'Really?'

'Yes, Ernie Franklyn Junior reckoned she'd just had a big bust-up, you know, end of some long-standing affair.'

'Oh.'

'I think it's daft to get yourself involved in that sort of thing. I believe in short flings, not getting involved.'

Charles quickly invested in the future by saying that he fully agreed, before going on to ask if Janie had any idea who the man in Sadie Wainwright's life had been.

But no. it seemed that Ernie Franklyn Junior's information service could not supply this answer.

'But he reckons it was suicide?'

'Oh yes.'

'In spite of the findings of the inquest?'

'Oh yes. Ernie Franklyn Junior says inquests always try to avoid suicide verdicts.'

'Why?'

'Well, so that people can collect on the insurance.'

'Oh. You wouldn't happen to know who was likely to collect on Sadie's insurance?'

'No. Mind you, Ernie Franklyn Junior says –'

But the Ernie Franklyn Junior Report on the British Legal System was interrupted by the approach of Scott Newton with the Casting Director, Tilly Lake. 'Janie,' asked the director, 'could you get some copies of Script Number Five. You know, the one with the old Army friend of Colonel Strutter's in it. Tilly's got some interesting ideas on casting and wants to send some scripts out for it.'

'Yes,' Tilly Lake trilled, identifying herself (for anyone who missed the hint of the Indian silk shawl and feathered cloche hat) as an ex-actress, 'you see I'm so terribly *anti* conventional casting. I mean, especially in sit com. All directors always seem to end up using the same repertory of actors who do their job awfully well, but with no...depth. I mean, like this part of Colonel Strutter's army friend. I mean most sit com directors would go for someone like...I don't know, say, Toby Root, who's a *perfectly* good actor – lovely actor, lovely person – but I'm sure we can aim higher.'

'Ah.'

'I always try to be unpredictable. I mean, take you, Charles. By no means obvious sit com casting. I mean, so many casting directors, looking at the part of the golf club barman, would go for some old comedian, some actor who's famous and well-loved for a part in another sit com, but whoever booked *What'll The Neighbours*...said, no, let's not go for the obvious, let's think laterally and go for someone who...who...' Her sentence lost momentum. 'And they booked *you*,' she finished lamely.

'Mmm.' Charles suppressed a grin.

But Tilly Lake was only subdued for a moment. 'So, anyway, with this part of the Colonel's friend, I think we should aim high. Not a Toby Root, but why not a Trevor Howard?'

'Just any old Trevor Howard?' asked Charles.

But she appeared not to hear him. 'Why not an Olivier?'

'The simple answer is, because he'd never do it.'

'Ah, but, Charles, you don't *know* that. You never know until you ask. Perhaps he's never taken a guest role in a sit com because he's never been *asked*. I mean, we'd be able to sort out a special fee. Anyway, Scott and I think we should send him a script.'

'Certainly – what,' agreed the Director gnomically.

'Incidentally, Charles...' Tilly Lake purred with sudden intimacy, 'your agent hasn't sent your contract back yet.'

'Ah, no.'

'I hope that doesn't mean there are any problems.'

'Problems? Good Lord, no. That's just the way he works.'

'Ah.'

At that moment Aurelia Howarth wafted up to the group, nursing the vile Cocky in her arms, and followed by George Birkitt. 'Scottie darling,' she cooed, 'have you any idea what time we'll be finishing today? I promised I'd ring Barton and tell him when to come round with the car.'

'Oh, Dob...' Tilly Lake cooed in turn. 'Don't bother Barton. The PA'll order a car for you.'

'Or I could give you a lift,' suggested Scott. 'If you don't mind the Mini. You're more or less on my way and I wanted to have a chat about –'

'No, no, Barton'll pick me up. He always does. He loves driving the Bentley. So what time, Scottie darling?'

'Let me think. I would like to have a quick word with you about something before you go, so, if we reckon to read the scripts in about...'

As Scott tried to estimate the shape of the afternoon, Charles sidled up to George Birkitt. 'Does she really mean that the old boy still drives?'

'Very much so.'

'God, what a terrifying thought. I'm glad I haven't got a car. I wouldn't have a moment's peace if I thought I might meet the old loony careering around in a Bentley.'

'Oh, I dare say he's safe enough. It's only his mind that's gone.'

'That's quite enough. I like to think that most people driving cars have got minds.'

'Hmm' George seemed distracted. 'What do you think of the scripts?'

'They seem remarkably like the pilot.'

'I wonder. I think there are things that'll have to be changed,' George Birkitt said ominously. 'And I'm rather annoyed with the Wardrobe girl.'

'Really?'

'Yes. Well, as you know, I'm the last person to make a fuss about something that isn't important, but I just asked her if she could guarantee that I'd have the same dresser right through the series. It's only a small thing, but it does make a big difference. I mean, when you're concentrating on a performance, you don't want to be thinking about costume changes and things. You want to be sure that all that side is in the hands of a regular dresser you can trust. Don't you find that?'

'Oh, certainly,' agreed Charles Paris, whose eminence in his chosen profession had never merited the attentions of a personal dresser, regular or irregular.

He was pleasantly sedated with wine for the afternoon's readings, but felt a great glow of righteousness from the fact that he did not actually go to sleep. What was more, he didn't miss any of his cues. In both of the remaining scripts, he delivered his fourteen lines impeccably (impeccably, that is, in the character of Reg, the golf club barman, a character chiefly humorous for his drink problem). He felt very professional.

Round about four o'clock they finished the last script. Rod Tisdale appeared unmoved by the rendering of his *oeuvre*. Only once during the day had he spoken. That was at the end of the fourth script, when he had said, 'Peter, I think there should be a change to that line on page 17 of Part Two.'

'Which one, Rod?'

'The Vicar's line. Where he says, "It got stuck in my cupboard".'

'Yes, got it, Rod. What should it be?'

'Can we change it to "It got stuck in my drawers"?'

'Yes, sure, Rod.'

'Silly of me, I should have thought of it earlier. Cupboard not funny, drawers funny – old rule of comedy.'

'Okay, have you all got that change?'

After all the scripts had been read, Peter Lipscombe said again that he thought it was all very exciting and Scott Newton said he thought it was all very exciting too and everyone could go, except for those who were taking part in the filming, whom Wardrobe and Make-up wanted to see. Charles Paris needed no second bidding and made off.

'Charles, Charles!' He was almost out of the building before Mort Verdon caught up with him. The tall Stage Manager had come flapping down some side stairs in pursuit and was breathless. For the read-through he had selected a pale biscuit boiler suit and changed the diamond stud in his ear for a plain gold one.

'Charles, dear, have to give you your calls for the filming. And Wardrobe wants a word. You're a naughty boy to go off like that.'

Charles felt his hand lifted and a mock slap administered.

'But I didn't think I was in any of the filming. I thought I just stayed behind my bar.'

'No, Charles...You must read your script, dear. At the end of Episode Four it said quite clearly "Film. Golf Club Exterior. Reg the barman chases Colonel Strutter off the premises and into his house as the captions roll".'

'So there are no words?'

'No. Just ad lib shouting.'

'Oh well, that explains why I didn't notice it. I only read the speeches.'

'Oh dear.' Mort Verdon made a *Dame aux Camelias* gesture against his forehead and then said, but not vindictively, 'I can see we're going to have trouble with *you*.'

A revolutionary thought struck Charles. 'Does this mean I'll be seen below the waist?'

'Of course.

'But barmen are never seen below the waist. Primary rule of television.'

'First time for everything, dear. Now you come back like a good boy and have those lovely ladies in Wardrobe measure your inside leg for some trousers. I dare say you'll enjoy that.'

'These trousers'd do.'

Mort Verdon narrowed his eyes. 'That I *doubt*.'

'They were a nice pair of trousers ten years ago.'

'I was a very beautiful young man ten years ago, but it doesn't make the crows' tootsies any less prominent now.'

'I'd better come back then.'

'Yes, boofle, that would be best.'

They were alone in the lift, so Charles hazarded a detective probe. 'Pity about Sadie, wasn't it?'

'Yes. Terrible.' As far as it was possible to judge through the drawl, Mort Verdon sounded as if he meant it. 'I'll miss her.'

'Really?'

'Oh yes, she was so much fun.'

'Fun!'

'Yes, dear. Wicked sense of humour.'

'That I can believe.'

'Oh yes, I know her manner was brusque and all that, but underneath she had a...'

He paused, gesticulating for the right word.

'You aren't going to say "heart of gold", are you?'

'Nooo,' he replied, lengthening the vowel into a long swoop. 'No, dear Sadie had a lot of qualities, but I don't think a heart of gold was among them. But she could be very funny sometimes.'

The lift stopped and they walked towards the conference room. Charles persisted with his questioning. 'Had she got a husband around?'

'No, dear, not exactly around. There had been a husband at some point, but I think she left it in South Africa when she came over here.'

'How long ago was that?'

'Don't know exactly, boofle. Must be ten years, I should think, because she was a pretty senior PA here. And of course they don't – or didn't then – have the telly in South Africa, so she must have done all her training here.'

'Ah.' Soon they would be back with the hordes of Strutters. Charles had to be quick. 'Did Sadie have a particular boyfriend?'

'Oh, lots on and off. Most more off than on.' Mort screwed up his face in self-parody and said limply, 'Men can be bastards'. Then he dropped back to his customary level of exaggeration. 'She had just finished something that had been going on for...ooh, six months, I think.'

'Who was the lucky fellow?'

Mort Verdon looked at Charles with mock severity. 'Now there's no need to be ironical, boofle. I doubt if you'd know the guy. anyway. He did a series here about six months ago.'

'What was his name?'

'Walter Proud,' said Mort Verdon as he swept back into the conference room.

CHAPTER FOUR

THE MORNING AFTER the *Strutters* read-through, Charles's eyes opened with their customary reluctance and closed again with their customary promptness, hoping to recapture the dwindling oblivion of sleep.

But it was no good. He was awake. After a few moments of tight-eyed pretence, he let them open again.

He supposed he should be grateful that he slept as well as he did. A lot of his contemporaries complained of long watches through the night and assumed sleeping pills to be a regular part of their diet for the rest of their days.

Charles felt a perverse righteousness from the fact that he hardly ever took sleeping pills. Such a solitary activity. His own solution to the sleep problem, alcohol, was at least taken socially. Usually. Taking sleeping pills was never social. Except in the case of a suicide pact. And that was hardly convivial.

Of course alcohol had its disadvantages, but it was so long since he hadn't woken up with a furred tongue and tender head that he hardly noticed them.

He looked round his bedsitter, trying to delay thinking about things he didn't want to think about. The room had changed little during the seventeen years of his occupancy. He had moved into Hereford Road within a year of walking out on Frances and, except for periods of working out of town or the occasional good fortune of finding a lady willing to share her bed, he had been there ever since.

The fixtures and fittings of the room were unaltered. Still the same low upholstered chair and asymmetrical wooden one, both painted grey by some earlier occupant. The same low table, masked by magazines and papers. The fact that these now covered the portable typewriter expressed well the likelihood of Charles ever getting down to serious writing again. His own contributions to the decor, yellow candlewick on the single bed and a different plastic curtain suspended to hide the sink and gas-ring, had now been there for over ten years, and reached a kind of dull middle age that made them impossible to distinguish from the rest.

Contemplation of the room didn't cheer him.

Perhaps he should get up.

He gave this unwelcome thought a minute or two to settle in his mind.

Charles always envied people who could spring gazelle-like from bed and bound straight up the gradient of the day. He awoke always to the North Face of the morning, and usually held long internal discussions about whether or not to call the whole expedition off, before achieving the precarious base camp of a cup of coffee, from which he could at least contemplate the arduous climb ahead.

So it was on this occasion. When he had made the coffee, he animated it with a slug of Bell's whisky. This was a practice which in principle he deplored, but increasingly he found his principles would waver in the face of life's practicalities.

With the coffee in his hand, he could delay thinking no longer.

There were two things he didn't want to think about. The first was his wife. The school of which Frances was headmistress would soon be breaking up for Easter and he really felt he should get in touch to find out whether she was going away for the holiday. In spite of their estrangement, he liked to know her movements and, though they met comparatively rarely, he could still miss her when he knew her to be away. Also, he wanted to see her.

Still, thinking of Frances did raise all kinds of emotional questions whose answers he wished to continue to evade, so he focused his mind on the less personally challenging subject of Sadie Wainwright's death.

Though he had satisfactorily accepted the common verdict of death by accident or perhaps, following the Ernie Franklyn Junior thesis, death by suicide, there was still one jarring element he couldn't reason away.

It was what he alone had heard in the Production Control cubicle on the day of *The Strutters* recording. Sadie Wainwright saying, You couldn't kill me. You haven't got it in you.'

If only he had heard just a few seconds more, so that he could identify whom she had been addressing. The words, out of context, sounded ominous, but it was quite possible that they were just another example of show-business hyperbole.

He wished he knew a bit more about television studios and their sound systems. He knew that a variety of people could talk back into the Production Control box. Certainly the Sound and Vision Controllers on either side could. So could the four cameramen...and of course the Floor Managers with their little walkie-talkies. Then he was sure he'd heard PAs talking to people or places with technical names like VTR and Telecine. And there was always sound from the studio microphones on their booms.

In fact, Sadie could have been speaking from almost anywhere in the immediate studio area. That didn't give him any clues as to who she was with. Maybe it could be investigated, but two months had passed and, apart from the dauntingly technical nature of the enquiry, Charles thought it unlikely that anyone was going to remember exactly which microphone might have been left open to catch Sadie's words.

But he did now have another line of enquiry. It was one he was reluctant to pursue, because it involved a friend. But he could no longer pretend that he knew nothing of the dead girl's private life. And he had got Walter Proud's phone number.

He decided that they perhaps should meet for a drink.

Walter was very apologetic that they had to meet in a pub. 'I'd have said come round to my place, but really, I've hardly got a place for anyone to come to now.'

'Well, never mind. I'm always happy with a pub.'

But it still seemed to worry Walter. 'Thing is, I've moved from that service flat in Kensington. I'd have invited you round there, but the place I'm in now…well, it's really just a bedsitter.'

The emphasis he put on the last word amused Charles. 'Oh, come on, that's not the end of the world. I live in a bedsitter, you know.'

'Yes, I know. I mean, it's all right for someone like you, but for someone with…' Walter Proud realised he was on the brink of being insulting and stopped. Charles, who wouldn't have been offended anyway, wondered what the next word would have been. Standards? He certainly had standards, but on the whole they didn't concern material possessions.

Walter tried to cover up. 'What I mean is, the last few years have been a series of shocks for me. Angela and I had been married for eighteen years, you know, and we'd been in that house in Datchet for twelve. So when we split up, it was quite an upheaval. I mean, don't get me wrong – I wanted the divorce, no question, but it was…an upheaval. And then leaving the BBC so soon after, and I'd done…what?…fifteen years with the Corporation…well, it all made sense at the time, and it was the right thing to do, careerwise, but…er…'

He seemed unable to resolve the sentence.

'Do you see Angela at all now?'

'No.' Walter Proud sounded very hurt. 'No, she won't see me. I see the girls occasionally, but…'

'I'm sorry,' said Charles formally, giving Walter the opportunity to move on to another subject.

But the producer was unwilling to do so. 'What makes it worse is that she's ill.'

'Angela?'

'Yes. She had a growth, apparently, on her breast, about a year ago and had a…what do they call it…mastectomy. But apparently it didn't get rid of it all. It's spreading.'

'Oh.'

'I only hear this from the girls, you know. I keep offering to go and see Angela, but they say, no, she doesn't want to see me and…I don't know, it makes me feel terrible.'

'Let me get you another drink.' Charles tried another way of breaking the flow, but when he returned with a large gin and tonic and a pint of bitter for himself (still irrigating the brain, move back on to the scotch later), Walter continued.

'You break up a marriage because it doesn't work and because you want to get around a bit, see a few more other women, have a bit of life for God's sake, before you're too old, and then you come up against something like this. And you realise perhaps you are too old, that you're now in the generation to whom illnesses happen, and you should have just stuck together, because there really isn't any time.'

Charles felt a cold pang of depression. Walter's situation was too close to his own for comfort. Suppose something happened to Frances. Suppose she became ill or, worse, was suddenly killed in an accident, and he was nowhere around...He must ring her.

Walter's tale of woe wasn't making it easy for him to get round to the real purpose of their meeting. It was bad enough suspecting a friend of murder, but to interrogate a friend in this sort of state was really kicking a man when he was down.

Fortunately, Walter seemed to realise how low he was getting and made a determined effort to pick himself out of his slough of despond. With something approaching the old bravado Charles remembered, he said, 'Still, a man has to do what a man has to do. I don't really regret any of it. Okay, I was very cosy at the BBC, and, to some extent, at home, but I was dying on my feet. At least I've seen a bit more of life and things by cutting loose.'

'Things...being women?' Charles fed gently.

Walter responded to this man-of-the-world approach. 'Oh yes, there have been one or two. It's only when you're on your own that you realise quite how many of them there are.'

Charles laughed conspiratorially, hoping to stimulate further information, but got nothing more than an answering chuckle. He would have to be a bit more direct in his approach. 'Down at W.E.T., the other day, someone was saying you'd had a bit of a fling with someone there.'

'Oh yes.' Walter smiled a Lothario smile, but then seemed to recollect something unpleasant and changed his manner. 'Yes, it was very unfortunate. The girl died.'

'Really?' said Charles ingenuously.

'Yes, she was...well, you were there.'

'I was there?'

'When you were making that pilot, you remember, the girl who fell off the fire escape.'

'Oh, Good Lord, you mean that PA? What was her name...Sadie?'

'Sadie Wainwright.' Walter nodded. 'Yes, we had a thing. It went on... well, on and off. . . for two or three months.'

'How awful for you, for her to have...'

'Yes, it was pretty upsetting. But in fact the affair was over, had been for a month. Didn't work.'

'But I seem to remember...' (Charles tried to disguise the interrogation in casualness) '...that you said you'd talked to her on that evening.'

'Oh, talked to her, yes. We were still on speaking terms...at least I'd thought we were.

'You mean she wasn't pleased to see you?'

'She was bloody rude, if you must know.'

'Seems to have been a habit with her.'

'Yes, she had a sharp tongue. Mind you, that was only her manner. She could be very…well, different.' Walter Proud seemed to recollect some moment of tenderness, but quickly snapped out of the mood. 'No, I'd gone to see her because she knew everything that was going on at W.E.T.. I thought she might know of something coming up for me. The fact is, Charles, not to put too fine a point on it, I am out of a job. I've been out of a job now for five months. I've tried writing round all the companies, going to see people, using every contact I've ever made, and all of them lead to the same answer – nothing doing.'

'Couldn't you go back to the Beeb?'

'No chance. They're in as bad a state as anyone else. Worse. They've got no money and can't think of taking on new staff. And if they did, I don't think people who resigned three years ago at the age of fifty-four would be top of the list. The BBC is very paternalistic and looks after you very well, so long as you remain on the staff. But if you commit the unforgivable affront of resigning, well, you look after yourself, matey. It's fair enough, but I'm afraid it means, in answer to your question, No, under no circumstances could I go back to the Beeb.'

'Something'll come up,' Charles offered meaninglessly.

'It'd better. Needless to say, I've screwed up the full pension I would have got if I'd stayed.'

'Have you got any savings?'

Walter laughed shortly. 'Never had many. By the time I'd sorted out the divorce and moved a couple of times…And then being out of work is bloody expensive. Trying to get jobs is, anyway. I mean, if you're chatting up an old friend who happens to be a Programme Controller somewhere, then you take him out to the sort of lunch you would have taken him out to in the old days. Except of course in the old days, you would have had an expense account. When you're paying with real money, boy, you notice the difference.'

'So Sadie…' Charles steered the conversation back on to the course he required.

'Yes, Sadie was a last-ditch attempt. A contact. I thought she might know the scene at W.E.T.. Tell me if they'd got all the producer/directors they needed for the new stuff they were doing. I mean, I know they've got *Wragg and Bowen* coming up, and I worked with them at the BBC. And then there's this series for the elderly. A real F.G., if ever I heard one.'

'F.G.?'

'Franchise-Grabber. You may have been aware, Charles, that all the ITV companies' franchises run out in a year or so. And so suddenly all of them have started doing very worthy programmes – stuff for minorities, heavily subsidised operas, all kinds of noble enterprises that they wouldn't normally do in a million years. It's just so that they can show the IBA what public-spirited and responsible companies they are, and why they ought to continue to have their franchises and continue to make huge amounts of money from their usual run of crap.'

This cynicism was unlike Walter, who had always been one of those people, like Peter Lipscombe, who found television enormously *exciting*. He read Charles's reaction. 'Well, I'm just sick of the whole bloody business. God, I wish I'd just stayed in the BBC and coasted quietly down to my pension. Even taken an early retirement. I don't think I'd have any pride left about that sort of thing now. Have you any idea what it's like going round to people all the time, begging them to employ you?'

Charles shrugged. 'I'm an actor.'

'Yes, of course, so you know all about it. But at least you've had practice. I find it's a bit late in life for me to learn how to cope with it.'

'But Sadie,' Charles insisted mildly, 'couldn't help?'

'Wouldn't help certainly. Probably couldn't either.' He looked very doleful. 'Oh, she was probably right.'

'What did she say?'

'That I was past it. Past everything, she said. Certainly washed up as a television producer.'

'Oh, come on. You did some terrific stuff in the past.'

'In the past, yes. And what have I got to show for it? A few press clippings, some stills, cassettes of the later stuff – though that's ironical; I can't afford to keep up the rental of my video cassette recorder, so that's gone back. So I've got nothing. Not even Angela. She's dying quietly in Datchet and here am I drinking gin I can't afford and…'

Walter Proud seemed to be on the verge of tears, which Charles didn't think he could cope with. He wrenched the conversation brutally on to another tack. 'That evening of the pilot, when you came to see Sadie, when did you arrive?'

'When did I arrive?' the producer repeated blankly.

'Yes.'

Suddenly Walter started to laugh. It was a weak and not a jovial sound. 'Oh, Charles, I don't believe it.'

'What?'

'You're off on one of your bloody detective trips, aren't you?'

'Well…'

'Now you think Sadie was murdered and – '

'I think there may have been something strange about the death. I mean, she was a grown woman, she hadn't been drinking, why should she suddenly fall off the fire escape?'

'The railing gave way.'

'Or was helped to give way.'

'Oh really.'

'I'm not the only person who said that.'

'What, you mean all those self-dramatising fools at West End Television think someone gave her a shove?'

'Not that, necessarily. She might have done it herself.'

'Suicide?'

'Possible.'

'Not if you knew Sadie.' Realisation dawned on Walter. 'You mean, you thought she might have...because of me? Because we'd broken up, you thought she might...oh, Charles. It's so wrong it's almost flattering. No, I'm afraid I didn't rate that highly on her list of priorities. I was a few bouts of sex before she decided I was...what was her expression...past it? I don't think I was bloody past it, I think anyone would have found the same with her. I really think she was a nymphomaniac. I don't mean the kind of avid partner one dreams of, but the real thing, someone with a pathological and insatiable desire for sex. It's not very pleasant when you encounter it.'

Charles, who never had, agreed uncertainly. And, since any cover he might have had had been thoroughly blown, asked, 'And you didn't kill her?'

'No, no, sorry. There were times when it might not have been a bad idea, but I'm afraid I never thought of it.'

'So what time did you arrive at W.E.T., that evening?'

'Oh, I see, the full interrogation. I don't get off the hook so easily. Right, I got there about nine. I have cause to remember that, because the doorman wouldn't let me in. Good God, I've produced two or three series for the company, and he wouldn't let me in to the building. Said I had to be vouched for by a member of staff. I got him to page practically every name I could remember ever having met there before I found someone who'd vouch for me and let me in to get a drink. That's the sort of thing that destroys you, Charles. You don't think about it when you've got a job, but, God, it tears you up when you find yourself crawling to doormen like some unwanted alien.'

Charles felt relief. He hadn't wanted to suspect his friend, but he had had to check it. If Walter really had arrived at nine in the evening, and that could be confirmed, then he could not possibly have been the person whose death threat Sadie Wainwright had treated with such contempt. And since those few overheard words were the only real reason why Charles had any suspicions about the accident, Walter seemed effectively to have left the list of suspects.

'So you saw Sadie after the pilot recording finished at ten?'

'That's right. I met someone in the bar who told me what she was doing that evening and waylaid her as she came out of the studio. I suggested a drink and got my head bitten off, so I said what I really wanted to ask her and...'

'Had your other head bitten off?'

'Exactly.'

'So you didn't see her for long?'

'No, she was very short with me. Said she had other fish to fry. And from the tone of her voice I could have believed she meant it literally. I knew the signs well enough to recognise them. She was spoiling for a row with someone.'

'You don't know who?'

'I know where. She didn't even stop to talk to me. I had to tag along by her side while she marched ahead to sort out the next poor sod. She just marched into his dressing room and I heard her say before the door closed, "Right, what is all this, you bastard?"'

'Who was in the dressing room?'

'Ah, I don't know.'

'Which number was it?'

'Number Three.'

Number Three, the dressing room whose allocation to him had caused such affront to Bernard Walton.

CHAPTER FIVE

FILMING DAYS ALWAYS start uncomfortably early. Charles had had a make-up call at seven o'clock. A car had been sent to fetch him, which he might have thought was a flattering recognition of his raised status as an actor if he hadn't seen the prodigality with which television companies send out cars to deliver scripts, pick up cassettes or collect take-away meals. Needless to say, at six-thirty in the morning the driver's tattoo on the front door at Hereford Road had failed to wake Charles, but had disturbed the hive of lumpish Swedish girls who occupied the other bedsitters. With their sing-song remonstrances and the driver's belligerent complaints at being kept waiting, he had left the house in some confusion.

But as he was made up, he relaxed. He always found it a pleasant experience. In the theatre he was used to doing it himself, and to have someone doing it for him was a great luxury. Besides, make-up girls are by tradition extraordinarily attractive. And to sit half-asleep in a comfortable chair while a sweet-smelling girl caresses your face must be the definition of one sort of minor bliss.

Its only disadvantage is that, like all blisses, it is too short. Only seconds after he had sat down, it seemed, the gentle facial massage stopped, a discreet tap on the shoulder made him open his eyes, he had another second to gaze deeply into the brown eyes of the make-up girl, and then it was time to go and join the rest of the cast in the coach which would take them to the location. *Sic transit gloria mundi.* (So it is that transport brings us from the glorious to the mundane.)

On the coach, Charles saw that George Birkitt had an empty seat beside him and made towards it, but the actor indicated a pile of scripts and said, 'Sorry, old boy, lot of studying to do. I seem to have a damned lot of lines to learn for this bloody filming.'

So Charles went and sat by Debbi Hartley, the actress who played the Strutters' *au pair*. She was a pretty little blonde of about twenty-five, but he had never fancied her. She was the clone of too many other pretty little actresses of twenty-five, and her self-absorption was so great that it was almost impossible to think of her in a sexual context.

She did not seem to object to his company, and started animatedly into a monologue about the wisdom of having her hair cut short once the *Strutters* series was over. Whereas her agent thought it would make her look younger, certain of her friends were of the opinion that it might make her look older. This was obviously of enormous relevance because when one went up for an interview (Charles had noticed how the new generation of actors never used the word 'audition'), first impressions were vital and if the director thought of one as too old, one wouldn't stand a chance for ingenue roles, or if he thought of one as too young, then one wouldn't get the sort of *femme fatale* parts, because no one ever realised how versatile one was and it was so difficult to avoid getting typecast, but she, Debbi, thought she was just at the stage in her career to do something a bit different, so showing she could do other things as well as the little-bit-of-fluff parts, what did Charles think?

Since he didn't really think anything, he didn't say anything, but his lack of response did not deflect Debbi from the course of her debate.

Charles looked round. The coach was filling up. Mort Verdon stood at the front, checking names against a clipboard. Janie Lewis entered importantly, carrying piles of bits of paper. He contemplated joining her and exchanging discussion of hair length for that of the relative merits of film and mobile VTR recording, quoted directly from Ernie Franklyn Junior or some other guru of the W.E.T. canteen. There wasn't much to choose in conversation; the only difference was that he did fancy Janie, whereas he didn't fancy Debbi.

On the other hand…By the time the coach was on Westway, his eyes had closed. Beside him, Debbi Hartley continued to enumerate her virtues as an actress. It was half an hour before she noticed he was asleep.

Bernard Walton lived in a large house, set on a hill between Cookham and Bourne End. Charles woke up as the coach turned off the main road into his drive. The house was at this point invisible because of the steepness of the incline, but the approach was impressive. A gravel drive zigzagged up through immaculately planted gardens. Neat stone walls bordered it and on these, at intervals, stood tall terracotta urns from which variegated displays of flowers spilled.

As the coach groaned and protested through its lowest gears on the hairpin turns, its occupants could see the view the house commanded. At the foot of the hill, green, flat water-meadows spread to the broad gleam of the Thames. Beyond, woods obscured most signs of human habitation.

Round one last corner and they saw the house itself. It was Thirties Tudor, black and white, not scoring many aesthetic marks, but impressive just for its bulk and position. A tennis court and a service cottage brought right angles to the landscaped curves of the garden. Beyond a neat privet hedge could be seen the polite undulations of a golf course. If the whole location had a manufactured air, it was very fitting for the character of its owner.

Bernard Walton stood in front of the large oak door waving welcome. More than welcome, he was waving possession and condescension. By allowing *The Strutters* to use his home, he had given the series his seal of approval. But he had also diminished it, as if it existed only by his mandate.

Charles caught George Birkitt's eye. 'Ostentatious bugger,' murmured the star of *The Strutters*.

'All part of the image,' said Charles lightly.

'Yes. God, if I had his money, I hope I'd show a little bit more reticence.' But there was a note of wistfulness in George Birkitt's voice. Bernard Walton's house had struck a psychological blow against him. He might be the star of *The Strutters* and he might be about to make a great deal of money. But he hadn't made it yet. Whatever his fantasies, he had still a long way to go to catch up with a real, established star.

Bernard Walton greeted them effusively. 'Do make yourselves at home. I'm just pottering around today, so ask if there's anything you need. The *Sun*'s coming down to do an interview this morning and I'm recording a few links for some radio show this afternoon, but otherwise I'm completely at your disposal. Do remember you're my guests.'

This was pure Bernard Walton and Charles couldn't help admiring it. He felt sure the star had deliberately set up the newspaper and radio bits to coincide with the filming day, so that no one should forget his importance. The pose of the self-denying host was also typical, and it was a gesture that was very easy to make. The usual filming back-up services, location caterers, make-up caravans and so on, already had their transport drawn up on the gravel. Even lavatories were available in the various vehicles, so the demands on Bernard Walton's hospitality would be minimal. And he would certainly have arranged a suitable fee with the Location Manager to cover any mild disruption which the filming might occasion.

Already there were a few signs of activity around the location. Men in blue nylon anoraks moved cables and huge lights on wheeled tripods. Make-up girls checked for any deterioration in their handiwork that the coach trip might have caused. Dressers inspected costumes for invisible flecks. Mort Verdon flounced around checking props. The men whose only function seemed to be to wear lumberjack checked shirts wore their lumberjack checked shirts and discussed overtime rates ominously. Midge Trumper (yes, the Midge Trumper), the cameraman, inspected his camera. Janie Lewis, her neck festooned like a Hawaiian princess s with pens on thongs and stopwatches on thongs, moved about, aimlessly purposeful.

But there seemed no momentum to any of the activity. It wasn't just the slow pace of everything, which is *de rigueur* in television, there was an even greater lack of purpose. It took Charles a minute or two to realise that this was due to the absence of the Director.

Scott Newton had not been in the coach; he had insisted on coming to the location under his own steam.

Even as Charles remembered this, the throaty roar of an engine and a fusillade of gravel announced both Scott Newton's arrival and the nature of the steam under which he was arriving.

A brand-new silver Porsche screeched to a halt beside the coach and the young television director bounced out, looking, in his tinted glasses, his ginger corduroy blouson suit and his white soft-leather French boots, exactly as a young television director should look.

'Morning, crew and artists,' he cried. 'Let's get this show on the road. Is everyone here?'

Mort Verdon fussed up to him. 'Not quite everyone, dear. Dob wasn't coming in the coach. Hasn't arrived yet.'

'Okay, let's start with one of the other set-ups that doesn't involve her. What about the Colonel being chased by Reg the barman?'

Slowly this message filtered through, and men and equipment started to move slowly to the side of the house where the first set-up was to be. Even the men whose only function was to wear lumberjack checked shirts deigned to wear them over there.

Charles couldn't help noticing the new confidence that illuminated Scott Newton. He decided that it was because they were filming. Film still has a glamour and tradition, and it is easier for a director to fit into the supercool Hollywood stereotype on location than it is in the prosaic and crowded setting of a studio. But Scott Newton was also obviously in the money. The new clothes and, more than that, the new car made it clear that his agent had negotiated a very favourable contract for *The Strutters*. Scott Newton no longer looked like a man with financial worries.

Charles found himself beside the young man while they waited for George Birkitt to change into the relevant tweeds for the scene ahead and, because he thought Scott would appreciate it, commented that the Porsche was a very smart motor.

Scott's reaction proved him right. Clearly not enough people had made the observation. 'Yes, not bad, is it?' he agreed airily. 'Really good to feel a bit of power under your foot. Drinks petrol, of course, but...' he shrugged, '...if you want the power...'

'Must have set you back a bit.'

'It's leased, actually. Makes sense. My accountant says I'm going to have to pay so much in tax this year that I may as well offset what I can.'

Yes, his agent had certainly negotiated a good contract. Life seemed to have come right for Scott Newton. Any agonising he might have had about the wisdom of leaving the BBC had dissipated. He was now director of a major series, which would lead to other major series and...Nothing could stop him.

Charles couldn't help thinking of Walter Proud. He had once talked in exactly the same brashly confident tones.

A further scrunching of gravel and the sound of an altogether more sedate, but no less powerful engine than the Porsche's, now interrupted the proceedings and announced the arrival of Aurelia Howarth and Barton Rivers.

The vintage Bentley was a green monster with its hood fixed back in honour of the warm weather. The couple behind the windscreen looked like its first owners. Aurelia wore a large hat bound round with a silk scarf, and Barton Rivers had added a white flat cap and white gloves to his uniform blazer. When he tottered, spidery, from the car and went round to open his wife's door, he revealed again white flannels and black shoes.

The arrival, like that of visiting royalty, suspended all other activity and everyone drifted over towards the car. Scott Newton got there first, still full of his new possession. 'What do you think of the car, Dob?'

'Very nice, dear.'

As with Charles, he couldn't resist boasting of his affluence. 'Expensive to run, mind.'

'I'm sure you'll manage, dear.'

'I'm sure I will, Dob.'

At that moment Bernard Walton, who was going to miss no opportunity of asserting his authority over the day, once again materialised from the house and, throwing his arms around Aurelia, gushed. 'Dob darling, lovely to welcome you here again. Always such a pleasure to see you, whether the call is purely social or, as today, when you're working. Hello, Barton, old boy.'

Barton Rivers did his death's head grimace. 'Nice to see you, dear boy. Lovely day for the match, what?'

Mort Verdon busied up to the leading lady. 'Aurelia boofle, sorry to interrupt, but I have to chivvy you, dear. Time to get into your cossy and have your slap done.'

'Yes, of course, darling. Must just see to Cocky. The little darling's in his little basket in the back of the car, and he does so hate his little basket.'

'Of course,' sympathised Mort, whose pressure was always discreet, and who knew that Aurelia wouldn't settle until she had settled the dog. He followed her to the car, in case she needed any help with her darling.

George Birkitt, standing beside Charles, was less sympathetic. 'Bloody dog. I thought she'd have left it behind. This whole bloody production seems to revolve round that pooch.'

'Doesn't do much harm,' said Charles mildly.

'Huh. It offends me. I wonder if they make mousetraps big enough,' George Birkitt mused.

Charles chuckled, but when he looked at his fellow-actor, there was no smile on the other's face.

Cocky was released from his wicker prison and celebrated his freedom by leaping around everyone's legs, yapping. 'How is the little love?' asked Bernard Walton with a great deal of warmth, though, shrewdly, he kept his distance.

'Ah, he's not a very well boy. The nasty old vet says he's not a well boy.'

'Good,' murmured George Birkitt. 'That's the best news I've heard all week.'

'Come on, boofle,' urged Mort Verdon tactfully. 'I think we'd better get changed for the filming.'

'Of course, darling. Now where are the dressing rooms?'

'It's just caravans, I'm afraid, dear.'

'Oh.'

She spoke the word coolly, without real disapproval, but Bernard Walton saw another opportunity to demonstrate his magnanimity. 'Dob darling, come and change in the house. Honestly, I hate to think of you cramped in some awful caravan, while the house is just here. Come on, love, you can go into the guest room where you stayed last time you were down. Barton, you come along, old boy.'

And, before anyone could remonstrate, Bernard Walton led the royal pair into the house, with a rabble of commoners, dressers and make-up girls trailing behind.

'Make you bloody sick,' said George Birkitt savagely. 'Turning up bloody late, disrupting everything, no apologies. I just don't think it's professional.'

Charles shrugged. 'I think it's remarkable she gets here at all, at her age. Particularly with dear old Barton Rivers driving.'

But George Birkitt was not mollified. 'What I object to is the fact that I got up at six to get to W.E.T. for my make-up call, came in that bloody coach with everyone else, and she has the nerve to just roll up about ten o'clock, and of course she isn't in make-up, so everything's behind. And no one ticks her off or anything, everything just bloody stops and we all bow and scrape and grin inanely for a quarter of an hour until her ladyship allows us to get on with our work. I mean, you know I'm the last person to make a fuss, but I do think somebody ought to say something. Peter, or Scott. God, how I hate all this *star* business.'

'Oh, come on. She's an old lady. Deserves a few allowances.'

But George Birkitt wasn't listening. 'I think, for the next day's filming, I'll drive myself down.'

The filming started, and made its usual, infinitesimally slow progress. Once again Charles realised why film stars were paid so much. If they could stand the constant repetition, the constant disruption, the tiny daily advance, then they earned every penny. For him, working in film had all the appeal of building a ten-foot model of the World Trade Centre out of match sticks.

He was fortunate, or not, according to how you looked at it, to get his scenes out of the way early on. Under Scott Newton's perfectionist direction, they only spent about an hour and a half on Reg the barman chasing Colonel Strutter the twenty yards from the privet hedge to the house. Another day, in another location, they would have to film the beginning of the chase, the segment from the golf clubhouse to the privet hedge. (Because the clubhouse adjacent to Bernard's house was in the wrong style for the decor of the studio set already built, they were doing that sequence at a different club.)

Charles was told that an hour and a half for thirty seconds of film without written dialogue was not bad going, though to him it seemed very slow. It meant that by twelve o'clock he had discharged his obligations for the day, and was in theory free to leave. On the other hand, he was a long way from a station, and no one seemed likely to be driving anywhere until the day's filming was over. So he might as well stay around until the coach returned.

He didn't really mind. He had noticed that there were some crates of wine in the location caterers' minibus. He felt relatively content.

The only thing that made him feel less than completely content were the trousers that Wardrobe had reckoned to be right for Reg the barman. Charles liked trousers better the longer he wore them. His two main pairs had a combined age of twenty-one years and now he never noticed that he had them on. The ones Wardrobe had chosen for the rare, probably never-to-be-repeated appearance of a barman's bottom half, felt stiff, tickly and alien.

At twelve-thirty sharp they all broke for lunch. (The Union rules were no less closely observed because they were on location. Indeed, over the few days Charles had been involved with *The Strutters* series, he had noticed an even greater consciousness of Union rules. Maybe this was another symptom of the approaching industrial trouble which George Birkitt had forecast at the time of the pilot.) Bernard Walton was in no way inconvenienced by the arrangements, though it appeared that he had swept Aurelia Howarth and Barton Rivers off for a private lunch in the house. The location caterers opened up their double-decker bus to reveal rows of tables and chairs, and served a substantial meal of truffled pork pâté, cold duck with a wide variety of salads, and fresh strawberries (not cheaply available in May), washed down with a choice of, or, if you felt like it, a mixture of, red and white wines.

Since he hadn't been involved in the recent filming, Charles was early in the queue and sat down alone with his loaded plate and a large glass of red wine. Two of the men whose only function was to wear lumberjack checked shirts, and therefore hadn't been involved in the filming at all, sat down opposite and, oblivious, proceeded to discuss their profession.

'You reckon he'll overrun?' asked the older one.

'Don't know. He seems to be more or less up to schedule.'

The other one grimaced. 'Might pass the word round to the lads to cool it a bit, or we won't get into the overtime.'

'Yeah.'

'Incidentally, I need a flyer off of you.'

'What for?'

'Oh, do own up. You come in my car with Rog and Bill, we're all going to claim the first-class rail and taxi link, I got to get a cut for depreciation on my motor.'

'Have Rog and Bill paid up?'

'Sure.'

'Okay then. There you are.'

'You on this filming for the *Wragg and Bowen* thing next week?'

'Yeah.'

'Reckon we're on to a flier there.'

'What, you mean we'll have to stay overnight?'

'No, no, sonny. The location's only an hour and a half down the motorway. No, we only *claim* the overnights, don't *do* them.'

'Sure.' A pause over the truffled pâté. 'You reckon it's all all right today?'

'Filming? Yeah, okay, I reckon. Mind you, I'm just waiting for him to do a shot that's got one of the greens of the golf course in it.'

'Why's that?'

'Haven't you noticed, son? They've got the sprinklers on.'

'So?'

'Oh, come on, where was you brought up? If you got running water in the shot, then you got to have a plumber on the set, haven't you. Specialist work, son. Need a fully paid-up plumber when you're using sprinklers.'

'Didn't know that.'

'You got a lot to learn, son. Have a word with Rog, he'll fill you in about your rights.'

'I must do that. Oh well, cheers.'

They raised their glasses and drank. The older one grimaced at the taste. ''Ere, I don't reckon this lot's château-bottled. Might have a word to Rog about that, and all.'

The arrival of George Birkitt beside him prevented Charles from concentrating further on this illuminating conversation. Colonel Strutter's mood had not improved.

'Did you see that? Bloody Bernard Walton's taken bloody Aurelia and her lunatic husband off to lunch.'

'They've known each other a long time.'

'Huh. Well, I don't think there should be any discrimination of that sort. We're all of us actors, for God's sake, neither more nor less.' He took a mouthful of pate. 'And notice I wasn't invited to the private lunchipoos.'

'Don't worry, the food's not bad here.' He reached out to fill his glass a third time from the bottle of red wine.

'Not too much of that, Charles. Got to work this afternoon.'

'You have, George. I haven't. I'm finished.'

'Oh yes. Well, Charles, do watch it in future. I've got a lot of scenes with you in this series, and I've got enough to do without worrying whether you're going to be sober enough to remember the lines.'

'I'll be very careful,' said Charles, mock humility masking his annoyance.

'Good.'

'Mind you, though, George, I am one of those actors who has always been said to be B.W.P.'

'B.W.P.?'

'Better when pissed.'

The location caterers had no sense of economy. W.E.T. was paying, so they didn't mind the half-finished plates left by technicians who had overestimated their capacity. They seemed content to scrape half-full terrines into their rubbish bins. And they had no objection at all to Charles Paris appropriating a bottle of red wine to see him through the afternoon. (In fact, when he offered to pay them for it, they looked at him as if he were the first of some newly hatched species hitherto unseen on this planet.)

So, since it was a nice sunny day, and since Bernard Walton's garden was a very pleasant place to loll in, Charles spent a pleasant afternoon lolling. Occasionally he would stroll back to the filming to show a token interest, but nothing ever seemed to be happening. They were always waiting. Waiting for the sun to emerge from behind a cloud. Waiting for an aeroplane to pass, so that its sound wouldn't affect the recording. Waiting, on one occasion as Charles passed, for Debbi Hartley to complete a costume change.

This had clearly been taking some time. The men whose function it was to wear lumberjack checked shirts were looking at their watches and smiling, as the odds on overtime shortened. Scott Newton and Peter Lipscombe, who had appeared at some point during the day to see that everything was okay, were looking extremely frustrated. At last the director could contain himself no longer. 'Oh, for Christ's sake!' he cried. 'What the hell is she changing into?'

'An actress?' Mort Verdon asked, almost inaudibly.

Once, just for a change of scene, Charles wandered down the steep zigzag of the drive towards the main road. He had it vaguely in his mind to walk along by the river. An interest in fishing, which he had not recently indulged, drew him to rivers. But when he got to the bottom, he saw that the Thames was a good deal further away than it had looked. There was a two-mile stretch of fields to traverse, so he turned round and started back up the drive.

It really was steep. It made him realise, gloomily, just how out of condition he was. Not enough exercise, too much booze. He knew he should take more of the first and less of the second, but something stubborn within him resisted the notion. It made him think of Frances. That was the sort of advice Frances would give him. She was nearly always right. That was what at times annoyed him about her and made him, perversely, turn against her advice.

He must ring her, though.

Half-way up the drive he felt puffed and sat on the wall for a moment by one of the tall flower-filled urns. He leant his back against it, but it wobbled, so he sat upright and looked over the deep green to the Thames.

Must start fishing again, he thought. Must start fishing, and must see Frances. In some way, the two intentions seemed related. Could it be that both of them offered the prospect of a kind of peace?

The day's filming finished in time. At twenty past five, Scott Newton said the magic words, 'It's a wrap,' and it was all over. The director looked buoyantly confident. The men in lumberjack checked shirts looked disgruntled for a moment, and then started dismantling everything with a speed and efficiency that hadn't been approached during the day. There were fixed payments for their tidying-up time, so there was no point in hanging about.

Everyone was now in a hurry to be off. The actors made for the coach. They still had ahead of them the tedious business of returning to the W.E.T. dressing rooms where their day clothes were. Aurelia Howarth, to the annoyance of Wardrobe, said that she and Cocky were tired and so she'd go home in her frock and bring it back the next day. Barton Rivers appeared, white-gloved and grinning, to squire her to the Bentley. He shook everyone's hands and urged everyone ghoulishly to play up, play up, and play the game.

The traffic jam on the gravel in front of the house was increased when Bernard Walton brought his dark blue Rolls-Royce Silver Cloud out of the garage. He had to be up in Town for the Charity First Night of some new movie, and was suddenly dressed in a midnight-blue dinner suit, with a midnight-blue butterfly bow at the neck of a froth of pale blue shirt. He didn't lock the house, since his housekeeper remained. (Bernard Walton was unmarried. He and his Publicity Manager had not yet found a woman who would keep her fashion value long enough for him to justify this step.)

Charles, in the mellowness of the afternoon's wine, felt confident that however the traffic was sorted out, the coach would probably he the last to leave, so he didn't rush into it to sit and wait.

The Bentley went first, its huge power held back to cope with the dangerous curves of the hill. Aurelia turned and waved, while Barton grinned ahead. They looked like something out of a Thirties film. The noise of the engine faded quickly to silence as they passed out of sight. The steep bank cut off sound quickly and ensured that the domestic calm of the great Bernard Walton should not be disturbed by the vulgar sounds of traffic on the main road below.

Bernard himself set off next, the Rolls moving faster than the Bentley, secure in its knowledge of every contour of the steep drive. Once again the powerful engine sound died quickly.

Scott Newton moved over to the side of his Porsche, his face beaming the unrestrainable smile of a father with his first daughter. But once there he hesitated. He wanted to make a departure which would be noticed, or rather by which his car would be noticed, but he wasn't sure how to time it.

The sight of Peter Lipscombe came to his rescue. The Producer, having checked with everyone that everything was okay, was about to get into his company BMW and return to London. Scott Newton called across to him, 'Last one back to W.E.T.'s a sissy.'

The producer smiled. 'I'll be back before you, Scott.'

'No chance. Yours doesn't go as fast as this.'

'I'm not saying it does. But I know the back ways when we get to Town. You may get there first, but I'll beat you through the rush hour. I've done it back from here within the hour.'

'Want a bet on it?'

'Fiver.'

'You're on.'

The Producer and Director walked towards each other and shook hands. 'What's more,' said Peter Lipscombe, 'I'm so confident I'll beat you, that I'll let you go first.'

Scott Newton thought for a second, but then decided to take advantage of the offer and make his exit while everyone was still watching. He leapt into the silver Porsche, gunned the engine and shot off in a burst of gravel.

The sound of the engine faded, but just before it disappeared, the note changed to a scream of metal. This was followed by a series of heavy thuds, and then a great boom which seemed to shake the hill on which the house stood.

Charles Paris reached a viewpoint of the accident a little behind the younger men who had rushed down the drive. There was no doubt what had happened.

Round one of the hairpins in the drive, an urn lay in the middle of the gravel, its bright confusion of flowers spilled in the fall. The ridges swept up by the Porsche's tyres showed how Scott, coming on the obstruction blind and too fast, had swerved to avoid it. And how the car had got out of control.

The scarred flower beds and uprooted shrubs charted its passage down the hill. The jack-knifed TIR lorry from Spain showed what it had met when it reached the main road.

And, because there was nothing else in sight that could be it, the shapeless mass like crumpled kitchen foil must have been the silver Porsche.

CHAPTER SIX

West End Television Ltd,
W.E.T. House,
235–9 Lisson Avenue, London NW1 3PQ.
30th May, 1979.

Dear Charles,

Just a note to fill you in on developments on *The Strutters* front. Obviously we were all very shocked by what happened but we mustn't let our imaginations run away with us. People are talking about our two misfortunes and saying they must be connected and that it's a bad luck show and...All rubbish! The show must go on and the show will go on. There is no danger of anything stopping the advance of this very exciting project.

I am delighted to be able to tell you that we now have a new Director for the series, and even more delighted to say that he's Bob Tomlinson, whose work I'm sure you know from such hit series as *No Kidding*, *O'Reilly and Truly*, *Last, But Not Least* and, last but not least, that smashing show set in a municipal rubbish dump, *Hold Your Nose and Think of England*! From that list of credits, I don't need to tell you that Bob certainly knows his stuff when it comes to sit com!

I can't think that Bob's going to want to make major changes to the schedule, but I'm sure you'll hear in plenty of time if any of your calls are different. I look forward to seeing you at the read-through next Monday, 4th June, and am confident that, after this rather unfortunate start, we are going to have a really exciting and successful series.

With the warmest good wishes,

Yours sincerely,

Peter

PETER LIPSCOMBE

Producer *The Strutters*

The payphone on the landing at Hereford Road rang the morning Charles received the letter. The various Swedes were out at their various Swedish occupations, so he answered it.

'Hello, Charles, it's Walter.'

'Oh, hello. How are things?'

'So-so. I hope you don't mind my ringing, but I want to pick your brains.'

'You're welcome to anything you can find there.'

'It's a slightly ticklish thing, actually. I read in the paper about that poor boy's terrible accident...you know, your Director. Obviously I was terribly shocked, but I couldn't help thinking, you know, the way one does, that that must leave your series without a Director. So I thought I might give Peter Lipscombe a buzz and see what gives, but I though I'd check with you first, just to make sure nothing's been sorted out yet.'

Charles didn't like the drift of the conversation, and said rather shortly, 'I've just heard. We've got a new Director.'

'Oh. Who?'

'Bob...Tomlinson I think it was.'

'Ah, yes. He's never out of work. Yes, of course. He would be free. He was going to do that series about the dance band called *Hands Off My Maracas*, but it's been cancelled because of problems with the Musicians' Union. Oh well, never mind...We must meet up for a drink again sometime, maybe.'

'Sure.'

'And you will let me know if you hear anything coming up, won't you?'

'Yes. Of course.'

Charles went back into his room feeling depressed. Of course Walter had to follow up any job possibility that might emerge, but it was unpleasant to hear him reduced to the role of professional vulture. For a moment suspicion of Walter returned. Certainly he was someone who might hope to gain from Scott Newton's death, and he'd made no secret of his resentment of the young man's success.

But there were many arguments against casting Walter in the role of the director's murderer. The first, and most potent, was that he hadn't been at the scene of the crime. Short of introducing a conspiracy theory or the use of a hired killer, there was no way he could have toppled the flower urn which had caused Scott's death.

And why should anyone want Scott dead? He had seemed pleasant enough, not the sort to raise instant antipathy like Sadie. Just an ambitious young television director with money problems.

Mind you, the money problems seemed to have resolved themselves. The new clothes, the new car...Charles's mind did a little spurt. Suppose Scott had witnessed the first murder and blackmailed the killer, thus providing a motive for his own death...? Hmm, there might be something there, but there was a distinct lack of hard evidence.

And, anyway, was there even a murder to investigate? There seemed no real reason to think that the young man was the victim of anything more sinister than an accident. The police, who had made extensive investigations at the scene of his death, seemed satisfied with this solution. And, after all, a young man, flushed with success after a good day's filming, showing off a powerful and unfamiliar car, was unlikely to be concentrating much on his driving. And the urn of flowers could have fallen of its own accord. Charles knew from having leant against one that they weren't fixed, just balanced on the wall.

Yes, it could have fallen of its own accord. But it was a substantial piece of terracotta and there had been no wind. Perhaps a bird could have flown into it or a rabbit or something brushed against it...or maybe the vibrations of one of the passing cars had dislodged it, but it all seemed pretty unlikely.

Maybe one of the cars had scraped against the wall and bumped the urn off...But logic was against that too. Whereas one could imagine that the ancient Barton Rivers, at the wheel of his huge Bentley, might be less than secure on the tight turns of the drive, he and Aurelia had not been the last people to go down it. Bernard Walton had followed them and, apart from the fact that he must have known every curve of the approach to his house perfectly, he was unlikely to scrape the gleaming surface of his precious Rolls. And he wouldn't have been able to drive over the urn if Barton's Bentley had dislodged it before him.

So either it just fell, or someone deliberately moved it. And if it had been deliberately moved, it must have happened just after Bernard's Rolls had driven past.

If it was a murder, and if it had been planned, then the perpetrator was likely to be someone who knew the layout of Bernard's grounds, someone who had been there before. The list included Bernard himself, obviously, and, from what they had said during the day, Aurelia and Barton and Peter Lipscombe. Presumably the unfortunate Scott had also been down on a recce to check the location, and who knew how many people would have accompanied him? Certainly the Designer, certainly the Location Manager, possibly Janie Lewis, the PA, possibly dozens of other people. That was the trouble with a crime committed in television – there were always so many people about, it was difficult to reduce lists of suspects.

Charles concentrated, and tried to remember where everyone had been at the moment of Bernard Walton's departure in the Rolls. The conjectural saboteur of the urn need not have been in a car; he, or she, could have walked down the hill and moved it. But the picture didn't come back to him with any clarity. He just remembered a lot of people milling about, clearing up; he couldn't place individuals.

No, he came back to one fact: if the urn was moved in order to cause an accident, then the person with the best background knowledge and the best opportunity to do it was Bernard Walton.

And it was also Bernard Walton with whom Sadie Wainwright had had a blazing row just before her death.

But why? Why should a highly successful television and theatre star hazard everything by committing murder? Charles supposed that if *The Strutters* had been being made at the expense of *What'll the Neighbours Say?*, then Bernard might be seen to have a motive for sabotaging production of the new series, so that it would have to be cancelled and replaced with the older one.

But that motivation didn't work, because the options on the next series of *What'll the Neighbours Say?* had been taken up and, though Bernard didn't know that at the time of Sadie's death, he certainly did when Scott died. Nope, it didn't work.

But, as a theory, it did contain one attractive element, and that was the idea of sabotage to the production. If the violence was directed against the whole series rather than individuals, then the random nature of the murder schemes made more sense. Maybe the saboteur had fixed the railing on the fire escape to injure Sadie Wainwright *or anyone else* connected with *The Strutters* pilot. The dislodged urn, too, might have been a random act of violence.

This idea answered a doubt that had been nagging at Charles ever since Scott's death. Any theory that assumed murder directed specifically at the young director also assumed an enormous amount of luck. There was no guarantee that Scott was going to be the next person down the hill after Bernard. He might well have chosen to leave last of all and demonstrate the powers of his Porsche by overtaking everyone else on the motorway back to London. Even if the murderer could have predicted the bet with Peter Lipscombe, he couldn't have known that the producer would offer the opportunity for the director to go first. (Unless of course the producer *were* the murderer...But no, that was a blind alley; it was Scott who had suggested the race.)

And, as well as having no guarantee who his victim would he, the conjectural murderer had no guarantee that he would murder anyone. A more prudent driver than Scott Newton might have been going slowly enough to stop safely when he saw his path obstructed. And, even given Scott's precipitous speed, he might well have survived his descent on to the main road. No murderer, however much of a criminal mastermind, could have arranged the simultaneous arrival of a Spanish juggernaut to finish off his victim.

So, if any crimes had been committed, it looked as if they were just random sabotage. And the only person who had ever had a motive for such actions, Bernard Walton, had had his motive removed by the guarantee of a new series of *What'll the Neighbours Say?*

Unless, of course, the acts of sabotage were the work of a psychopath. Oh dear, Charles did hope not. Psychopathic crimes offered no prospect of satisfaction; if their motivation was without reason, then no amount of reasoning was going to provide a solution to them.

So what was he left with? Two deaths. Both, according to police findings, accidental. And nothing to make him disagree with those findings except for a few ambiguous overhead words relating to the first one.

All he could do was watch and listen, and wait to see if anything else happened.

On Monday, June 4th, Charles arrived at the Paddington Jewish Boys' Club for the first *Strutters* read-through, and found Peter Lipscombe predictably cooing over Aurelia Howarth. She appeared just to have given him a brown paper parcel.

'Of course I'll read them, Dob love, of course I will.'

'I don't know, I just think there might be something there, darling. They're old-fashioned, but might adapt into a rather jolly series. Just an instinct I have about them.'

'And when have your dramatic instincts ever been wrong?' asked the Producer with a sycophantic laugh.

Charles moved over to sit beside George Birkitt, who was reading the *Sun*. 'How's tricks, as the white rabbit said to the conjuror?'

George brandished the newspaper. 'Look at this – bloody Bernard Walton all over it.'

Charles glanced at the page. 'MY FIRST DATE – In our series of the Famous with Two Left Feet, BERNARD WALTON, hilarious star of TV's *What'll the Neighbours Say?* describes the visit to the pictures that went riotously wrong...' He didn't read any further. There was a half-page picture of Bernard, pulling one of the gauche expressions that was a feature of the character he played in the sit com (and indeed of every other character he played; whatever the part, he always gave the same performance).

Charles shrugged. 'So what?'

'I don't know. I just get a bit sick of it,' George Birkitt complained. 'I mean, you just can't get away from him. He's always doing all these bloody interviews, and popping up on quiz shows and all that rubbish. All the *Blankety-Blanks* and *Star Games* and *Celebrity Squares* when that was around. Or he's opening supermarkets or being photographed at premieres.'

'I agree, it must be hell. But that's the life he's chosen. One of the penalties of being a star, you have to be on show all of the time.'

'Yes,' said George, with a tinge of wistfulness.

'Surely you don't want to get involved in all that, do you?'

'Good Lord, no,' he protested. 'No, no, I value my privacy. I'm the last person to want to become a public property. No, no, I was just thinking from the financial point of view. I mean, there is quite a bit of money in all those spin-off things. And I think, you know, if you get the chance to do them, well, you shouldn't turn them down from high-minded principles about the sanctity of your art. You should take advantage of whatever's going.'

'Oh, I agree.'

'And, if there's money going for all that sort of rubbish, I don't see why it should always go to the same circle of boring professional personalities with heads too big for their bodies. Because, to be quite frank, Charles...' George Birkitt lowered his voice, 'I wouldn't mind a little more money. They're getting me damned cheap for this series. Okay, I know it's the first time I've had my name above the title – as if I cared about things like that, for God's sake – but they are still getting me damned cheap. No, if they want to do another series after this lot, I'm afraid they'll find my agent in more of a negotiating mood. It's not that one wants a huge amount of money, it's just that one doesn't want to be undervalued.'

Further demonstration of George Birkitt's unwillingness to fall into a star stereotype was prevented by the arrival of *The Strutters*' new Director. Bob Tomlinson, the man who certainly knew his stuff when it came to sit com, proved to be a thickset individual in his fifties whose appearance behind a market barrow would have been less remarkable than behind a television control desk. He was dressed in a shiny blue suit and wore an expression of belligerent boredom.

'Okay,' he said. 'Let's sit down and read this rubbish.'

'Bob!' cried Peter Lipscombe heartily. 'Sure you'd like to be introduced to everyone, wouldn't you?'

'I'll get to know them soon enough in rehearsal,' said Bob Tomlinson, and sat down.

'But you haven't worked with Dob Howarth, have you?' Peter Lipscombe persisted.

'No.'

'Well, do allow me to introduce you to our lovely leading lady.'

Bob Tomlinson looked up briefly. 'Hello. Right, PA got the watch ready? Let's start reading.'

Peter Lipscombe intervened again. 'Er, yes. Just a moment, Bob. If I could say a few words…'

'Why?'

'Well, er, as Producer, I would like to –'

'Oh yeah, I forgot you were Producer. All right, be quick. I'll get myself a coffee.' And Bob Tomlinson got up and walked across to the coffee machine, while Peter Lipscombe started his pep-talk.

'Right, first let me say how nice it is to see you all looking so well. Now we've all had a horrible shock and there's no use pretending what happened didn't happen, but what we've all got to do is to put it behind us and look ahead, just remember what a jolly exciting series this is going to be. Now, because of circumstances, we've lost a couple of days' filming, but we'll be able to pick them up in the course of our schedule. And, incidentally, I'd like to warn you now that I've just received Script Number Six from Rod and that's going to involve some of you in a night's filming. We'll let you know the date as soon as it's been sorted out, but I thought you'd like to know.

'So…here we all are and by this time next week we'll have recorded the first episode – second, if we include the pilot – of this really exciting new series-*The Strutters*! Let me tell you, ladies and gentlemen –'

'Have you finished?' asked Bob Tomlinson, returning with his cup of coffee.

'Well, er, yes, I, er, um…'

'Okay, read from the top. Start the watch, girl.'

Maybe it was the inhibiting expression of boredom on the director's face, or perhaps it was just that the script was inferior to the pilot episode, but the read-through didn't seem very funny. Peter Lipscombe and Tilly Lake provided their usual sycophantic laughter for the first few pages, but soon faded to silence.

As the pay-off to the episode was spoken, Bob Tomlinson turned to Janie. 'How long?'

'Part One: 10–17, Part Two: 9–41,' she supplied efficiently. 'Making a total of 19–58.'

'That's near enough.' Bob rose with the enthusiasm of a man about to put three coats of paint on a forty-foot wall. 'Let's block it.'

Peter Lipscombe raised a hand to intervene. 'Um, just a few points before you do that. Debbi, that line you have on 1–7, where you say, "No, I'm not that sort of girl"...could you –'

''Ere, what is this?' asked Bob Tomlinson, with all the anger of a barrow-boy who'd arrived at market to find someone else on his pitch. 'I'm the Director of this show. I give the bleeding artists notes.'

Peter Lipscombe didn't want a scene. His voice took on a mollifying tone. 'Yes, of course, Bob, of course. I wonder if you'd mention to Debbi that I think *one* way – not by any means the only way, but one way of delivering that line would be to emphasise the 'that'. 'I'm not *that* sort of girl.' I think it points up the joke.'

'All right,' Bob Tomlinson conceded. 'Which one of you's Debbi? Right, on that line, could you hit the "that"? Okay, let's get this bloody show blocked.'

'I've got a point, Bob,' said the colourless voice of Rod Tisdale.

'And who the hell are you? Another bloody producer?'

'No, Bob, this is our writer, Rod Tisdale.'

Bob Tomlinson glowered. 'I don't like writers round my rehearsal rooms.'

Rod Tisdale showed no signs of having heard this. 'It's Page 3 of Part Two.'

'Oh, don't bother me with bloody details on the script. Tell the producer.'

'Peter,' said Rod Tisdale obediently, 'on that page, I think the line, "I can't stand it any longer" would probably be better as "I can't stick it out any longer." You know, probably pick up the laugh on the double meaning.'

'Yes, nice thinking, Rod. Um, Bob, Rod's had rather a good idea, I think. On Page 3 of Part Two, wondering if we could change "I can't stand it any longer" to "I can't stick it out any longer"?'

'Change it. See if I care.'

'No, but I don't want us to force it on you. We all want to be in agreement on things. So do say what you'd like.'

'I'd like you and the bloody writer to clear out and let me get on with this rubbish.'

As rehearsals progressed. Charles found his respect for Bob Tomlinson increasing. He realised that the director's manner was not just rudeness for its own sake, but a way of getting on with the job quickly. And his contempt for the material he was directing (a feeling for which Charles found in himself considerable sympathy) did not seem to make the performances any worse. Nor did it lower the morale of the production; after the agonising of Scott Newton over every comma, the more practical approach was quite a relief. The atmosphere in the rehearsal room was rather jolly.

Bob Tomlinson just got on with the job and didn't waste time with socialising or toadying to his stars. He was an efficient organiser and ensured that every part of the production came together at the right time. He was a good example of the huge value of competence in television. Flair may have its place, but flair is not always coupled with efficiency and, given the choice between a director with flair and one with competence, many actors would opt for the security of the latter.

Certainly the cast of *The Strutters* didn't seem put out by the offhand manner of their new Director. They seemed to respect his lack of obsequiousness. It made them more equal, a group of people who had come together to get on with a job of work. Aurelia Howarth, used to cosseting and cotton-woolling from generations of producers, seemed totally unworried by Bob Tomlinson's directness and his undisguised lack of interest in the welfare of Cocky.

The atmosphere between Director and Producer remained. The fact was that Bob Tomlinson was not used to working to a Producer. For many years he had combined the roles, and his agent had ensured that the final credit read: 'Produced and Directed by Bob Tomlinson'. It was only because of the last-minute nature of his booking on *The Strutters* when his other series was cancelled that he found himself in this unusual position.

But he didn't let it worry him. He didn't let anything worry him. *The Strutters* was just another three months of well-paid work, and soon he'd be on to something else. The secret of Bob Tomlinson's success and his formidable track record in sit com was his ability not to let anything get to him. He was the first person Charles had met in that world who seemed to have an accurate estimate of the value and importance of the product.

He continued to be cheerfully rude to Peter Lipscombe and continued to allow no notes to be given directly from the Producer to the artists. So there were more conversations in which people with a common language talked through an interpreter. But Peter Lipscombe's role, which under Scott Newton's inexperienced regime had increased, dwindled back to grinning a lot, asking everyone if everything was okay and buying drinks. Which was, after all, what he did best.

The actual recording of Episode One (or Episode Two, if you counted the pilot) of *The Strutters* did not go particularly well. This was in no way due to Bob Tomlinson's direction. There was, after all, only one way to shoot a Rod Tisdale script, and that was the way he did it. All that was wrong with the evening was that the script was slightly inferior, and after all the euphoric generalisations about new eras in comedy which had followed the pilot, anti-climax was inevitable.

After the recording, Charles overheard a conversation between the writer and Director. Rod Tisdale, in a voice that almost betrayed some emotion, asked, 'How d'you think it went?'

Bob Tomlinson shrugged. 'All right. How does any sit com go?'

Rod Tisdale shook his head. 'I don't know. I reckoned there were sixty-eight jokes in that script. We only got fifty-three laughs.'

'It'll look fine after the sound-dub.'

'You mean you'll add the laughs?'

'You bet I will. By the time I've finished, you won't be able to tell the difference between this and a really funny show.'

'I've always resisted having laughs dubbed on to my shows.'

'Sod what you've always resisted, son. I'm directing this show and I'll do it my way.'

Which was of course the way it would be done.

Charles decided to go up to the bar in the lift. (Though no one actually mentioned it, the fire escape had been used much less since Sadie's death.) He had changed with his customary rapidity out of his top half (Reg the golf club barman's legs, after their brief airing on film, had once again retreated to proper obscurity), and reckoned only Peter Lipscombe would have beaten him to the bar. Where he could once again demonstrate his skill in buying drinks.

There was an argument going on outside the lift. A small balding man with glasses, who carried a duffle bag and wore a thin checked sports jacket and a yellow nylon shirt, was being moved on by a uniformed commissionaire.

'No, I'm sorry, sir, show's over. I have to clear all the audience out of the building. Now come along, please.'

'But she will see me, she will. She always does.'

'No, I'm sorry, sir, I've got to clear the building. So, if you don't mind...If it's an autograph you want, you're welcome to wait outside the main door until the artists come out.'

'I don't want her autograph. I've got her autograph a thousand times over. I've got autographed programmes of every show she's ever been in. I've collected them all.'

'Sorry, sir, I must –'

'No, listen, my name's Romney Kirkstall. She knows me. Really. You just tell her I'm here and –'

'She know you were coming tonight?'

'No, she didn't actually, but she's always glad to see me. I come to all the *What'll the Neighbours...*recordings and –'

'If the lady's not expecting you, sir, I'm afraid I must ask you to –'

'No, really, she will want to see me!'

Before the commissionaire could produce further verbal or physical arguments, the truth of Romney Kirkstall's assertion was proved by the zephyrous arrival of Aurelia Howarth, saying, 'Romney, darling, how good of you to come!'

'You're lucky I'm still here, Dob,' said the little man. 'This...gentleman was doing his best to throw me out.'

'I'm sorry, Miss Howarth,' the commissionaire apologised sheepishly. 'I didn't know who he was. We get a lot of types wanting to worry the stars and that. I thought he might be some kind of freak.'

The wildness of Kirkstall's appearance justified that supposition, but Aurelia cooed lightly, 'No, no, Romney's my most loyal fan.'

The lift arrived at that moment, so she continued, 'Come on, darling, let's go up and have a drink. Sorry about the mix-up.'

Charles went into the lift with them and they all arrived together in the bar. Where, predictably enough, Peter Lipscombe bought them all drinks. And he did do it very well.

Gerald Venables had once again come to the recording and Charles met him in the bar. The actor was becoming suspicious of the solicitor's constant appearances at West End Television. Though he always claimed disingenuously he had just come to see the show, Gerald was notorious for investing in the lucrative areas of show business, and Charles wouldn't have been at all surprised to discover he had a stake in the company. He seemed to know everyone altogether too well to be a mere casual visitor. And his constant discussions with W.E.T.'s Head of Contracts suggested more than idle conversation.

But Charles never expected to have his suspicions confirmed. Gerald was masonically secretive about his investments.

'Still think we're on to a winner?' he asked ironically, after Peter Lipscombe had bought Gerald a drink too.

'Oh yes,' asserted the solicitor confidently. 'Minor hiccup tonight, but it'll be fine. Yes, this series is going to make the autumn schedules look very healthy. What with this and *Wragg and Bowen*, the BBC'll be knocked for six.'

Gerald was talking so exactly like Peter Lipscombe that Charles once again suspected him of complicity with the company's management. He seemed to know altogether too much.

But Gerald's interest in television was subsidiary to his interest in criminal investigation. He had helped Charles on one or two cases in the past and was evidently avid for more.

'Well? Two suspicious deaths now. What do you make of it, bud?'

'A coincidence of two accidents, I think.'

'Oh, come on, you can do better than that.'

'I don't know. I've thought it through a lot, but I can't seem to get any line on it at all. Either there are two totally unrelated crimes, or only one crime and one accident, or no crimes. I can't get any consistent motivation for anyone.'

And he gave Gerald a summary of his thinking to date. 'The only person for whom I've got even a wisp of motivation,' he concluded, 'is dear old Bernard Walton. If he thought the future of his own series was threatened by

The Strutters, then he would in theory have a motive to sabotage the show. And, if you think on those lines, it becomes significant that the two people who have died have nothing to do with *What'll the Neighbours Say?* I mean, say Aurelia or George had gone, then that might jeopardise the future of the series, but as it is, there's nothing to stop it going ahead. As indeed – and here's the one fact that makes the whole theory crumble in ruins about my ears-it is going ahead. I'll have to think of something else.'

'I've got news for you, Charles,' Gerald announced portentously.

'What?'

'I was just talking to the Head of Contracts. The proposed series of *What'll the Neighbours Say?* has been cancelled.'

'It can't have been. The artists' options have been taken up.'

'Oh, sure. But they're all going to be paid off. Head of Contracts has been ringing round the agents today. Were you optioned for the series, by the way?'

'No. They just did an availability check. Said it wasn't definite that Reg the golf club barman would be a regular character.'

Gerald grimaced. 'If your agent was worth his commission, he'd have got some sort of contract out of them. Who is your agent, by the way?'

'Maurice Skellern.'

'Oh. Say no more.'

'But just a minute, Gerald, they wouldn't just pay everyone off.'

'Why not? Happens all the time.'

'But it's a huge amount of money.'

'A huge amount of money for the actors involved, maybe. A very nice little pay-off for doing nothing. But, as a percentage of the budget of a major television production, it's peanuts, really. So long as you actually keep a show out of the studio, you're still saving money. In fact, there are producers who have built up considerable reputations by keeping shows out of studios.'

Once again Gerald was showing more than a layman's knowledge of the workings of television, but Charles didn't comment. Instead, he said, 'Anyway, even if that has happened, and I still don't quite see why it has...'

'Nigel Frisch has lost confidence in the series. And they need the studio dates for *Wragg and Bowen*.'

'Okay, but coming back to our little problem of a murder motivation, we're no further advanced. If the artists' agents were only told about the cancellation today –'

'Yes, most of them were. But Bernard Walton, because he was the star, was given the honour of knowing the bad news before anyone else. Nigel Frisch, who, whatever else one may say about him, is never one to shirk responsibility, rang Bernard personally.'

'When?'

'Last Tuesday.'

The day before Scott Newton's death.

CHAPTER SEVEN

THE ATMOSPHERE at the Paddington Jewish Boys' Club Hall for the read-through the following morning was distinctly subdued. Partly, this was because the previous night's recording had been less than successful, but there was also a communal consciousness that they were now all into a weekly turnaround of shows; they would have to work harder and there would be less time for anything else. And there were some sore heads. The very human tendency to have a few drinks and go out for a meal after a recording that finishes at ten rarely takes account of a ten-thirty call the next morning.

George Birkitt was the only one who seemed cheerful. His agent had come to the recording and told him about the *What'll the Neighbours Say?* pay-off. Not only did this give him financial encouragement, because the contracted fees for thirteen programmes came to a very considerable amount, it also seemed a promising augury for *The Strutters* series. The company was clearly backing the new show at the expense of the old one. And, though he didn't quite say it, he reckoned that meant they thought George Birkitt was now a more bankable star than Bernard Walton. 'The other thing is,' he confided to Charles, 'it means I'll be able to take some other work. My agent keeps having calls from casting directors offering quite nice stuff, but always has to turn it down, saying, no, sorry, love, he's under contract to W.E.T.. Exclusive contracts have their advantages, but they do restrict your movement.'

Charles Paris, whose experience of exclusive contracts was small, nodded wisely.

But George was the only one in a sunny mood. Even Aurelia, whose diaphanous charm rarely varied, seemed distracted. Apparently it was something to do with Cocky, who had been sick during the night and had to have the vet summoned. The lack of sleep this disturbance had caused made the actress look slightly less ageless than usual. Charles was more aware of the strains a television series must impose on a woman in her seventies.

And she was obviously worried about the dog. Throughout the read-through, she kept going across to his little basket to check on his welfare. 'If anything happened to Cocky,' she said, 'I don't know what I'd do.'

Janie Lewis was also less than her beaming efficient self. Dark circles under her eyes suggested she hadn't had any sleep the night before and a strained atmosphere between her and one of the regular cast, Nick Coxhill, suggested why. Charles once again thought he might continue his desultory pursuit of her, but his first overture was met with the sharp retort that she was henceforth to be known as Jay, and that she was busy.

Tilly Lake emoted round the rehearsal room, implying enough sighing heartaches to keep a romantic novelist in business for a decade. Charles, rather cheekily, asked her whether she'd heard from Trevor Howard or Laurence Olivier about playing the part of Colonel Strutter's friend in Episode Five.

'Both got other commitments,' she said elegiacally. 'Otherwise, of course...Still, I'm not downhearted. Going to continue to aim high. Such a smashing script, after all, lovely part. I've been rereading it and I think the character might be rather younger than I first thought. So I think I might try for an Alan Bates, or a Michael York maybe...or a Derek Jacobi. Keep away from the obvious, anyway, the Toby Roots of this life. Nothing against him, but you know what I mean.'

Charles mumbled some ambivalent response.

'Casting so easily becomes predictable, so one always admires the people in television who don't do the obvious. I mean, have you heard, on this programme for the elderly, they haven't gone for the boring competent sort of presenter like Robert Carton. They've chosen Ian Reynolds, who's nearly eighty.'

'Yes, I heard that.'

'Well, isn't that inventive? And people sometimes say casting isn't a creative business.' She laughed tragically, setting up a ripple through the feathers of her hat.

'What does Bob Tomlinson think about your ideas of casting?'

'Oh, he doesn't care. He just told me to get on with it.'

That was Bob Tomlinson's great quality, the ability to get on with it and to delegate. But he wasn't slapdash. He had his own standards, as was apparent when he clapped his hands for attention.

'Before we start this read-through, got another filming date for your diaries. This Friday, the 15th. We're meant to be rehearsing here, but if we get our skates on, we can miss a day.'

'Where's the location?' asked Debbi Hartley.

'Back at Bernard Walton's place.'

'But I thought we'd done all that.'

'Got to do it again.'

'Why?' Peter Lipscombe's producer's instinct picked up the implication of extra expense.

'Because I saw the rushes this morning of what was done last week, and it's all bloody terrible. I wouldn't have film of that quality in one of my shows.'

'What's wrong with it?'

'It's all bloody arty-farty. All shot over people's shoulders or up their trouser-legs. Every new director's first day with a film camera. Just bloody wanking. I don't know what that little tit thought he was up to.'

Peter Lipscombe still seemed more worried about the prospect of spending money than any disrespect to the dead. 'Are you sure there isn't any of it you can use?'

'Bloody certain.'

'Well, look, I'll have to talk to the Cost Planners about this. And then to Film Department to see if they can find us a day to –'

'I've done all that. Don't you bloody listen? It's all set up for this Friday.'

'Oh.' Peter Lipscombe had one more try. 'I'm sure the film can't be that bad...'

'It's self-indulgent crap. Totally wrong for this show. Don't ever forget, what we're making here is just a second-rate sit com, not bloody Ingmar Bergman.'

And so – not that there had ever been any doubt that he would – Bob Tomlinson won the day. All of the people who had been present at Scott Newton's death were to be reassembled at the scene of the crime.

Charles wondered if Bernard Walton would also be there.

In the Birthday Honours, announced the next day, Aurelia Howarth was made a Dame of the British Empire. This caused considerable excitement at the Paddington Jewish Boys' Club, which was invaded by newspaper reporters, and even had a sycophantic royal visit from Nigel Frisch.

His legs once again encased in Reg the golf club barman's alien trousers, Charles Paris went through his second day's filming at Bernard Walton's house. If doing it once had been boring, doing it twice was excruciating. The only improvement on the previous occasion was that Bob Tomlinson moved a lot faster than Scott Newton. While the younger man had spent hours composing every shot, the older one just got the camera lined up and went ahead. He had a cameraman with a comparably prosaic approach to the job. The inestimable Midge Trumper had shared Scott Newton's concern to make every frame a Rembrandt; the new man's only worry seemed to be making sure that there was film in the camera.

The result was that the men in lumberjack checked shirts' prospects of going into overtime faded fast. By the time they broke for lunch (pâté de foie gras, steak au poivre and raspberries with – thanks to the intervention of the Union representative – a rather good 1973 Mouton Cadet), only four set-ups and a couple of establishing shots remained to be done. All Dame Aurelia Howarth's scenes had been completed, and she and Barton Rivers had already set off in the Bentley back to London. She still looked very tired and would no doubt benefit from a half-day's rest. The excitements of all the congratulations on her award must have added to her exhaustion.

But, though the progress of the filming was rapid and efficient, Charles made little or no progress in the business of criminal investigation. He did wander down the drive to the point where Scott's Porsche had skidded off, but the scene of the accident told him nothing new.

Bernard Walton must have had efficient staff, because most traces of the car's descent had been erased. Walls had been repaired, broken shrubs replaced, and scarred lawn returfed. Only the difference in colour between the old grass and the new bore witness to the spectacle of the previous week.

Charles once again weighed one of the urns in his hands. Their centre of gravity was high, so it wouldn't take much of a nudge to shift them, but, even so, they were heavy and it would require more than a gust of wind to do the job.

He looked around the area. Maybe some vital clue remained, maybe the vital stub of a cigarette only available from a small shop in Burlington Arcade, maybe the unmistakable outline of a shoe with callipers, maybe the return half of a railway ticket to Auchtermuchty...But he was not optimistic of finding anything. People on the whole rarely leave clues to where they have been. And, if there had been any, he felt sure the police's more professional searches would have revealed them.

No, there was only one line of investigation open to him. And he was prevented from pursuing that by the absence of his chief suspect. Bernard Walton wasn't there.

He arrived just as the day's filming was finished, at about three o'clock. The Rolls scrunched to a halt on the gravel. Bernard's powder blue leisure-wear and the gleaming leather bag of clubs he removed from the back of the car revealed that he had been on the golf course. His breath revealed that he had also been in the bar.

He greeted Charles warmly. 'Is Dame Dob around?' he asked.

'No. Her bits were finished early. She went off about lunchtime.'

'Ah.' Bernard Walton hesitated. He had had a hospitable urge, but now he knew Aurelia and Barton weren't there, didn't know what to do with it. 'Are you through, too?'

'Yes. It's all done. The magic words, "It's a wrap," have been spoken.'

'Uh-huh.' Bernard was still undecided. But only for a moment. 'Look, would you like to come in and have a drink?'

'That's very kind, but I think the coach'll be going back shortly and...'

'Don't worry about that. I've got to drive up to Town later. Got to go on some radio chat show. Live at ten o'clock – ugh. Bloody inconvenient, but I'd better do it.'

'Well, in that case...' A snag. 'But I'm in costume.'

'Oh tell them you'll take it in tomorrow.'

'They won't like it.'

They didn't, but Charles was too determined to grab his chance of talking to Bernard to worry about the affronted flouncing of a dresser.

They sat by the window of Bernard's sitting room with glasses of brandy and watched the cavalcade of buses and cars depart.

'How's it going?' asked the star of *What'll the Neighbours Say?*.

'Hard to judge, really. I'm not very good at assessing comedy, least of all this sort of stuff.'

'I think it'll probably be very successful,' Bernard condescended.

'Hmm. Of course, it's got off to rather a disturbed start...'

But the opportunity to talk about Scott's death was ignored. 'You've heard they're not going to proceed with *What'll the Neighbours ...*'

Charles nodded. 'Still, nice big pay-off, I gather.'

'Yes.' Bernard's tone did not suggest that the money was a great comfort. 'Oh well, maybe I should go back to the theatre. Might get a job in rep. at Cardiff,' he suggested ruefully.

This reference to their first meeting released a variety of reminiscences. Charles played along. He wanted to bring the conversation round to the deaths of Sadie and Scott, but he had to do it gently. Also, there was something about Bernard's manner, the way he had buttonholed Charles and insisted on his staying, that suggested he might want to unburden himself of some confidence. But it mustn't be hurried.

It was about half-past five when Bernard suggested they should leave for Town. 'I have a call to make on the way. It won't take long. I hope you don't mind.'

Charles didn't. His social calendar was as empty as ever. Whether he arrived back at Hereford Road at seven or midnight or indeed three a.m. made little difference. He had had a vague intention to ring Frances that evening, but it'd keep.

The call Bernard had to make proved to be at a home for spastics. Charles said, no, he didn't mind coming in with him.

It was a strange experience, prompting mixed reactions. On one level, Charles knew that it was a carefully engineered public relations exercise. He felt sure that Bernard had made his call before in other more eminent company. After all, there was little point in impressing Charles Paris with the great star's big-heartedness. They had known each other too long. Charles knew the kind of calculation that went into everything Bernard did, and had a shrewd suspicion Bernard knew he knew.

On the other hand, it was undeniable that, whatever his motive, the star was doing good. The expressions on the distorted faces of the children he addressed spoke their welcome. And his familiarity with names and interests vouched for the regularity of such visits. As did the gratitude of the nursing staff.

Charles was brought back to a conclusion that he had often reached before: that a good action remains a good action, whatever its motivation. The fact that Bernard was making capital out of his work with the handicapped, the fact that he was very deliberately supplying a lack of natural humanity, that he was consciously building up an image of caring, and quite possibly scoring points to be recognised in some future Honours List, did not detract from the pleasure that he brought to the objects of his manufactured concern.

Charles found himself disarmed by this discovery. Having seen Bernard in action on the hospital visit was not going to make it any easier to challenge him over the deaths of Sadie Wainwright and Scott Newton (though he knew that, if Bernard had an inkling of his suspicions, the star was quite capable of deliberately fostering such a mood of doubt).

The visit only took half an hour. The matron and a few giggling nurses saw them to the main door. 'Haven't seen you on the television so much recently, Mr. Walton,' commented the matron.

He grinned. 'Ah no. Have to ration myself. Don't want the public to get bored with me.'

'Oh, I'm sure that wouldn't happen.'

'All too easily, matron, all too easily.'

'I bet you've got another big series coming up soon, haven't you?'

Bernard Walton laid his finger slyly along the side of his nose. 'Big secret, matron, big secret.'

'Ooh, I bet you have got something coming up.'

'All,' he announced mysteriously, 'will become clear at the proper time.'

Back in the car, Charles asked the blunt question, 'Have you really got a new series coming up?'

'No,' replied Bernard gloomily, 'but I can't tell them that, can I?'

As they approached London, Bernard asked if he had any plans for the evening. Charles, whose plans rarely aspired beyond a visit to the Montrose, said he hadn't.

'I'd thought of dining at my club, the Greville. Be delighted if you'd join me.'

'Oh, but I...' Charles instinctively thought of his usual dress (once dignified by Gerald Venables with the description 'neo-woodcutter'). But no, of course. Reg the barman's blazer and ungiving trousers were quite suitable for dining in a gentleman's club.

So it proved. As they entered the splendid hallway of the Greville, an elderly member, mellowed by alcohol, seized Charles by the hand and confided that he'd always recognise an Old Millingtonian tie and had he heard anything from Stubby Harbottle.

They dined well in a small, darkly panelled room. It was still early and they were alone. As Charles had suspected, Bernard was now in confiding mood. Not only confiding, but morbidly realistic.

'I don't need to tell you, Charles, the news about *What'll the Neighbours*: ...was pretty serious for me.'

'Oh, something else'll come up,' Charles assured him easily.

Bernard Walton shook his head. 'No sign of it. I need a starring vehicle and there just ain't another one around.'

'Oh, come on. You're not going to be out of work.'

'No, not out of work, but out of the right sort of work. Okay, I can do a few guest appearances on other people's shows, I can do panel games, that sort of stuff, but I need the continuity of my own show. Everything else springs from that. You heard that Matron – "Haven't seen you on the television so much recently, Mr. Walton.." It doesn't take long for the public to forget a face, you know.'

'And, apart from that, there's the money. It takes a few bob to maintain the sort of establishment I do.' Charles could well believe him. 'It isn't just the money for the television series that counts, it's all the other spin-off stuff. You get booked for cabaret or after-dinner speaking or other shows because you're seen regularly on the box. And now, it seems, I'm not going to be seen regularly on the box.'

'I'm sure some other series'll come up for you.'

'I hope so. I've been talking to a few writers to see if they've got ideas. I'm prepared to put up development money. I'm trying to get Rod Tisdale. He's the best for my sort of comedy, but he's always got so much work. Still, there's an idea of his that might work out, but it's early days yet. I need another property.'

It was interesting to hear how Bernard thought in properties. He didn't just want a job, he wanted a personal setting for his own personality. It was an attitude to show business which Charles had never found necessary.

But as Bernard talked, the precarious nature of his position became clearer. The top-rating series was essential to his operation. Without it, the celebrity bookings would only continue for a short time and he would degenerate into a professional celebrity, a tree without roots, famous for being famous, without any basis of other work to justify his status. The stakes were high and a character with a star complex like Bernard Walton might go to considerable lengths to maintain his position.

He was surprisingly aware of his limitations. 'What worries me about it most, Charles, is that I think this is a symptom. Nigel Frisch stopped *What'll the Neighbours.*, saying that there was nowhere left for the series to go. Rod had worked out every possible permutation of the basic situation. Okay, that's true enough, but it's not a reason for cancelling. Almost every sit cam continues long after the basic situation's been exhausted. No, I'm afraid that what Nigel was saying was that he reckoned the public's getting sick of me. After all, I do only do one thing, and they may just have had enough of it. If that is the case, then I really have got problems.'

There was a pause. They both drank from their glasses of wine. What Bernard said next took Charles completely by surprise. 'Which is why,' he pronounced slowly, 'I need your help.'

'I'm sorry?'

'I need your help. I need someone involved in *The Strutters* to keep me informed as to how things are going.'

'What?'

'Listen, that series is thriving at the expense of my series. The company's decided they can't do both. That's been obvious since the spin-off was first mooted. They can't give Dob and George Birkitt star billing in one series and then put them back as supports in *What'll the Neighbours...*'

'So you've known from the start that they wouldn't make any more of yours?'

'No, no, I thought they'd make more with new neighbours. Pay off Dob and George and introduce a new couple. I talked to Rod Tisdale about it and we worked out a few story-lines. But now they've cancelled the series flat.'

Bernard looked at the light through his wine glass before continuing. '*What'll the Neighbours Say?* will only come back if *The Strutters* doesn't get made.'

Charles nodded, waiting.

'I keep trying to think what could stop it from getting made. The best thing I can think of is if Dob were to die.'

It was spoken very casually, but Charles felt a cold chill. It seemed incredible that he was with the same man whose philanthropy with the spastics he had witnessed a couple of hours earlier.

'Unfortunately,' Bernard went on, 'though she's the right sort of age to pop off at any moment, she seems remarkably robust. Have to wish for something else. That's why I'm glad you're there in the cast, Charles.'

'Why?'

'Well, I think you owe me a few favours. I mean, I got you the job, after all.'

'Are you asking me to sabotage the show?'

'No, no, no. Nothing as dramatic as that. I just want you to keep me in touch with the production, how it's going, you know. There may be something I can use. I mean, how did this week's recording go, for instance?'

'Not very well.'

'Good. That's exactly the sort of thing I want to hear.'

Charles tried to recover himself. The new direction of the conversation had come as a shock to him. It had confirmed his conjecture about Bernard's motivation, but he had not expected such a direct statement of the situation. 'I suppose then,' he began slowly, 'you must have been pretty pleased to hear about Sadie's death. And Scott's. Both liable to slow down the advance of the series.'

Bernard nodded. 'Yes. Except that neither of them slowed it down enough. No, I'm delighted so far. The series seems to have got off to a very unpropitious start. But it's not enough. It's still going ahead. I need something a bit more central than those two deaths. A rather more permanent spanner in the works.'

He stumbled a bit over the last sentence and Charles suddenly realised that the star was very drunk. He must have been at the bottle all day, maybe every day since he had heard of his show's cancellation. That would account for his atypical indiscretion and the strangeness of his approach. But it didn't explain away his desire to destroy *The Strutters*. That was real enough.

Simultaneous with Charles's realisation, the power of the drink seemed to get through to Bernard, who looked blearily about him.

'Sadie,' Charles nudged gently.

'Sadie.' The name was repeated without emphasis.

'She came to your dressing room after the pilot...'

'Yes.'

'And she called you a bastard.'

'Yes.'

'You had an argument and a little later she fell to her death from the fire escape.'

'Yes.'

'What did you argue about?'

Bernard stopped nodding and a look of cunning came into his face. 'I'd complained to the Producer about the allocation of dressing rooms. She regarded this as sneaking behind her back.'

'I see. And Scott?'

'Scott drove too fast.'

That was all he got. In a moment Bernard started drinking black coffee, suddenly aware of the state he was in. He clammed up, realising he had said too much already.

But Charles was pleased with what he had heard. There was now no doubt about the strength of Bernard's motivation and his desire to destroy *The Strutters* at any cost. And, though he hadn't confessed to either of the murders, he had been at least enigmatic about them. And he had effectively asked for Charles's help in his sabotage plan.

All that was needed was evidence to link the two deaths to Bernard. At least now Charles had a clear line of investigation. After rounding off the evening at the Montrose, he went to bed relatively content.

His content was broken the next day at lunchtime when the radio news announced the death of Rod Tisdale, who had been run over by a vehicle which didn't stop.

Not very funny. Minor accidents are funny, fatal accidents aren't. Basic rule of comedy.

More pertinently, Rod Tisdale had already delivered the six scripts he was writing for the series, so his removal did not impede the progress of *The Strutters* in any way.

What was more, he was a person to whom Bernard Walton looked to provide him with a new star vehicle.

And, most galling of all to any theorist trying to see a pattern of murders committed by the star, Rod Tisdale had been killed at nine o'clock the previous evening. At which time the main suspect was sitting in the Greville Club, dining with Charles Paris.

The case was once again wide open.

CHAPTER EIGHT

West End Television Ltd,
W.E.T. House,
235–9 Lisson Avenue, London NW1 3PQ.
18th June, 1979.

Dear Charles,

I thought I'd just drop everyone a note after recent events to assure them that, in spite of problems you all know about, everything is okay on *The Strutters* front and all of us here are still confident we've got a very exciting property on our hands.

Until recently we weren't certain whether Rod Tisdale was going to write the remaining scripts in the series or not. He was undecided about it. Obviously now the decision has been made for us, and I am delighted to be able to announce to you that the rest of the series will be written by none other than Willy and Samantha Tennison! I'm sure you're familiar with their work from hosts of successful sit coms, but if your memory needs any nudging, let me just mention such series as *Flat Spin, Daisy and Jonathan, Your Turn, Darling, Oh, What a Pair of Au Pairs!* and that charming show set in a cookery college, *Oh, Crumbs!*

Willy and Sam are delightful people and great chums and I'm sure will be absolutely *right* for *The Strutters*. I've asked them to come along to our next read-through, so that we can all get a chance to meet up.

Thank you, incidentally, for your continuing hard work on the series. We really have got a smashing cast and I think that's one of the most important ingredients in a really exciting show. Let's put our troubles behind us and look forward to the success *The Strutters* is inevitably going to be!

With the warmest good wishes,

Yours sincerely,

Peter

PETER LIPSCOMBE
Producer *The Strutters*

When Bob Tomlinson arrived at the Paddington Jewish Boys' Club Hall for the next read-through the following Wednesday and found Willy and Sam Tennison holding court, he said he was going out for a sandwich and would come back in half an hour, by which time everyone had better be ready to start work.

The atmosphere of the second read-through had cleared, and everyone seemed a lot more cheerful. Rod Tisdale's death, apart from shattering Charles Paris's murder theories, had not had much effect. He had been such an unobtrusive person to have around that his absence was hardly remarked at all.

And any void he might have left was more than filled by Willy and Sam Tennison. They were a roly-poly little pair of writers, a married couple who that day affected patchwork shirts and matching yellow jeans. They were awfully affectionate and flirtatious with each other all the time, and talked in a manner very similar to the scripts of their sit coms. Since most of their success had been based on a series of interchangeable shows which dramatised the small happenings of their own lives, this was hardly surprising.

The viewing public knew everything about them. Their student lives in adjacent flats had hit the screen in the hilarious form of *Flat Spin*. The early days of their marriage had been chronicled in the series *Daisy and Jonathan*. The wacky tribulations of having children took comic form as *Your Turn, Darling* and the increasing affluence these scripts brought them provided the basis for *Oh, What a Pair of Au Pairs!* Their revolutionary attempt to do something different with *Oh, Crumbs!* had been weakened by the fact that the catering college where the series was set was run by a couple called Rob and Mona Partridge, who bore a remarkable similarity to all their other couples.

The Tennisons also had a disconcerting habit of always talking as if they were being interviewed and volunteering information that no one had ever asked for.

Peter Lipscombe thought they were wonderful. He laughed constantly at their shared monologue.

'Well, I don't know, darling,' said Willy Tennison.

'Don't know what, darling?' asked Sam Tennison.

'How we're going to get six scripts together in time, darling.'

'Oh, we'll manage somehow, darling. Lots of midnight oil.'

'But is it going to be worth it with the price oil is these days?'

'Oh, I've got a friend who's a sheik.'

'I thought your friend was the milkman.'

'Well, this guy's a kind of milk sheik.'

'You know people always ask us how we manage to work together all the time, you know, as man and wife. Don't they, darling?'

'They do, darling.'

'And I always say that there are four of us. There's a husband and a wife and a writer and another writer.'

'And never the twain and the twain shall meet.'

'Yes. Or at least one twain never meets the other twain.'

'Otherwise, darling, there'd be a twain crash.'

'Oh, lovely, darling. I'll write that one down.'

While her husband committed the gem to paper, Sam Tennison continued, 'Willy always uses a blue notebook, while I like pink ones. We never go anywhere without our notebooks, do we, darling?'

'Never, darling. Never know when the Muse will strike.'

'As one pussy cat shop steward said to the other.'

'Oh, darling, that's another one for the book.'

Charles prayed for the return of Bob Tomlinson. He also mentally fabricated a new series which would chronicle the remainder of Willy and Sam Tennison's lives if he had his way. There'd be *Mum's The Word!* for when their tongues were cut out, *There's a Funny Thong!* for when they were garrotted, and, to cover their funerals, *We're Only Here for the Bier!*

Eventually, Bob Tomlinson and belligerent sanity returned.

'Hello, Bob, I'm Sam...'

'And I'm Willy...'

'Shut up.'

'We're your new writers.'

'Are you? Well, I don't want you round my rehearsal rooms. Send your scripts in by post. You've already wasted enough time this morning. We've got a tight schedule. We're losing two days' rehearsal with the filming we've got to pick up. Incidentally, everyone, the overnight shoot for Ep. Six is fixed for Thursday fortnight. 5th July. Okay, read!'

'But, Sam and I had hoped –'

'But, Willy and I had hoped –'

'Didn't you hear me? Piss off.'

He was a good man, that Bob Tomlinson, thought Charles.

The overnight filming Bob had mentioned was for an insert into the last *Strutters* script Rod Tisdale wrote. In fact, it was the last full script of any sort that he wrote, but anyone who searched through its fabric for some final message from the writer to the world would have been disappointed. All he would have found was a predictable plot, dressed up with sixty-seven familiar jokes, fifty-two of which were destined to receive laughs from the studio audience and the remaining fifteen to have artificial ones imposed in the dubbing suite. Not a great memorial to a human being (which is what Rod Tisdale must have been, though he never gave any sign of it).

Charles had found out as much as he could about the writer's death, but there was not a lot. His relaxed rehearsal schedule (given a pragmatist like Bob Tomlinson as director, fourteen lines and two moves didn't take long to perfect) allowed him time to go to the inquest, but information seemed to be scarce.

Rod Tisdale had lived in a block of flats in a quiet road in Maida Vale. At nine o'clock on the previous Friday evening, 15th June, he had left the block and started out across the road, where he had been knocked over and killed by a vehicle travelling at considerable speed.

There had been no witnesses of the accident, though people in other flats had heard the impact. By the time they looked out of their windows, only parked cars were visible.

Rod Tisdale had lived alone, and had apparently spent the day in his flat working. Investigations so far suggested that he had not spoken to anyone on the telephone except for his agent, and had not then mentioned any plans to go out. There was nothing in his diary to indicate why he set out at nine o'clock. He might have been walking towards Maida Vale tube station. He might have been going to the local pub (though he was very rarely seen in there). He might just have been going out for a walk.

Police investigations would continue to try to track down the errant vehicle which had killed him, so an adjournment was requested. The coroner granted it in a voice that did not expect much more to be discovered and commented on the alarming increase in hit and run accidents.

There was no one Charles Paris recognised at the inquest. so he left little the wiser. The death could just have been an accident. On the other hand, if the potential murderer were someone Rod Tisdale knew, the murder would have been fairly easy to set up. He had only to ring the writer, fix a meeting-place which would involve his crossing the road, and sit and wait for him to come out.

So, just another death, and apparently an accidental one. Every attempt at a pattern Charles started was soon frustrated. He had been on very promising lines with Bernard Walton cast as villain, but that approach had been mined by the latest incident. Rod Tisdale's death would do nothing to halt the progress of *The Strutters*, and was, on the contrary, a positive loss to Bernard, who had looked to the writer to come up with a new star vehicle for him.

So, even if Bernard Walton hadn't got the one alibi Charles could never crack, his motivation was gone, and, with it, fantasies of the star bringing in hired killers to do his dirty deeds.

Charles tried to contact Bernard a few days later with a view to checking a few facts about Scott Newton's death, but the housekeeper said Mr Walton had gone for a month's holiday to his villa in Sardinia. Since this was supported the next day by a photograph of the star beaming farewells at Heathrow Airport, there was no reason to disbelieve it. (Charles's first cynical reaction to the news had been that Bernard's Publicity Manager had packed him off to Sardinia in the hope that a well timed kidnap might bring his client back to public attention.)

So, if any further accidents hit *The Strutters* team during the next month, it was pretty unlikely that Bernard Walton had anything to do with them.

But for the next couple of weeks there was no sign of any sort of accident. Charles began to think that the first three must after all be just unfortunate coincidences.

All that happened was that *The Strutters* continued to be made, and that was quite a tiring process for all concerned. The basic pattern for the first burst of the series had been for Tuesday evening recordings, with a read-through for the next episode the following morning. Six weeks of this was already a heavy schedule, but the need to fit in extra filming days to replace those lost after Scott's death made it very heavy indeed. Saturday rehearsals crept in, then Sunday ones. Even Charles, on whom the demands of fourteen lines and two moves a week were not onerous, began to get tired. The strain on the principals must have been enormous.

George Birkitt reacted by occasional bouts of temperament. He was not used to learning so many lines every week and was often still to be seen with script in hand at the Dress Run on recording day. He got very cross when the poor little Assistant Stage Manager charged with the task prompted him, and kept complaining that he found the lines difficult to remember because they were so badly written.

Aurelia Howarth, on the other hand, always knew her lines after a couple of days and generally showed professionalism and stamina which would have been remarkable in an actress half her age. She still appeared very anxious, no doubt worried about Cocky's health, but did not let this interfere with her work. She lived up to the theatrical standard of a 'trouper' and, by contrast, showed up George Birkitt's relative immaturity.

In spite of her worn looks, she did not seem to have lost any of her enthusiasm for the business. Indeed, a couple of days after Rod Tisdale's death, Charles was amused to hear her asking Peter Lipscombe whether he'd yet read the books she'd lent him. She was sure there was series potential there.

Peter apologised, promised they were next on his list, really. Charles had heard that from too many producers to take it too seriously. Though many television producers can read scripts, it's a very rare one who can manage a whole book.

So there didn't seem much prospect for Aurelia's idea. But Charles was impressed that at her age and in the middle of such a tight schedule she was still on the look-out for a new project.

With all the pressures, a kind of peace and community spirit came over the production. They all spent so much time together that they had to choose between constant arguments or conviviality and fortunately most opted for the latter. Even Charles began to see the advantages of television. It was almost like having a regular job.

The audience reaction to the recordings didn't change much, but everyone seemed quite happy about it, and Charles came to share the indifference to, or even contempt of audiences, which is common to most people who work in television. Bob Tomlinson was all set to come in with his electronic hilarity in the dubbing suite, so it hardly mattered what the people shovelled out of coaches into the studio seats thought of the show. The only function of their reaction was to tell the viewing audience at home where the jokes were intended to be.

Charles also got closer to Jay Lewis. The young PA seemed to have ended her relationship with Nick Coxhill and to be more or less available. She seemed to enjoy Charles's company and, though he got a little sick of the received wisdom of Phil Middleton and Ernie Franklyn Junior, news of the progress of VTR editing and the doings of Jay's flatmate who worked in Film Research, he enjoyed hers. She really was very pretty.

Sometimes Charles wondered if his continuing attraction to girls young enough to be his daughter arose from his incomplete relationship with his real daughter, Juliet. But, since it didn't change facts or get him anywhere, he never indulged such speculation for long.

He didn't make any move with Jay for the time being. They were working too closely together for him to risk a rebuff or any awkwardness. But he made his interest clear, and planned in a vague way for some sort of advance just before the break in recording sequence in mid-July.

Thoughts of crime receded. When he spoke to Gerald Venables after one of the recordings, he said he'd decided there was nothing to be investigated, except for a sequence of coincidences. The only thing that had ever made him think differently was the words of Sadie which he had overheard. And there was no chance of finding out any more about them.

After the recording before the overnight filming, the usual group of cast (including Toby Root, who'd played the part of Colonel Strutter's friend) and camp followers (very camp, in some cases) gathered in the bar for a quick drink, because the week ahead was busy. Read-through the following morning and rehearsal all day. Then, because of Union regulations covering the Thursday night's shoot, no rehearsal on the Thursday or Friday. Pick up again Saturday morning, rehearse Sunday, somehow be ready for the Crew Run Monday at noon, and into the studio on the Tuesday. It wasn't long to get a half-hour of television together.

With this in mind, neither Dame Aurelia Howarth nor George Birkitt went up for a drink. Both no doubt (though the latter would never admit it) had gone back to do a bit of work on the week's lines.

The absence of his idol left Aurelia's Number One Fan at something of a loose end. Since his first contested appearance, Romney Kirkstall had come to every recording and hung around on the fringe of Aurelia's circle in the bar afterwards. He never had a drink, neither buying for himself nor accepting anyone else's offer.

He looked so helpless that once he had got a large Bell's (very skilfully bought by Peter Lipscombe), Charles went across to him.

'Dob not coming up?' asked Romney Kirkstall anxiously.

'Don't think so. Busy schedule this week. I expect she's gone back to catch up on some sleep.'

'Oh dear.' The little man looked very upset. The focus of his whole week had been removed.

'I'm sure she'll come up for a drink next time,' Charles comforted. 'It's just that we've got an overnight shoot on Thursday, so it's a tight week.'

Romney Kirkstall still looked distraught. 'I wanted to see her. I've got a book I wanted her to autograph.'

'Oh. Well, next week.'

'I suppose so,' Romney Kirkstall conceded dismally. 'I was so excited to find it, though. It's a biography of Dab that I've been looking for for ages. Found it on a barrow outside a second-hand bookshop in Putney.'

'Oh, really.'

'It's very rare, you know. Called *I Dream of Dancing*. You know, after the song.'

'Oh yes. I've heard of it.' It was difficult not to have done. The song had been a big hit in a revue in the early Thirties and had virtually become Aurelia Howarth's signature tune.

'Oh, I did want to get her signature today.' Romney Kirkstall still sounded desolated.

'You'll get it in a week.'

'Anything can happen in a week.'

Charles looked up sharply, his dormant detective instinct aroused. But no, there was no threat in Romney Kirkstall's words. He was a little man with an obsession, but that obsession wasn't murder.

Charles thought perhaps showing an interest would cheer him up, so asked Romney if he might look at the book.

It was the right question. There was a scurry into the duffle bag and the precious trophy was presented to him.

The book was a battered little blue volume. Presumably it had had a decorative dust jacket, but that was long gone. Charles turned instinctively to the date of publication – 1940. It was not surprising that Romney Kirkstall had had difficulty in finding it. Most books vanish pretty quickly, but show business biographies must be the most quickly dated and evanescent forms of literature.

The name of the book's author was Max de Pouray, which meant nothing to Charles. He glanced at the text as he flicked through and recognised the breathless sycophancy of the genre.

And of course Dob appeared in his famous Midnight Revue at the 'Pav'. All the stars in London's theatrical galaxy were there, and she outshone them all. Dressed in the simplest gown of white silk, in such company as the Prince of Wales, Lord and Lady Louis Mountbatten, Mrs Dudley Ward, the Duchess of Portland, Lady Victoria Wemyss, the Duke and Duchess of Westminster, the Duke of Norfolk and half the noble scions of Debrett's, a glittering company that must have left most of this sceptred isle's stately homes empty, it was Dob who was the 'wow' of the evening…

There was a lot more in similar vein, but Charles found the photographs more interesting. They were brownish, and many had the posed quality of publicity stills. What they revealed most forcibly was Aurelia Howarth's natural beauty. At fifteen, while she was a humble member of the chorus, she already had a remarkable purity of line and, maturing through the photographs, she retained the softness of youth. In spite of the vagaries of hair-styling and the ridiculous nature of some of her revue costumes, her quality shone through. And the soft studio lighting of the period gave her outline that blurred indistinction which she somehow still retained.

There were a few less posed shots, though they still looked pretty formal. Over dinner at the Café Royal. In a deck chair on a transatlantic liner. Relaxing on the beach at Nice with a handsome young man... It was with shock that Charles realised that her escort must be her husband. A photograph of their wedding confirmed it.

It was hard to imagine from the grinning skeleton he now was that Barton Rivers had once been such a dashing figure. With his body fleshed out and a thick crop of dark hair sleeked back on his head, he looked very much the matinée idol.

But the photographs did not offer much evidence of his career. After all, the book's subject was Aurelia, and it seemed that they had rarely worked together. There was one shot of them with two other couples dancing in front of a backdrop of a desert island. The caption read '*In the Palm of My Hand with a Palm Overhead* from *Careless Feet.*' And there was a picture of the pair sitting in a Bentley over the legend, 'Husband and Wife – from *Death Takes A Short Cut.*' The photograph looked like a film still.

What was remarkable about it was that they looked so familiar. The photograph was only a half-page and the whole of the Bentley was in shot, so it was difficult to see much detail of their faces. Aurelia wore one of her floating gowns, and a hat tied on with a scarf. Barton wore a blazer and cravat, and his hair was obscured by a large white flat cap. The car, which must have been a lot newer when the photograph was taken, was identical to the one they now drove around in.

In fact, to the casual eye, the photograph could have been taken a few weeks before, when the couple drove away from Bernard Walton's house after the day's filming.

'Do you know anything about this film?' Charles asked.

Romney Kirkstall shook his head. 'Never heard of it. But then I've always concentrated on Dab's theatrical work. That is, until she stopped doing theatre and started television.'

Charles looked again at the photograph, but was aware of Romney Kirkstall's hands reaching out for the book. 'If you don't mind...'

There was a note of paranoia in the little man's voice, as if he were genuinely afraid Charles was going to appropriate his prize.

'Okay, thank you very much for letting me look at it.' He handed the book back and, without another word, Romney Kirkstall stuffed it into his duffle bag and scuttled off.

Jay Lewis was chattering to some other young PAs. She turned round angrily when he ran a finger down her spine, but softened when she saw who it was.

Which was nice.

'Hello, Charles.'

'Hi. I wondered if you fancied coming out for a meal.'

'Now?'

'Uh-huh.'

'I've just fixed to go and eat with Dinky and Lucretia.' She indicated the other girls. 'You could come with us, I suppose.'

'Not really what I had in mind.'

She grinned a grin that suggested she knew what he did have in mind. And didn't object too much.

'Another time, maybe,' he proposed.

'Hock – A.'

'And do you think your flatmate in Film Research could find out something for me?'

'I'm sure she could.'

'Good. I'll tell you about it when we have our meal.'

He got another drink (had to buy his own – Peter Lipscombe had left) and looked round for someone to talk to. Most of the cast had gone. Jay and her friends were collecting their coats by the door. Knots of cameramen still drank lager. Men in lumberjack checked shirts grumbled ominously. Robin Laughton, the hearty Floor Manager, held court to some young men at a low table. Charles drifted over to join them.

Robin seemed pleased to see him. He was showing off his savoir-faire to a group of trainee Floor Managers, and wanted to demonstrate his easy familiarity with the stars. Since there weren't any stars in the bar, he would make do with Charles Paris.

'Charles, just passing on a few wrinkles to the lads here. Charles Paris, this is Bob, and Tony and... er....'

'Dick,' supplied the youngest young man, who looked vaguely familiar. 'Actually. Charles, we met on *The Strutters*' pilot. I was trailing Robin on that.'

'Ah yes.' That would explain the familiarity. 'What've you been doing since?'

'Oh, trailing other stuff. I went and did some of the *Wragg and Bowen* filming, and then I've been following this series for the elderly. Do you know they've got this presenter on that called Ian Reynolds, who's nearly eighty?'

'Yes. I had heard.'

'He's a great old boy. He's not got a nerve in his body when it comes to-',

Robin Laughton decided that the trainee had held the floor long enough and interrupted. 'I must tell Charles about you and the walkie-talkie.'

'Oh.' Dick did not look keen on having the anecdote repeated.

But Robin Laughton pressed on with enthusiasm. Clearly it was a story that was going to show up Dick's inexperience. 'Charles, you know we all carry round these walkie-talkies, so that we can talk back to production control?'

'Yes.'

'Well, one thing you've got to remember is to switch them off, otherwise you're wired for sound at all times…'

'Yes.'

The other two trainee Floor Managers snickered in anticipation of the story they had heard before, and Dick looked even more uncomfortable, but Robin continued inexorably. 'Well, when Dick was very new, two or three months back, he was all wired up and he forgot about it and went off to the Gents to have a shit.'

This was the cue for the other trainees to burst into open laughter, which they dutifully did.

'Everyone,' Robin Laughton continued, 'heard everything. You got a round of applause when you came back into the studio, didn't you, Dick?'

'Yes.' He grinned and, reckoning that his baiting was now finished, tried to change the subject. 'What interests me, Charles, about –'

But Robin Laughton wasn't going to let him off the hook that easily. 'Oh, Dick kept doing things like that when he started. After the lavatory incident, he went and lost his set one day.'

'Well, I mislaid it.' Dick was not enjoying this crude masculine teasing. 'I just put it down somewhere. There's a lot to think about when you start.'

'Oh yes, a great deal,' Robin Laughton mocked. Charles saw the Floor Manager for what he was, the sort of man who would offer no sympathetic assistance to trainees in his charge, but would take delight in watching them make mistakes. Having started niggling at Dick, he couldn't leave the subject alone. 'Actually, it was on *The Strutters*' pilot you lost it, wasn't it? Lost it for the bloody Dress Run. My, you were a useful Floor Manager, weren't you?'

The other trainees laughed obediently. Dick spoke angrily. 'Look, I found it straight after. Right at the beginning of Line-up.'

Robin Laughton continued his mockery. 'He'd left it switched on, needless to say. Relaying anything it picked up into Production Control. Lucky the batteries weren't completely flat.'

'Where had you left it?' asked Charles, suddenly interested.

'In the Quick Change Room.'

'And you found it just after six?'

'Yes.'

'And was there anyone in the Quick Change Room?'

Dick was relieved at the change of interrogator and replied readily. 'Yes. Sadie Wainwright was in there, being her usual bad-tempered self.'

'Bad-tempered to you or to someone else?'

'Both. She appeared to be in the middle of an argument when I went in, and then bit my head off.'

'Who was in there with her?'

'Aurelia Howarth.'

CHAPTER NINE

ROD TISDALE's FINAL message to the world, the sixth (or, if you count the pilot, seventh) episode of *The Strutters* was on a theme he had used before. In *What'll the Neighbours Say?* much of the comedy had derived from the conflict between the wildly bohemian (if slightly overmature) Bernard Walton character and his more conventional neighbours, the *Strutters*. In *The Strutters*, the reactionary disapproval of the Colonel and his wife was moved to the centre of the action, and directed at everything in general and at their son in particular. This character, played by Nick Coxhill, became increasingly indistinguishable from the Bernard Walton character in *What'll the Neighbours Say?* He it was now who turned up in episodes with black girlfriends or wearing kaftans (sit cams must be the only places in the world where kaftans are still worn as a symbol of Bohemianism) or playing music too loud. (In the original script for this last plot, Rod Tisdale had gone daringly modern and had the character smoking pot, but West End Television, feeling this was a bit strong, had changed it to playing music too loud, which, as they said, 'made the same point'.)

Having reasserted the basic polarities of his traditional script, Rod Tisdale seemed determined to adapt all his old plots for the new series. But for the unfunny intervention of death, there was little doubt that all of the *What'll the Neighbours Say?* storylines would, in time, have reappeared in the guise of episodes of *The Strutters*. However, it was not to be, and with the appointment of Willy and Sam Tennison, who knew what direction the series would take? (Actually, one could have a pretty good guess. It was only a matter of time before the Nick Coxhill character was supplied with a dizzy wife to exchange darlings with, and Colonel and Mrs Strutter were moved back into subsidiary roles.)

All this preamble is necessary to explain the reason for the night filming that was so disturbing the rehearsal schedule of *The Strutters*. In Episode Six (or, if you count the pilot, Seven) the plot, simplified (bit not much) was as follows:

Colonel Strutter and his son argue violently about politics. The Colonel is a true-blue Conservative (jokes about being blue in the face too) and the Nick Coxhill character is a follower of Marx (sequence of jokes about Groucho, Harpo and Chico, which are compulsory in all sit coms which mention Marx). The son, in a kaftan, then meets a friend, also in a kaftan, who has just started a new political party, the Conservation (jokes about recycled paper and brown rice) and Union (brassiere jokes about 'One out, all out') Party. Friend suggests son should bridge the gap between the generations and invite his father to come and speak at the inaugural meeting of the new party. Son rings mother, who takes message and, daffily, mishears 'Conservation and Union Party' as 'Conservative and Unionist Party'. End of Part One. Commercial Break.

Part Two opens with Colonel and Mrs Strutter (on film) in the street, looking for the venue of the meeting and being amazed by the Bohemianism of the people they see going in. (All the extras involved wear kaftans to demonstrate their Bohemianism and have long hair and beards, thus adding considerably to the make-up bill for the episode.) The rest of Part Two is a studio sequence of the actual meeting in which misunderstandings abound, and everyone gets the wrong end of every available stick with, as in all good sit coms, 'hilarious consequences'.

The above plot had appeared in a very early episode of *What'll the Neighbours Say?*, in which Bernard Walton formed a new political party called 'The Brigade of Hard Red Unions', which his father (a character who didn't get on with Bernard and was quickly dropped from the series) misheard as 'The Brigade of Guards Reunion'. With, once again, 'hilarious consequences'.

The only difference between the two was that in *The Strutters* episode, all the other regular characters went along to the meeting to witness the Colonel's discomfiture. Which meant that Reg the golf club barman once again displayed his trousers, and Charles Paris had to turn up to West End Television for a nine p.m. make-up call, before being taken by coach to the condemned road in Clapham which the Location Manager had selected for the night's filming.

All the impedimenta of filming lay ready when the coach arrived. The crew had been booked for the full night and so were guaranteed 'Golden Time' (the best rate of overtime), regardless of when they finished. As a result the men in lumberjack checked shirts hadn't told them to slow down and they had been very efficient.

It was still a warm summer evening and not quite dark. But a fierce glow brighter than daylight came from the terrace of houses which was to be used as the location. Huge lights on tall metal stands were trained on them ready for filming. Cables ran from these to a variety of vans and lorries. Make-up caravans and mobile dressing rooms spread down the street. The double-decker bulk of the location caterers' bus loomed to one side. Extras in beards and kaftans sat around, plotting as ever how to get personally 'directed' by the director, thus raising their status (and fee) to that of 'walk-on'. There could be no doubt that a film crew was around.

So was a large crowd of gawpers. This was inevitable. The paraphernalia always attract an audience, and the clemency of the weather increased their numbers. Many had been standing outside local pubs and followed the film transport with interest. It was not an area where a great deal happened.

There was some raucous shouting from the crowd, but they seemed fairly good-humoured. Robin Laughton, the Floor Manager, walking round with his walkie-talkie, was of the opinion that they would soon disperse once the novelty had worn off and it got later.

The Location Manager, looking a little anxious, said he hoped that was the case. 'There seem to be a lot more people round here than I expected. I thought all the houses were empty. Most of them are boarded up.'

'Squatters, I should think,' said Robin Laughton. 'What time of day did you do your recce?'

'Afternoon. Hardly anyone around then. Just the old couple who live in that house right in the middle. I fixed a fee with them all right.'

'If you get trouble, maybe you'll have to pay some of this lot off.'

The Location Manager nodded uncertainly. It was part of his job to carry round pockets full of flyers to buy off anyone who objected to the filming. 'There are a lot of them, though.'

'They'll soon clear off once they see how boring it is. Don't you worry, my son.'

'Is Bob ready to start filming?'

Robin Laughton shook his head. 'Dob's not here yet.'

'Wasn't she coming in the coach?'

'No, special dispensation, she was to come and get made up here.'

'What, that old looney coming here in the Bentley? He's probably driven her to the wrong place.'

'No, no, we've sent a hire car for her. Old Barton'll be safely tucked up in bed by now.'

George Birkitt, standing by Charles, had overheard the end of this conversation. 'Oh no, it's the bloody limit!'

'What is?'

'Bloody Dob. Coming straight here. Not getting made up at W.E.T. like the rest of us.'

'Oh, come on. She's tired. Needs as much rest as she can get.'

'Don't you think I'm bloody tired?'

'I'm sure you are, but you're not seventy-five.'

'Huh. It's all very well, everyone kow-towing to her all the time, but who's carrying this bloody show, that's what I want to know. I mean, really, I'm the one who has to keep the thing going. I carry the story-line every bloody week, while she just twitters around charmingly. And yet who gets the top billing? Huh. You know I'm not the sort of person to fuss over details, but I think that billing'll have to be looked at on the next series.'

Aurelia arrived soon, clutching Cocky's basket, full of apologies for being late. The minicab driver, like all minicab drivers, hadn't known the way and had got lost. But she wouldn't be a minute honestly, darling. And she hurried into the make-up caravan.

Charles strolled over to the lit area and leant against one of the tall light-stands. ''Ere, keep off that. Not stable,' said the voice of one of the men in lumberjack checked shirts.

Charles moved away and looked at the stand. It was perfectly stable, in fact, mounted on a wheeled tripod. Metal locks were fixed down on the wheels to prevent it from slipping down the incline of the street. Still, television is full of people telling you not to touch this or that. Charles didn't want to precipitate a demarcation dispute by arguing.

Rather than getting smaller, the crowd of sightseers had increased. He looked at his watch. Of course, pubs just closed. The thought made him feel in his pocket, where his hand met the reassuring contour of a half-bottle of Bell's. Essential supplies for a night's filming.

There was irony in the scene before him. Here was a television crew setting out to film television's idea of an Alternative Society scene, and being watched by genuine members of the Alternative Society. It wasn't just their make-up which distinguished the television extras from the people they were meant to represent. Even those who weren't wearing kaftans looked far too groomed, far too designed. Television, particularly colour television, is a glamorising medium and it is very bad at reproducing authentic shoddiness.

But there was no doubt that the crowd of spectators was authentically shoddy. They were dusty and poor and bored. The interest the filming was arousing suggested that nothing else much happened in their lives.

Probably a lot of them were unemployed. And, as their numbers grew, their good humour seemed to diminish.

Charles heard another whispered consultation between the Floor Manager and the Locations Manager.

'You have cleared the filming with the police, haven't you?'

'Of course I have. First thing I always do.'

'Oh well, if they don't disperse once we start filming, we can get the cops to move them on.'

'I thought you were the one, Robin, who said they'd all disperse without any bother.'

'There weren't so many of them then.'

'Hmm.'

'Well, I think if you slip the noisiest ones a fiver, you'll be all right.'

'I might try it. See how things go.'

Bob Tomlinson bustled up to Robin Laughton. 'Come on, where are the bloody artists? We don't want to fart around all night, for God's sake.'

'I think Dob's nearly ready.'

'Then get her out here. And George. And the others. Come on, if we move, we can knock this lot off in an hour.'

But progress did not prove to be so fast. The artists were assembled and their first set-up, a walk along the road looking at house numbers, was rehearsed. The actors spoke their lines, and the director was satisfied.

'Okay. Let's go for a take.' There was silence. The clapper-board was duly filmed and the item identified verbally by the Floor Manager. 'And – Action!'

But the cast weren't the only people who took the cue. As soon as the word was spoken, the crowd behind the camera started up their noise again, shouting and baying, chanting in unison.

Bob Tomlinson tried again. Again there was silence while the shot was set up. Again, as soon as he cued the actors, the crowd started up. 'Talk to them, Robin,' he said tersely.

Robin Laughton went across towards the crowd in his most jovial Floor Manager manner. He spread his arms wide for attention. 'Listen, everyone, could we have a bit of hush while we're working? We're in a filming situation for a series called *The Strutters*, which you'll be able to see on your telly screens in the autumn. It's going to be a jolly funny show and I'm sure you'll all enjoy it. So we'd be really grateful if you could give us a bit of hush while we're doing our filming. Okay?'

'Why?' asked a tall black youth in a Bob Marley T-shirt.

'Why?' echoed Robin Laughton.

'Yes, why? Why should we let you disrupt our lives just for some tatty television show?'

Robin was baffled. It was a question that had never occurred to him so he had never considered the answer to it.

The black youth spoke very fluently. He was obviously well educated and not randomly obstructive. He was making a political point. What was more, the rest of the crowd listened to him. He was their leader and they did what he said. The disruption seemed to be an organised protest.

Robin Laughton, unable to provide any sort of answer to the black youth's question, wandered back to Bob Tomlinson and beckoned the Location Manager across. They conferred.

Then the Location Manager went across to the crowd. The black youth had his back turned and was talking to a group of other young men. The Location Manager joined the group and appeared to make some suggestion.

Suddenly the black youth leapt in the air, waving a piece of paper in his hand. 'Hey, look, man – five pounds. You ever see one like that, man? Come on, everybody, this man's giving away five pound notes. Make sure you all get one.'

'No, no,' protested the unfortunate Locations Manager. 'I haven't got enough for everyone. I just wanted to persuade everyone that –'

'What is it – bribery now?' The black youth was suddenly very quiet. 'Oh yes, money buy off everything, eh? Well, listen, man, why should we put up with you coming round here? What you say it is – comedy show? So you think the way we live's funny, eh?'

'No, not at all. We just want to get on with our work. Look, you wouldn't like it if we came along and interfered with your work now, would you?'

This proved an unfortunate thing to say. 'Our work, is it? Sorry, brother, we don't have any work. That's why we live here, you know. That's why we live in these houses. That's why we don't like you making fun of our houses.'

The Location Manager was beginning to lose his temper. 'But they're not your houses. You're only bloody squatters.'

'And why are we squatters, man? We're squatters because this lousy government don't build no houses. We're squatters because this government don't care about anything except making the rich richer.'

Hearing the political turn of the conversation, Bob Tomlinson decided to join in with his common touch. 'Listen, mate, I'm with you. I vote Labour, just like you do. I don't want this lot in. But they're here and all we have to do right now is to get the work I got to do done, and get into bed for a good night's sleep. So what do you say? You give us no bother and we'll give you no bother.'

He chuckled disarmingly, but didn't persuade his audience. 'What do you mean?' asked the black youth. 'You don't give us any bother, huh? You take over the whole bloody street, and half the side streets of it. You fill the whole place with your bloody vans and buses and your big cars – all your bloody BMWs and Rovers and Bentleys and Daimlers and Mercs – and you say you don't give us no bother. Why should we be put out by you fat cats, eh?'

The Location Manager nodded to Bob Tomlinson and walked away. 'Now listen, son,' said the Director in a new, hard voice. 'He's gone to phone for the police. We have police permission to be here, you know, and if they come along, I think you'd be wise to be out of sight.'

'Oh, I see, it's threats now, is it? What d'you think we care about the bloody pigs. Okay, so you've got police permission. Big deal. Did you ever ask our permission? Eh?'

'We got permission from the couple in that house over there, who, as I understand it, are the only people with a legal right to live here.'

'What do you know about legal rights?'

'I know who deserves them.'

'What do you mean by that?'

'I mean I know the difference between someone who works for a living and someone who just scrounges on the state.'

'Hey, who you calling a scrounger, man?'

'You know bloody well who I'm calling a scrounger.'

'You want a punch in the mouth?'

'Why, do you?'

Slap on his cue, at this moment Peter Lipscombe appeared beaming through the crowd. 'I say, is everything okay?'

His appearance did at least avert the incipient fight between Bob Tomlinson and his antagonist, but it didn't bring the start of filming any nearer. He tried to explain the complex costs of filming to the crowd, but they didn't seem susceptible to budgetary arguments.

The actors were still standing round in the lit area, ready to resume work if required, but eventually Robin Laughton came across and suggested they should go into the caravans until the atmosphere settled a bit.

Charles found himself in the make-up caravan with Aurelia Howarth. The actress busied herself with Cocky in his little basket.

'Quite frightening, all those people, aren't they?' he observed.

She shrugged. 'I suppose so. It reminds me of entertaining the troops during the War. You got that same feeling of the power of a crowd.'

'And you don't find that frightening?'

'Not really, darling.' She sounded genuinely unconcerned, though a note of anxiety came into her voice as she turned back to the dog. 'How's my little boy then?'

'Do you think we'll get anything done tonight?'

'Oh yes, surely, darling. They'll get bored and go away.'

The noise had certainly died down. Charles looked through the caravan window. The crowd was dwindling.

'Yes, they've made their point. And if the police do come...'

'I think it would be as well if the police didn't come,' Dame Aurelia Howarth observed shrewdly. 'That might just antagonise them further.' But her attention was elsewhere. 'How's my little Cocky then?'

'Is he okay?' Better show an interest.

'He's not a well boy.'

'He means a lot to you.'

'Of course. If anyone hurt Cocky, I'd...' She looked at Charles very straight and he felt the daunting power of those famous blue eyes. When she continued, her voice was very quiet, but very determined. 'I'd kill them.'

Everything fell into place. As well as determination, there was obsession in the eyes. On three occasions Aurelia Howarth had had the opportunity. She had been definitely identified as the one who had threatened Sadie Wainwright. The PA had certainly spoken dismissively of Cocky. Was it not likely that Scott Newton and Rod Tisdale had done the same? Or was he back to his earlier blackmailing theory? Had Scott Newton witnessed Sadie's death and...?

Well, if there had to be a confrontation, there was no time like the present. Charles took a deep breath. 'Aurelia, when Sadie Wainwright died –'

But before he could say more, they were disturbed by a sudden shout of anger from outside. The crowd had once again erupted in fury. Charles and Aurelia rushed to the door of the caravan to see the cause.

It was the location caterers. Oblivious to the commotion, they had started to lay out a lavish selection of salads and meats and wines on trestle tables outside their bus. A section of the crowd had seen this and, infuriated by the ostentation, screamed for the others to join them as they rushed forward.

The horde descended, seizing plates and bowls and throwing them to the ground. When the film crew tried to intervene, they had food hurled at them. Within seconds, everyone was involved in a bizarre fight outside the location caterers' bus.

Terrines of pâté cracked against skulls, rare beef slices slapped in faces, glazed chicken wings rediscovered flight, strawberries spattered, mayonnaise flowed down denim shoulders, coleslaw matted into layered hair.

How the fight would have developed was impossible to say. An awful thud and a scream froze the action and drew everyone's attention back to the lit area.

In the middle of it lay the still body of Robin Laughton, pinned beneath the metal mass of a toppled light.

'Oh no.' Aurelia Howarth's face had lost all its colour. 'Not another death. Oh, my God, no!'

But there was no doubt that the Floor Manager was in a death situation.

CHAPTER TEN

SINCE THEY HAD already been summoned to move on the crowd of spectators, the police were on the scene of the death quickly. They took charge and were very efficient. Technicians and actors were asked to wait in the caravans until the police were ready to take statements from them. The crowd who had disrupted the filming seemed to have melted away. They would have stayed and argued their rights with the police over the filming, and enjoyed the exercise; but now there was a death to be investigated they made themselves scarce.

Two plain-clothes detective-sergeants were taking the statements. The one Charles got looked bored and seemed keen to get the basic questions over as quickly as possible. 'You see anything unusual?'

'Well, the whole scene was fairly unusual. With the fight going on, food flying in every direction.'

'Yes, I know all that. I mean, anything unusual near the light that fell and killed Mister ...' He consulted notes. '...Laughton.'

'No, but I did notice that the wheels of the light were firmly locked earlier.'

'Yes. What I'm really asking is did you see anyone tamper with the light-stand. I gather the crowd was trying to break up your filming, so I suppose we can't rule out the possibility of sabotage. Did you see anyone go near the lights?'

'No, but everything was such chaos that –'

'Yes, Mr Paris. At the time of the fight, did you see where John Odange was?'

'Who's John Odange?'

'He's the black guy who was apparently leading the crowd.'

'Oh yes. I saw him by the food. I remember, because he emptied a lemon meringue pie over our producer, Peter Lipscombe.' Charles couldn't help smiling. The image was one that would stay with him and bring comfort in his old age.

'So you didn't see Odange go near the lights?'

'No.'

'Hmm.' The detective-sergeant sounded disappointed. 'We've had trouble with him before.'

It seemed that the black youth's view that society was conspiring against him may have had some justification. 'No,' said Charles firmly. 'He was right at the centre of the crowd all the time. If he had tampered with the lights, everyone would have seen.'

The detective-sergeant nodded in a bored way. 'We'll have to pull him in and talk to him anyway. Okay. Mr Paris, if you could ask the next member of the cast to –'

'There is one thing,' said Charles. There was no point in keeping all his suspicions to himself. After all, it was the police's job to investigate crime and they were much better qualified to do it than he was.

'Yes?' There wasn't a lot of interest in the word.

'Of course this death could just have been an unfortunate accident...'

'That's rather the way it looks, Mr Paris. Unless we can get any evidence to the contrary.'

'The only thing is...it's not the first accident that's happened on this show. First there was a PA who –'

'Yes, yes, Mr Paris, thank you. I'm well aware of all that. Every one of your colleagues who I've talked to has mentioned the sequence of accidents, and I'm sure it's been very worrying for you. Maybe someone quoted *Macbeth* in a dressing room or something.'

The detective-sergeant spoke as to a tiresome child. It was something Charles had got used to through his career. For a lot of people, actors would always remain a self-dramatising and infantile breed.

He kept his temper. 'Okay, it may sound fanciful. All I'm saying is that, if you are thinking of sabotage, then it need not have been perpetrated by someone in the crowd; it could have been someone connected with the production.'

'Thank you very much for your invaluable advice, Mr Paris. Yes, I admit it does sound a little fanciful, but we will certainly bear every possibility in mind in our investigations. I can assure you that we are already aware of the coincidence of accidents which have surrounded your precious production, and if there is any link between them, you can rely on us to find it. Now, if you will allow me to get on...'

Charles wasn't sure. Maybe the police had got the show under surveillance, maybe they had followed all his reasoning through step by step, maybe they were way ahead of him and just waiting to make an arrest. All he knew was that it would be a long time before he shared his suspicions with the police again. Their opinion of amateur detectives was all too clear.

Outside in the street, where the apparatus of filming had mostly been cleared up, he met Jay Lewis, looking young and waif-like in the moonlight.

'Have you been through the grilling too?'

She nodded. 'Not very nice. Poor Robin.'

'Has Aurelia gone?'

'Yes. I organised a car for her about an hour ago. She looked exhausted. I'm just waiting for mine to come.'

'Ah.'

'Actually, Charles, you're Bayswaterish, aren't you? I'm Notting Hill. You could share the cab.'

'Great. If you're sure that's okay.'

She was. In the cab she still seemed waif-like, so it was only kind for him to put his arm round her. On the journey, with the predictable interruptions to give directions to the driver, who appeared never to have driven in London before, a degree of intimacy was established.

They arrived outside her flat first. She didn't seem keen to leave him. 'My flat-mate's away. I don't really like to go in on my own. After what happened to Robin.'

Charles, ever the obliging gentleman, dismissed the cab. As they climbed up the stairs, he said, 'About your flatmate, you know I said I wanted to pick her brains on Film Research...'

'Oh yes.'

'I wonder if you'd mind asking her about a movie Aurelia did with her husband. Late Thirties, I should think. Called *Death Takes a Short Cut*.'

'I've never heard of it.'

'Nor have I, sweetie. That's why I'm asking.'

'Hock-A. I'll ask her.'

Jay Lewis opened the door of her flat. Once she had closed it, she came into Charles's arms.

In bed he disentangled himself lazily. 'Very nice indeed.'

'Really. You mean it?'

'Certainly do.'

She sighed. 'There's so much to learn.'

'As a PA?'

'Yes, and...'

'And sex?'

'Uh-huh.'

'Well, I think you have a natural aptitude for it.'

'Good.' She snuggled into his shoulder. 'You know. Ernie Franklyn Junior says a PA should really be prepared to sleep with anyone.'

'Oh, does he?' said Charles Paris. 'Thank you very much.'

West End Television Ltd,
W.E.T. House,
235–9 Lisson Avenue,
London NW1 3PQ.
6th July, 1979.

Dear Charles,

I enclose some revised pages for the beginning of Part Two of this week's script. As we lost last night's filming and are working so close to time, Bob and I have decided it'll be simpler to do a rewrite and replace the exterior scene with a new scene in the hall. I turned to Willy and Sam who, at incredibly short notice, have come up with the enclosed, which I think is terrific and well up to the standard of the other scripts I'm getting from them for later episodes. I think we really are on to a very exciting series!

On a slightly sadder note, I heard this morning that Dob's little dog, Cocky, died during the night. As you know, she doted on him and is bound to be very upset. I'm sending this letter to you by taxi to ensure that you get it before going to rehearsal on Saturday. Do be gentle with Dob.

Once again, many thanks for all your hard work on the series. See you at the Crew Run on Monday.

With the warmest good wishes,

Yours sincerely,

Peter

PETER Lipscombe

Producer *The Strutters*

The detective part of Charles's mind was in confusion. Every time he got near a theory which linked the deaths around *The Strutters*, something new came along to break it up. On the Thursday night he had been convinced that Dame Aurelia Howarth had arranged the murders of Sadie Wainwright, Scott Newton and Rod Tisdale, because she had gone slightly dotty and was convinced that they all meant harm to her precious little dog.

But, even as he had reached that conclusion, another death had occurred, a death in which Aurelia could not possibly have had any hand. He was getting rather sick of providing alibis for his main suspects.

And now, to add to the confusion, Cocky had died. So any motivation the dog might have provided for Aurelia was gone. If any more deaths happened, there would have to be another reason for them. Just as there had to be another reason for Robin Laughton's death.

Again Charles was struck by the random nature of all the deaths, except for Rod Tisdale's. If anyone did unlock the wheels of the huge light and push it over, they can't have had Robin Laughton as a specific target. There was no guarantee that the Floor Manager would be standing in the right place at the right time (or, from his own point of view, the wrong place at the wrong time). Like Scott Newton's death, the latest accident seemed a random act of sabotage. There was no guarantee that the light would hit anyone, and certainly no guarantee that it would kill anyone it did hit.

So he was back to indiscriminate violence against the whole series. And the only person to whom he could attribute a motive for that was currently sunning himself in Sardinia and maybe waiting for a well-publicised kidnap.

Maybe it was all just coincidence, after all. Maybe, as the condescending detective-sergeant had said, someone had quoted from *Macbeth* in the dressing room, and *The Strutters* was just a bad luck show.

And yet he felt he was missing something. There was something he had heard recently that was important, something that he should have been able to relate to the sequence of deaths. But he couldn't for the life of him remember what it was.

The final recording of the first batch of *The Strutters* on 17th July went well. The cast was relaxed and the tested old formula of the *What'll the Neighbours Say?* script about the political meeting pleased the studio audience.

'Rod Tisdale – what a great writer!' Peter Lipscombe was heard to observe in the bar between buying drinks for people. 'What a terrific talent! Tonight's episode just said it all – still experimenting, never content, always looking for new avenues in the comedic field. What a loss he'll be. You know, I reckon, if someone brought out a book of his scripts, he'd really get the recognition he deserves. He'd be up there with the Sheridans and the Wildes and the Shaws, no question. But of course no publisher would ever do it, no publisher would have the imagination to do it.'

Willy and Sam Tennison, the archpriest and priestess of the arch, were also there, and, while agreeing absolutely, but absolutely with what Peter said about Rod, who really had been a terrific writer and such a good chum, they had been delighted with the way their little scene had gone, promised well for the future, didn't it, darling, oh yes, darling, really promising, darling, whole show going to be such fun, wasn't it, darling, yes, darling.

The cast was animated, too. They were lifted by the audience's reception of the show, but, more than that, they had the prospect of a couple of weeks' rest after the hectic pace of the recent schedule. In fact, given extra filming days and an early read-through, the break was only going to be nine days, but that was better than nothing and they were all looking forward to it.

George Birkitt put his complaints to one side and, with the prospect of no new lines to forget for a few days, was jovially expansive. Even Dob Howarth seemed to be bearing up pretty well after her loss. She and the grinning Barton stood in the bar like royalty, accepting the servile tributes of its inmates.

Only once did her gracious exterior crack and emotion threaten. Romney Kirkstall was there, as ever, and eventually engaged the attention of his idol. 'Dob,' he said, 'I was terribly upset to hear what happened.'

'Thank you.' She inclined her head and very deliberately changed the subject. 'It'll be good to have a few days' rest. Imagine the luxury of the occasional breakfast in bed.'

But her fan persisted. 'Cocky meant a lot to me as well as to you. Anyone who's important to you is important to those of us who hold you dear.'

'Thank you.' She was polite, but wanted the subject dropped.

'So I've made you a small tribute.' Romney Kirkstall reached into his duffle bag and produced a large cross, made from silver cardboard and decorated with sprays of silver tinsel. In the centre of it was a colour photograph of Cocky under a fur-clad arm, cut out of some magazine.

'It says on it,' Romney Kirkstall continued inexorably, '"To Cocky, for many years a dear friend and companion".'

Tears glistened in Aurelia's huge blurred blue eyes. 'Yes, darling, it's very sweet of you, but –'

'And I've written a poem that goes with it. I do occasionally write poems,' Romney Kirkstall admitted modestly. 'It goes:

> Ah, Cocky, though you're far away,
> I dream of dancing with you still.
> In stead of a Good Boy chocolate drop,
> How sad you ate death's bitter pill.'

A deep sob broke Aurelia's customary self-restraint, but her fan did not seem to notice the effect his tribute was having. 'I hope you noticed I got in the reference to *I Dream of Dancing*. I was rather pleased with that. And I remembered that Cocky used to like those Good Boy chocolate drops.'

'Yes,' Aurelia managed to say, but she was suffering intensely. 'Barton,' she hissed, 'get rid of him.'

The angular blazered skeleton moved forward with surprising speed and took a firm hold on Kirkstall's sports-jacketed arm. 'Look here, old boy,' he said with a ghastly grin as he steered the fan away, 'little lady's a bit upset. Want to talk to you about the team the selectors are putting up for the Oval. A bit rummy, to my way of thinking.'

The language was still bizarre and dislocated, but the actions were very positive. When it came to defending his wife, Barton Rivers was a daunting figure.

Charles Paris was left with Aurelia.

'I'm sorry,' she said, dabbing at her eyes with a lace handkerchief. 'It's just it's so recent. I had managed to put the poor darling out of my mind, and then to have him going on and on about it…He's a dear boy, but…'

'I understand. Can I get you a drink or…'

'No, I'll be fine in a second. I just…' She sobbed again.

The gentlemanly thing to do would have been to start a new inoffensive subject, but Charles couldn't leave the little dog's death yet. Romney Kirkstall's inept rhyme had started a new train of thought. Suppose Cocky's death had been another in the sequence of apparent accidents…Suppose he had been poisoned by someone who wanted to get at Aurelia…It opened up a whole new range of motivations.

'Dob,' he began. He used the pet name to increase their intimacy. 'Dob, we are all very upset to hear about Cocky's death.'

'Thank you, darling. I just want to forget about it, please.'

'Of course.' He'd have to be direct. 'I'm sorry, I have to ask. Did you think there was anything strange about it?'

'Strange?'

'You don't think he could have been poisoned?'

Shock registered on her face, but very swiftly understanding followed. 'I see what you mean, darling. Another of these unfortunate…*évènements*…?'

Charles nodded.

'No, darling. He was just a very sick boy. The vet had said he hadn't long. No, he just…slipped away in the night.' A sob broke her voice.

'I'm sorry. I had to ask.'

'Of course. I understand.' She took his hand between both of hers. 'And I do appreciate what you're doing for us. There have been too many deaths. They must stop. I'm sure they're just accidents, but, if there is a sequence, if there is a solution, then I'm sure you're the one to find it.'

And she gave him the full beam of those wonderful eyes.

Charles reeled. He was flattered that she seemed to know about his hobby of detection, but he felt much more than that. He felt inspired by her confidence. Here now was a lady in whose honour to pursue his knightly quest. He understood more than ever before why princes had courted her, and young men toasted her, why husbands had dreamed of her while they made love to their wives, and why young soldiers had marched to their deaths with her image imprinted on their minds.

He returned the pressure of her hand. From now on he was determined to solve the accumulating mysteries. For her.

She and her husband left soon after and Charles went across to comfort Romney Kirkstall, who stood forlorn in the bar, drinkless as ever, his duffle bag dangling ineffectually from his hand.

'Do you think she didn't like it?'

'I think it was just the wrong moment, that's all. It made her think about the dog too much.'

'Mmm. I mean, I have done her things before. You know, cards and so on. And poems too. She's always liked them before.'

'And I'm sure she'd have liked this one, but it was just too soon after the event.'

He mulled that over. 'Yes, I suppose so. I could post it to her.'

'I'd leave it a week or two, if I were you.'

'Yes.'

The little man seemed downcast, so Charles tried to make conversation. 'What do you do, Romney?'

'Do? I collect stuff about Dob.'

'Yes, I know that, but what job do you do?'

'I don't have a job. I came into a bit of money when my mother died, so I gave up my job. I just do the collection now.'

'Oh, I see. And are you going to use all the material to write a book about her?'

'Oh, no, I couldn't write a book. It's just an interest, you know,' Romney Kirkstall replied in a voice which suggested that the only thing strange about the conversation was Charles's need to ask the question.

'So you spend your days collecting?'

'Yes, looking around for stuff a lot of the time. I'm a lot younger than her, you see, I'm only forty-three, so I wasn't around to collect programmes and things at the time. But I go around junk stalls and book shops. It's an interest,' he repeated.

Only forty-three. Charles was surprised. Romney Kirkstall could have been any age, but forty-three seemed very young to have developed this kind of obsession. Maybe, Charles reflected, it was a sign of his own age. When the loonies start looking young .

'Actually,' Romney Kirkstall continued, 'I thought of you today.'

'Oh?'

'I was looking for some stuff in a bookshop in the Charing Cross Road – a place Barton Rivers recommended to me, actually – and I came across that book you were talking about.'

'What book?'

'Well, you were talking about the film, but it had the same title. *Death Takes A Short Cut.*'

'Oh yes?'

'They'd got a copy of it there. I looked at it, but it hadn't got anything to do with Dob, so I put it back. But, since you asked about it, I thought you might be interested.'

'I am. Thank you. Who was the author?'

'R. Q. Wilberforce. Didn't mean anything to me. You heard of him?'

Charles grimaced. 'It's vaguely familiar. Think he could have been one of those Thirties detective story writers, like E. R. Punshon or Freeman Wills Croft.'

'Never heard of them either,' confessed Romney Kirkstall.

'Well, if you could give me the name of the bookshop...'

Romney supplied it. 'I must go,' he said. Then he hesitated, as if to impart some vital piece of information. 'Do you know why I was called Romney?' he asked.

'No.'

'My mother named me after Romney Brent. Friend of Noel Coward's.'

'Ah.'

'Yes.' Romney Kirkstall turned tail and scuttered out.

Jay Lewis was still in the bar and seemed to be looking his way. He sidled up to her and whispered, 'What does Ernie Franklyn Junior say about PAs sleeping with the same person twice?'

'Oh, he says that's all right. He says it's inevitable that relationships develop.'

'Oh, does he? That's very nice of him.'

Charles thought he would like to meet Ernie Franklyn Junior one day, and smash his teeth in. Or perhaps set a posse of indignant PAs on him to revenge his unflattering generalisations. Charles's previous experience of PAs had taught him (by the unquestionable empirical method of trying to get off with them) that their inclination towards promiscuity was no greater than that of other women. They weren't all as gullible as Jay Lewis.

But he couldn't really complain, as he seemed currently to be a beneficiary of the Ernie Franklyn Junior teaching. He was in no position to argue.

Nor, for the first hour after they got back to Jay's flat, was he in a position to think much either. But he was in some nice positions that didn't involve too much thinking.

There came a lull and they lay back on the pillows.

'You're just using me for experience, aren't you, Jay?'

'Yes. Ernie Fr –'

'Sure, sure.'

'You don't mind, do you?'

'Why should I mind?'

'You know,' she said slowly, 'I may be coming off *The Strutters*.'

'Oh yes.'

'They need an extra PA on *Wragg and Bowen*.'

'Ah.'

'I'll see if I can get it. Learn more on a big variety show.'

They turned the light out and dozed.

'Oh, by the way...' Jay said suddenly.

'Hmm.'

'I did ask my flatmate about that film you mentioned and she found out about it.'

'What did she find out?'

Was this going to be important? Was this going to be the key that unlocked the Chinese box of mysteries?

Apparently not.

'It never got made,' said Jay.

'Oh.'

'No, it was all set up in 1939. They started, did a couple of days' filming, then war was declared and the whole production was cancelled.'

'Ah,' said Charles Paris, and went to sleep.

CHAPTER ELEVEN

West End Television Ltd,
W.E.T. House,
235–9 Lisson Avenue,
London NW1 3PQ.
18th July, 1979.

Dear Charles,

Just a quick note to say how super last night's show was and to thank you for all the hard work you're putting into this very exciting series.

A few days rest now, which I'm sure you'll be glad of, and then…on with the fun! We've got some smashing scripts from Willy and Sam and I think the series is going to go all the way to the top of the ratings!

Look forward to seeing you at the next read-through on Friday, 27th July.

With the warmest good wishes,

Yours sincerely,

Peter

PETER LIPSCOMBE

Producer *The Strutters*

Good God, did the man never stop writing notes, Charles wondered. Where did he get the time? On the other hand, of course, he was a television producer and there must be a limit to the hours in the day you can spend buying people drinks.

The only other mail he had that day was something offering him a piece of leatherette if he applied for an American Express card and a photocopied sheet from the Red Theatre Co-operative, demanding workers' solidarity against the Right Wing Fascist take-over of Equity. He put these two, together with Peter Lipscombe's note, straight into the wastepaper basket, and decided he might go for a stroll down the Charing Cross Road.

The man in the bookshop was desolated, but the book was gone. 'Sold it to a dealer yesterday. Know him well. He's always on the look-out for that sort of stuff. You a collector?'

'Well, not really. I was just interested in that particular book.'

'Oh. 'Cause I could do you a nice 1930 Austin Freeman. *Mr Pottermack's Oversight*, first edition. Or I got a few early Ngaio Marshes. *Died in the*

Wool, 1945. And I think I still got a couple of S. S. Van Dines.'

'But no R. Q. Wilberforces?'

'No, sorry, don't get many in. He didn't really do that many, don't think he did any after the War. Maybe he was killed, don't know. I could take your number, if you like, and if I get an R. Q. Wilberforce, give you a buzz.'

'OK. Thanks.' Charles gave his number. 'But don't worry. It isn't important. You say a dealer bought the one you had...'

'Yes. Of course, if you're really keen, I could put you in touch with him.'

'I would be grateful.'

'Right. I know him well. Comes in here about once a month. His name's Gregory Watts and he lives down in Kew, I think. Here's his number.'

'Thank you very much.'

'And you're sure it's just the R. Q. Wilberforce you're interested in?'

'For the moment, yes.'

''Cause I mean, far be it from me to tell you your business, but if you are starting a collection, you ought to go for a few more in the genre. I mean, there aren't many R. Q Witberforces and they're fairly rare, so I reckon you should widen your sights a bit. I mean, I got a nice early American edition of *The Lady in Black*. That was the title of *Trent's Last Case* over there. You know, Bentley.'

With a loud clang, a penny that had been jammed for some days in a slot in Charles' brain, dropped.

'I've got it!' he shouted.

'Have you really?' asked the bookseller, with some surprise at his vehemence. 'Well, that's quite rare. Now that's a very good basis for a collection.'

But he spoke to an empty shop. The potential collector of R. Q. Wilberforce had shot off down the Charing Cross Road.

Charles contemplated making up for the job, but reckoned it was too risky. Part of him wanted to appear in the tramp guise he had worn as Estragon in *Waiting for Godot* at Glasgow ('Never mind Godot, I spent the entire evening waiting for some distinguished acting' – *The Scotsman*). Another part suggested a socially committed researcher, using the earnest Midlands voice he had perfected for some forgotten *Play for Today* ('Tried to fit a quart into a pint pot and drowned the unfortunate actors in the resulting spillage' – *Sunday Times*).

But he rejected both of these. His prospective quarry had seen him before, and Charles knew from experience that disguise in such circumstances could all too easily lead to discovery.

No, he had to go in his own persona, but he had to have a reason to justify his presence. And it had to be something that would disarm the prejudice his appearance was bound to arouse.

His quarry hadn't heard him speak, so he could certainly do something with his voice, which might help. Perhaps he could use the Liverpudlian he'd used in *The Homecoming* at Leatherhead ('I laughed till I left' – *Leatherhead Herald*). Or the non-specific East Anglian he'd developed for a small-time villain in *Z Cars* ('As regular as clockwork and about as interesting' – *Evening Standard*). Or the Midlands one...?

But that wasn't really the problem. He could choose a voice when he got there. The difficulty was a reason for his appearance. He thought.

It came in a flash. Of course, nothing is wasted. Everything is meant.

He went through the contents of his wastepaper basket until he came to the photocopied sheet from the Red Theatre Co-operative.

And he studied it hard.

It was strange revisiting the scene of the near-riot and Robin Laughton's death. The weather was benign, early summer sun washing the old frontages of the condemned terrace and giving them a kind of apologetic grandeur, as if they had somehow regained their youth. In the brightness of the sun he wasn't so aware of the boarded windows and padlocked doors, the flaking paint and angry graffiti.

He wasn't sure what a Red Theatre Co-operative member of his age would wear, because he had never met one. In fact he rather wondered whether there were any members of his age; the ones he had come across were all in their twenties and thirties. They were angry young men – no, he mustn't say that, the use of the expression dated him – *committed* young men – that was better – and girls, often with very short hair, tight jeans and leather blousons, who tended to interrupt rehearsals with queries about what the Equity representative intended to do about the rising unemployment figures, or whether Shakespeare was inextricably allied to the capitalist system. Charles had even, briefly, worked with a Red Theatre Co-operative director on a production of *King Lear*, which saw the play as a socialist parable. To justify this reading, the King had to be seen as a symbol of traditional landowning conservatism and the division of his kingdom as a necessary step towards public ownership. As a result, the political sympathies of the audience had to be with Regan and Goneril in their attempts to reduce the power of the traditional hierarchy and impose a socialist state. Cordelia became a symbol of wishy-washy bourgeois uncommitted apathy, and the entrance of Lear with her dead in his arms showed how non-participation was tantamount to alliance with the corruption of capitalism. The tragedy of the play was the deaths of Cornwall, Regan and Goneril, martyrs to the cause of progress, but the production ended on a note of hope. Albany's lines in the final scene,

> All friends shall taste
> The wages of their virtue, and all foes
> The cup of their deservings,

were transposed to the very end of the play, and signified the start of the revolution. They were greeted by a great shout from all the company, dead bodies included, who all sang *The Red Flag*. The production, in spite of being hailed by *Time Out* as 'a milestone in political theatre, showing that traditional plays need not just be commercial bullshit', played to small houses throughout its short run.

The same director's productions of *Othello* (about a black school-leaver unable to get a job) and *Macbeth* (an interpretation based on the lines

> No, this my hand will rather
> The multitudinous seas incarnadine,
> Making the green one red)

also failed to reach more than a minority audience.

Given the lack of middle-aged models for his chosen role, Charles wore his own clothes. He went first to the house which had been cleared for filming, and summoned the elderly couple who lived there to the door.

'Hello. My name's Charles Paris. I was involved in the filming that West End Television was doing here the other week.'

'Oh yes.' The old man did not look unwelcoming. 'I wondered when you lot would be back.'

'Oh'

'I said to Rita, they're bound to be back, didn't I, Rita?'

'You did, Lionel.'

'Why?'

'Well, the way I saw it was, you didn't get no filming done that night, did you? So I put two and two together and realised that you'd want to do it another night, because you need it for your show.'

'No, in fact –'

'And before you say anything else, let me say that I'm going to want twice the money you paid last time. The disruption and noise was much more than what you said it would be.'

It took Charles some time to explain that the filming had been covered in the studio and there wouldn't be another fat facility fee going into the old couple's coffers. Once he understood this, the old man was less accommodating. 'What the bleeding hell d'you want then?'

'I'm looking for someone who was around on the night of the filming. The black youth called John Odange. I wondered if you knew where I might find him.'

'I don't know nothing about that scum! We're respectable people. We got a right to live in this house. We ain't going to move on till the council comes up with what we think's proper accommodation. Are we, Rita?'

'No, Lionel.'

'We're quiet, respectable people,' the old man shouted. 'This used to be a nice road. Now we've got all these bloody squatters, living ten to a house, drinking, taking drugs, playing music! Bloody foreigners, and all! They aren't even house-trained, a lot of them. They're all...'

He continued in the same vein for some time. Under this splenetic fusillade, Charles retreated and went to ask someone else where he might find John Odange.

He knocked on one of the doors from which the council's padlock had been unscrewed and was answered by a pretty and very clean young mum with a baby. Yes, John Odange lived three houses down. She didn't know whether he was likely to be in, but it was worth trying.

He was in. His tall frame filled the doorway. He wore a faded mauve T-shirt and black jeans. There was no sign of recognition when he asked what he could do for Charles.

He sounded wary, but not, as Charles had expected, deliberately aggressive.

'I was involved in that filming which West End Television was doing a couple of weeks back.'

'Uh-huh.' Still no overt hostility.

'I was one of the actors in the show and I...I wanted to talk about it.' To his annoyance, Charles found he was speaking in his own voice. Also he had difficulty in getting round to his prepared speeches about actors being workers as much as anyone else and the need for education and the vital role of the entertainer in spreading the Marxist message. He was daunted by John Odange, not by the man's size and vouched militancy, but by the sharp intelligence in his eyes. He was not going to be easy to fool.

'Come in.' The tall youth moved to one side and Charles went into the house. Inside it was spotless. The old man up the road wouldn't have believed how clean and sweet-smelling it was.

John Odange indicated a room to the right. It was a bedsitter lined with books. It too was immaculately tidy. By the window was a desk piled with more books and files. A portable electric typewriter still hummed, suggesting Charles had interrupted composition.

'Are you a writer?' he asked.

The black youth shook his head. 'Only incidentally. I'm a student really. An unaffiliated student.'

'What does that mean?'

'It means I was at the London School of Economics, and I got involved in certain political activities, and suddenly there was trouble over my grant, and I found I was no longer at the London School of Economics. So I continue my studies here.'

He spoke without bitterness. There was no doubting his commitment, but the violent resentment which had been evident on the night of the filming had gone.

'You want coffee?'

'Love some.'

While John Odange went to fill the kettle, Charles wondered how to proceed. Faced with the young man's quiet sincerity, his pose as a member of the Red Theatre Co-operative diminished to an insulting charade. But he had to get the information somehow.

John Odange returned, plugged the kettle in, sat down in his typing chair and looked straight at Charles. 'So, you were an actor in the West End Television filming and you want to talk to me about it.'

'Yes.' Charles hesitated.

'Hmm. So why would you want to come and talk to me? To tell me I'm a naughty boy to disrupt your precious show? To tell me I should allow other people the right to work? Well, if that's your line, I can argue it through with you point by point. Okay, the evening degenerated. All that fighting with the food was pretty childish. And the fact that someone got killed, no one wanted that. But the basic point we were making, that remains valid. The filming was set up to make fun of the way we live.'

'I don't know exactly that that was the –'

'Now, come on, man. All those Sixties hippies around in the kaftans, they were meant to be funny, right?'

'Well. I suppose so.'

'Right. And the places they live got to be funny too. Okay, let's find somewhere really run down, somewhere really bad, that'll get a good laugh.'

'That wasn't the intention in –'

'Listen, man, I found a script lying about in the road. I read it, man.' In that case, there was not much point in Charles continuing his enfeebled defence. It was probably the first time one of Rod Tisdale's masterpieces had been subjected to serious political scrutiny, and he didn't think it would have come through the test well.

'It said in the Stage Directions, 'Film of grotty, condemned street. Establish till audience laughs, then zoom in to shot of Colonel.' Now, okay, that's very funny if you don't happen to live here. If you do, it gets kind of insulting.'

'I can see that. I didn't actually come here to –'

'No, no, that's clear. So why did you come here? Now let me see. Have you come here as a politically-committed actor to say how much you support my actions over stopping the filming and how we're all brothers working for the same glorious revolutionary cause...?'

Here, if ever, was the cue. 'Well, I –'

But John Odange answered his own question. 'No, you don't look the sort for that. Under the sloppiness, man, you're really bourgeois.'

It wasn't said offensively, but with a note of pity. And Charles had an uncomfortable feeling that it was probably an accurate assessment of him. He didn't feel encouraged to proceed with his cover story and start extolling the virtues of solidarity and the coming revolution.

'So what is it?' mused John Odange. But he still preferred to supply his own answers to his questions. 'Perhaps your watch disappeared on the night of the filming and you think I stole it...'

'Good Lord, no. Nothing like that.'

'Don't sound so surprised, man. That's what a lot of people would think. And if you went to the local police station, they'd believe you. In fact, they'd welcome you with open arms. They're just longing to pin something on me, man, and a nice stolen watch could fit the bill nicely.'

'You've had a lot of trouble with them?'

'Always hassles. They think I spend all my time here building bombs, you know. Yes, I've had more than a bellyfull of the pigs recently.'

'Since that Floor Manager died, you mean?'

'Yes. That was a gift for them. If they could pin that on me – wow! they'd all go home happy. They dragged me in and talked to me for a long time about that. They were very sorry to have to let me go. Unfortunately, every witness they could rustle up said the same thing – I didn't go near that light at any time during the evening. I didn't arrive till late and then I made such an exhibition of myself, my every movement was watched. Were they disappointed? Be a long time before they get another chance like that.'

'Actually, it was about –'

'Oh, I think I get it now.' The large brown eyes opened wide and a huge grin irradiated the face. 'You the little amateur detective investigating the crime? You think you've got new evidence that can really pin it on me?'

'No. Well, yes and no.'

'Which answer to which question? Kind of important to me, you know.'

'It's okay. Yes, I am investigating the murder. No, I have no suspicions of you.'

'Nice to hear that, man. And interesting to hear you call it a murder.'

'I meant "death".'

'Not what you said, man. Classic example of Freudian slip.'

'Maybe.' Charles grinned. The atmosphere between them had relaxed and he felt he could ask his question. He also felt a bit sheepish about the elaborate charade he had prepared for this interview. Direct questions so often succeed in getting direct answers.

But John Odange was still conducting the conversation. 'Okay. I'll tell you anything I can, man. Though I don't think there's much. I didn't see anything odd. I was too busy pouring cream over the fat cats from television.'

'It's not something you saw, it's something you said.'

John Odange shrugged and smiled disarmingly. 'I said a lot that night. Man, did I say a lot that night.'

'Yes, what interests me is that at one point you complained about all the film vehicles and cars that were blocking the roads.'

'Perfectly justified complaint, man. It was like there was a Cup Final on.'

'Yes, I agree. But what I want you to remember is exactly what you said. You gave a great list of all the cars there were blocking streets...'

'All company cars too, I bet.'

'Probably. What I want to know is, was that just a random list you made up, or had you actually seen all the cars you mentioned?'

'What you mean exactly?'

'You said, as I recall, that the streets were full of BMWs, Rovers and Mercs.'

'Sure.'

'Did you actually see all those?'

'Certainly did.'

'You also mentioned Daimlers .

John Odange smiled wryly. 'Ah, I think I might have been guilty of a little poetic licence there. I didn't see a Daimler; it just fitted in the rhythm of my rhetoric.'

Oh dear. That didn't augur well for the next question, the important question. 'You also mentioned Bentleys.

'Yes.'

'Does that mean you saw a Bentley?'

'Sure did.' Charles breathed a sigh of relief. 'Yes, there was a dirty great brute of a Bentley hidden behind an old garage in a side street. I saw it as I walked along here.'

'What colour was it?'

'Green. Great big green bugger. Vintage, I'd say.'

There was only one person connected with *The Strutters* who possessed such a car. And that was a person who was supposed to be at home in bed on the night of the filming, while his wife went to the location in a minicab.

Charles had got the information he required. He might have felt a little more satisfaction with his detective skills, though, if he had actually interviewed his informant, rather than being interviewed by him.

CHAPTER TWELVE

BARTON RIVERS HAD had the opportunity on every occasion. When Sadie Wainwright died, he had been in W.E.T. House and would have had plenty of time to arrange the broken railing and help her on her way. The Bentley had been the last car down before Bernard's Rolls on the day Scott Newton met his end. There was no reason why Barton shouldn't have parked for a few moments out of sight by the gates and slipped back after Bernard Walton had passed to topple the flower-urn. A Bentley made a very effective weapon to run over Rod Tisdale, and its presence near the filming location made it quite possible that Barton had slipped out in the confusion to sabotage the light that killed Robin Laughton.

Four deaths, and he could have done them all. In fact, it made much more sense to suspect Barton than his wife. Charles now felt rather sheepish about his suspicions of Aurelia. Even if her supposed motivation, the protection of her little dog, were not now irrelevant, there was still a strong incongruity of her in the role of murderer. She seemed a remarkably sane woman and, particularly in the case of Rod Tisdale, very unlikely to have been able to commit the crimes, even if she had wished to. So far as Charles knew, she couldn't drive, and the idea of that wispy beauty deliberately running someone over was ridiculous.

And yet it had been definitely to her that Sadie had addressed the words which had stimulated thoughts of murder in the first place. That still fitted rather uncomfortably into the new scenario. Charles's only possible solution was that Aurelia had threatened the PA in a fit of anger, never meaning to carry out her threat, but that Barton, in his unhinged gallantry, had leapt to his wife's defence and done the deed.

And had he had the same motivation for the other crimes? Were they all born of some perverted sense of honour? Or was there perhaps no continuing logic to them at all? Were they just random blows from a madman?

Because there was no doubt that Barton Rivers was mad, but whether there was any method in his madness, Charles could not yet work out. The only consistent thread in the deaths was that they were all directed against people connected with *The Strutters* (though, as yet, no member of the cast had been injured). Maybe that fact supplied logic; maybe this massacre was the actor's revenge on all the production staff he had ever worked with. It seemed far-fetched.

But if a madman were stage-managing all the deaths, that did at least explain their random nature. Rod Tisdale's was the only one aimed at a specific target. All the others could have struck at a variety of people, or could have misfired and injured nobody.

But was Barton just gleefully playing the role of an unselective god of destruction, or was there somewhere in his fuddled mind a pattern to the killings?

Another question that worried Charles was the unavoidable one of how much Aurelia knew of her husband's activities. Obviously she wasn't an accomplice, but, as the deaths mounted, she must have come to suspect something. If Barton had stopped and slipped back to move the urn at Bernard's place, even if she didn't think it odd at the time, subsequent events must have made her suspicious. Equally, she must have known that he was out in the car at the time of Rod Tisdale's death.

And yet she seemed to want the business sorted out and ended. Charles could not forget her appeal to him which had filled him with such crusading fervour. 'And I do appreciate what you're doing for us. If there is a solution to all this, then I'm sure you're the one to find it.'

In the light of his recent thinking, her words took on a different emphasis. The important word became 'us'. I appreciate what you're doing for us. Was she tacitly admitting that the problem was one that she and her husband shared? That she knew what he was doing, but was powerless to stop him?

Another thought followed hard on that. He remembered when he had asked whether Cocky had been poisoned, Aurelia's face had registered shock. Perhaps the dog had been killed, and perhaps Barton had done it, as a threat to buy his wife's continuing silence. Maybe he had threatened her own life too. Charles knew that many things happened inside marriages which were invisible to outsiders. Was it fear that kept Aurelia Howarth so tightly bound to her lunatic husband?

He didn't think he was going to find out any answers to these questions until *The Strutters* got back into production again. Three of the deaths had taken place on production days, and the fourth, Rod Tisdale's, had been right in the middle of a very busy rehearsal schedule. Charles somehow didn't think much would happen until they started work on the next batch of shows. And then he was determined to watch Barton Rivers like a hawk whenever he came near the production. There was still no real evidence to trap the madman. But Charles was determined to find some before there was another 'accident'.

He got a batch of new scripts through the post a couple of days before the next read-through. Willy and Sam Tennison had made predictable changes in the show's direction. Not only, as anticipated, had they brought in a semi-permanent girlfriend for the Nick Coxhill figure, they had even got the Colonel and Mrs Strutter exchanging darlings like newly-weds. This softening of their relationship weakened the aggressive crustiness of the Colonel's character and, since that was the main basis of the series' comedy,

Charles thought George Birkitt might have something to say about it at the next read-through.

But Peter Lipscombe must have been happy with the scripts or he wouldn't have issued them. Though it seemed to Charles that the producer was so much under the writers' spell that he would never dare find any fault with their scripts.

Episode Eight was, for those trained to spot such things, a version of a plot that Willy and Sam Tennison had used in an episode of *Oh, What a Pair of Au Pairs!* In that, a Japanese family had moved in next door to the au pair-owning young couple and, after a lot of misunderstandings, jokes about tiny transistorised instruments and the line 'There's a nip in the air', a kind of peaceful coexistence had been achieved, symbolised by the Japanese family's gift of a geisha girl as a third au pair (an hilarious consequence if ever there was one).

The Strutters version of this saga of racial stereotypes had a Japanese family moving next door to Colonel and Mrs Strutter. The same misunderstandings, jokes about tiny transistorised instruments and the line 'There's a nip in the air' ensued, but a less total rapprochement resulted. In a pay-off which was, by Willy and Sam Tennison's standards, satirical, the Japanese family presented Colonel Strutter with a samurai sword and, when he asked what it was for, told him that it was for committing hara-kiri when he got too depressed about Japanese car imports.

Charles predicted that George Birkitt wouldn't like that either. But he paid scant attention to the scripts, because by the same post arrived a much more interesting communication. It came from his agent, Maurice Skellern, which already made it a rarity, and it contained a very large cheque, which made it rarer still. It was in fact the money owing to him for the first batch of *Strutters*, which Maurice, as was his wont, had sat on for some weeks. But also, as was his wont, he had not forgotten to deduct his commission.

Even so, it really was rather a gratifying amount of money. So long as he didn't consider paying tax bills or anything like that (which he didn't), he felt quite well off.

The day before the next read-through, he started to worry about .what Barton Rivers was going to do next, and to doubt his capacity to avert it. He couldn't really watch the man all the time; it would be simpler if he had someone to help him.

He rang Gerald Venables. Polly, the solicitor's secretary, whose sexy voice always gave Charles erotic fantasies, put him through.

'Hello, Charles, how are things going?'

'Not so bad. I think I may have a line on the deaths.'

'Good, good,' said Gerald breczily. But he didn't sound very interested. Not his usual panting schoolboy reaction to talk of murder.

'Perhaps we could meet and talk about it.'

'Love to. Trouble is, I'm a bit tied up at the moment. In a couple of days I'm –'

'Thing is, I think you could help me.' This appeal shouldn't fail. Gerald was usually delighted to get involved in a murder investigation. Real crime had so much more to offer than sorting out show-biz contracts.

'Love to, love to. Trouble is, we're off on holiday day after tomorrow.'

'Ah.'

'School holidays just started, you see.'

'Going far?'

'Have to go some way these days to get away from the crowds.'

'Where?' asked Charles with jealous resignation.

'Seychelles.'

'Just the Seychelles?'

'Mmm. Well, if you only get one holiday a year, you like to be able to guarantee the weather.'

'But you don't only get one holiday a year.'

'No, that's true.'

'You're always off on bloody holiday.'

'Have to have the odd break, you know. Recharge the batteries. I do work for it,' Gerald added in an aggrieved voice.

'Hmm.'

'You ought to have a holiday. Go off with Frances somewhere. Are you speaking to her at the moment?'

'Haven't for some time.'

'Oh dear.'

'No great rift. Just haven't got round to it.'

'Well, you should.'

'I will.'

'Anyway, about these deaths...are you going to bring me up to date?'

'No. It'll keep. I'll tell you when you get back. Probably be a few more by then.'

'Good. I'm only away the fortnight.'

'Just the fortnight?'

'Yes.'

'Right. I must say, as a Dr Watson, you're hopeless. Sherlock Holmes never had this trouble. He didn't have his faithful acolyte zooming off to the Seychelles whenever his assistance was needed.'

'No, but on the other hand, he solved crimes.'

Charles thought about what Gerald had said when he put the phone down. Not the final gibe, that hadn't hurt, such rudeness was well established between them; no, he thought about what Gerald had said about Frances.

It would be rather good to go on holiday with her. He was already getting bored with Jay Lewis. The sex was all right, but there was a limit to how much quotation from the luminaries of West End Television he could take.

Frances, though...They'd always said, in the old days, that when they could afford it, they'd go to Greece. Just the two of them, without Juliet. Thanks to the cheque from Maurice, he now reckoned he could afford it. And Juliet, in her late twenties with a husband and twin sons, no longer presented a problem.

He rang Frances's number. There was no reply. He'd try again.

He was just going back to his bedsitter when the payphone rang. The Swedes all being out, he returned to answer it. Some cock-eyed logic suggested it might be Frances ringing him back.

It wasn't. It was a man s voice he didn't recognise. 'Hello, could I speak to Charles Paris?'

'Speaking.'

'Oh, hello, my name's Gregory Watts...'

'Oh yes.' It didn't ring any bells for Charles.

'I'm a bookdealer specialising in detective fiction.'

'Oh yes.' With more understanding.

'Just talking to a friend of mine who runs a bookshop in Charing Cross Road and he said you'd been looking for an R. Q. Wilberforce...'

'Yes, I was. In a vague sort of way.'

'Well, look, I've got this first edition of *Death Takes A Short Cut*. Very Good Condition. 1938 it is, but of course you'd know that.'

'Um, oh, er, yes.'

'If you do want it, I'm asking five pounds.'

'Ah.'

'I've got other collectors who might be interested, But I rang you first, because my friend said you only collected R. Q. Wilberforce.'

'Well...' It rather appealed, the idea of being the nation's specialist in Wilberforciana. Even if it wasn't true.

'Have you met the old boy, by the way?'

'Which old boy?'

'R. Q. Wilberforce. He's still about. Must be in his eighties. I wrote to him to see if he'd got any old editions he wanted to get rid of.'

'Ah.'

'He said he'd got rid of them all. I didn't believe him. Not many of these authors want to part with their private copies of their own works. Mind you, the widows often don't care so much, if you come in with a reasonable offer.'

'Really? No, no, I haven't met him. Don't know much about him.' Anything about him, in fact.

'Well, do you want to buy it?'

Charles couldn't remember exactly why he had thought the book important. It was part of some train of thought that had been shunted off into a siding to make way for the Intercity express conviction of Barton Rivers' guilt. On the other hand, he did feel fairly flush and this bloke had taken the trouble to ring up .

'Yes, please, I would like it.'

'Okay, well, if you can send me a cheque for £5.32 – that's with postage – I'll send the book as soon as I receive the money.'

'Fine.'

Be nice to have something to read while he watched to see who Barton Rivers tried to eliminate next.

He felt a chill. Of course it was possible that the old madman might start on members of *The Strutters* cast.

CHAPTER THIRTEEN

'NOW PLEASE DON'T worry. Everything's going to be okay,' Peter Lipscombe assured the cast at the read-through on the 27th July, 'but I should just put you in the picture about the news on the industrial front. You'll have heard that there was a one-day strike last Monday, and there have also been one or two other go-slows and things happening, but I think the atmosphere's clearing now, and I don't think we need worry about our recording next Friday. You may find odd things happening in the W.E.T. building – I mean, for instance there may not be any canteen service and the bar may suddenly be closed.'

A communal groan broke from the cast.

'But I think basically everything's going to be okay. We'll get the show made, don't you worry about that. Now one thing I should tell you – I don't think it's likely to happen, but we should be prepared for any eventuality – when we get into the studio, we may have to rehearse/record the show during the day. You see, at the moment – and I'm sure this will have changed by next Friday – at the moment the security men have got an overtime ban on, which means that they won't work evenings, which means we can't have an audience in the studio because of safety regulations. So if that ban hasn't been lifted – and I'm sure it will have been – we'll get the schedule changed and do the show during the day.'

'And dub the laughs on afterwards?' asked Bob Tomlinson.

'Yes,' replied the producer with distaste.

'Good,' said Bob Tomlinson.

'Okay, sure it won't happen, but thought you'd like to know. Oh, one other thing about the studio. We're not in Studio A this week, we're in B.'

'The small one?' asked George Birkitt, affronted.

'Smaller,' conceded the producer.

'Why?'

'Well, *Wragg and Bowen* are in the big studio.'

'Why?'

'It is a big prestige show.'

'And what about us? Aren't we a big prestige show?'

'Of course, of course. But not quite as big a prestige show as *Wragg and Bowen*.'

'Just because of the bloody money they're being paid...' George Birkitt muttered darkly.

'You finished?' asked Bob Tomlinson, with his customary lack of grace.

'More or less,' said Peter Lipscombe.

'Right, let's get this rubbish read. You ready on the watch, girl?'

Jay Lewis was ready for the read-through, but George Birkitt wasn't. 'I'm sorry, before we start, there are a few things in this script we've got to change.'

'Why?' asked Bob Tomlinson belligerently.

'Because they're just wrong. I mean I've spent seven episodes of this series – not to mention all the *What'll the Neighbours* before it – building up Colonel Strutter into a recognisable, rounded comic character, and now I'm handed a script in which not only does he have considerably less lines than in previous episodes, but the ones he does have are unfunny and out of character.'

'Oh, but we've worked so hard to maintain the character,' wailed Sam Tennison, dressed today in a Mister Men T-shirt and strawberry coloured jeans. 'Haven't we, darling?'

'Yes, indeed, darling,' concurred Willy Tennison, also dressed today in a Mister Men T-shirt and strawberry coloured jeans.

'Then obviously you just haven't worked hard enough,' said George Birkitt. 'I mean, I know Colonel Strutter, and these lines aren't Colonel Strutter. I can't learn lines that are out of character.'

'You can't learn lines that are *in* character,' was the thought that went through every mind in the room. But nobody said it.

'I mean, for a start, since when has Colonel Strutter called Mrs Strutter 'darling'?'

'Oh, but all married couples call each other "darling". Don't they, darling?'

'They certainly do, darling.'

'Not Colonel Strutter. He wouldn't go in for that sort of sentimental nonsense. He never calls his wife anything.'

'But he has to call her *something*,' complained Sam Tennison.

'Well, he doesn't.'

'But everyone calls everyone *something*. Don't they, darling?'

'They most certainly do, darling.'

'Anyway, that's only a detail,' George Birkitt steamrollered on. 'The plot is full of silly things too, which are just out of keeping with the rest of the series that we've already made. I mean, that business at the end with the samurai sword. Have you ever met a Japanese with a samurai sword?' He turned to the Japanese actor who was playing the *Strutters* new neighbour. 'I mean, have you got any samurai swords?'

'Yes, many,' replied the Japanese with a polite smile.

'Well, that's neither here nor there. As a pay-off for an episode of *The Strutters* it's just hopelessly out of keeping.'

'Oh no,' murmured Mort Verdon, who was sitting by Charles. 'Don't cut the samurai sword. I spent most of last week finding somewhere that would hire the thing to us. They're about as easy to come by as a banana in a convent.'

'Now come on,' Peter Lipscombe was saying bonhomously. 'I'm sure everything's really okay with this script. Just change the odd word here and there and...'

Charles relaxed. Barton Rivers had delivered Aurelia to the rehearsal and then driven away. If anything was going to happen, it wouldn't be yet a while.

Idly he wondered what form the next attack would take. Shooting? Stabbing? Bombing?

He also wondered idly who would be its target.

But the week passed very quietly at the Paddington Jewish Boys' Club. Those whose work took them into W.E.T. House, like Mort Verdon, came back speaking of strikes and rumours of strikes, but the atmosphere in the rehearsal room remained peaceful. All of the *Strutters* team had benefited from the few days' rest and seemed relaxed. George Birkitt, whose objections to the script had really only been a way of asserting himself, was content with a few minor word-changes. The offending 'darlings' were excised, which made the script a revolutionary new departure in the literary careers of Willy and Sam Tennison, and George became quite mellow. He didn't really mind about having less lines than usual; if the truth were told, he was quite relieved – there was now a chance he might be able to learn them. But the tantrum had been necessary to him. As he said to Charles, 'Well, you know I'm the last person on earth to throw a scene, but occasionally one does have to put one's foot down and remind them who one is, or they trample all over you...er, one.'

He had also been persuaded that the pay-off should be left unaltered.

This was not because he thought it was right, but to avoid trouble; he had finally accepted it with a don't-say-I-didn't-warn-you shrug. After all, if the whole show was likely to be dubbed, it didn't really matter whether the jokes were funny or not. The viewing audience would laugh with recorded hilarity just as much as they would with the sounds of a so-called live audience.

Because, as the week progressed, there seemed less and less chance of the show's being recorded on the normal schedule. The security men's go-slow was unlikely to be resolved; the worry was how many more unions were likely to join them. The threat of the strike that Charles had jokingly predicted, of ITV staff for greater disparity of pay from BBC staff, loomed larger.

As a result of this, the rehearsal room saw more of Peter Lipscombe than it had since Bob Tomlinson took over as Director. The Producer appeared almost every day, bringing news of fresh possibilities and contingency plans. Nothing dented his Little Noddy image, though. Everything was still going to be okay, they were still working on the most exciting series to have hit television since Logie Baird's early experiments. Maybe the pitch of these assertions rose to a more hysterical level as the week went on, but nothing stopped them pouring out.

And everything seemed to be normal with Dame Aurelia Howarth and her husband. The senile homicide delivered his wife to the rehearsal room in the

Bentley and picked her up at the end of the day's work. On no occasion did he come inside the building.

The only significant moment came when Aurelia, who always did the correct thing, asked Bob Tomlinson, 'Darling, if this beastly go-slow happens and we have to rehearse/record the show through the day, do you mind if Barton sits in and watches? He does so enjoy coming to the recordings.'

'No, that's all right, love,' said the director, who, in spite of his resistance to show-biz schmaltz, had, over the weeks, like everyone else, developed a soft spot for Dob Howarth.

She turned to Charles, who was standing nearby, and gave him the exclusive benefit of her smile. 'How are things?' she asked lightly.

'Getting somewhere,' he said confidently, the intimacy between knight errant and damsel in distress re-established.

Aurelia looked up with sudden understanding. Once again he felt sure that she suspected Barton too.

And he also felt sure that, if the old lunatic was going to strike again, he would do so on the studio day.

Just as he was about to leave Hereford Road for rehearsal the day before the recording, Charles received a package through the letter-box. It was in a padded brown envelope and for a moment he couldn't imagine what it might be. Then the Kew postmark and the feel of the contents told him it must be his rare copy of R. Q. Wilberforce's *Death Takes A Short Cut*.

Because he was late, he shoved the package into his pocket and caught a cab to the Paddington Jewish Boys' Club. The cab was just another example of how having money in his pocket made him feel wealthy. He still hadn't managed to get through to Frances about the Greek idea; must try again.

Not much rehearsal ever gets done the day before studio, because the timing revolves around the Crew Run. This is the occasion when, as actors often put it, 'the anoraks move in'. In other words, all the studio staff, cameramen, sound-boom operators and so on, come to see the show in rehearsed form and follow it in their camera scripts (often typed up by the PA into the small hours of the previous night).

The Crew Run on this occasion was scheduled for twelve noon and, as the hour drew near, tension mounted. No one was quite sure of the latest on the industrial front and there were constant calls for various union members to go to meetings, which might or might not lead to strike action. Until all the crew turned up, it would not be known whether the show could go ahead. In their present militant mood, the technicians were liable to regard one member's absence as an instance of under-manning which would not allow the rest of them to proceed.

Mort Verdon twittered around with gloomy cautionary anecdotes from W.E.T. House. How the waitresses in the Executive Dining Room had walked out, leaving the Catering Manager to serve a lunch party of ten, given by Nigel Frisch. How a fellow Stage Manager had been having his bacon roll handed over the canteen counter when the call for a meeting came over the loudspeakers, and how the sweet-smelling breakfast had been whisked back from under his hungry nose. How a particularly bolshie studio team had insisted on reboiling a kettle and remaking tea for every rehearsal of a brief scene in a drama production. Mort got very dramatic about it all.

But gradually the anoraks assembled. Peter Lipscombe was for once silent and even anxious as he counted the crew members. One by one they came in through the rehearsal room door and, with the instinct of their breed, homed in on the coffee machine and tins of biscuits.

So the Crew Run was achieved. It even went quite well. George Birkitt remembered most of his lines. Peter Lipscombe thought it was a terrific episode and the whole series was jolly exciting.

Afterwards, as everyone disbanded, the mood was cheerful. The crew had been friendly and no one doubted that the show would get made the next day.

George Birkitt, flushed with the success of his feat of memory, asked if he could buy Charles a drink. Charles conceded the requisite permission. He felt relaxed. Nothing would happen till the studio day.

'Stupid thing came up the other day,' said George Birkitt with a sheepish grin, as they sat outside a mews pub drinking pints of Guinness. 'Had a call from the headmaster of my old school – asked if I'd open the school fête. I must have "arrived", they usually get some retired Colonel or something.'

'It's the Colonel Strutter image.'

'I suppose it is. Flattering in a way, mind.'

'Are you going to do it?'

'Oh, I'm not sure. Depends what else I have on round the date. I've referred him to my agent.'

'Oh.'

'Well, you do have to be bloody careful. I mean, you do one of these things as a favour, word gets out, and suddenly they're all clamouring round.'

'I hadn't thought of that.'

'Believe me, it happens. Anyway, it's easier if my agent sorts out the financial side.'

'I hadn't thought of that either.'

'Got to be canny, Charles, got to be canny.'

They both drank deeply into their Guinness. George Birkitt continued, 'Rang my wife the other day.'

'Oh, really?'

'Do you know her? Stephanie Roscoe.'

'I know her as an actress. I didn't know you were married.'

'Oh yes. We've been separated for a few years. You know, her career really took off when she got that part in the Royals telly series.'

'I read about it.'

'Made life very difficult for us. I was going through a bad patch, you know, professionally. Puts strain on a marriage, when one partner's very successful and in demand, and the other...ain't. So, after a lot of fighting, we split up. Best thing at the time.'

'Hmm.'

'You're divorced, aren't you?'

'Not actually divorced. Just separated.'

'Uh-huh.'

'I found an actor's life incompatible with matrimony.'

'It's difficult, certainly.'

'Must be even more difficult if you're both in the business. When you've got professional rivalry to add to the other pressures.'

'Doesn't help, Charles. You very rarely get show-biz marriages where the two careers balance exactly. For every pair of Lunts, there must be a hundred Dobs and Bartons.'

'Yes.'

'Of course, I was never jealous of Stephanie. Problems were just logistical. I mean, she was – is – a sweet girl, but really no great shakes as an actress. Just had a couple of lucky breaks. So jealousy was never really appropriate.'

'No. Haven't heard much about her recently. What's she been up to?'

'Not a lot, poor darling. Got a bit over-exposed, I think, with the Royals thing. So I thought I'd just ring, see how she was.'

'And how was she?'

'Fine, fine. Pity about this damned go-slow. I was going to ask her to come along to one of these recordings.'

So that she can see George Birkitt's name above the title, thought Charles, as the other continued, 'Still, I'm taking her out to dinner in a couple of days. See if there's anything left.'

'Hope there is, for your sake.'

George Birkitt shrugged. 'Doesn't worry me one way or the other. Just be interesting to see her, though.'

'Yes.'

'Strange, you know, during the time she was successful with that series, while I was spending a lot of time sitting around at home while she was off at rehearsals and premieres and things, I got really paranoid about it. You know, began to doubt my own abilities.' He laughed. 'Even started to believe Stephanie's publicity and think she was more talented than I was. Huh, but strange how quickly one gets like that. Most difficult part in the world, second fiddle, specially for a man.'

'But you don't have any worries about that now?'

'Good Lord, no. Everything's turned out fine recently. I really think this series could do me a lot of good, you know.'

'I'm sure it will. Same again?'

'That would be very pleasant.'

As Charles went into the pub with the empty glasses, he mulled over what

George had said about the pressures of being second fiddle. A lifetime of it could unhinge someone. Suppose you married a wife when you were both at about the same level in the business. And then you watched her rise to international success, while your career made no noticeable advance. You saw her become the toast of London and New York, you heard her name on everyone's lips, you saw her picture everywhere. You stood by while she became a pin-up of the Forces, you witnessed her career mature with her years, you saw her break into television with the same unerring success, you read the announcement that she had been made a Dame of the British Empire...

That kind of pressure could drive a man insane. And who knew what revenge he might take on the world which had put him in a position of such constant inequality.

He wondered again where Barton Rivers would strike next.

With four pints of Guinness inside him, he wandered back to Hereford Road through the bleary sunlight. It was really too nice an afternoon to go back to the bedsitter, but he had a vague intention of ringing Frances. The school of which she was headmistress must have broken up by now. It would be good to speak to her. George's words about the pressures of show business marriages had reminded him of the advantages of his own.

Then, after he had spoken to her, he might go out to the park. Walk round the Serpentine, maybe.

It was when he was inside the stuffy bedsitter that he became aware of the bulky package in his pocket. Oh yes, of course, his R. Q. Wilberforce. In his Guinness-sodden state, he couldn't really think why he had it.

He pieced it together slowly. Oh yes, it had started with that book Romney Kirkstall had had, the biography of Aurelia Howarth in which there had been a still from an aborted film called *Death Takes A Short Cut*. Then later Romney said he'd seen a copy of a book with that title in a Charing Cross Road bookshop Barton Rivers had recommended to him. So Charles had gone to the bookshop, been put in touch with Gregory Watts and...yes, yes, of course.

He took the brown padded package out. There was a little red plastic tag which would open the bag along a line of perforations.

He took hold of the tag and pulled it.

CHAPTER FOURTEEN

DEATH TAKES A SHORTCUT
by
R. Q. Wilberforce

CHAPTER 1
THE TRAVELLER'S RETURN

Maltravers Ratcliffe had risen and broken his fast early, so that he was already installed behind his desk, with a long black cigarette holder between his teeth, reading through his accumulated correspondence, when his wife appeared at the library door.

'So my bonny has come back to me,' she announced with joy.

'Over the sea to Skye,' he rejoined merrily, as he rose to greet her. 'Except, in my case, it was over the sea and through the sky. I came on the aeroplane to Croydon. Podd brought the Bentley down to meet me at the 'drome, and we fairly flew again as we drove back here!'

'You should have wakened me on your arrival.'

'No, no, Eithne my love. Even the nonpareil of beauty can reap benefit from a little beauty-sleep.'

Nor was his description fanciful; Eithne Ratcliffe was possessed of a beauty that would quicken the blood in any man's veins. Though slight, she was perfectly proportioned, and her carriage was superb. The golden hair that was her chiefest glory had been cut in the modern style, but its waves owed nothing to the artifice of coiffeurs. And her eyes! What eyes! Their hue of purest blue would have made a cornflower despondent; sapphires could offer but feeble comparison to them.

'Was your business in Paris successfully concluded?' she enquired of her handsome spouse.

'Successfully enough,' he conceded carelessly. 'Although, as is ever the case, I trapped the small fry in the certain knowledge that the big fish swam away unscathed.'

'Was it…?' Eithne questioned tremulously.

'Our old enemy?' Maltravers nodded with gravity. 'That same Teutonic devil was behind this latest outrage. Backed by an international conglomerate of Jewish bankers, he was planning to flood the gold bullion market with counterfeit ingots. Had he succeeded, he'd have crippled all the major

economies of the Western world! Shares would have gone down to cat's meat prices and hundreds of perfectly decent small houses would have gone smash!'

'But you prevented the swindle?' demanded Eithne, her wonderful eyes sparkling as she looked at her husband.

'Oh yes, I scotched his scheme easily. It was like eating jam. Once I had worked out that someone must be manipulating prices on the Bourse, I found out who it was first pop. A little Jewish thimblerigger, who I may say won't be seeing much scenery except the inside of a prison for the next twenty years. The Sûreté were very grateful. I've been awarded one of their croix d'honneurs'.'

Charles' concentration on the words wavered, but his interest was fiercely aroused. He skimmed verbose description of Maltravers Ratcliffe's cricketing prowess and a long, somewhat precious discussion about where the couple should spend the weekend. This was resolved at the end of the first chapter...

With a merry laugh, Maltravers cried, 'I've had my fill of crime for a while! Let's away to Derbyshire to play cricket. I happen to know Lord Wainscott fields a scratch team that's none so dusty. Tell Podd and Smithers to commence packing for us immediately! We'll take the Bentley and they can follow along in the Sunbeam. Oh, and tell Wallace to prepare a luncheon-basket, so that we are free to lunch where the scenery's good. Then we'll leap into the Bentley, my angel, point the bonnet towards Derbyshire, and be there in two twos!'

The second chapter assembled a house party of suspects at Wainscott Hall, in the time-honoured style of its genre. One of them, a foreign gentleman called Mr Akbar, did not endear himself to the rest of the guests...

The presence of this last personage was an unaccountable mystery. Neither his appearance nor his manners qualified him as a likely social acquaintance of Lord Wainscott, and yet the peer seemed ready, nay, eager, to welcome the foreigner into that proverbial castle of the Englishman, his home. Mr Akbar did not commend himself to the Ratcliffes by appearing at dinner in a silken cummerbund of the hue favoured by Romish cardinals and diamond studs of such ostentatious size that they might have looked less out of place amongst the regalia of a Babylonian Coronation! And Maltravers Ratcliffe, in front of whom the newcomer pushed as they proceeded to dinner, was not a little shocked to feel his nostrils assailed by a distinct whiff of perfume!

All that the book needed now, apart from a plan of the ground floor of Wainscott Hall (which soon appeared duly printed in the text), was a crime. After dinner Maltravers and Eithne Ratcliffe repaired to the billiard room...

'You know, my love, there's something deuced rummy going on here,' mused Maltravers as he chalked his cue. 'Deuced rummy. Something that makes my flesh creep. Do you feel it too?'

His wife answered in the affirmative.

'It's something to do with that gigolo, Akbar. I've a feeling he's out to spoke somebody's wheel. And what's more…I've a feeling I've seen the bounder somewhere before.'

At that moment Maltravers Ratcliffe froze, his face suffused by a ghastly pallor, his eyes transfixed by some object on the floor.

'Oh no,' he breathed. 'Oh no, oh no, oh no!'

He moved forward and picked up a monocle, whose silver setting was curiously wrought in the shape of a coiled snake. 'See, he has left his visiting card.'

'Are you sure?' murmured Eithne, unwilling to accept the sheer ugliness of the truth.

'Sure, ' her husband confirmed with unearthly calmness. 'Yes, it's von Strutter!'

Eithne Ratcliffe gasped. Their arch-enemy! Here, at Wainscott Hall!

'What's behind there?' Maltravers demanded, pointing to a door in front of which the monocle had lain.

'That's where Lord Wainscott keeps his collection.'

'Quick!'

He tried the door. It was locked, and there was no sign of a key. Fortunately he always carried a set of pick-locks, fashioned for him by the versatile Podd, and to open the door was a matter of moments.

One look inside sufficed to tell him all!

'Don't look, my love, don't look!' he commanded Eithne as he entered the room.

The walls were hung with many splendours of the Orient, but he had eyes for none of these. All he saw was the ghastly spectacle staining the fine Turkey carpet in the middle of the room.

It was the offensive Mr Akbar, destined never more to give offence! He lay face down on the floor. Upright from the back of his coat rose the bloody blade of a Japanese samurai sword!

CHAPTER FIFTEEN

THE EFFECTS OF four pints of Guinness vanished. Charles's mind was working very clearly. And fast.

It was incongruous, and yet it might be true. Could the pattern to this apparently meaningless sequence of deaths lie in a series of forgotten detective stories?

There were too many coincidences for him to dismiss the idea with his customary cynicism. The old still from the never-completed film of *Death Takes A Short Cut* told him that Barton Rivers and Aurelia Howarth had once been cast as Maltravers and Eithne Ratcliffe, and the old man's bizarre dress and style of speech suggested that in some mad way he was still playing the part. It made sense of the white flannels and all the inconsequential cricketing jargon, as well as Barton's permanent air of demented gallantry.

But the greatest coincidence was in the name, von Strutter. There had to be some connection there. If somewhere in the fogs of Barton Rivers mind, he was convinced he had an arch-enemy called von Strutter, he might well seek revenge on a television series which was called *The Strutters*. It was lunatic logic, but it was the only form of logic Charles had so far been able to impose on the random accidents.

The most chilling thing he had read, though, was R. Q. Wilberforce's choice of murder weapon. The coincidence of a samurai sword in the book and in the script of the next day's *Strutters* episode seemed to offer too much temptation to Barton Rivers' insane motivation. The accident with the sword must be averted.

But Charles needed more information. All he had so far was an idea, a new theory into which some of the known facts fitted. Many more would have to fall into place before he could dignify the theory with the title of a solution.

That meant finding out a lot more about the books of R. Q. Wilberforce. He went to the payphone on the landing.

'Hello. Gregory Watts.'

'This is Charles Paris.'

'Oh, good afternoon. Did you get the book all right?'

'Yes, thank you.'

'What else can I do for you?'

'I seem to remember when we spoke, you said Wilberforce was still alive.'

'Was last year, certainly.'

'Look, I need to contact him very urgently. Have you got a phone number for him?'

'No, I've got an address. Incidentally, when I wrote to him, I wrote to R. Q. Wilberforce, but his reply was very firmly signed in his real name, so perhaps you should use that.'

'You mean R. Q. Wilberforce is a pseudonym?'

'Certainly.' Watts laughed. 'I can't imagine too many people are actually called R. Q. Wilberforce.'

'It's possible.'

'Oh yes. Mind you, his real name is pretty odd, too.'

'Oh. What is it?'

'Barton Rivers.' There was a long silence. 'Are you still there, Mr Paris?'

'Yes, I...yes. Good God.'

'Shall I give you his address?'

'Yes...no. I mean, no, I don't need it now.'

'Oh, but I thought...'

'No, what I do need are copies of his books. All of them. And fast.'

'I told you, that's the only one I've got – or rather had. They're pretty rare.'

'But they must exist somewhere. Don't you know of any libraries or....'

'I suppose they might be around in a library, but you could spend weeks looking.'

'I've got to find them. It's really important.'

'Hmm...Well, the only thing I can suggest – I don't know if any of them would have any – but there are one or two collectors who specialise in detective fiction. You could ask.'

'Anything's worth trying.'

Gregory Watts gave him three names and phone numbers.

Stanley Harvey's cottage in Hampstead was, like his speech, precise to the point of being precious. On the telephone he had admitted with pride to being the possessor of an almost complete set of R. Q. Wilberforce, but he had been unwilling to have them inspected that evening. Charles had to use all his powers of persuasion and even resort to the phrase (for once used in a literal sense) 'a matter of life and death', before he achieved grudging consent. 'But I'm going out at eight,' said Stanley Harvey, 'so you'll have to be through by then.'

And no, there was no possibility of Charles borrowing any of the books.

When he opened the front door, Stanley Harvey lived up to the impression of his voice and cottage. He was a dapper little man in his early sixties, with a white goatee beard. A tweed Norfolk jacket and a Meerschaum pipe gave a Sherlockian image, which was reinforced by prints on the walls, models and memorabilia of the great detective.

Stanley Harvey seemed unimpressed by Charles Paris. 'This is really extremely inconvenient. I hope you meant what you said about it being important.'

'You must believe me. It is. It's far too complicated to explain but it is important.'

Stanley Harvey sniffed. 'I rang Gregory Watts and he confirmed that he had given you my number. Can't be too careful. The collection is pretty valuable and I can't let *just anyone* in.'

The emphasis, and the look that accompanied it, suggested he suspected Charles might be *just anyone* and still contemplated refusing admission. 'Gregory Watts said you were an R. Q. Wilberforce collector.'

'Hardly. I've only got one of the books. *Death Takes A Short Cut*.'

Stanley Harvey gave a superior smile. 'Oh, I've got that, of course. I've got five of them, and there only ever were the six.'

'First editions?' Charles felt he had to ask, only to give Stanley Harvey the satisfaction of saying a supercilious 'Of course.'

It had been a good question, because now Stanley Harvey's desire to show off his collection was greater than his distrust of his visitor. 'Come through,' he said curtly.

They went to the back of the cottage and through a passage to what appeared to be a modern extension. As they walked, Stanley Harvey continued to parade his knowledge. 'Of course, the reason R. Q. Wilberforces are so rare is that so few were printed.'

'Oh?' said Charles humbly.

'Yes, he never really caught on as an author. He was too larky and the plotting was too slack, I believe. He had the books printed at his own expense.'

'Really?'

'Oh yes.' Stanley Harvey had perked up now he saw what a humble student he had to lecture. Yes, he must have been a schoolteacher, he obviously enjoyed pontificating so much. A schoolteacher who had come into money.

Quite a lot of money, Charles reckoned when they went into the library. It was a purpose-built circular room. Packed bookshelves rose to the ceiling, alternating with tall windows protected with metal grids. All their books, arranged with the pernickety neatness that characterised their owner, were hard-backs of this century.

Charles made suitably appreciative noises.

'Yes, not bad,' said Stanley Harvey smugly. 'One of the largest private collections in the world, so I believe.'

'Of what?' Charles couldn't resist saying.

'Detective fiction. All first editions of course. I have my own private cataloguing system.'

Yes, you would.

'Conan Doyles along there – complete set of English and American firsts. Agatha Christie, the same. Raymond Chandler...Dorothy Sayers, of course. Simenons in the original, English editions and some selected translations and –'

'What about R. Q. Wilberforces?' asked Charles. It was twenty past six, the eight o'clock curfew was approaching fast, and he felt a desperate urgency to find out if he was on to something or just caught up in an elaborate fantasy.

'Yes,' said Stanley Harvey, with a *moue* of annoyance. 'Of course. Right, if that's all you're interested in, over here.'

He moved across the room and pointed to a row of matching blue spines. 'Here we are. R. Q. Wilberforce. The only one I haven't been able to track down yet is *Death Takes A Back Seat*. But here we have *Death Takes A Tumble, Death Takes The Wrong Turning, Death Takes A Drive, Death Takes A Stand* and *Death Takes A Short Cut*. I also have some manuscripts and drafts of stuff that was never published, if that's of interest.' He gestured towards a rank of metal filing cabinets.

'Did you collect them all one at a time?'

'No, not the R. Q. Wilberforces, actually. I do with most of the stuff, get it from publishers or through dealers, but in fact I got all this lot together. Just after the war I wrote to R. Q. Wilberforce and asked if he'd got any material he wanted to get rid of. To my surprise he sent me the lot. With a very strange letter. Said that he had been going to throw it all away, said that the War had changed everything, that there was no time for frivolity any more, that life had been shown up in its true colours and it was a tragic business. He said that R. Q. Wilberforce was dead and he never wanted to hear anything about him again. The letter was very odd, sounded a bit unbalanced.'

'Did he sign his own name?'

'He signed R. Q. Wilberforce, I don't know whether that was his name or not. I've got the letter filed if –'

'It doesn't matter.'

Stanley Harvey smiled a self-satisfied smile. 'So I got a nice little haul there for nothing. Shows what a letter arriving at the right time can do. Always worth writing a lot of letters if you're building up a collection.'

'Yes.' Charles looked at his watch. Half-past six. And he looked at the thickness of the five blue books on the shelf. 'Look, perhaps you could save me a bit of time. All I need to find out is about the deaths in the books. Perhaps you can remember something of the plots.'

Stanley Harvey looked at him in amazement and stroked his little beard. 'Good Lord, no. I only collect this stuff, I don't read it.'

Stanley Harvey perched watchfully at his desk in the middle of the library while Charles did his research. The circular room strengthened the impression of a spider at the centre of his web, as did the little man's suspicious eyes. He clearly expected Charles to try to leave with an illicit Margery Allingham under his jacket.

But once he got into the books, Charles was too intrigued to be inhibited by any hostile spectator. He read with fascination as the pattern he had suspected unfolded in all its lunacy.

He soon realised that he wouldn't have to read all the text. The relevant bits were not hard to find.

He opened each book and checked the date to confirm their sequence. There was a dedication in each one, too. In the first, *Death Takes A Tumble*, it read 'To Darling Hilary', and in the subsequent ones, 'To Hilary again, with all my love'. That introduced a new element. Barton and Aurelia's had always been hailed as the great example of a show business marriage that remained faithful, and yet who was this Hilary to whom he had dedicated five books? Charles knew he would have to find that out.

But for the moment he was more concerned with the deaths. They were easily found. Barton Rivers, in the guise of R. Q. Wilberforce, wrote his books to an unerring formula. In Chapter One, Maltravers Ratcliffe would return to his wife, Eithne, from some gallant exploit, arid they would decide to go away somewhere to escape all thoughts of crime. In Chapter Two they would arrive at their destination, and, on the last page of the chapter, someone would die. Maybe this total predictability was one of the reasons why R. Q. Wilberforce couldn't find a publisher and had to produce the books himself.

The murders made fascinating reading. *In Death Takes A Tumble*, the victim apparently fell from a fire escape on the tower of a baronial castle. In *Death Takes A Wrong Turning* a rock, cunningly placed round a hairpin bend in the Dolomites, caused a young playboy to drive his Hispano-Suiza to destruction down the face of a cliff. In *Death Takes A Drive* the victim was run down by a Bentley that didn't stop (thus causing, because of the make of car, suspicion to fall on the spotless Maltravers Ratcliffe). And in *Death Takes a Stand* a young man in a stately home was killed by the apparently accidental fall of a heavy wall-mounted light-stand.

In each book the manner of the death was, either punningly or directly, suggested in the title.

And, in every case, whoever had actually committed the crime, behind it, masterminding the operation, had been 'the evil genius of von Strutter' (usually followed by an exclamation mark!).

And so, in these old blue volumes were prefigured the deaths of Sadie Wainwright, Scott Newton, Rod Tisdale and Robin Laughton. Their individual identity had not been important; so long as they were connected with the series called *The Strutters* they had earned the right to die.

Charles returned the four volumes to their shelf long before Stanley Harvey's deadline. He didn't look at *Death Takes A Short Cut*. He knew what happened in that one.

Someone got impaled on a Japanese samurai sword.

CHAPTER SIXTEEN

THE TOWER BLOCK of W.E.T. House looked unchanged, modern, impassive, but internally it was crippled. There was no canteen or bar service, the security men's go-slow continued and members of other unions formed little mumbling groups. The company was like a very old man's body, in which no one knew which organ would fail next. Senior management sat like anxious doctors in their offices, waiting for the loudspeaker announcement or phone call that would signal the end, or at least the lapse into coma, of their patient.

But Peter Lipscombe was not the man to let that sort of atmosphere get him down. With Boy Scout brightness he welcomed each member of *The Strutters* cast into the building, and assured them all that everything was okay.

And so indeed it seemed. Costumes were laid in dressing-rooms, make-up girls waited to administer their tantalisingly short caresses, cameramen and sound-boom operators drifted towards the studio, Vision Mixer and PA to the control box, Sound and Vision Controllers to their adjacent stations. The set was up, and there seemed to be no reason why the rehearse/recording of Episode Eight of *The Strutters* should not start on camera at ten o'clock as scheduled.

Charles Paris wasn't there on the dot of ten, because, from force of habit, he had gone to the big Studio A, where *Wragg and Bowen* were having an uphill struggle with new directors and scriptwriters, and beginning to question the wisdom of their hugely expensive transfer from the BBC. (Why did they think they could change the inalienable law of television – that no comedy star was ever improved by moving from the BBC to ITV, and that for most a commercial offer was a sure sign that they had passed their peak of popularity?)

Charles realised his mistake as soon as he saw the set of garish tinsel and dangling silver bicycle wheels. As he turned to leave, he nearly bumped into a familiar, and not unattractive, figure. 'Jay!'

Actually, I call myself Jan Lewis now. It looks better on the roller caption.'

'Uh-huh. Well, how are things?'

'Fine. This *Wragg and Bowen* show is so complicated. There's lots to learn.'

'I'm sure.'

'Did you hear what happened yesterday?'

'Don't think so.'

'Oh, it was an absolute *disaster.* You know, this programme for the elderly...'

Oh yes, the Franchise-Grabber. He nodded.

'Well, you know they'd got this wonderful old boy in to front it. Ian Reynolds, he's nearly eighty.'

'Yes, I had heard.' A few times.

'Well, yesterday was their first day in the studio and when he got in front of the cameras – he dropped dead.'

'Oh dear.'

'Yes, they lost the whole studio day.'

Charles tut-tutted appropriately.

'They're going to get Robert Carton in instead. I'm sure he'll do it awfully well.'

'Oh, I should think so.' There was a silence. 'It'd be nice for us to get together again soon .

'Charles!' She looked at him as if he had made an improper suggestion. Which indeed he had. But not one that had worried her before.

'What's the matter?'

'But, Charles, I'm on a different *programme* now.'

His dilatoriness in getting to Studio B didn't matter. He had checked with Mort Verdon, who assured him that the samurai sword would be kept locked in the prop store until required for the final scene. 'Can't leave things like that lying around, boofle. For a start, it's worth a few bob, and things have been known to disappear, you know...Also, it's an extremely businesslike weapon, dear. Very sharp. If somebody started fooling about with that, there could be a very sudden influx of new members to the Treble Section...'

Maybe Mort Verdon's protective eye would be sufficient to ward off any 'accidents', but Charles knew Barton Rivers was cunning in his madness, and didn't feel confident. As soon as the sword appeared on the set, he would watch Barton Rivers's every move. Any attempt to touch it and he'd pounce. He needed evidence to ensure that the old maniac was put away where he belonged. But he'd have to be quick. He wanted evidence, but he didn't want another corpse.

Studio B, when he found it, looked quite a bit smaller than Studio A, but he was informed that it had the same floor area. The difference was that the larger studio had permanent audience seats, while when Studio B had audience shows, banks of seats were brought in, thus reducing the acting area. The seating was built *in situ* on frames of bolted metal sections, and stood up in great wedges away from the studio back wall. (A large gap had to be left between this wall and the back of the bank of seats because of fire regulations.)

Charles slouched in the front row and watched the recording with mild interest. The atmosphere was different to the usual studio day. Normally the tension mounted as the day went on, building to the mock-climax of the Dress Run, and then the final release of the end of the recording. On the revised schedule, each scene was rehearsed until satisfactory, and then recorded. It made everyone more relaxed. In spite of the industrial stormclouds outside, in the studio all was cosy. Many of the actors commented how much they'd rather rehearse/record the show every week, forget the moribund studio audience and either dub on the laughs or – heretical thought to any traditional Light Entertainment mind! – dispense with them altogether.

Peter Lipscombe explained at considerable length how much more expensive this would be because of the cost of VTR machine time, but soon lost his audience in a welter of budgetary jargon.

Through the slow processes of the morning Charles kept an eye on Barton Rivers. The old man sat in the audience grinning inanely and watching the every move of his wife. Whatever had happened to his mind, his devotion to Aurelia seemed absolutely genuine, a devotion reflected in such overblown and dated terms by the relationship between Maltravers and Eithne Ratcliffe.

Once again Charles wondered who on earth Hilary could be and where she fitted into the bizarre picture.

At one point he chatted to Barton. The old man, with his zany politeness, used a lot of 'dear boys', commented that doing the show this way was 'a rummy business' and asked Charles what chance he thought our chaps had against the Indians at the Oval.

Now that he had the key, Charles could hear the intonations of Maltravers Ratcliffe in every word. And, remembering the photograph of the fine young man in the Bentley, he could see that, if ever the filming of *Death Takes A Short Cut* had been feasible, Barton Rivers would have been ideal casting for it.

He contemplated challenging the old man with all he knew, but he didn't think it would work. The ruined mind would not be able to respond. No, he had to wait for the sword and see what happened.

They proceeded quickly on the new schedule and by lunchtime had recorded the bulk of the show. Of course, there were no canteen facilities, but Peter Lipscombe demonstrated that he did have his uses by laying on large supplies of take-away food in the dressing rooms. Mort Verdon was of the pessimistic opinion that this might be construed as strike-breaking and twitched visibly every time there was an announcement on the loudspeakers.

There were quite a few announcements on the loudspeakers that lunchtime, calling meetings of various branches of various unions, but, remarkably, the entire studio crew reassembled to continue work at two o'clock.

Charles began to feel nervous as the final scene of the episode drew near. He was taking a terrible risk. If something went wrong, another person could die.

Perhaps he should have gone to the police. But even as the idea came to him, he dismissed it. His story was so fanciful, so ridiculous, that no one would believe him. He remembered from his interview after the night's filming in Clapham how little the police cared for the romantic notions of amateurs.

The recording continued. The penultimate scene was completed and the set had to be redressed before the final one, in which Colonel Strutter's Japanese neighbour was to present him with a samurai sword.

Dob Howarth, whose work for the day was finished, came into the audience, yawning. She smiled at Charles, giving him once again the full beam of her eyes. 'Oh, I think we'll get it all in the can now.'

'Looks like it.'

'I'm exhausted. Come and sit with me and tell me sweet stories, darling.'

Charles was torn. Barton Rivers sat two rows in front of him and he wanted to keep within range of the old man. Equally, he didn't want to arouse Aurelia's suspicions by not accompanying her up to the back of the audience seats.

It'd be all right. The sword wasn't even on the set yet. And it would only take a second to get down on stage. He moved up to join Aurelia in the back row.

'Be a relief when all this industrial trouble's over, won't it, Dob?'

'Will rather, darling. I must say it doesn't make the whole process any less tiring.'

Her voice was intimate and close. He decided to talk to her about Barton. She must know a bit of what was going on. Maybe, if he told her all of it, she would agree to having the old man put away. It could all be sorted out without further risk.

Charles put his arm along the back rail of the audience seating and asked gently, 'How *is* Barton, Dob?'

She sighed. 'Not getting better, I'm afraid.'

Charles looked down on to the set. Mort Verdon walked into the light bearing, like Miss World with her sceptre, the samurai sword.

Six rows down, the long figure of Barton Rivers rose to his feet.

Immediately, Charles did the same and started down the steps.

But Barton didn't go for the sword. Instead, with his fixed gentlemanly grin, he came up towards them.

Charles subsided back into his seat with relief. The danger had passed for the time being.

'Barton's mind works strangely, doesn't it, Dob?' he murmured.

She sighed. 'I'm afraid so, darling.'

There was a sudden commotion on the set. Charles tensed, but Barton Rivers was still moving away from the sword.

Everyone seemed to be flooding into the studio looking bewildered. At last Bob Tomlinson emerged from the melee. He turned to the audience seats and shouted in his coster's voice, 'That's it, folks. A.C.T.T. has called a strike. We're all out. It's over.'

Then everything happened fast. Charles saw Mort Verdon put the samurai sword down on the sofa. Barton Rivers, who was now almost at the top of the audience steps, turned back towards the set.

But as Charles rose, the old man's arm suddenly swung round and caught him in the chest, toppling him backwards.

As the rail behind him gave way and Charles felt himself falling, falling backwards, his last thought was he wished he'd read *Death Takes A Back Seat*.

CHAPTER SEVENTEEN

HE LANDED WITH a terrible jolt that rearranged every cell in his body. He was winded and may have passed out for a few moments. Time seemed to have elapsed when he became aware of his surroundings.

Two men in lumberjack checked shirts lay on the studio floor with him. Both looked dazed and were rubbing various of their extremities. Around the three prone figures a little semi-circle of technicians had gathered.

One of the men on the floor found his tongue. 'Bloody strike-breaker,' he grumbled. 'Where the hell did you come from?'

Charles pointed weakly up to the top of the bank of seats, where the back rail hung loose and the outline of his tipped-up seat showed.

'You're bloody lucky we're not seriously injured,' continued the man in the lumberjack checked shirt. 'Bloody lucky.'

'He didn't fall on purpose,' a voice said defensively.

'Comes to the same thing whether he did or didn't. Falling down on top of union members – that's the sort of thing that could cause a strike.'

'But we're already on strike.'

'Oh yes. Bloody lucky for him we are.'

The other lumberjack checked shirt groaned.

''Ere, you all right?' asked his mate.

The only reply he got was another groan.

The speaking shirt turned accusingly to Charles. ''Ere, you really hurt him. I reckon falling actors comes under industrial accident. We'll take the company for a lot of insurance on this.'

That thought seemed to make his own injuries worse, and he too groaned.

'You've chosen a bad time for that,' observed one of the watching cameramen. 'Now we're on strike, the company's not liable. In fact, with the security men on total strike, even the building isn't insured.'

'Bloody hell.' Both the lumberjack checked shirts stopped groaning, stood up, and walked off, grumbling.

Charles lay still. He didn't know if it was shock or genuine injury, but he felt numb, unable to move. There was no pain, just a lassitude, an unwillingness to come back to the real world.

He vaguely heard voices asking if he was all right and vaguely felt hands lifting him. With infinite caution, he put weight on first one foot, then the other.

'Are you sure you're all right?' He focused on the anxious face of a young cameraman. There should be a nurse on duty in the building. I don't know if she'll have gone on strike yet. I could ring. I think the phones are still working.'

Slowly, Charles's faculties were coming back to him. He tried his voice and it seemed to work. 'No, no, I think I'm all right. Just shock, really. And I feel as if I'm a bit bruised. Let me go. I'll see if I can walk.'

He could. Just. It hurt. The feeling had come back to his body as well as his mind.

'Thank you. Thank you very much. I'll be okay.'

'Are you sure?'

'Yes. Thanks.'

He moved very slowly out of the studio. Each footstep, however gently he tried to place it, jarred his back, and he felt himself sweating with the pain.

But he had no doubt about what he had to do. Or where he had to go. With pain, but determination, he moved slowly towards Dressing Room Number One, which had been allocated by *The Strutters* new PA to Aurelia Howarth.

He knocked, and her husky, cultivated voice gave him permission to enter.

She was sitting at the mirror adjusting her make-up. Her usual diaphanous gowns and the ones she wore for the show were so similar that he couldn't tell whether she had changed or not.

Barton Rivers was not there.

Charles's appearance shocked her. 'You survived,' she gasped.

He nodded, which he found a rather painful action.

Aurelia seemed to be in the grip of a strong emotion and it was a moment before she managed to murmur, 'Thank God.'

'Yes, I survived. Unlike Sadie and Scott and Robin.'

Tears glinted in huge unfocused eyes. 'I'm so sorry. I kept thinking he'd stop.'

'*Death Takes A Back Seat*,' said Charles. 'I never got to read that one.'

She looked at him with surprise, but also a touch of relief, relief perhaps that now her terrible secret was shared. 'So you worked it out from the books?'

'Yes. But I was stupid today. I kept thinking it'd be the samurai sword.'

She gave a strained smile. 'Of course. *Death Takes A Short Cut*. I'm afraid I'd given up trying to work out what would happen next. I just kept praying it would all stop, but it went on, and on.'

'He'll have to be put away,' Charles said gently.

Aurelia inclined her head. 'I suppose so. That's what I feared. That's why – once I knew – all I could do was beg him to stop. I couldn't actually betray him. Not my husband.'

'No.' Charles felt the stirring of a deep emotion, sympathy for her pain. 'But why? I see that he was following the murders in the books, but he must have had some reason, some logic, however bizarre.'

Aurelia Howarth shrugged. 'Barton just said it had to be done. He said that von Strutter was the mastermind behind every evil and the series of *The Strutters* was part of a plot to take over the country.'

'But in the books it's von Strutter who commits the crimes, not Maltravers Ratcliffe.'

There was a little humourless laugh. 'It'd be funny if it weren't so tragic. Barton said that the only way to counter the Teutonic devil's schemes was to use his own methods.'

'I see.' Yes, in the mind of a madman, that was a kind of logic. 'How long has he been like this?'

Strangely, as he said it, the line seemed to echo Claudius' response to the demented Ophelia, 'How long hath she been thus?'

Aurelia sighed. 'It was the war. The war left many scars, and the worst of them were invisible. For Barton, it destroyed everything. First, there was the film of *Death Takes A Short Cut*. That had been set up with great difficulty, with a great deal of money, but it promised so well. It would have been the two of us working together, as equals, working on scripts from his book. Barton hoped it would be the first of a series of films and would make his career. But it was cancelled as soon as war was declared. So the war, the Germans, to Barton's mind von Strutter, ruined that chance.

'And he wasn't even allowed to revenge the affront personally. He was turned down for active service because he was too old. I went off to entertain the troops all over the place, and once again Barton was left behind.

'But that was not the worst...' Aurelia's voice broke, but she regained control quickly. 'Our son was of an age to fight for his country. In January 1944, we heard that he had been killed on active service.'

'Your son's name was Hilary?'

She nodded, unable for a moment to speak. Charles waited until she could continue.

'From that time on, Barton was changed. He stopped writing, said that he would never write again. And he started to get ideas, strange, grotesque ideas. He started to dress and talk like this character and to plan revenge on von Strutter. At first he was convinced that Hitler was von Strutter in disguise, and that he would win the war and we would be overrun by the Germans.'

'His mind went?'

She nodded again, very slowly. 'But I always thought he was harmless. And then...this started. At first I couldn't believe it was true, then I just hoped it would stop. Now I still wish it could be kept secret. But you've worked it all out...' Her hands dropped helplessly on to her lap.

So there it was. Bizarre, yes, ridiculous, yes, but true. Charles' grotesque theory had been proved correct. He felt a slight dissatisfaction. He'd never liked the idea of psychopathic murders; always felt more comfortable with a logic of motivation he could understand. Still, Barton Rivers was his culprit, and Barton Rivers had to be found. One crime, the murder from *Death Takes A Short Cut*, had not yet been recreated.

'Where is Barton now, Dob?'

'In the building. Not far away.' She spoke distractedly.

'He must be found.'

'Yes.' A listless monosyllable. Then, in a different tone, 'I still think it's remarkable how you worked it out. I suppose you saw the books in Peter's office.'

'In Peter's office?'

'Yes. You know I lent them to him. Barton gave me a set years ago, and forgot about them when he threw out all his copies.'

'Those were the books you thought might make a series?'

'Yes.'

Charles felt a great surge of excitement. Something had happened. He hadn't worked it out in detail yet, but his mind was suddenly racing away in a new direction.

He looked piercingly at Aurelia. 'I don't believe you.'

'What on earth do you mean?'

He thought out loud, piecing it together as he went along. 'Those books would never make a television series.'

'That's a matter of opinion,' she said frostily.

'No, it's not, it's a matter of fact. They would have made a pretty peculiar set of films in the 1940s, but a television series in 1979 – never.'

'Perhaps not. I just thought, hoped that –'

'No, you didn't. The idea is a bummer and you know it.'

'I don't understand.'

'Yes, you do. If there's one quality which has distinguished every moment of your career, it's your judgement. You have always done the right thing, chosen the right show, the right part. You know what works and what doesn't.'

'Perhaps I did once, but as we get older, our judgement gets less reliable.'

'Your judgement is as good as it has ever been. And yet I heard you say to Peter Lipscombe on two occasions that you thought those books would make a good television series. I didn't know what the books in question were at that stage or I'd have smelt a rat earlier.'

'I don't know what you mean.'

'Nor do I completely, but I'm getting there.' Charles paused and built his thoughts up slowly. 'You knew, of course you knew, that those books had no potential at all for television and yet you still very deliberately brought them to Peter Lipscombe's attention. Why? I think you wanted them read, you wanted someone to see the parallels with the crimes that surrounded the *Strutters* series. Yes, in spite of what you say about wanting to keep your husband's crimes quiet, I think you were deliberately trying to draw attention to the books' parallels with what he was doing. And, if you'd given them to anyone other than a television producer, the connection might have been made a lot earlier.'

Aurelia looked crestfallen. 'All right, so what if I did? I couldn't actually betray Barton, but by offering the books I was at least opening up the possibility that someone might work out what was happening.'

Charles was almost seduced by her meekness, but not quite. 'If that was the case, why didn't you offer more help, show the books to the police or something, tell someone? And why did you sound so disappointed when I said I'd worked out the connection just now?'

Aurelia now looked angry. 'You're talking nonsense, Charles. Why else would I lend the books?'

He looked at her very straight. 'I think you lent them as an insurance policy. So that they were there if anyone started connecting the deaths. And so that if suspicion started to move towards you, it could be diverted towards Barton.'

He wasn't sure, but he knew that he had to hold her stare until she gave way if he was to have any chance of finding out the truth.

It took a long time, but eventually she lowered her eyes. 'So...it's confession time, is it?'

'I think so.' With caution and discomfort, Charles sat down. 'You killed Sadie Wainwright?'

'It was an accident. Really, an accident.' The wonderful blue eyes looked totally sincere, but Charles was getting suspicious of their messages. 'It was a stupid thing. She had been being unpleasant about Cocky all day, really offensive. Then, when we were walking up the fire escape, she said something even viler and I lost my temper. I pushed her and the railing gave way. That is the truth.'

'So Cocky *was* the motivation?'

'Yes. And after that night's filming, I thought you'd worked it out. That's why I poisoned him.'

'Poisoned Cocky?'

She nodded. 'I thought if you saw how little I was affected by his death, you'd discount him as a motive against Sadie. But then Romney came along with his wretched card and I broke down, so it...'

Charles tried to slow things down, so that his mind could accommodate the new information. 'Okay, Sadie's death you say was an accident.'

'Yes, and she was such a peculiarly unlovely person I can't think that anyone was too upset by it.' She spoke with a kind of blind selfishness, the murderer s immunity to other people's existence. 'Anyway, I didn't want investigations and things. I had my image to think of.' Image – the star's eternal motivation. Was the perfect marriage to Barton just another reflection of the image?

Charles nudged on. 'But Sadie's wasn't the only death.'

'No. As I say, she was an accident, really. I thought she would soon be forgotten, but...'

A new set of facts fell into place. Scott Newton had been in a terrible state after the recording of the *Strutters* pilot, Scott Newton had wanted a private word with Aurelia at the first read-through, Scott Newton had been suddenly affluent at the filming at Bernard Walton's house. 'But,' suggested Charles, 'Scott Newton had seen Sadie die and, being under a certain amount of financial pressure, had started to blackmail you.'

Aurelia nodded. 'I gave him one big pay-off, but he wasn't going to be satisfied with that. So he had to go.' It was said very matter-of-fact.

'You moved the flower-urn yourself?'

'Barton did it.'

'You told him all about the –'

She laughed unattractively. 'I told him that Scott was one of von Strutter's spies, and that we had to destroy him. And I said the only way we could thwart the Teutonic devil was to use his own murder methods. The way Sadie died had been a coincidence, but I suddenly saw that it could fit very conveniently into a pattern.'

'And Bar ton didn't question what you were suggesting?'

'Not at all. He took to it instantly. It was what he'd been waiting for all his life, for someone to share his delusions.' She spoke of her husband as one might of a large and inconvenient pet.

'And it was after Scott's death that you gave Peter Lipscombe the books, so that he could make the connection between the two crimes if he chose to?'

'Yes. He mentioned the possibility of their being connected in one of his little notes and that got me worried.'

'And, if they ever were discovered, you'd set it up so that Barton would get the blame.'

'He'd never betray me. Never betray a *lady*,' she said dismissively'.

Charles sighed. 'That still doesn't explain the deaths of Rod Tisdale and Robin Laughton.'

'No' Aurelia agreed. 'It doesn't.' She let out a sudden peal of laughter. It was a famous sound, a sound that had been heard on millions of recordings of *I Dream of Dancing*, but at this moment its gaiety was not infectious. 'I'm afraid I was hoist with my own petard.'

'What do you mean?'

'I am afraid I had planted the idea of a von Strutter conspiracy rather too firmly in my poor husband's head. He started recreating the other murders completely off his own bat. Obviously what I had asked him to do had struck a chord. Barton was happy, happier than he had ever been. I think he felt that murder was going to be the one thing in his life that he had ever been good at.'

'So you had nothing to do with the last two deaths?'

'Nothing at all. Mind you, they were not without convenience. They shifted suspicion from me. The death of that tiresome Floor Manager put you off the scent, for a start.'

She smiled. It was the same famous smile, but its charm had gone. Charles recoiled from the image of this woman playing on her husband's illness, winding him up like some demented clockwork mouse to the random murders of people she regarded as irrelevant. That was it, he realised –

through all the charm, she had never recognised the relevance of anyone in the world but herself. Perhaps, given more understanding, more care from his wife, Barton's descent into insanity could have been checked.

But it wasn't the moment for conjecture. 'And Barton's attack on me – was that just random?'

She shook her head slowly, with another little smile. 'No, I'm afraid that was my suggestion. I planted the idea, I have to confess. Your inquisitiveness was becoming rather disturbing, and I saw a good way of satisfying my husband's lunacy and removing a danger to me.'

'I'm honoured.'

'Yes.' She paused. 'Now, of course, you represent even more of a danger to me.' She looked at her watch and Charles realised why she had vouchsafed him this long confession. She had been playing for time, awaiting the return of her demented assassin.

The door opened, and Barton Rivers entered with his customary idiotic gallantry. He seemed totally unsurprised to see Charles. 'Bung-ho, old boy,' he said. 'Lovely weather for it.'

'Barton,' commanded Dame Aurelia Howarth, 'Mr Paris is being rather tiresome.'

The death's head turned to face him. 'I say, old boy. Mustn't worry the little lady. Perhaps you ought to be off.'

'I didn't mean that, Barton,' she snapped. 'I mean, get rid of him.'

'Eh?'

'He's one of von Strutter's spies.'

'Oh, can't have that, eh? Don't understand the rules of cricket, that lot.'

'Kill him, Barton!'

The old man stepped forward, the claws shot out and Charles felt himself lifted out of his chair. The strength was enormous and terrifying. His arms were clamped to his sides and, in his weakened state, he was unable to move.

The eyes in the skull-face glinted at him, horribly close.

But then they seemed to lose focus, to waver, and change to the confused eyes of a senile old man.

'Difficult, you know, old girl,' said Barton. 'Only one of the Teutonic devil's tricks we haven't used is the old samurai sword, and I'm afraid I haven't got one of those on me.'

'It doesn't matter how it's done,' Dame Aurelia Howarth hissed. But she was up against the unassailable logic of lunacy. 'Oh, but it does, old thing. There's a right way and a wrong way, you know.'

'Just kill him!'

'Have to find a sword first, my angel. Have to think. I wonder if there's anything else we could do, or has von Strutter finally triumphed?'

Charles Paris felt very tired, while this surreal discussion about his death went on. He wanted to laugh. but hadn't got the energy.

Then the door opened again and he looked up with relief to see the startled face of Mort Verdon. 'Oops, sorry, boofles. Thought you'd all gone.'

Barton Rivers did not appear to notice the new arrival, but relaxed his hold on his victim's arms. Aurelia fixed Charles with an expression of hatred, but seemed to recognise that nothing could be done with Mort there. 'Come on, Barton.'

The living skeleton did not react.

'Maltravers,' she murmured.

He came to life. He gave her a gallant little bow, and offered his arm. 'Of course, Eithne, my angel. We'll soon get this ghastly business sorted out.'

She took his arm almost reluctantly. She seemed hypnotised by him, half-attracted, half-repelled. And there was something else in her look, which with a shock Charles recognised as fear. As Barton led his wife out of the dressing room door, he seemed very much in command of their relationship.

'Come, let's away, my fair one, and we'll be there in two twos.'

Relief, and the expression of amazement on Mort Verdon's face, reduced Charles to helpless laughter. As amazement changed to concern, he realised he was hysterical.

'Oh God,' he finally managed to say, 'I've never been so glad to see anyone.'

Mort Verdon flicked an eyebrow with his little finger. 'I bet you say that to all the boys.'

Charles giggled again and then sobered up. 'You look a worried man, Mort.'

'I am, boofle, I am.'

'Why?'

'Always the same when you've got something valuable in the studio. It gets nicked.'

'What are you talking about?'

'The samurai sword has completely disappeared, dear. Completely.'

'Oh, my God!' Charles realised that his ordeal was not yet over.

'That's why I'm going round the dressing rooms and –'

'Mort,' said Charles.

'Yes, dear.'

'Would you mind walking out with me?'

Mort Verdon's eyebrows shot up. 'Well now,' he said, 'there's a novelty!'

There was no sign of the Bentley or its owners as they left the dead stillness of W.E.T. House, but a cruising taxi was passing and Charles hailed it. He'd feel safer inside than exposed on the streets.

He was going to give the Hereford Road address, but suddenly panicked that Aurelia might know it. He felt certain they'd be out to get him, but he didn't know how. Perhaps there would be a clue in the R. Q. Wilberforce books. He asked the driver to take him to Hampstead.

Stanley Harvey objected that it was very inconvenient and ill-mannered, but Charles was in no mood to be stopped. He bulldozered his way into the little man's library and flicked quickly through *Death Takes A Short Cut*.

It was unhelpful. Then Charles remembered Stanley Harvey had mentioned some other R. Q. Wilberforce papers in the filing cabinet, and he demanded to see them.

It was the only thing he could think of. Perhaps there would be some further clue, some pointer that might help him avert the final tragedy.

With bad grace, Stanley Harvey opened the filing cabinet. Charles riffled through the piles of manuscript and letters at speed, not certain what he was looking for, but convinced that there must be something.

In a few minutes he found it. A pointer, yes, but it didn't point in the way he had expected.

There was just one sheet. It was headed as if it were the start of a new book, but at the bottom of the page, a thick line had been ruled. All that was written below that was the date, 30th January 1944.

DEATH TAKES THE HONOURABLE COURSE
by
R. Q. Wilberforce

CHAPTER ONE
THE TRIUMPH OF EVIL

Maltravers Ratcliffe looked at his wife as he put down the 'phone, and felt the glow of wonder and gratitude that her visage always aroused in him. The golden hair! The heavenly blue eyes, more precious than a Rajah's treasure store! Eithne's small face was set in the lines of courage, as together they listened to the distant, ominous boom of the guns.

'London has fallen, my angel,' he announced with his same old debonair carelessness.

She gasped; though it was the news that she had feared, to hear it confirmed was still a profound shock to her sensibilities.

'So von Strutter has triumphed!'

'Triumphed over this sceptred isle,' her husband rejoined with the spirit, 'but never over Maltravers Ratcliffe!'

'It is inevitable that the Teutonic devil will seek you out to exact his ghastly revenge.'

'Inevitable,' he confirmed. 'But let him seek! To seek is not to find! Come, my angel, we will go for a drive! Tell Wallace to provide a luncheon-basket and tog up in your gladdest rags!'

They drove towards the South. The Bentley swallowed the miles keenly, relishing the open road. Never had the Garden of England looked more beauteous! Never had Maltravers and Eithne Ratcliffe been so much together, so equal in their love! They took their luncheon in a flowery dell and chattered amiably of cricket and of their happiness.

Then the great Bentley, smoothly seeming to sense its destination, headed towards the sea, towards those white cliffs which, until this last devil, had hitherto daunted every foreign invader.

As they neared the cliff-top, Maltravers Ratcliffe, without diminishing the great car's speed, took his wife's small hand in his. 'Take heart, my angel!' he cried cheerily. 'We may thank our stars that we have had each other. Onward now, my fair one – and we'll be there in two twos!'

The news of Aurelia Howarth and Barton Rivers's fatal car crash was on the radio the following morning. It wasn't the first item. That was of course the ITV strike.

CHAPTER EIGHTEEN

DAME AURELIA HOWARTH

The death of Aurelia Howarth, who died in a car accident together with her husband, Barton Rivers, robs the British theatre of one of its most glittering and best-loved stars. Born Anne Howarth, she was the daughter of a grocer and spent her early years near Guildford. Her great natural talents led to her enrolment in the stage school from where she progressed to the chorus of a West End revue, *Careless Rapture*, at the tender age of fifteen. She was 'spotted' in this show by the great Andre Charlot, who gave her solo spots in some of his revues, and later taken up by the impresario C. B. Cochran, one of the most famous of whose 'Young Ladies' she became. Her biggest successes of this period were in *Parisian Trifles, Only the Night* and *Shimmering Stars*. It was in this last show that she first sang *I Dream of Dancing*, the song that she made her own and which virtually became her signature tune. She also went with *Shimmering Stars* to Broadway where, under the title of *Box of Tricks*, it became one of the hits of the season, and established Aurelia Howarth as an important new star in America. During the Thirties she played leading roles in many British films, of which the most memorable are probably *Lovers' Moon, Princess of Dreams* and *Tomorrow's Gone*. During the War she worked indefatigably entertaining the troops, services which were recognised by a CBE in 1947. In the post-war years her career took a new turn and she started to build a reputation as a straight actress. Long runs in the West End in such shows as *The Long Climb, Here We Go A-Wassailing* and *The Former Mrs Wellington* demonstrated her versatility. Then, at an age when many people contemplate retiring, Aurelia Howarth started to work in the growing medium of television, where she proved very popular, particularly in the role of the scatty Mrs Strutter in the comedy series, *What'll The Neighbours Say?* She was working on a new series in the same character at the time of her death. Throughout a long career in the theatre, Aurelia Howarth was one of the few performers who commanded universal love and who never did a malicious action to anyone. Both in the profession and with the public, her popularity never waned. She was created a Dame of the British Empire in the recent Birthday Honours List. She married Barton Rivers, a revue performer, in 1918 and their one son, Hilary, was killed in action in 1944.

There was no separate obituary for Barton Rivers. Neither his reputation as an actor nor as a writer justified it.

Charles Paris tried ringing his wife Frances on and off for about three days and, when he still didn't get any reply, he rang their daughter Juliet at her home in Pangbourne.

'No, Mummy's not there at the moment.'

'Where is she?'

'It's school holidays. She's away.'

'Where?'

'Naxos.'

'That's Greece, isn't it?'

'One of the islands, yes.'

'Do you happen to know if she went on her own or...'

'She went with a friend.'

'You don't know who?'

'No.'

'Oh.'

'She'll be back in about ten days.'

'Ah. I'll ring her then. How are things with you?'

'Oh fine. Hectic with the twins.'

'I'm sure.'

'Still, they start play school in September. And I'm going back to work. Just mornings.'

'Ah.'

'Miles and I would love to see you if you're free. Give us a buzz if you're about.'

'Yes, I will.'

'I must dash. Damian's pulling Julian's hair. 'Bye.'

'Goodbye.'

West End Television Ltd.
W.E.T. House,
235–9 Lisson Avenue, London NW1 3PQ.
29th October 1979.

Dear Charles,

Now that the strike's over and life here is getting back to normal, I wanted to drop you a note to thank you for all your hard work over the series of *The Strutters*.

Obviously, with Dob's tragic death, there is no possibility of the series being completed. Recasting such a major role is out of the question. Still, you should by now, I hope, have received your outstanding contractual payments.

Plans here are still rather fluid, so the future of the programmes in the series that were completed is uncertain. There's still a bit of editing and sound-dubbing to do on them, and since the demand on those facilities here is pretty heavy at the moment, it'll be some time before they're ready to be transmitted. But the 'powers that be' have spoken of the possibility of putting the seven completed programmes out as a mini-series in the Spring or Summer. We'll have to see.

Now that we don't have *The Strutters* there's a possibility that we may do another series of *What'll The Neighbours Say?* at some point. Obviously, without Dob, it'll have to be rather different and so I can't really say whether your character would be likely to recur or not. Anyway, it's a long way in the future and will depend when Bernard Walton's free. He's currently in Australia doing a tax year (and, incidentally, remaking a *What'll The Neighbours Say* series out there with an Australian supporting cast!).

I haven't heard much from the *Strutters* crowd, though I did see George Birkitt with his wife at a première the other week. Oh, and also I have to pass on the bad news that Willy and Sam Tennison have split up. I've just had a very exciting new script from Willy, provisionally titled *Marriage on the Rocks*.

Once again, many thanks for all you did to make *The Strutters* what it was. I look forward to working with you again on some other project.

With the warmest good wishes,

Yours sincerely,

Peter

PETER LIPSCOMBE
Producer *The Strutters*

MURDER UNPROMPTED

To Dany, with love

CHAPTER ONE

CHARLES PARIS was in the Number One dressing room.

True, the Number One dressing room at the Prince's Theatre, Taunton, was distinguished from the other dressing rooms only by the white plastic numeral screwed on to the door. In size and lack of amenities they were all identical.

And true, Charles was sharing the Number One dressing room with another actor, Alex Household, who had a larger part in the play.

But the fact remained that, for the duration of the three-week run of *The Hooded Owl*, Charles Paris would be in the Number One dressing room and, though publicly he always affected lack of interest in such petty distinctions ('Men are led by toys', he would say, loftily quoting Napoleon), he was secretly delighted. However cynical he appeared, however logical he was about the likelihood of a sudden breakthrough at the age of fifty-four, his actor's imagination could still leap in seconds to the pinnacles of theatrical success. Dreams of sudden public recognition of his talents had survived almost unchanged from his teens, and reality, in the form of modest achievements and much 'resting' since he had started in the business in 1949, could make little impression on them.

So, though he would never actually speak of it, even in his most drunken moments (which in his case were *quite* drunken), Charles still nursed the tiny hope that *The Hooded Owl* would be the one, the play on whose crest he would ride into the West End, where his true worth would be instantly appreciated, and he would spend the rest of his life 'reading scripts' rather than grabbing any job that came within reach, becoming a regular on television chat shows, participating in 'Nights of a Thousand Stars' for charity, and describing his favourite room to the *Observer* Colour Supplement.

Since he lived in one room, a dingy bed-sit in Hereford Road, London W.2., this last part of the fantasy had not been fully thought through. In fact, none of it had been fully thought through, because, in small measure, he had tasted success. He had been in long runs in the West End, he had even had his own play running in the West End, he had done bits in television and films, and his logical self knew how insubstantial such satisfactions were.

And yet the fantasies persisted. It was just as it had been in his teens. In the early years of adolescence, he had put down all his feelings of dissatisfaction to the fact that he hadn't got that all-important amulet, a girl-friend. But, to his surprise, at the age of nineteen, after a steady two-year relationship, he had found he was still attributing his discontent to the same cause. Like the horizon, a sense of fulfilment kept its distance, regardless of his position.

But, in spite of that bleak conclusion, hope survived.

Hope for the future of *The Hooded Owl* was not quite as baseless as it might be for the average production in a provincial theatre. The staple diet of Taunton's theatre-goers was set-book classics, creaking but well-built thrillers and last year's West End cast-offs, none of which had any prospects beyond the three weeks of their run. *The Hooded Owl*, on the other hand, was a new play, and not a bad one at that. If all of the thousands of variables which govern such a process came right, it was not impossible that the play should transfer to the West End.

One person believed that possibility with sufficient conviction to back his belief with money. His name was Paul Lexington, and he called himself a Producer. He certainly had a letterhead on his note-paper to prove it, though details of his actual productions seemed a little less well-defined. He talked confidently of tours he had set up with Music Hall shows and even mentioned putting on a pantomime, though at what level these productions had been mounted, it was difficult to assess. A tour of a Music Hall show could be anything from a glamorous parade of the country's Number One provincial theatres down to a glorified pub-crawl, with a motley band of barnstormers passing the hat round after a few songs at the piano.

Since Charles Paris had not heard of any major Music Hall tour in the previous few years, he inclined to the opinion that the operations of Paul Lexington Productions had been at the more modest level. On the other hand, impresarios have to start somewhere, Paul Lexington seemed a pleasant and knowledgeable young man and, in a business peopled with the incompetent and the frankly criminal, Charles felt inclined to give him the benefit of the doubt.

After all, without Paul Lexington, he would not be currently employed, and, if there was one thing that Charles's experience in the theatre had taught him, it was the inestimable advantage of having a job over 'resting'.

The sequence of events which had brought *The Hooded Owl* to its first night at the Prince's Theatre, Taunton, had been that usual circuitous trip through an obstacle course by which new plays reach the stage. The work had been written by a schoolmaster called Malcolm Harris who, though of undoubted talent, had no contacts in or knowledge of commercial theatre. He had lavished three years of his spare time on the work and, when he had the final draft neatly typed up with a Letrasetted front page and a transparent plastic folder, the only person he could think to send it to was the Professor of English at the university he had left twelve years previously. The Professor, after a few months' delay and an apologetically nudging letter from the playwright, had written back in terms of vague praise, which a professional writer would have recognised as a confession of not having read the script, and said he had passed it on to the Professor who headed the university's recently-inaugurated Drama Department. This gentleman, after a few months' delay and an apologetically nudging letter from the playwright, had written back to say he had passed it on to an actor friend who was setting up a new fringe theatre company in Surbiton. After quite a few months' delay, and three apologetically nudging letters from the playwright, the actor scribbled a note back, from an address in Gloucestershire, saying he was sorry he hadn't yet had time to read the play. And also he was sorry that he seemed to have lost the manuscript. And, anyway, he had decided that the theatre wasn't for him after all and he'd set up an antique shop with a friend.

Phase One of the offensive was thus over, and Phase Two started with the top carbon of the play, a newly-Letrasetted front page and a new transparent plastic folder. This time, on the advice of his wife's mother, who'd just read a biography of some playwright out of the library though she couldn't remember what his name was, Malcolm Harris had sent the play to his local repertory theatre. After a few months' delay and an apologetically nudging letter from the playwright, the General Manager had returned the script with a duplicated letter, saying thanks very much for sending it, the Play Selection Committee had found it really interesting, but unfortunately it wasn't the sort of show they were looking for at that time, why not try sending it to an agent? This Malcolm Harris had done, but, unfortunately, due to the random selection method of sticking a pin in the 'Theatrical and Variety Agents' section of the *Yellow Pages*, he had sent it to one who specialised in booking blue comedians and strippers into Working Men's Clubs. After a few months' delay and an apologetically nudging letter from the playwright, the script was returned, together with a photograph of 'Sadie Masso: 38–26–36: Just the Thing to Liven Up your Stag Night or Rugby Club Dinner', in an envelope without a stamp on it. At this point, that infallible source of advice, his wife's mother, told Malcolm Harris that she was sure she had seen something about a play-writing competition in some magazine she'd been reading at the hairdresser's, why didn't he go in for that? Painstaking research having tracked down the competition, sponsored by a local Arts Festival in the Midlands, the playwright had received his application form and copy of the rules. Obeying these implicitly, he had sent off his manuscript, together with the stamps for return postage and the entrance fee of one pound, and sat and waited. Four months later, he received back through the post a copy of *Psychosymbiosis,* a Monodrama by George Walsh. Repeated letters to the adjudicating committee of the Arts Festival, trying to retrieve the right manuscript, elicited no response.

Eighteen months had now passed since Malcolm Harris had completed *The Hooded Owl*, and so far there was no evidence that anyone vaguely connected with the professional theatre had even read it. The playwright was gloomily resigning himself to spending the rest of his days teaching history to recalcitrant adolescents, but the confidence of his wife, who had read the play, and his wife's mother, who hadn't, would not allow him to give up. His wife's mother had heard some successful playwright or maybe it was a producer talking on the radio she thought perhaps on *Woman's Hour* and saying that nowadays a successful play needed a star name, so often the star's interest came first. This suggestion coincided with Malcolm Harris reading a letter to *The Times* about VAT on theatre tickets from that popular British film and television star, Michael Banks. Since the letter gave his address, and since Michael Banks, in the playwright's wildest fantasies, would have been ideal casting for the main part, Malcolm Harris took his courage in both hands and sent *The Hooded Owl* off to the star. Needless to say, Michael Banks didn't read it, but, being an amiable old boy, he passed it on to his agent, whose organisation had a Plays Department. They didn't read it either, but a girl on the switchboard was having a brief affair with a young man who wanted to be a theatrical producer and claimed to be 'on the look-out for a good property', so she passed it on to him. The young man read the play, recognised its potential, and bought an option to produce it within six months for a sum which delighted Malcolm Harris, but which would have appalled his agent, had he had one.

The young producer's name was Paul Lexington, and he then set about finding a theatre that would put the play on.

The Hooded Owl was an expensive production for the average provincial company. Though it only had a cast of eight and its contemporary setting limited the Wardrobe costs, it did require three solid representational sets, a very big outlay for a three-week run. Whereas a theatre might spread its budget to allow that kind of expenditure on a certain crowd-puller like a Shakespeare or the annual pantomime, it was very unlikely to invest so much in the uncertainties of a new play by an unknown playwright. Money was tight enough, and no provincial theatre wanted to hazard its local authority or Arts Council grants by rash speculation.

But this was where Paul Lexington had something to offer. He had money. No one quite knew where it came from; he always spoke airily of 'my investors', but he gave no clue to their identity. And no one knew how much he could raise, though from the confidence of his tone the amount seemed to be infinite.

So this was the deal that he offered round the provincial theatre companies during the spring and summer of 1979: if they would put on a production of *The Hooded Owl*, a good play for which he held an option, he would invest the necessary extra production costs for the expensive sets and, ideally, the import of a star name. Then, if the play did transfer to the West End, his production company would present it and the originating company would be credited and receive a small percentage. If it didn't transfer, then the theatre would have had a more expensive production than their normal budget could run to, and Paul Lexington and his investors would have lost their money.

Only Paul Lexington himself knew how many companies had been offered the deal and turned it down before he got to the Prince's Theatre, Taunton, but common sense dictated that he must have tried the better-known ones nearer London first. The chances of getting all the people necessary for a transfer, the London theatre managers and the big investors (whose aid, in spite of Paul Lexington's confident assurances, would almost definitely be needed), diminished the further one got away from the metropolis.

However, the producer was determined to get the show on and was confident enough of the property to think it could make the transfer, even from this West Country base, whose record of getting shows into the West End was not remarkable. (In fact, it had never in its history had an original production transfer, though a few shows had passed weeks there during their pre-London tours.)

But there was a new Artistic Director at the Prince's Theatre, a young man called Peter Hickton, whose confidence at least matched that of Paul Lexington. He had got the Taunton job some six years out of Cambridge and was determined to maintain his whizz-kid image and make a mark on the theatre nationally. He was ambitious to make the Prince's Theatre a power-base and incubator of productions for London, in the way that the Royal Exchange, Manchester, and the Arts Theatre, Cambridge, had become in recent years. So, when Paul Lexington arrived with his proposal, Peter Hickton was already looking for a show with transfer potential.

His one condition for backing the production was predictable: that he should direct it. If that was agreed, he was prepared to put all his energies, even down to the *enfant terrible* tantrums that his track-record required of him, into persuading the Plays Selection Committee that *The Hooded Owl* should be one of the productions in the 1979–80 season at the Prince's Theatre, Taunton.

Paul Lexington at first demurred. He had hoped to get a director of greater stature for his production, but he soon had to face facts. Peter Hickton was the only Artistic Director who had shown enthusiasm for the project and, if Paul Lexington Productions were to get their first major show under way at all, there would have to be compromises. (And it was not lost on the producer that Peter Hickton's residence at Taunton meant directing the show would be part of his job. Sure, he'd have to be on some percentage when the play got to the West End, but at least a director's fee would be saved for the try-out.)

So the two ambitious young men came to an agreement, and Peter Hickton set to work on the Plays Selection Committee. His success was not total. He managed to get a commitment that the Prince's Theatre should do *The Hooded Owl*, but he could not persuade them to do it in the 1979-80 season. He tried all his tricks, being sarcastic, going dead quiet, shouting, walking out of the meeting, even threatening (carefully) to resign: but the best date he could come up with was September, 1980. Seeing that to protest further would be pushing his luck, he agreed with bad grace that *The Hooded Owl* should be the first production of the 1980–81 season.

Paul Lexington didn't welcome this delay to his plans, but he was a realist and he wanted to get the show on, so he accepted it. He rang Malcolm Harris to say he had some good news and some bad news: the good news – that the play would definitely go into production at the Prince's Theatre, Taunton; the bad news – that it wouldn't happen for another year. He did not mention to the playwright that the six-month option he had bought on the play would be some eight months out of date at the proposed production date, nor did he offer more money to renew the option. He knew that Malcolm Harris was still in a flush of naive excitement about the play actually being produced and wasn't thinking about money.

So for a year Paul Lexington continued with his other activities, whatever they might be. Nobody knew. Maybe he mounted another Music Hall tour, maybe a pantomime. Maybe he involved his investors in some other production; maybe he made contacts with London theatre managements, so that the delay should be kept to a minimum when the production actually happened.

The one thing he was known to have done during that period was to try to get a star name for *The Hooded Owl*. As with theatre companies, only he knew how many he approached with the script, how many refusals he got, how many tentative agreements dependent on dates and money. There were two main male parts and one female, so presumably stars of both sexes were approached.

All that was known was the result of his machinations. A fortnight before rehearsals were due to start, which was the time when Charles Paris was engaged to play the second male lead, it was bruited about in the business that the female lead was to be played by a young lady who had recently, 'in order to concentrate on her career as a serious actress', left the cast of the interminably-long-running television soap opera, *Cruises*.

The fact that she wasn't much of an actress, serious or any other sort, was irrelevant. The audience would flock to see her. It didn't matter if she just stood on stage, they would still love her. (In fact, people who had worked with her thought it might be better if she *did* just stand on stage; they knew the hazards of trying to push her beyond her range.)

Once Paul Lexington had his star name, he was happy to fall in with Peter Hickton's suggestions for the rest of the cast. So long as they were cheap, competent and available in the event of a transfer, he didn't much mind who they were. As a result, Peter Hickton cast largely from his regular Taunton company; he knew them, they worshipped him, and he fancied himself in the role of star-maker.

In the lead he cast Alex Household, an actor in his late forties, who had had early success then a rather bad patch culminating in a complete breakdown, but was now coming back, in the view of Peter Hickton, twenty years his junior, 'stronger than ever'.

In the part of the daughter, Peter Hickton cast Lesley-Jane Decker, an actress eight years his junior, who he thought had 'enormous potential'. And the way he looked at her didn't suggest he thought that potential was limited to the stage.

For the part of Alex's failed brother, Peter reckoned he had had a brainwave. There was no one in the regular Taunton company of the right age, but he remembered an actor he had worked with when Assistant Director at Colchester, who had exactly the right 'smell of failure' that the part required. Peter rang the guy's agent and found, to his delight, that he was free.

To the agent in question, Maurice Skellern, his client's 'freeness' was no surprise. Charles Paris's engagement diary was a joke on the level of all those corny old lines about *The Kosher Book of Pork Recipes*, *Britain's Economic Miracle* or *The Pope's Book of Birth Control*. 'I've sorted out a great job for you, Charles,' the agent asserted when he rang.

'Oh yes?' Charles had replied sceptically.

'Sure. Great new play called *The Head Owl*..'

'Where?'

'Taunton.'

'Ah.'

'Director asked for you specially.'

'Oh.'

'Said he wanted someone who really smelt of failure.'

'Thank you, Maurice.'

So it was that Charles Paris joined the cast of *The Hooded Owl*.

It was the day before rehearsals started that the agent of the former *Cruises* star rang to say that she had just signed up to do a series for West End Television of a new sit. com. set in a lingerie shop and called *Knickers*; so, because that was going to keep her very busy, she had flown off the day before to Kenya for a safari holiday. And no, sorry, she hadn't actually signed *The Hooded Owl* contract.

Frantic phoning ensued. Paul Lexington tried in vain to produce a star in twenty-four hours, but eventually had to accept Peter Hickton's casting of Salome Search, a Taunton regular, 'who's awfully solid, Paul, and, you know, has never really had the breaks, but could be massive'.

So it was that, while the former *Cruises* star pointed her camera at world-weary rhino, her predestined dressing room at the Prince's Theatre, Taunton, was shared on the first night of *The Hooded Owl* by Alex Household and Charles Paris.

CHAPTER TWO

NERVES, LIKE hopes, Charles found, didn't go away, however long he worked in the theatre. The fact that he had survived a few hundred first nights did not make each new one any easier. In some ways it made it more difficult; he now had more experience of the things that could go wrong than he had in his twenties, and so the dark side of his imagination had more to work on.

But two things delayed the full impact of his nerves about the opening of *The Hooded Owl*. The first was having a large part, a fortune that was not often his lot. He began to realise how stars could remain cool right up till the first night. Their responsibility was greater, but the mechanics of learning all their lines and rehearsing kept them pretty busy. It was those with small parts and long gaps in rehearsal who had time to sit around twitching over endless diuretic cups of coffee.

The other factor which staved off the assault of nerves was the work-rate Peter Hickton demanded of his cast. Because most of them had worked with him so much, they knew what to expect, that he would rehearse every waking hour (and a good few normally allocated to sleep). Equity rules about maximum hours were ignored. There was an Equity representative in the cast, duly elected by the rest, but he was one of the Peter Hickton rep. too, so he made no demur.

Peter Hickton was one of those people who gained ascendancy over others by demonstrating how little sleep he needed. Charles, whose ideal was a whisky-sodden eight hours, found this was a contest in which he did not wish to participate, but he had no alternative. He couldn't turn up for a nine o'clock call in the morning and complain that he hadn't finished rehearsing till one the night before, when he knew that the director had been up till four working on the lighting plan.

Charles also found this relentless rehearsal made serious inroads into his drinking time, a part of the day he had always regarded as sacrosanct. He wasn't an alcoholic (he kept telling himself), but he did enjoy a drink, and he found resorting to a half-bottle of Bell's in his pocket somewhat undignified. Apart from anything else, it gave his antiquated sports jacket a lop-sided look. And it tended to clink against things. Also it gave the wrong impression. When Salome Search caught him one day taking a surreptitious swig in the Green Room, she gave him a look that showed she had got a completely false idea of his relationship with drink. She obviously regarded it as a till-death-do-us-part marriage, whereas he liked to think of it more as a casual affair, in which either partner could drift off at will (though, when he came to think of it, neither often did).

Peter Hickton's rehearsal schedule (probably a misnomer for a process that was simply continuous) intensified towards the end. The Monday night's Tech. Run, which followed a full day in the rehearsal room, finished at three-thirty a.m.. As a special concession, the next morning's call for notes was not until nine-thirty, then rehearsal of odd scenes continued till it was time for the evening's Dress Rehearsal, which, though intended to be played as per performance, did not end till a quarter to two a.m.. Because of this, Peter Hickton demanded a second Dress Rehearsal, on the Wednesday afternoon before the first night. This was followed by notes, taking everyone right up to 'the half' (the time half an hour before curtain-up, by which all members of the cast have to be in the theatre).

So Charles didn't even have time for the half-hour in the pub over a couple of large Bell's, which he regarded as such an essential preparation for the full realisation of his art.

What was more, he was down to about half an inch in his pocket-bottle thanks to the pressures of the previous days. He had been sure there'd at least be time for him to nip out and buy a replacement.

But there wasn't. And all the A.S.M.s and hangers-on were too busy to have this important commission delegated to them.

It was a serious situation.

And it didn't improve the half-hour before curtain-up, when all the pent-up nerves came crashing in with devastating force. Normally he could control the incipient nausea and limit the number of rushes to the lavatory by judiciously-spaced doses of Bell's whisky, but now he felt as if he was having a leg off without anaesthetic.

He drained the half-bottle to attain some sort of stability, but five minutes later, when something started doing macramé with his intestines, he wished he had saved it.

Alex Household's method of building up to a performance did not involve alcohol. He did not believe in the use of stimulants, being an advocate of the use of the mind's internal resources to control the waywardness of the body. It was part of an elaborate philosophy he had developed from reading the first chapters of a few paperbacks about Eastern Religion and talking to other actors over cups of jasmine tea.

His build-up method involved lying dead straight over three chairs, with the head free and lolling back and breathing deeply. A deep intake of air sounding like a gas central heating boiler igniting, a long pause, and then exhalation over a muttered phrase, which may have been some potent *mantra*, but to the casual observer sounded like 'Rub-a-dub-a-dub-a-dub-a-dub'.

Charles was becoming a decreasingly casual observer as the half-hour ticked away and his nerves were twisted tighter. Alex's charade didn't help. Charles, normally most accommodating about the foibles of others, began to think sharing the dressing room might have its drawbacks.

Alex was that very common theatrical type, a faddish actor. He believed in vegetarianism, transcendental meditation, homeopathy, transmigration, the occult and a variety of other semi-digested notions. Alex was always talking about communion with nature and being at one with the world. He had a habit of producing herbal snacks in the dressing room, seeds, grasses, nettles and other less identifiable greenery. He had read a few chapters of a book called *Food for Free*, and kept going on about 'the earth's plenty'.

Normally, Charles could accept all this with good humour – after all, he did quite like the man – but, as he again suffered the interminable pause between the intake and the inevitable 'Rub-a-dub-a-dub-a-duba-dub' he thought he was going to scream or lash out. To avert both these dangers, he left the dressing room to go to the lavatory, though he couldn't resist slamming the door as he went.

In the corridor he met Lesley-Jane Decker, whose arms were full of purple tissue-wrapped parcels. She was an attractive red-head of about twenty, still full of breathless excitement about actually 'being in the theatre'. She was quite talented, and devoutly believed Paul Lexington's and Peter Hickton's conviction that *The Hooded Owl* was going to sweep triumphantly into the West End and make them all stars.

It had been obvious from rehearsal that Peter Hickton fancied her, but whether he had got anywhere, Charles could not judge. In fact, he couldn't imagine how the director's rehearsal schedule would leave any time for thoughts of sex, though, of course, all things were possible.

On balance, Charles thought that probably nothing had developed. Apart from the logistics, Lesley-Jane was so naive and bubbly, he could not imagine her keeping quiet about a love affair. He even suspected that she might be that remarkable rarity, a theatrical virgin.

And it was more likely that Peter Hickton was saving his assault on her for the less hectic time when the play was actually running. There would be two and a half weeks then, which should give the young director plenty of time.

'Oh, Charles darling, this is for you.' Lesley-Jane thrust one of the packages into his hands.

'Oh,' he said blankly.

'First-night present.'

'Ah.' Theatrical camp, he thought. What would it be? A fluffy toy? No, felt too hard. A plaster statuette of a pierrot? Yes, that'd be the sort of thing. 'Oh, er, thank you. How are you feeling?'

She opened her green eyes wide. 'Scared witless, darling. Paul says he's hoping there'll be some people from London out front.'

'Oh really?' Charles had heard that a few too many times to get very excited about it.

'And, even worse...' She paused dramatically.

'What?'

'My mother's come down from London to see it.'

'Is that bad? Is she awful?'

'No, she's an absolute angel. But she's got awfully high standards. Used to be in the business, you know.'

'Oh.' The need to get to the lavatory was suddenly strong again. 'If you'll excuse me .

'Yes. Is Alex in the dressing room?'

'Sure.'

Sitting on the lavatory, Charles opened his first-night present. Oh, good, that girl would go far. He took back all his thoughts about her naiveté and theatrical camp.

It was a quarter bottle of champagne. He drained it gratefully.

As he went back to his dressing room, he met the author of *The Hooded Owl*, hanging around in the corridor like a schoolboy outside the headmaster's study. The expression of agony on Malcolm Harris's pallid face made Charles's own nerves seem less crippling.

'Don't worry. It'll be all right. It's a good play.'

'Do you really think so?' The schoolmaster's pouncing on this crumb of praise was almost pathetic.

'Yes, of course it is. We wouldn't have put in all this work on it if it hadn't been.'

'Oh, I do hope so. It's just no one seems to have talked about anything for the past few days except the bits that don't work and all the technical problems it raises and...'

Poor sap. Yes, it must have been strange for him, religiously attending the last week of rehearsals, and knowing nothing about the workings of the theatre. Everyone would be far too busy to waste time assuring the author that his play worked; there would be a lot of complaint about its inadequacies and difficulties. Anyone who had had a play produced before would have been prepared for that; but for Malcolm Harris, snatched from teaching the Causes of the Thirty Years' War to fourteen-year-olds, it must all have been a profound culture shock. Charles felt guilty for not having realised earlier what the author had been suffering.

'It'll work. Really.'

Malcolm made a grimace that might have been intended for a smile. 'Maybe. My main worry is everyone getting the lines right.'

That's what every author wants, thought Charles. And occasionally they get it, though most actors are highly skilled in the art of paraphrase.

'I do hope Alex gets that big speech about the Hooded Owl itself right. I mean, that is the key to the play, and he got the rhythms all wrong this afternoon.'

'Don't worry,' Charles soothed. Poor old Alex was having a bit of difficulty with the lines, he thought complacently.

'Oh, and Charles, could you watch your line at the end of Act One.'

'What?'

'At the Dress Rehearsal, you said, 'I'll tell you one thing – it's the last time I'll come running.'

'So? Isn't that right?'

'No. It should be, 'I'll tell you *something...*''

Oh really! thought Charles. Bloody authors!

But he didn't say it. Instead he asked, 'Anyone out front tonight?'

'Oh, just my wife and my wife's mother.'

'Ah.' Then reassuringly, 'And maybe lots of impresarios and film producers waiting to snap up the rights. How would you feel about a film offer on the play?'

'Oh, I'd...I'd get my agent to deal with it,' replied the author, with an unsuccessful attempt at insouciance.

Still, good. At least he'd got an agent. Slowly he was sorting himself out.

Charles looked at his watch. Twenty past seven. 'Must just go in and check the old slap,' he said, gesturing to his make-up.

'Yes, I'll come in and wish Alex all the best.'

Charles opened the dressing room door to discover that Alex Household had stopped his 'Rub-a-dub-a-dub-a-dub-a-dub' routine. In fact, though they sprang apart quickly, he appeared to be doing his giving-Lesley-Jane-Decker-a-cuddle-on-his-knee routine. Well, there's a novelty, thought Charles.

Alex tapped Lesley-Jane on the bottom in a way that was meant to suggest the contact had just been theatrical excess, but he didn't convince Charles.

'And thank you so much for the ginseng, darling,' said Alex, to reinforce the impression of casual contact.

Ginseng. Of course. It would be. Lesley-Jane had got Alex's number all right.

'Um...' Malcolm Harris began awkwardly. 'Um, Alex, just came in to say good luck –'

'Oh Lord!' shouted the actor. 'For Christ's sake!' The author looked mystified by the outburst.

'Don't you know anything, you bloody amateur?'

'I don't understand...'

'You mustn't say what you've just said.'

'What? I mustn't say good –'

'Don't say it again!' Alex shrieked. 'It's bad luck.'

'Well, what should I say?'

'Oh Lord – break a leg or...anything but that!'

Charles should have remembered: amongst Alex Household's other fads was devout observance of all the theatrical superstitions.

Malcolm Harris's minimal confidence had now deserted him completely.

'I'm sorry. I don't know these –'

'No, you don't know anything!' snapped Alex. 'Don't even know how to write a decent play!'

In a second the author's hand clenched into a fist and was raised to strike. But in the fractional pause that preceded the blow, the Stage Manager's calming voice came over the loudspeaker.

'Beginners, Act One, please.'

Malcolm Harris lowered his fist, glowered at the lead actor of his precious play, and scurried off to find the pass-door to join his wife and his wife's mother in the auditorium.

Alex Household, Lesley-Jane Decker and Charles Paris hugged each other wordlessly, and passed through the corridor to the stage.

The eruption of applause as the final curtain fell left no one in any doubt that *The Hooded Owl* had worked, at least for the good burghers of Taunton. Whether it would work for the supposedly more sophisticated audience of the West End remained to be seen.

But for the cast there was no doubt about anything. Each of them had felt the momentum of the play build up through the evening, each of them had felt his doubts about its worth evaporate, each of them felt the relief of consummation after the exhausting preparations. They were all euphoric.

Charles and Alex tumbled back into the Number One dressing room, arms around each other's necks, giggling like schoolgirls. 'Yippee, yippee. It works, it works!' cried Alex.

They both felt emotionally drained – the parts they played were taxing – but lifted above exhaustion on to a high like drunkenness.

As Charles became aware of this, he realised that he had given a performance – and a good one – on an alcoholic intake of only a swig of Bell's and a quarter bottle of champagne. This was something of a record for him, and momentarily the heretical thought traversed his mind that maybe his talent could flourish without constant irrigation.

Mind you, he really needed a drink now.

As if in answer to his thought, Paul Lexington poked his head round the dressing room door. 'Terrific, both of you! We have a hit on our hands, babies! Soon as you're out of your cossies, up to the bar. Drinks are on me tonight!'

'That's very generous of you, Paul,' said Charles.

'Oh, it's nothing. I'd laid it on for anyone who came down from London.'

'And has anyone come?'

A shadow passed over the producer's boyish face. 'No, not tonight. I expect they'll be along later in the week.'

But he was incapable of pessimism. 'Don't worry, I'll be on the phone first thing in the morning. Tell 'em the quality of what they're missing. They'll be falling over themselves trying to snap this one up.'

At that moment Lesley-Jane Decker burst in, as effervescent as the champagne she had handed out. She threw her arms round Alex Household's neck. 'God, you were wonderful tonight.'

'Oh Lord, praise, praise,' he said, with a shrug.

'You were super too.' Paul Lexington patted Lesley-Jane on the shoulder. 'See you up in the bar.'

'Terrific.'

As the Producer turned to leave, he was met in the doorway by a tall lady in a light-brown fur coat. She looked as if she was in her forties, but slightly over-elaborate make-up and hair that had been helped to recapture its former redness made putting an exact date on her difficult.

'Excuse me,' she apologised in a rich, elocuted voice. 'I don't want to intrude.'

She was looking at Alex and Lesley-Jane still clasped together, a sight for which she seemed to have slight distaste.

The young actress turned at the voice and rushed across to the older woman. 'Mummy! Mummy, *do* come and meet everyone.'

Paul Lexington, after being introduced, nodded politely and said he hoped she'd join them for a drink in the bar. Alex Household said he was enchanted, *but* enchanted to see her at last, he'd heard so much about her.

'And, Mummy, this is –'

'Ah, but I know you, don't I, Charles?'

Charles Paris looked up warily at the woman's face. Maybe there was something vaguely familiar about it, but he couldn't for the life of him say where he had seen her before. 'Um...'

'Long time ago, darling.'

'Oh...er...' He was going to need a bit more of a clue than that.

Malcolm Harris blundered in through the door flanked by ferret-faced women who had to be his wife and his wife's mother, and there was a pause for more introductions.

'Wonderful play, Malcolm,' Alex cooed. 'Oh Lord, what a wonderful play.'

But the diversion didn't let Charles off the hook. 'Have you placed me yet?' asked Lesley-Jane's mother seductively.

'Um, no...,' he had to admit, wondering whether their previous encounter had been under embarrassing circumstances.

'You remember Cheltenham...?' she nudged.

'What? Cheltenham Rep.? Back in the early sixties?'

'Sssh.' She raised an elegantly manicured finger to her lips. 'Don't let's talk dates. But yes, Cheltenham Rep. it was.'

Given a context, he did begin to place her. 'Oh yes.' But he still couldn't for the life of him remember what her name was.

She seemed to realise this, and gave in. 'Valerie Cass.'

'Of course! Valerie Cass! Well, how are you? Talk about long time, no see.'

As he brought out the platitudes of recognition, he placed her exactly. Yes, of course, early sixties, Cheltenham, young actress, playing *ingenue* roles. Now he knew the connection, he remembered that she had had that same quality of naive enthusiasm that Lesley-Jane demonstrated. Not as good an actress, though. No, his recollection was that Valerie Cass had been a pretty bad actress.

As if to apologise for this thought, he continued fulsomely, 'Valerie Cass! You know, you haven't changed a bit. Have you got a picture up in the attic that grows old instead of you?'

This was the right approach – or at least the approach she liked. She fluttered coquettishly.

'I've followed your career with interest, Charles. Read *Stage* every week, you know.'

Oh, thought Charles, there must have been a few thousand weeks when you've searched it in vain for any mention of me. 'Are you still in the business?'

'Oh goodness me, no, Charles. I gave up when I married Lesley's father. Had my time fully occupied bringing up my baby girl.'

'Yes, I'm sure.' It seemed a good solution to Charles. Valerie Cass had probably been quite good as a mother; whereas, had she stayed in the theatre, it would only have been a matter of time before her lack of talent had been exposed.

'No, no, Lesley-Jane carries on the theatrical tradition in our family. Of course, I give her any help I can, but...' She shrugged. 'I'm afraid my career was cut short. So I'm just left with my dreams of what might have been.'

Charles hoped, for her sake, the dreams weren't accurate. No, no doubt like his own, they were pure wish-fulfilment.

He still felt apologetic for not having recognised her. 'Sorry, it was so out of context. I mean, Lesley-Jane's name gave me no clue.'

'No, she got that from her father,' said Valerie Cass rather tartly. Mother and daughter, and Malcolm Harris and his womenfolk eventually left the two actors to change out of their costumes.

'Last one in the bar's a sissy,' said Charles, the euphoric giggliness returning.

They both plunged for the door and, as they collided, Charles felt something heavy in Alex's jacket pocket thump against him.

'You great fraud! All your talk of "no stimulants" and you're another of the flask-in-pocket brigade!'

'Oh no,' said Alex Household gravely. 'It's not a flask.'

'Then what...'

'I got mugged last year, walking back from the theatre in Birmingham.' His voice became unsteady. 'I got beaten up. It won't happen again. I never go out after dark without this.'

He withdrew his hand from his pocket. It was clasped around the butt of a Smith and Wesson Chiefs Special revolver.

CHAPTER THREE

THE LOCAL paper thought *The Hooded Owl* was a success. It even raved about it. The last sentence of the notice read, 'It is rarely that down here in Taunton we are treated to a show of such excellence. I urge everyone to go and see *The Hooded Owl* now, before you have to pay fares to London and West End prices for the privilege.'

So, as far as the local paper was concerned, the transfer was a certainty. Unfortunately, it wasn't local papers that arranged such things. It was London theatre managements and, at the end of the first week's run, even Paul Lexington's unpuncturable buoyancy could not hide the fact that no one relevant had been down to see the show. Still, as he kept asserting cheerfully, two weeks to go, and a lot could happen in two weeks.

The local paper review, as well as backing the whole show, was also extremely gratifying to Alex Household and Charles Paris. The sentence which kept recurring in both their minds for some days was this: 'After witnessing acting of such power and emotional truth, it is hard to imagine why these two actors are not considerably better known than they are.'

Exactly, they both thought, that's what we've been saying for years. For Charles, the review was particularly welcome. For one thing, the sort of part he usually played didn't often get reviewed. And for another, on the past three occasions when critics had deigned to mention him, their comments had been as follows:

'Charles Paris was an odd choice for the part of the solicitor' – *Guardian*

'Charles Paris wandered through the play like one of Bo-Peep's sheep looking for its tail' – *Evening Standard*

And - 'Among the rest of the cast was Charles Paris' – *The Stage*.

In spite of the fact that nothing was happening on the transfer front, the cast could not keep down their optimism. The experience of playing in a success, endorsed nightly by the audience's reaction, was an invigorating one, and Paul Lexington's so-far-groundless confidence was infectious.

'You know,' said Alex Household, as he made up on the Tuesday evening of the second week, 'I think it is going to work. I think we will make it.'

Charles grinned. Closer acquaintance with the other actor had increased his liking for the man. His antagonistic feelings of the first night had just been the product of nerves. Now he found that, so long as he arranged to be out of the dressing room for the 'Rub-a-dub-a-dub-a-dub-a-dub' routine, he could cohabit with Alex quite happily. He had also found, to his surprise, that Alex had some sense of humour about his various fads and would even respond to gentle teasing on the subject.

'Yes, it's going to happen,' Alex continued. 'I feel my luck is due for a change.'

'Hmm. I gather you've had a fairly rough few years.'

'You can say that again. First I had a long patch out of work, then my marriage broke up – are you married, Charles?'

Difficult question, really. He had married Frances back in 1951, and they weren't divorced. They had a grown-up daughter, Juliet. On the other hand, he had walked out after ten years and, though he still saw Frances and felt a lot of ill-defined emotion for her, theirs was not what most people meant by a marriage.

'Um, not unmarried,' he replied cagily.

Not that Alex was really interested. He continued his own catalogue of disasters. 'Then I had the breakdown. It was an awful time. I went through everything – drugs, psychotherapy, the lot.'

'But that was three years ago. Everything's going to be all right now. I am going on on that assumption. I've just bought this new flat in town, so a nice West End run is just what the mortgage and I need.'

'And if the transfer doesn't happen…'

'Treason, Charles. Don't even say it.'

'No, I mean have you got another job lined up after this one?'

Alex shook his head. 'You?'

'Good Lord, no.'

A tap on the door prefaced the bursting-in of Lesley-Jane Decker, even more effervescent than usual. She threw her arms round Alex's neck and looked at him in his mirror. 'Have you heard, darling?'

'What?'

'Wonderful news.'

'Your mother's gone back to London?'

Lesley-Jane giggled, then, guiltily, stopped. 'No, no, Alex. Denis Thornton's in tonight.'

'Really?' said both the actors together.

The name meant a great deal. Denis Thornton had been a successful juvenile in a long string of undemanding West End comedies, but had of latter years turned his talents and money towards management. Though he would still occasionally come back for a sixth-month run in a tailor-made comedy vehicle, most of his energies now went into Lanthorn Productions, which he owned with his partner, Gerard Langley. They were lessees of three or four London theatres and, in difficult times, made commercial theatre work. The shows they put on may have contributed little to the nation's cultural heritage, but they certainly brought in the coach parties.

'Ah.' Alex looked complacent. 'I heard that show at the King's was doing fairly bad business.'

'King's would be a bit big for this, wouldn't it?' said Charles. 'It's more for your grand musicals and..'

'It'd do…' Alex preened himself with a hint of self-parody. 'Yes, I wouldn't mind having my name in lights above the title at the King's.'

'I'm sure you will, darling.' Lesley-Jane kissed the top of his head. 'Got to go. I left Mummy in my dressing room. See you.'

'See you.'

She fizzed out. Charles gestured towards the door with his head.

'She part of your new start, Alex?'

'Why not? As I say, about time my luck changed.'

'Hmm. I thought Peter Hickton had earmarked her.'

'So did he, dear, but experience does tell, you know. It's my belief that all young girls should have their first affair with an older man. Anyway, dear Peter's always so busy.'

'You've been pretty busy too. Don't know how you've had time or opportunity to…'

'Time, my dear Charles, can always be made. And you forget that Lesley-Jane and I joined the company at the end of last season. As for opportunity…well, always sort out a bolt-hole for yourself, Charles.'

'What do you mean?'

But he only got an enigmatic and rather smug smile by way of answer. 'Lesley-Jane's a sweet kid,' Charles volunteered magnanimously.

'Oh yes. Only one thing wrong with her.'

'What's that?'

'She's not an orphan.'

'Ah, doesn't the lovely Valerie approve of you?'

'Not really.'

'Because you're too old?'

'No, I think simply because I'm a man.'

Charles nodded and started to powder down his make-up.

'Still, sod the lot of them!' said Alex Household with sudden venom. 'I am going to win through. I am going to have all the successful things I should have had years ago. And none of the buggers are going to stop me!'

Once again Charles detected the unstable note of paranoia in the other's voice.

There was a call for all cast on stage at the 'half' for the next day's matinée. Most of them reckoned they had a pretty shrewd idea of what it was for.

And sure enough, when Paul Lexington addressed them, his first two words were the ones which had been the cause of much discussion and speculation since the previous evening.

'Denis Thornton,' he announced, 'as you may or may not know, came down to see the show last night. And I have some good news for you – he liked it!'

The cast burst into shouts of delight, but cut them off sharply, waiting to hear what followed from this.

'And basically what has happened is – he has offered us a theatre to transfer the show to the West End!'

This was greeted with more euphoria. As it died away, Salome Search, who plumed herself on knowing a bit about the mechanics of 'going in' to the West End, having once spent a week in the chorus of an ill-fated musical at the Apollo, asked, 'Does that mean Lanthorn Productions will be presenting the show?'

'Oh no. I will be presenting the show. Denis's company will just be renting us the theatre. It gives us a lot more freedom than if Lanthorn actually took over.'

And a lot more chance to fail, thought Charles cynically.

'So when will we be going in to the King's?' asked Alex.

'Ah, it's not the King's,' said Paul. 'No, Denis reckons the King's is far too big for this show. We'd get lost in there. No, he's offering us the Variety.'

'Oh,' said all the cast at the same moment, trying not to sound disappointed.

The Variety Theatre had had a chequered history. It was called a West End theatre, but its position, in Macklin Street, was a little too far from Shaftesbury Avenue for the designation to sound convincing. It had been a popular Music Hall venue before the First World War, and come back to prominence in the fifties with a series of intimate revues. Since then it had justified its name by the variety of managements who had tried to make a go of it and the variety of fare they had presented there. Mime shows, light shows, nude shows, drag shows had all been washed up there as theatrical fashions ebbed and flowed. Religious rock musicals had followed on modern dance extravaganzas; one-man shows based on eighteenth-century letters had succeeded abortive attempts to revive the art of stage revue; poetry readings had drawn the same size audiences as South African jail diaries; laser shows, a punk rock musical and a gay version of *Romeo and Juliet* in black leather had all been tried, and failed.

It was currently occupied by an entertainment based on Maori song and dance, which had somehow maintained its sickly life there for nearly three months.

'Now I know what you're all thinking,' said Paul Lexington hastily. 'That the Variety hasn't had a success for the past twenty years. Don't worry. *The Hooded Owl* is going to change all that. Listen, Denis Thornton has just taken over the lease and he's no fool. He's been looking for a property to reopen the theatre under his management and we are it. If we go to the Variety, we'll go in with maximum publicity and really put the place back on the map!'

The cast were so willing to believe the best that Paul Lexington's rabble-rousing techniques worked and they instantly forgot their reservations and shouted again with excitement. Yes, of course they could succeed where others had failed. They were good. *The Hooded Owl* was good. Not only were they going to take the West End by storm, they were going to redefine its boundaries.

Alex Household adjusted his question. 'So when do we go in to the Variety?'

'If all goes well, we'd open there in about four weeks. 30th October.'

The date seemed very near and was greeted with renewed cheering.

'Now there are a few things to sort out,' the producer continued. 'I'll have to go back to my investors. Because of the guarantees required I'm going to have to raise a bit more money. But that shouldn't be any problem.'

In the ecstatic mood of the company, no one was so cynical as to think of the last sentence as understatement. In order to be allowed to go into the West End, Paul would have to put up in advance all of the rehearsal money and two weeks' running costs for the production. The rehearsal money would be paid back when the show opened, the rest when it closed. Couldn't be that much, the cast all thought; as Paul said, it shouldn't be any problem.

'So I'm going to be very busy for the next couple of weeks, rushing around, raising the loot. I'm also going to be getting lots more people down to see the show, so remember – give of your best every night, you never know who's going to be in.'

'But basically – don't worry. I'll sort it all out. And *The Hooded Owl* is going in to the West End!'

Malcolm Harris reappeared for the Friday performance of the second week. No one had really noticed his absence, just as no one had really noticed his presence when he had been there. Presumably the previous weekend his ferret-faced women had taken him back to his ferret-faced children, and he had spent the week teaching history.

He came in to the Number One dressing room after the performance. Alex Household looked at him in the mirror and asked, 'Well, happy with the way your little masterpiece is shaping up?'

'Not very,' the author replied awkwardly.

'Why not?'

'Well, the lines are all over the place.'

'What do you mean?'

'Well, I'm sorry, Alex, but I have to say it – you're really killing the big speech about the Hooded Owl.'

'Killing it? Oh, come on. That's the high spot of the evening. Not a sweet-paper rustles, even the chronic bronchitics are cured at that moment.'

'Well, of course. That's how it's meant to be. But you're not saying the lines as written. Again tonight you said, "And this bird has seen it all, lived through it all, silently, impassively".'

'That's what I say every night.'

'Well, you shouldn't. The line, as written, is, "And this bird has lived through it all, has seen it all, impassively, in silence".'

'Oh Lord – really! What difference does it make? I think my version flows better, actually, sounds more poetic.'

'It's not meant to sound bloody poetic, for God's sake! It would be out of character for the father to sound poetic.'

'Oh, look –'

Charles decided a tactical intervention might be in order. As if he had suddenly walked into the room and heard none of the preceding exchange, he asked naively, 'What do you think of the news about the Variety, eh, Malcolm?'

'Oh, it's very encouraging,' said the schoolmaster. 'Salome told me before the show tonight.'

Oh dear, that was a slip-up on Paul Lexington's part. The author should have been told as soon as the Producer knew, not hear the rumour from a third party. Fortunately, though, Malcolm did not seem aggrieved. His ignorance of the theatre encompassed a great deal of humility (about everything except the actors getting his lines right).

'Do you think you can cope with fame and all those royalties?' asked Charles playfully.

The schoolmaster gave a shy smile. 'I think I'll manage.'

'Hmm. Make sure your agent sorts out a good deal for you. Remember this axiom of theatrical business – all managements are sharks.'

'Oh, I'm sure it'll be all right.'

'Who is your agent, by the way?'

Malcolm's smile grew broader. 'That's the wonderful thing. When Paul heard I hadn't got an agent, he was shocked.'

'I should think so. And he recommended someone to you?'

'No, better than that, Charles. He said he'd represent me himself. Keep it all in the family, he said. Isn't that terrific?'

'And you've signed up with him?'

'You bet. And no messing about with short contracts. He's really showing his confidence in me and agreed to let me sign up for three years.'

'Ah.' It was all Charles could say. The damage was done; the contract was signed. He found it incredible that every day produced new innocents to fall for the oldest tricks in the business. But there was no point now in telling Malcolm the folly of signing up with the same person as agent and manager, no point in making him think what would happen when he was in dispute with the management and needed an agent to represent his interests. The schoolmaster would have to find out the hard way.

But the knowledge did put Paul Lexington's image in a different light. If he was capable of that sort of old-fashioned sharp practice, maybe his other dealings should be watched with a wary eye.

Further speculation about the producer was interrupted by the ebullient entrance of Lesley-Jane Decker. 'Alex, Alex, have you heard? Bobby Anscombe was in tonight.'

'Was he?' said Alex and Charles in impressed unison.

'Who?' asked Malcolm Harris ignorantly.

But his question didn't get an answer, so he siddled out into the corridor and away.

The answer he didn't get was that Bobby Anscombe was a very big theatrical backer, or 'angel', whose instincts had directed his money into a string of lucrative hits. He was rich, shrewd, and prepared to take risks, to rush in, indeed, where other angels feared to tread. His style had paid off handsomely in the past, and the fact that he had come all the way to Taunton to see *The Hooded Owl* was the most encouraging boost so far for the transfer prospects.

Alex Household rubbed his hands slowly together. 'That is very good news, Lesley-Jane, very good news.'

'Yes, darling. Let's hope he liked it.'

'I don't honestly see how he could have failed to.' Alex's confidence these days seemed to be unassailable. He reached out and took Lesley-Jane's hand. 'Tell me, do you fancy a *drive in the country* tomorrow morning? I could do with some fresh air.'

The way he italicised the words showed they had some private meaning for the couple.

'Oh, I'd love to, darling, but I can't. Got to go to the station to meet Mummy.'

'Oh Lord, is she coming down again?'

'She's terribly lonely in town with only Daddy for company.'

'Of course.' Alex turned back to his mirror and started rubbing grease on to his face.

'See you up in the bar?' asked Lesley-Jane tentatively.

'Possibly,' said Alex Household.

'Oh yes,' said Charles Paris.

He had a good few drinks inside him as he left the theatre. The quickest way back to his digs was by a path near the car park and, as he walked along, he heard Paul Lexington's voice from the other side of a wall.

'Good,' it said. 'Excellent. I'm delighted at your reaction.'

'We'll talk on Monday about the points I made,' said an unfamiliar voice, 'but I think we can assume that, in principle, we have a deal.'

'Terrific,' said Paul Lexington's voice.

A car door slammed, a powerful engine started, and there was a screech of tyres. As Charles came to the end of the wall by the car park exit, he was nearly run over by a silver-grey Rolls Corniche.

As he watched it go off up the road, its BA registration left him in no doubt that it belonged to Bobby Anscombe.

And the conversation he had overheard left him in no doubt that Bobby Anscombe was going to back *The Hooded Owl*.

He didn't mention what he had overheard to anyone when he went in the next day for the Saturday matinée. After all, they'd all know soon enough when Paul made an official announcement.

But the Saturday passed and no official announcement was made.

The final week of the run began. The Monday passed, the Tuesday, the Wednesday, and still there was no official announcement. No one would say that the transfer was definite.

Paul Lexington was around that week, though he kept on rushing up to town for unspecified meetings. As the days went past his cheerful face began to look more strained and the shadows around his eyes deepened. His manner was still confident, and, if directly asked, he would say everything was going well, but the old conviction seemed to have gone.

The cast felt it too. As the time trickled away, there was less talk of the transfer, fewer fantasies of what they were going to do when they got to the West End, more discussion of other potential jobs. Though no one dared to put it into words they were all losing their faith.

And by the Saturday night, when the run ended, the atmosphere was one of gloom. The final performance was good and was received with more adulation than ever by the Taunton audience, but all the cast could feel their dreams slipping away. It was over, the play was finished, the right people hadn't made the effort to come all the way from London to see it, *The Hooded Owl* was destined to begin and end its life at the Prince's Theatre, Taunton.

So the mood of the cast party, held in the bar after the last performance, was more appropriate to a wake than a celebration. Still no one would voice the awful truth that faced them, but everyone knew. Any gaiety there was was forced.

Alex Household looked stunned and uncomprehending. Charles Paris was glad to pull out his old armour of cynicism and don it once again. Serve him right. He was too old to be seduced by that sort of childish hope in the theatre. Never mind, his old stand-bys would see him through. Cynicism and alcohol. He made the decision to get paralytically drunk.

He found himself, not wholly of his own volition, talking to Valerie Cass, who had appeared for yet another weekend. 'You see,' she was saying, 'one does lose so much by being married. I mean, realising one's full potential as a woman.'

She was obviously making some sort of sexual manoeuvre, though he wasn't quite sure what. He tried to reconstruct their previous meeting back at Cheltenham. Had he made any sort of pass at her then? Was she trying to pick up some previous affair?

But no, surely not. Round that time he had been breaking off with Frances and it had, surprisingly, been a time of celibacy. No, if her motive was sexual, this was something new.

'Of course,' she went on, 'one wouldn't have had it any other way. I mean, bringing up a child can be very fulfilling, but occasionally, when one stops and thinks, one does realise the opportunities one has missed – I mean, both in career terms and...emotionally. I think there comes a point where one is justified in being a little selfish, in thinking of oneself and one's own priorities for a moment. Don't you?'

'Oh, er, yes,' replied Charles uneasily.

She seemed almost to be offering herself to him, and Charles was not in the habit of turning up such offers. And she remained an attractive woman. But something in the desperation of her manner turned him off.

'I always thought you were the sort of man who understood a woman's needs,' she murmured to him.

Definitely time to change the subject. He looked around the bar. 'No sign of Paul, is there?'

Valerie Cass looked rather piqued, but replied, 'No, I expect he's sorting out the details of the transfer.'

So she still believed in it. Presumably, her daughter did, too. It would be in keeping with her habitual breathless optimism.

He didn't know whether to disillusion Valerie or not, but the decision was taken away from him by the arrival of Paul Lexington.

The cast drew apart to make room for him, drew apart with respect or loathing, as if uncertain whether they were dealing with royalty or with a leper. It all really depended on what news he bore.

Paul Lexington seemed aware of this as he clapped his hands for silence.

'Ladies and gentlemen, I'd like to thank you all for all the hard work you've put into making *The Hooded Owl* such a great success in Taunton.'

The silence was almost tangible. Was that all he had to say? Was that it? Was Taunton the end?

The Producer looked absolutely exhausted, but seemed almost to be playing with them, timing his lines to maximise the suspense.

'And I would like to say,' he continued after a long pause, 'that today I have finally persuaded Bobby Anscombe to come into partnership with me to transfer the production to the West End! *The Hooded Owl* will open at the Variety Theatre on 30th October!'

The last sentence was lost in the cast's screams of delight. Everyone leapt about, hugging each other, laughing, crying, howling with relief.

Charles Paris joined in the celebration, but he felt a slight detachment, a reserve within him. Because of the conversation he had overheard, Paul Lexington's words did not quite ring true. The producer had had Bobby Anscombe's assent a full week before.

Sure, there must have been details to sort out, but Charles couldn't lose the feeling that Paul Lexington had deliberately prolonged the cast's agony for reasons of his own.

What reasons? Hard to say. Maybe just to delay sorting out contracts for the West End, to avoid paying an extra week's retainer or rehearsal money..

Charles regretted his suspicions, and tried to convince himself that they were unworthy. But he couldn't. After the fast one Paul Lexington had pulled on Malcolm Harris, it was going to be a long time before he regained the trust of Charles Paris.

CHAPTER FOUR

'HELLO, FRANCES, it's me.'

'Charles! Where are you? How are you?'

'I'm in London and I'm fine.'

'I'm so glad you rang. There are things I need to talk to you about.'

'That sounds ominous.'

'Not too ominous. Just business.'

'Business is by definition ominous. Still, if you want to talk to me, I would like to talk to you. Can I take you out to dinner tonight?'

'Oh, Charles...I'm meant to be doing some marking.'

'I thought when you were headmistress you delegated such menial tasks as marking.'

'Don't you believe it.'

'Oh, come on. A quick dinner with me and then you can do the marking when you get back.'

'I know quick dinners with you, Charles. You'll get me back late and too drunk to read the stuff, let alone mark it.'

'Oh, Frances...I am your husband. Don't I have any rights to your time?'

Shouldn't have said that. Not a very good argument, as Frances was quick to point out. Rather frostily.

'I think you've allowed any claims you might have on my time to lapse for too long, Charles.'

'O.K., forget I said that. Just come out to dinner with me for the pleasure of coming out to dinner with me.'

There was a silence from the other end of the line. Then she gave in. 'All right. It'd be good to see you. But, by the way, what is all this inviting ladies out to dinner? Not your usual style. Have you won the pools or something?'

'Better than that, dear. I'm just about to star in a West End show.'

'Are you? Well, in that case, I'll expect a big bunch of red roses too.'

He arrived at the Hampstead bistro first (almost unprecedented), with a big bunch of red roses (totally unprecedented), and asked the waiter for a vase to put them in. He then hid behind the foliage, and waited.

The expression on Frances's face when she saw the flowers showed what a good idea they had been. He was always slightly amazed at how effective such corny old gestures were, and surprised that he didn't resort to them more often.

'Charles, how sweet of you.'

'And how spontaneous,' he said wryly as he kissed her.

She sat down and saw the glass of white wine he had ordered for her. 'You even remembered what I drink. You're in danger of becoming a smoothie, Charles Paris.'

'Really?' He was drawn to the idea.

'No, not really. There's no danger so long as you keep that sports jacket. Cheers.'

They clinked glasses and drank.

'So what's this West End thing?'

'Well, you know the play I've just been doing down at Taunton...?'

'No.'

'But I thought I –'

'Charles, it's three months since you've been in touch.'

'Oh, is it?' Putting that behind him, he pressed on. 'Well, I've just been doing a play at the Prince's Theatre, Taunton, thing called *The Hooded Owl*, and, quite simply, it's coming in!'

'That's terrific. Have you got a good part?'

He smiled complacently. 'Not bad.'

'So when do you open?'

'Thursday, 30th October. We have this week free – well, there's a meeting on Friday to sort out rehearsal schedules and what-have-you – then start rehearsals on Monday, two weeks of polishing it up, three previews from the 27th – and then the grand opening, which will of course make my fortune, so that, in the evening of my life, I become a grand old man of the British Thea-taaah.'

The irony of his tone was very familiar to her. 'Don't you be so cynical, Charles Paris. Why shouldn't it work?'

'I have been here a few times before.'

'And this may be the time that it really takes off.'

'Maybe.' And he couldn't help grinning as she voiced his secret dream.

He told her more about the play and then asked about his daughter, Juliet.

'Oh, she's fine. And Miles. And the twins.'

Of course. Juliet didn't really exist on her own any more. It was Juliet and husband Miles, who was in insurance and, to Charles's mind, without doubt the most boring man in the world. Not only Miles, but also the twins, their lives already blighted, in their grandfather's view, by having been christened Julian and Damian.

'How old are they now?'

'They were four in April. I sent them presents from both of us.'

'Ah,' said Charles awkwardly. 'Thank you.'

'I wouldn't be surprised if Juliet didn't start another one soon.'

'Another what?'

'Baby.'

'Oh.'

So Miles reckoned the international financial scene could cope with another child. Hmm, maybe the recession was bottoming out.

'They'd love to see you.'

'Sure, I'd love to see them,' he replied automatically. 'Incidentally – apropos of Miles - you said there was something boring you wanted to talk to me about.'

Frances grinned guiltily. 'You must stop saying things like that about Miles.'

'Why? It's true. Or have I missed something? Go on, tell me, I'm anxious to know – have you ever heard an interesting word pass our son-in-law's lips?'

'I decline to answer that. Juliet's very happy with him.'

'Thank you. You have answered it.'

'Anyway,' said Frances, heavily changing the subject, 'what I wanted to talk to you about was the house.'

'Our house in Muswell Hill?'

'Yes. I want to sell it.'

'Sell it?'

'And move in somewhere smaller.'

'Are you hard up?'

'No, I'm better off than ever now I'm headmistress. But I'm also busier, and a house like that takes a lot of time.'

'I suppose it does. I'd never really thought about it.'

'And I'm over fifty now and have to start looking ahead to retirement. So selling the house seems the logical thing to do.'

'Hmm.'

'You don't mind, do you?'

'Mind? No, why should I mind?'

But he did. Somehow, through all the extravagations of his life, he still thought of Frances in the house in Muswell Hill as a fixed point, a moral and geographical norm from which everything else was a kind of deviation. He was surprised at the emptiness he felt at the prospect of her moving. That sort of thing, like Juliet thinking of having another baby, like the twins growing up, made him feel abandoned, immobile in a world where everything else was on the move.

He tried not to show his hurt, because he knew he had no justification for it, but for him the sparkle had gone out of the rest of the meal.

He saw Frances to her car, a bright yellow Renault 5, another symbol of her independence of him.

'Shall I…er…'

'No, Charles. I've got to do that marking.'

'Sure.'

She thanked him for a lovely evening and for the roses, with a strange formality, almost as if they had just met for the first time.

'We'll meet up again soon,' he said.

'Yes, I'd love that.'

She kissed him gently on the lips and was gone.

Charles found a cab and gave the driver the address of the Montrose, a drinking club off the Haymarket.

'Hello, Maurice Skellern Personal Management.'

'Maurice, it's me, Charles.'

'Oh, hello.'

'What's with all this "Personal Management"? I thought you were called "Maurice Skellern Artistes".'

'Yes, I was, Charles, but I decided it had a rather dated feel. "Artistes" is so…I don't know…so *Variety*. I thought "Personal Management" had a more with-it, seventies feel.'

'We're in the eighties, Maurice.'

'Oh yes, so we are. Well, you know what I mean.'

'Hmm. In my experience, "Personal Management" usually means the agent taking twenty per cent rather than ten.'

'Ah yes, well, Charles, we must talk about that sometime. Anyway, how did the play go down in Bristol?'

'Taunton.'

'Taunton, Bristol – it's all West Country. Anyway, how was it?'

'You mean you haven't heard?'

'Heard what?'

'Honestly, Maurice! I thought agents were meant to be the antennae of show business, alert to every rumour, every flicker of interest. I don't think you even know where the West End is.'

'You know, Charles, sometimes you can be very hurtful.'

'Listen. *The Hooded Owl* was a very big success in Taunton.'

'Oh, good.'

'And it's coming in to the West End.'

'REALLY?'

'Yes. Opening on 30th October at the Varietyoh.'

'What's the Varietyoh?'

'The Variety. It saves you the trouble of saying 'oh' in a disappointed voice.'

'Oh,' said Maurice, in a disappointed voice.

'No, it'll be all right. Denis Thornton's got the lease of the theatre now.'

'Has he?'

'And Bobby Anscombe's backing the show.'

'IS HE?'

'Yes, I'm surprised you haven't heard anything about it.'

'Now, Charles, I'm not as young as I was. I don't get about the way I –',

'No, I meant I was surprised the management hadn't been in touch to sort out the West End contract. You sure you haven't heard anything?'

'Not a squeak.'

'Oh well, they must be pretty busy this week. There's a meeting tomorrow. No doubt I'll hear more then.'

'Yes. You don't want me to ring anyone?' asked Maurice, with distaste at the prospect.

'No, don't bother.'

'You know, Charles, this is very good news. Very good news. It's really gratifying for me, you know, as an agent...'

'Oh yes?'

'Yes, when one feels that all one's hard work has not been in vain, that all that careful guiding of a client's career has not been wasted. Yes, moments like this make one understand the meaning of Personal Management.'

'Oh yes?'

'Now, Charles, about this rate of commission you pay me...'

The Friday's meeting for the company of *The Hooded Owl* was held in a superannuated gym near Covent Garden. Everyone was in good spirits, ranging from the quiet complacency of Alex Household to the Christmas Eve child's exhilaration of Lesley-Jane Decker. The week's break had relaxed them with that relaxation an actor can only feel when he knows he's got a job to go to. Those based on London had seen friends, seen shows, talked endlessly; those based outside had sorted out digs or friends to land themselves on, seen shows, talked endlessly. And when they all met up again in the gym, they talked further, volubly, dramatically, hysterically.

The meeting was called for three in the afternoon, but by three-fifteen there was still no sign of Paul Lexington. At one end of the gym there was a folding table with a couple of chairs, from which he would no doubt address them when he arrived. One chair was already occupied by a young man in a beige suit with immaculately waved hair. No one knew who he was or made any attempt to talk to him, but he didn't seem worried by this. He just sat at the table looking through some papers and playing with a pencil.

Peter Hickton wasn't expected at the meeting. He was still monitoring his next Taunton production, *Ten Little Indians* (called by its author, Agatha Christie, in less sensitive times, *Ten Little Niggers*), which had opened on the Wednesday. He would come up to town for the re-rehearsal, starting on the following Monday. In the view of most of die cast, two weeks was an excessive allocation of time to re-rehearse a show they had brought to such a pitch of perfection in Taunton. They reckoned they were in for a fairly lazy fortnight.

At three-twenty Paul Lexington arrived. He clutched a brief-case full of papers, and still looked pretty exhausted, but he had lost the wild look of the last week at Taunton. His confidence had returned a hundredfold.

'Sorry I'm late, everyone. There's been a lot to arrange, and one particular deal I only got signed half an hour ago. Have you all met Wallas?'

He indicated the young man in the beige suit. No, it was clear no one had met him. 'Ah, this is Wallas Ward, who is going to be our Company Manager.

Wallas Ward nodded languidly, and the company looked at him with new interest. The Company Manager would play a significant part in their lives during the run. He was the management's representative, responsible for the day-to-day running of the show. It would help if the cast got on with him, though, because of his allegiance to the management, they would never quite trust him.

'Right,' said Paul. 'I'm sorry that we haven't got round to contacting your agents during the last week, but it has been very busy. I've had to set up a Production Office, sort out the deals with Denis Thornton and Bobby Anscombe – there's been a hell of a lot to do.'

'Still, the important bits are now settled, and the result of it all is...' He paused, seeming uncertain, which was out of character for him. 'Well, let me say that I have some good news and some bad news for you.'

The cast was absolutely silent. This was the first discordant note since the euphoria of the Taunton party.

'Now, as you know, Bobby Anscombe is coming in with me on this production. The credit'll read: "Paul Lexington Productions, in association with Bobby Anscombe". Now this is excellent news for the show. I don't think I need to give you a list of Bobby's successes. He's got the best nose in the business, and the fact that he's with us means that we're going to have a hit.'

He paused again. The cast hardly breathed. They hadn't had the bad news yet.

Paul Lexington chose his words with care. 'Now Bobby Anscombe's success in the theatre hasn't been just coincidence. He knows what makes a show work, and, if all the elements aren't there, he has never been sentimental about making changes as necessary.'

There was a tiny rustle of unease from the cast. They were beginning to anticipate what was coming.

'Now I think it's no secret from any of you that when we opened the play in Taunton, we were hoping to have a star name in the cast.'

They all knew now. Imperceptibly, they all glanced towards Salome Search, whose face shone with tension.

'We didn't get a star name, but we got an excellent performance, and the show was still a huge success. And, for myself, I'd like to keep that success intact. I don't believe in changing a winning team.'

'However...'

Moisture glowed on Salome Search's eyes.

'Bobby Anscombe does not agree with me. Obviously he's more objective than I am, he doesn't know you all, he hasn't worked with you all. But his view is that to bring in a play by an unknown author *without any star names* is commercial suicide. He wants to make changes in the cast.'

'Now I've argued with him about this, but he won't budge. In fact, what it comes down to is, if we don't make cast changes, he'll back out. I've checked round other potential investors and there's nothing doing. Either we do the show with Bobby Anscombe – or the transfer's off.'

The cast was once again silent.

'I'm sorry I have to break the news to you like this. I'd rather have spoken quietly to the individuals concerned, but I'm afraid there hasn't been time. So

I'm going to be brutal and just tell you…'

He paused. Once again, as at the cast party, Charles wondered whether the producer wasn't rather enjoying the suspense he created. There seemed to be a kind of glee behind the apology, a relish in the role of hatchet-man.

'Alex,' Paul Lexington announced finally, 'I am afraid you're out. We've just done a deal with Micky Banks to play the part of the father.'

Now at last he got reaction, but it was a confused reaction. If he hadn't mentioned the name of the replacement, the cast would have been shouting at him in fury, in defence of the one of them who had been so savagely axed. But Michael Banks…Even in their moment of shock, they could recognise what a coup it was to get him. Now if ever a name was box office, it was Micky Banks. And though their hearts went out to Alex, their actor's fickleness could appreciate the commercial sense of substitution.

Alex Household himself was the slowest to react. The noise around him subsided and they all looked covertly towards him.

'I see,' he said, very, very coolly.

'I'm sorry,' said the producer. 'If it could have happened any other way, I'd've…I'm sure we can sort out some sort of deal for you. I mean of course, you haven't signed any sort of contract…'

I see, thought Charles. Maybe that was the reason for delaying the announcement of the transfer; maybe that was why no approach had been made to any of their agents. Paul Lexington hadn't wanted to get any of the original cast signed up until he had contracted his star.

'But I'm sure, Alex, we can sort out some sort of generous terms for you if you want to understudy –'

'Understudy!' the actor repeated, rising to his feet. 'Understudy…'

'I mean it's up to you. You just say what you want and I'll –'

'Say what I want, eh?' Alex's anger was beginning to build. 'Say what I want. Shall I tell you what I want? I want the world rid of all the little shits like you who run it. I want you all out – gone – dead – exterminated!'

'Look, Alex, I'm sorry –'

'Sorry, yes, but you're not as sorry as you will be! You dare to offer me the job of understudy to a part I CREATED! Well, you know what you can do with your job – stuff it! Understudy!'

And, with that sense of occasion that never deserts an actor even in the most real crises of emotion, Alex Household exited from the gym.

There was a murmur of mixed reaction from the cast. They were sorry, yes, angry, yes, but inside each felt relief. In each mind was the thought: It wasn't *me*.

'I'm sorry, this is very painful,' Paul Lexington continued, with the same hint of relish. 'It's not the part of the producer's job that I enjoy.'

'I mentioned cast chang*es*.'

They were all struck dumb again. In their relief they had forgotten that. The axe was still poised overhead. Eyes again slid round to Salome Search.

'Charles,' said Paul Lexington, 'I'm sorry…'

CHAPTER FIVE

CHARLES WAS no less hurt than Alex Household at losing his part in *The Hooded Owl*, but his way of showing the hurt was different. He was not quick to anger and confrontation; shocks caught up with him slowly and he usually faced them in solitary depression rather than by throwing a scene. A bottle of Bell's was the only witness of his lowest moods.

It was just the two of them. The rest of the cast had survived the axe. Charles stayed at the meeting long enough to hear when the rehearsal call was for the Monday; if he accepted Paul's offer of an understudy job, then he'd have to be there. But he wasn't sure whether he was going to accept. He said he'd think about it over the weekend, and let Paul know on the Monday.

When he left, the other actors offered him clumsy commiseration, as to someone who had been bereaved. And, as to the bereaved, their words glowed with the grateful confidence that their own worlds were still intact.

It was when he got outside into the sunlight of a newly-trendy Covent Garden that the disappointment hit him. His armour of cynicism was shown up as useless; all he could feel was how desperately he had wanted the job and how bitter he felt at the injustice that had taken it away from him.

Because it was injustice; he knew it wasn't a matter of talent. He had played that part well, certainly at least as well as the actor taking over from him.

George Birkitt.

He knew George Birkitt, had worked with him on a television sit. com. called *The Strutters*. He liked George Birkitt and thought he was a good actor. But to lose the part to George Birkitt...that he found hard to stomach.

And why? Simply because George Birkitt was a better-known name from television. After *The Strutters*, he had gone on to play a leading part in another sit. com. called *Fly-Buttons*. That had just started screening as part of the ITV Autumn Season and so suddenly George Birkitt was a familiar name. The sort of name which, on a poster – particularly if placed directly beneath that of Michael Banks – would in theory bring the punters in.

Whereas Charles Paris, who knew that he had given one of the best performances of his career in *The Hooded Owl*, was a name that the punters wouldn't know from a bar of soap.

So he was out, and George Birkitt was in.

Charles just walked. Walked through the streets of London. He often did at times of emotional crisis. He didn't really notice where he was going, just plodded on mechanically.

The sight of an open pub told him how much time had passed and also reminded him of his normal comfort in moments of stress.

But he didn't want to sit in a pub, listening to the jollity and in-jokes of office workers.

He went into an off-licence and bought a large bottle of Bell's.

But he didn't want just to go back to Hereford Road and drink it on his own.

He needed someone to talk to. Someone who would understand what he was going through.

There was only one person who would really understand, because he was going through exactly the same. And that was Alex Household.

The new flat was at the top of a tall house in Bloomsbury, round the back of the British Museum. Alex opened the door suspiciously and, when he saw who was there, was about to shut it again.

'I don't want your bloody sympathy, Charles!'

'That's not what I'm bringing. I've got the boot too.'

'Oh Lord.' Alex Household drew aside to let him into the flat. The interior was still full of boxes and packing cases, showing signs of recent occupation.

'I've bought a bottle of whisky and I'm planning to drink my way right through it.' Charles slumped on to a sofa. 'You going to help me, or are you still on the "no stimulants" routine?'

'I'll help you. What does it matter what I do now?'

'Transcendental meditation no good? Doesn't the "earth's plenty" –'

'Listen, Charles!' Alex turned in fury, his fist clenched.

'Sorry. Stupid remark. I'm as screwed up as you are.'

'Yes, I must say this is a wonderful "new start".' Alex laughed bitterly. 'For the last few months I've really been feeling together, an integrated personality for the first time since my breakdown. And now…Do you know, my psychiatrist spent hour after hour convincing me that it was all in the mind, that nobody really was out to get me, that the world wasn't conspiring against me…And I'd just about begun to believe him. And now – this. Something like this happens and you realise it's all true. The world really is conspiring against you. I'd like to see a psychiatrist convince me this is all in the mind. It's a –'

Charles interrupted him crudely. 'Glasses. Be too sordid for both of us to drink out of the bottle.'

Alex went off for glasses and Charles put the bottle down on a coffee table. As he did so, he moved a handkerchief that was lying on it.

He uncovered a gun. The Smith and Wesson Chiefs Special.

Alex saw him looking at it as he came back with the glasses.

'Yes, I'd just got that out when you rang the bell.'

'Thinking of using it?'

Alex smiled a little twisted smile. 'Had crossed my mind. Trouble was, I couldn't decide whether to use it on myself or on the rest of the bastards.'

Charles laughed uneasily. 'I'm sure your psychiatrist wouldn't recommend suicide.'

'No, he wouldn't. He was a great believer in *expressing* aggression, not bottling it up. If I were to take this gun and shoot...who? Paul Lexington? Micky Banks? Bobby Anscombe? Doesn't matter, there are so many of them. No, if I were to do that, my psychiatrist would reckon it proved my cure was complete.' He suddenly found this notion very funny and burst into laughter.

Charles poured two large measures of Bell's and handed one over. The laughter subsided, leaving Alex drained and depressed.

'So what are you going to do, Alex?'

'What do you mean?'

'About the understudy job.'

'I don't know,' the actor intoned lethargically. 'It'd be work, I suppose. I could keep on the flat.'

'And see Lesley-Jane...'

'Yes.' The name evinced no sign of interest. 'Give me another drink.'

Charles obliged, and filled up his own at the same time.

'Were you offered the same deal, Charles?'

'What – the great honour of understudying my own part? Oh yes, Paul nobly offered me that.'

'And what are you going to do about it?'

'God knows. Ask my agent, I suppose.'

'Hmm. Give me another drink.'

'Maurice, it's Charles.'

'I wish you wouldn't ring me at home. I try to keep work and my private life separate.'

'I know, but this is important. And it's the weekend.'

'You don't have to tell me that, Charles.'

'Was that your wife I spoke to?'

'Mind your own business.'

'Listen, Maurice, about *The Hooded Owl*...I've got the boot.'

'Yes, I know.'

'Oh, all of a sudden you know. On Thursday you didn't even know the show was transferring.'

'No, I had a call yesterday afternoon from Paul...Leamington?'

'Lexington.'

'Yes. Pleasant young man he sounded.'

'Oh, a great charmer.'

'Anyway, he told me about the necessity of recasting. And I said, of course, I fully understood.'

'Thank you very much.'

'Now what's that tone of voice for, Charles?'

'Well, really! You "fully understood" that your client had got the sack. Why didn't you stand up for me?'

'Now come on, Charles. We both know you're a very good actor, but you're not a *name*, are you?'

'Hardly surprising, with you for a bloody agent,' Charles mumbled.

'What was that, Charles? I didn't catch it.'

'Never mind.'

'Well, anyway, the good news is that Mr. Leventon –'

'Lexington.'

'Yes, has offered most attractive terms for an understudy contract for you.'

'Oh, terrific.'

'No, really very generous. I mean, a hundred and fifty a week – that's as much as I'd've expected you to get for actually *acting*.'

Blood money, thought Charles.

'Six-month contract, too. I mean, when were you last offered a six-month contract for anything?'

'So you reckon I should take it?'

'Well, of course, Charles. What's the alternative?'

'No other lucrative jobs on the horizon?'

''Fraid not, Charles. As you know, it's not a good time. All the provincial companies have sorted out their seasons, most of the big tellies are cast, there's not much on the –'

'Yes, all right, all right. In other words, things are exactly as usual.'

'Yes.'

'And you really think I should take it?'

'Yes. I can't think why you're havering. It's obvious. A very good offer.'

'Yes, but it is understudying a part I've already played – and played well.'

'So?'

'So…it becomes a matter of pride.'

'Pride? You, Charles? Oh, really.' And Maurice Skellern let out a gasping laugh, as if the joke had really cheered up his weekend.

It was inevitable that, when rerehearsals started on the Monday, the centre of attention should be Michael Banks. His theatrical successes exceeded those of all the rest of the cast added together (and the money Paul Lexington had agreed with his agent quite possibly exceeded their total too).

His face was so familiar that he seemed to have been with the production for weeks. Few of the cast would have seen him in the revues of the late thirties where his career started, but they would all have caught up with the films he had made in the immediate post-war years. He had had a distinguished war, being wounded once and decorated twice, and had spent the next five years recreating it in a series of patriotic British movies. Michael Banks it always was who gazed grimly at the enemy submarine from the bridge, Michael Banks who went back for the wounded private in the jungle, Michael Banks who ignored the smoke pouring from his Spitfire's engine as he trained his sights on the alien Messerschmidt.

He had then gone to Hollywood in the early fifties and stayed there long enough to show that he could cope with the system and be moderately successful, but not so long as to alienate his chauvinistic British following.

The West End then beckoned, and he appeared as a solid juvenile in a sequence of light comedies. He was good box office and managements fell over themselves to get his name on their marquees.

That continued until the early sixties, when, for the first time, his career seemed to be under threat. Fashions had changed; the new youth-oriented culture had nothing but contempt for the gritty, laconic heroism of the war, of which Michael Banks remained the symbol. The trendies of Carnaby Street flounced around in military uniforms, sporting flowers of peace where medals once had hung. Acting styles changed too, as did the plays in which they were exhibited. The mannered delivery of West End comedies sounded ridiculous at the kitchen sink, and became the butt of the booming satire industry.

'The wind of change', that phrase coined by Harold Macmillan in 1960, grew to have a more general application than just to Africa, or just to politics. It represented a change of style, and this new wind threatened to blow away all that was dated and traditional.

Amongst other things, it threatened to blow away the career of Michael Banks.

And it might well have done. He had reached that most difficult of ages for a successful actor, his forties. The audience who had loved him as a stage juvenile were themselves growing old, and could not fail to notice the signs of ageing in their idol. The rising generation was not interested. To them Michael Banks represented that anathema – something their parents liked. If they saw him in a play, they saw a middle-aged man pretending to be young, in an outdated vehicle that bore as much relation to their reality as crinolines and penny-farthings.

He did two more West End comedies, neither of which lasted three months, and theatre managements were suddenly less anxious to pick up the phone and plead with his agent. The British film industry, such as it was, was committed to making zany films about Swinging London and, if there were any parts for the over-forties, they went to outrageous character actors.

One or two offers of touring productions or guest star status in provincial reps came in, a sure sign that their managements were trying to cash in on the name of Michael Banks before it was completely forgotten.

It was the nadir of his career. He was all right financially – he had always been shrewd and he had made his money in days when the Inland Revenue had allowed people to keep some of it – but his prospects of regaining his former place in the public's esteem seemed negligible.

The way he had fought back from that position showed that the grit demonstrated in all those celluloid heroics was not just acting. He had survived by sheer determination.

His first decision had been to take on only older parts. He refused every sort of juvenile role that was offered, resisting lucrative inducements to recreate his West End successes in the diminished settings of the provinces or seasons in South Africa and Australia.

The result of this policy change was a very quiet three years. He played one Blimpish cameo in a short-lived play in Birmingham and a couple of small parts in television plays.

It wasn't an enjoyable period of his life, but he stuck it out, certain that he was on the right track. He deliberately courted very old parts, particularly on television. He realised the medium's power, and realised that, through it, he could reach a different public and establish a new image with them. The West End and even cinema audiences were tiny compared to the huge passive mass of armchair viewers. He reasoned that, if he could establish a new, older identity with them, he would be able to shake off the persona of faded juvenile.

Age was not the only criterion in his choice of parts. He avoided the trendy and the experimental, aiming ideally for costume drama, aware that his strengths were those of permanence and reliability, and would be dissipated by following the twists of fashion. And he had a gut-feeling that the values of that huge but silent force, the British middle class, were the same as his own. The television-viewing public was made up of the older stay-at-homes, not the swinging exotics whose exploits filled the front pages of the newspapers. They might not dare to admit it, but they didn't like the changes they saw around them; they enjoyed television's recreations of more confident times, when they had had a country to be proud of, when people had reached maturity at forty and had not pandered to youth. They liked seeing the old values reasserted.

And, gradually, through the parts he chose, Michael Banks came to symbolise those values.

His three years in the wilderness climaxed with a solid part in a BBC costume drama series. It was not the lead, but the character was in every episode, and had the advantage of ageing from week to week.

The public took the character to their hearts. Once again, they took Michael Banks to their hearts. Having watched him grow old before their eyes in their own sitting-rooms, they would thereafter accept him in parts of any age.

Since that time, his career had had no more problems. He had become increasingly selective in what he did, avoiding, on the whole, long runs in the West End, and concentrating on starring television parts or extremely lucrative cameos in international films. He became an institution of British acting, respected and loved. In the business, you never heard a word against Michael Banks.

And, when the cast of *The Hooded Owl* met him, they could understand why. He was an immensely likeable man. He was in his sixties, but had aged gracefully. The familiar acute face had thickened out, and the hair, remembered as darker than it actually was because of all those black-and-white films, had greyed becomingly. It was cut in a trendier style, worn longer than it would have been, but its shape still reminded one of all those gruff but infinitely reliable heroes. He dressed casually in a red golfing sweater, pale blue trousers, and deceptively ordinary-looking hand-made shoes.

The surprise about him was his size. As actors, they were all used to people looking different off screen, but none of them had expected him to be so tall. He must have been six foot four, with a frame to match. A most impressive figure. The reasoning behind casting him as the father in *The Hooded Owl* became clearer by the minute.

Clearer to Charles, anyway. He was at the rehearsal, needless to say, having, possibly for the first time in his life, followed his agent's advice. Through the haze of Bell's which had been the weekend, it had become clear that he had little alternative. He was being offered a job, being offered good money, and he'd be based in London. His dreams would have to wait, be returned intact to some cupboard deep in the recesses of his mind, whence they would arise, undaunted, at the next glimmer of hope in his career.

To his surprise, the strongest argument in favour of taking the job had been that it would keep him near to Frances. Her talk of moving, and the indefinable detachment he had felt in her when they had met, worried him. He felt he needed to rebuild the relationship – not, of course, to revive it as a total marriage, but to get back to the level of intermittent companionship which seemed to have gone.

Similar arguments must have weighed with Alex Household, because he was there too. His face looked strained and petulant, but he had clearly decided to put his mortgage and proximity to Lesley-Jane above pride.

If the cast had needed a demonstration of Michael Banks's genuine warmth, they could not have asked for a better one than the way he dealt with Alex Household.

The first thing he did on arriving at the rehearsal room was to ask Paul Lexington which one was Alex and, having had him identified, he immediately went across to the actor with hand outstretched.

'Alex, I'm sorry. This is a lousy way for me to get a job. I know exactly how you feel. Just the same thing happened to me on one of my first jobs. It was a revue back in the thirties. We were doing a pre-London tour. I got as far as Birmingham, and then was called into the manager's office. Just the same as you, I was offered the understudy.'

'Did you take it?'

'Oh yes.' Michael Banks grinned disarmingly. 'Oh yes, I took it. And it does mean I know exactly how shitty you're feeling at this moment, and all the horrible fates you're wishing down on my head.'

Alex blushed. 'Oh, I wouldn't say…'

'Yes, you would. You wouldn't be human if you didn't. Anyway, all I want to say is – I'm very sorry. This can be a rotten business at times. I sympathise. And, if you're willing, I'll be very grateful for your help. God, you must know this character inside-out by now, and I've got to get it presentable in a fortnight. Any tips you can give me, old boy, I will welcome as rich gifts.'

It was beautifully done. Had it been less well done, someone as prickly and paranoid as Alex Household would have bridled, would have pointed out that to lose a part at the beginning of one's career was rather different from losing it after twenty years in the business, would have made some bitter retort. But, as it was, Michael Banks had him eating out of his hand. Yes, of course, said Alex, no, he couldn't pretend he wasn't hurt, but thanks for saying it, and he'd be happy to give any advice that might be required.

George Birkitt didn't show quite the same smooth tact in his dealings with the actor he was replacing.

'Hello, Charles. Long time, no see,' he murmured after getting himself a coffee.

'Hello.'

'Rather strange circumstances for a meeting.'

'Yes.'

'I was very undecided when my agent told me about the offer...'

'Oh.'

'Well, it *is* second billing, no two ways about that. I mean, God knows, I'm the last person in the world to worry about that sort of thing, but there does come a point in your career where you *have* to think about it. I mean, with *Fly-Buttons* up there in the ratings, I do have to be a bit careful.' He lowered his voice. 'I tell you, Charles, it was only after I heard that they'd signed up Micky Banks that I agreed to do it. Of course, it is still second billing, but second billing to Micky Banks is no disgrace at this stage in my career.'

'No, I suppose not,' said Charles.

Peter Hickton was up from Taunton and keen to start working his cast as hard as ever. Now that the two main parts had been recast, there really was going to be a lot to do, and the company waved goodbye to their hopes of a cushy fortnight.

The director clapped his hands. 'O.K., loves. Now, as you all know, we've got a big job on, and we're going to have to work every hour there is to get *The Hooded Owl* up to the standard I know it can reach.'

This was very familiar to those who had worked with Peter before; he said it before every production, regardless of how complex or simple it was, and regardless of the length of rehearsal allocated.

'Now what I want to do is go through the blocking today, so that Micky and George can start to feel the shape of the production. Tomorrow we'll get down to Act One in detail, and then on Wednesday we'll –'

'Um, sorry, old boy...'

Peter Hickton looked to the source of the interruption. It was Michael Banks.

'Yes?'

'Sorry, can't do Wednesday.'

'What?'

'Can't do Wednesday. Got to do some Pro-Celebrity Golf thing for the BBC. Didn't the agent mention it?'

Peter Hickton looked round to Paul Lexington, who shook his head.

'Oh, I'm so sorry. The agent's an awful duffer when it comes to dates. Got the same thing the following Wednesday too.'

'Oh.' But Peter Hickton was only slowed down for a moment. 'Never mind. If we work hard over the weekend, we can –'

'Ah. Sorry, old boy, going away for the weekend.'

'Oh.'

'Going to stay with some chums in Chichester. Can't really put it off, been in the diary for ages. Sorry, this show came up so suddenly, there are a few dates we'll have to work round.'

'Yes ' said Peter Hickton. 'Yes, of course.'

Under normal circumstances, understudies would be expected to attend all the rehearsals to familiarise themselves with the production, but, because Alex and Charles knew the play so well, they were given a dispensation to take most of the first week off, which would save both them and their replacements the embarrassment of the early stumbling rehearsals while the newcomers were trying to memorise the lines. The two understudies were asked to come back on the Friday afternoon, when there was going to be a complete run of the play for the producers and Malcolm Harris.

When he arrived at the rehearsal room on the Friday, Charles found the author in a state of extreme annoyance.

'What's up, Malcolm?'

'Have you seen this?' He pointed to a printed handout on a table. It read:

THE VARIETY THEATRE
PAUL LEXINGTON PRODUCTIONS
in association with
BOBBY ANSCOMBE
presents
MICHAEL BANKS GEORGE BIRKITT
in
THE HOODED OWL

There was more writing beneath this, but it was printed too small to be legible.

'I see,' said Charles.

'It's a bit much. My name might just as well not be on it,' objected the author.

'Hmm. You see, what's happened is that this is a big design for a poster. They've economised by reducing it for the handout. Your name'd be legible on the big poster.'

'That's a fat lot of good. No, I'm really annoyed about this. I think these handouts should be withdrawn. I mean, look at the size of Paul's name – it's as big as Michael Banks's, for God's sake.'

'Producer's perk. He decides what the poster looks like.'

'Well. I'm furious. Who should I complain to about it?'

'Under normal circumstances,' said Charles gently, 'you'd go to your agent and get him to complain to the management.'

'Ah,' said Malcolm Harris, realising, perhaps for the first time, the folly of the contract he had signed with Paul Lexington.

'Good news about getting Michael Banks, isn't it?' said Charles, to cheer up the hangdog author.

It had the desired effect. Malcolm Harris brightened immediately.

'Yes, it's wonderful. From the moment I first thought of the play, I thought he'd be ideal for the part. Though, of course, I never dared hope...'

The run-through started. Charles could not judge George Birkitt's performance, he was too close to the part to be objective, but there was no doubt that Michael Banks was going to be very strong as the father. In his first scene he established an unshakeable authority, which, Charles knew, was bound to strengthen the total collapse of the character in the second act. Alex Household had been excellent in the part, but, in retrospect, he seemed to have been giving an actor's interpretation of a man fifteen years older than himself. Michael Banks actually seemed to *be* that man.

But, after the first scene, the performance weakened. The power of the acting remained, but its flow was constantly interrupted. The actor just did not know the lines and, though he could manage the exchanges of dialogue quite well, every time he came to a big speech, he would dry.

'Sorry, old boy. Sorry, loves. Prompt,' he would say. The Stage Manager would give him the line, he'd be all right for a couple more sentences, then, 'Sorry, it's gone again.'

The play tottered on like this for a quarter of an hour. Charles was sitting at the back of the hall with Malcolm Harris, and kept feeling the author tense as another of his speeches was chopped up and destroyed. Eventually, Michael Banks just stopped, looked out at the director, and said, 'Look, sorry, Peter old boy, I'd better use the book. Not getting anywhere like this.'

'I did want to do this run without books.'

'So did I, dear boy, so did I,' said the star lugubriously, and got a good laugh from the cast. He had managed to endear himself to all of them within the week, and they shared his agony as he groped for the lines.

'We open in less than a fortnight,' Peter Hickton continued to argue.

'Don't think I don't know it. But, honestly, I think we'll just be wasting time if I go on like this.'

'You've got to come off the book sometime.'

'I will, I will, love. I promise. Look, don't worry about it. I'm usually pretty good on lines. Once, when I was in rep, I learned Iago in three days. So it will come, just hasn't come yet. So I think for this run I'd better press on with the book.'

Michael Banks's charm didn't prevent him from being forceful, and Peter Hickton had to concede defeat. The play continued. With the support of the printed lines, Michael Banks's performance regained the stature it had shown in the first scene and left no doubt that he was going to add a new excellence to *The Hooded Owl*. Charles found he was watching much of the play as if seeing it for the first time.

Towards the end of the second act, the door beside him opened and a woman slipped in to the back of the hall. She was in her forties, smartly dressed in white trousers, *eau-de-nil* silk shirt and long camel-coloured cardigan. Very well-preserved. She flashed a well-crowned smile at Charles.

'Hi,' she whispered. 'I'm Dottie, Micky's wife.'

'Charles Paris.'

'How's it going?'

'Pretty good.'

She nodded and her alert hazel eyes flickered around the room, taking everyone in. They lingered on Lesley-Jane Decker. 'Who's that?' she hissed.

Charles gave the girl's name.

'Micky made a play for her yet?'

He was surprised. 'I don't know. I haven't been round much this week.' Then, curious, 'Why? Has he got a roving eye?'

'Haven't we all?' she said. Her tone was mocking, but she was fully aware of the sexual nature of her remark.

The play ended. Malcolm Harris started to applaud and some of the others joined in. Michael Banks grinned and went across to have a word with Lesley-Jane. After Dottie's remark, Charles couldn't help thinking that the two of them did look rather intimate.

Peter Hickton clapped his hands again. 'O.K., thank you all very much. We really are getting somewhere. There are a few scenes I'd just like to run through before we break and –'

'Sorry, love,' said Michael Banks gently. 'Got to go. Off for the weekend, as I said, old boy.' He waved vaguely to Dottie.

'But I really think we should –' the director began.

'Sorry. No can do.'

'Are you sure you can't just stay for –'

Michael Banks shook his head charmingly. 'Sorry, love.'

'Oh. Oh, well…You will have a look at the lines over the weekend, won't you? I mean, the performance is coming fine, but the lines are…'

'Course I will, old boy, course I will. Scout's honour. Cross my heart.'

'Oh, and I have got a note on –'

'Got to go.' Michael Banks went across to get his coat and brief-case.

'Lines a problem?' Dottie whispered to Charles.

'Seem to be.'

She nodded knowingly.

'He starts all right,' said Charles, 'but he can't keep it up.'

'You can say that again.'

Once again, there was no doubt of the sexual overtone in Dottie Banks's words.

CHAPTER SIX

THE WEEKEND with chums in Chichester did not seem, on the Monday's showing, to have left Micky Banks much time to look at his lines. If anything, he was worse after the break; even the words he had remembered the week before were now coming out jumbled and confused.

'Don't worry,' he kept saying. 'Don't worry, Peter old boy. They will come. Just out of practice learning, you know. That's the trouble with doing all these films and tellies – you just have to remember a little bit for a short take. Forget what it's like learning a long part. But don't worry – be all right on the night. I once got up Iago in three days when I was in rep. If we just press on with the rehearsal, it'll come.'

But it didn't. And indeed it was very difficult to press on with the rehearsal. In every production there comes an awkward jerky stage when the cast abandon their books for the first time, but for *The Hooded Owl* it seemed to be going on longer than usual.

And it had a knock-on effect. George Birkitt got lazy about learning his lines too. Charles remembered from working on *The Strutters* with him that George had always had an approximate approach to the text, relying, as did so many television actors, on a sort of paraphrase of the speeches which homed in on the right cue. Strong direction could make him more disciplined and accurate, but Peter Hickton was not well placed to bully George Birkitt. The latter could always turn round – and indeed did turn round-and say, 'Sorry, love, I don't mind working on them, but there doesn't seem a lot of point in my giving up my free evenings when *the star* is unwilling to do the same.'

He couldn't resist putting a sneer into the words. In spite of the success of *Fly-Buttons*, George Birkitt was not yet a star – and quite possibly never would be. He lacked the necessary effortless dominance of character. Deep down he was aware of this fact, and it hurt.

Charles hoped that George's assumption was right, that Michael Banks's difficulty in retaining the lines was just the product of laziness. If that were the case, then atavistic professional instincts and the terrifying imminence of the first night would ensure that he knew the part by the time they opened. But Charles had a nagging fear that it wasn't that, that Michael Banks really was trying, that he did go through the lines time after time in the evenings, but that his mind could no longer retain them. If that was the situation, it was very serious. And through the star's casual bonhomie at rehearsals, Charles thought he could detect a growing panic as the awful realisation dawned.

They were making so little progress on the Monday that Peter Hickton took the sensible decision and dismissed most of the cast at lunchtime; he would sit down with Michael Banks and George Birkitt all afternoon and just go through the lines. It was a ploy that often worked. Apart from the shame of being kept in like a naughty schoolboy, the constant automatic repetition of the lines taken out of the context of the play could often lodge them in the leakiest actor's mind.

And on the Tuesday morning it was seen to have had some effect. George Birkitt, whose main problem with the lines had been an unwillingness to look at them, showed a marked improvement. Michael Banks, too, started with renewed confidence and got further into the text than he ever had before without error. Relief settled on the rehearsal room. When he was flowing in the part, the company could feel his great presence and their confidence in the whole enterprise blossomed.

The first breakdown came about twenty minutes into the play. Needless to say, it was in a big speech. As ever, the start was confident. And, as ever, about three sentences in, Michael Banks faltered. The entire cast held their breath, as if watching a tightrope-walker stumble, and all let out a sigh of relief when he managed to right himself and make it through to the end of the speech.

But it was a symptom of things to come. In the next big speech, Michael Banks again stumbled. Again he extricated himself, but this time at some cost to the text. What he said was a vague approximation of what Malcolm Harris had written, and he didn't even give the right cue to George Birkitt, who spoke next.

This threw George, and he got his lines wrong. Being George, he didn't try to cover the fluff and press on; instead he said, 'Sorry, love, but I can't be expected to get my lines right if I get the wrong feed, can I?'

The scene lurched forward again, but its momentum was gone. Michael Banks's eyes were lit with the panic of a man about to dry. And sure enough, he did. Peter Hickton tried another approach and threw one of his little tantrums. This didn't help at all. It just soured the atmosphere of the rehearsal, and left Michael Banks looking pained, like some huge animal, beaten for a transgression he does not understand.

For a show due to open for its first public preview in a week's time *The Hooded Owl* was in far from promising shape.

There was a run on the Tuesday afternoon for the producers. Paul Lexington and Bobby Anscombe sat through the whole play in silence.

It was excruciating. Consciousness of the audience made Michael Banks nervous, and nervousness scrambled the lines in his head even further. George Birkitt got through with only one prompt, but his performance was spoiled by the smug smile he wore throughout at the star's expense.

Eventually, half-way through the second act, as the play's climax approached, Michael Banks could stand it no longer. He snatched the prompt copy from the Stage Manager and read the rest of his part. The strength of the performance, as ever, increased, but it was worrying.

The play finished and there was silence. The actors drifted away from the centre of the room to the safety of the walls, where they picked up crosswords, fiddled with knitting, lit cigarettes and gave generally unconvincing impressions of people who weren't worried about what was about to happen.

Paul Lexington and Bobby Anscombe were sitting at a table in the middle of the room, engaged in a fiercely whispered conversation. The cast couldn't help hearing odd words. Bobby Anscombe seemed to be doing most of the talking. 'Bloody terrible...amateur...when I put my money into something I don't expect...can't put that sort of thing into a professional theatre...These fag-ends did not augur well for any public announcement that might be made.

And when it came, the announcement lived up to their worst fears. With a gesture of annoyance at something Paul Lexington had just said, Bobby Anscombe stood up and banged his hand down on the table.

'This is bloody awful. I've backed more shows than you lot have had hot dinners and I've never seen anything like this. Do you realise, a week on Thursday you're going to play this show to all the West End critics? At the moment none of them's going to sit through to the end. If I don't see a marked improvement by the end of the week, I am going to take my money out!'

Shock registered on every face in the room. Even Paul Lexington's boyish mask was shattered.

Bobby Anscombe had intended his ultimatum as an exit line, but he was stopped by Michael Banks, who had worked with him in the past and knew his volatile temper. He stepped forward, diplomatically.

'Bobby, old boy, take your point. The show does look pretty shitty at the moment. Also take the blame myself. I just haven't got the hang of the lines yet. But don't worry. Give us a couple of days and you won't recognise it.'

'I'd better not. There is nothing in it at the moment that I would want my name associated with.'

'Now come on, Bobby. It's only me letting the side down,' Michael Banks volunteered nobly. 'I don't know my lines and I'm dragging down the rest of the cast.'

'And why don't you know your lines?' Bobby Anscombe snapped. 'Listen. You know how much money we're paying you. It's a bloody big investment. And when I invest that much, I reckon to get value for my money.' He thumped the table with his fist. 'I'm paying for a star actor who can do the job of acting, not some old has-been whose memory's gone.'

It was as if every person in the room had been slapped in the face. They all flinched. Michael Banks's charm had worked on every one of them, and they hated this savage attack on him.

The star himself took it with dignity. 'Fair comment. I agree, I should know the lines by now. And I will. Don't worry, once in rep. I learned all of Iago in three days.'

'I'm not interested in what you've done in the past. My money is invested in what you can do now.'

Once again, Bobby Anscombe intended this as a parting shot, but again he was stopped. This time the interruption came from an unexpected source, as Lesley-Jane Decker leapt to the defence of her idol.

'It's all very well you saying that, but do you realise that Micky only saw the script ten days ago? It's a huge amount to learn in that time.'

Bobby Anscombe looked at her contemptuously. 'I am not concerned about *actors' problems.* I don't give a toss how long he's had to learn the part or how difficult it's been. All I know is he's signed a contract to play the part properly, and at the moment he's not doing it. I am not getting my money's worth. I'm a business man with a reputation to think of. I've backed this show and I intend to make money out of it. The only way that's going to happen is if it looks like a professional West End production. At the moment it looks like amateur night. The only way for it to look any different is for Michael to learn the bloody lines. Unless,' he added with unpleasant irony, 'anyone has any other ideas for picking it out of the shit...?'

'You could revert to the original casting.'

It was Alex Household who had spoken. He hadn't intended to. He looked as shocked as everyone else at his words. They had just come out. The build-up of frustration he had felt ever since he lost the part would not allow him to be silent. When given such a cue, the reply had to emerge.

The investor wheeled on him. 'What, and put your name above the title? How many people do you think that'll bring in? At least, with Micky there, we can fill a few weeks of punters coming in to watch him dry. But who's going to come out to see a non-entity like you? I'll tell you – bloody no one!'

Alex may have had some response ready, but he got no chance to voice it, as Bobby Anscombe turned his fury on Paul Lexington.

'Not that anyone's going to come anyway at the moment. Where's the publicity? I haven't seen a single poster for this bloody show. I haven't heard anything on the radio, seen nothing in the press, nothing on the box. How are the punters meant to know there's a show on? Bloody E.S.P.?'

Paul Lexington looked subdued. 'Publicity is being handled by Show-Off Enterprises.'

'Never heard of them.'

'They're part of Lanthorn Productions. Denis Thornton recommended them.'

'Oh, did he? Well, you shouldn't trust him further than you can throw him. Are they doing the publicity for his new musical at the King's?'

'I think so.'

'Oh well then, you won't see anything from them. The musical opens next week as well. They'll be putting all their efforts behind that.'

'They've said they're going to do a big media blitz for us at the end of this week.'

'Oh really? And you believed them? Good God, the management of this outfit's as bloody amateur as the acting!'

And with that exit line, Bobby Anscombe succeeded in making his exit.

Rehearsals on the Wednesday were somewhat desultory, because the person most in need of rehearsal was not there. Michael Banks was fulfilling his previous commitment to play Pro-Celebrity Golf for the BBC. This was intensely frustrating for everyone, because logic dictated that he wasn't going to get much opportunity to look at his lines between strokes. It was just a wasted day.

But Peter Hickton could not resist working. Back with his own cast, he was determined to keep them at it as long as possible, fulfilling his own need for manic activity. (Charles had developed a new theory about the director's passion for working so hard. As well as giving him moral ascendancy over the rest of the company, driving himself to exhaustion might also cloud critical judgement, so that comments would be made on the effort that had gone into the show rather than on its quality.)

Because of the star's absence, his understudy took on the role. Alex Household performed this function punctiliously, making no comment, but demonstrating a fluency with the lines which contrasted significantly with Michael Banks's constant breaks for prompts.

And yet, even though Alex gave a performance quite as good as any he had given in Taunton, he was not as good as Banks. The artifice showed. Charles was aware of it, all the rest of the cast were aware of it. And the petulant set of Alex Household's mouth showed that he was aware of it too.

Malcolm Harris, whose school had Games on Wednesday afternoons, had managed to get away to see the rehearsal. When Peter Hickton was finally persuaded to stop for the day, at about seven, Charles Paris walked with the author to the pub round the corner.

Malcolm Harris was aggrieved. 'A complete waste of my time, coming to that rehearsal, with Michael Banks not even there.'

'Didn't anyone tell you he wouldn't be?'

'No.'

Oh dear. Another black mark against Paul Lexington, both as management and agent.

But not as black as the mark that the ensuing conversation was to put against the producer's name.

'I wouldn't mind,' said Malcolm Harris, 'but it does cost a lot, all this toing and froing up to London.'

'I suppose Paul hasn't mentioned anything like expenses?'

'No chance.'

'No. Few producers would, unless pressed by their client's agent.'

'I wouldn't mind, but I am pretty hard-up at the moment. Teachers aren't paid a fortune, as you know.'

'No. Still, you must have had some royalties from Taunton.'

'No.'

'No?'

'I did ask Paul about that. He said he couldn't pay me.'

'Couldn't pay you?'

'No.'

Charles could just picture Paul Lexington saying it, his plausible face earnestly puckered as he explained the situation to his gullible client.

Malcolm Harris brightened. 'No, but he offered me a very good deal.'

'Oh yes?' Charles couldn't keep the cynicism out of his voice. But the author did not appear to notice it. 'He said that he couldn't pay me because he had to maintain his cash flow for the London opening, but what he would do was to let me regard what he owed me as a stake in the show.' He grinned with triumph.

'So you become an investor?'

'Exactly. I'm now on a percentage, with the Taunton money as my stake. So, when the play starts making a lot, I get this extra money on top of my royalty!'

And if it doesn't make any money, thought Charles, you don't even get what's owing to you.

'And you accepted the deal just like that?'

'Oh yes, of course. I mean, it's a good deal. And, anyway, I didn't have any alternative.'

'Did he offer you any alternative?'

'Yes, he said, if I insisted on having my Taunton money, he wouldn't be able to afford to bring the show in.'

It was all horribly predictable. Once again Charles was astonished how easily Malcolm would fall for the oldest cons in the business. And once again, his estimate of Paul Lexington's integrity dropped a few notches.

'By the way,' asked the author, 'has Micky Banks learnt the lines yet?'

'Well...' replied Charles Paris evasively.

To his surprise, when they got to the pub, he found Valerie Cass sitting there over a large gin. She waved effusively and he couldn't pretend he hadn't seen her. 'Charles darling, how lovely to see you.'

'Yes, er...terrific. You know Malcolm, don't you?'

'Of course. We met in Taunton.'

'Did we?'

'Yes. I'm Valerie Cass. Though you might not think it, I'm Lesley-Jane's mother.'

'Why shouldn't I think it?' asked Malcolm Harris innocently. He was not skilled in the art of complimenting ladies.

Nor, as Charles had come to realise to his cost, was he skilled in buying rounds of drinks. Resigning himself, Charles asked, 'Get you another one, Valerie?'

'Oh, just a teensy gin. Thank you, Charles.'

'Malcolm?'

'Half of lager, please.'

While he was getting the drinks, Alex Household came in to the pub, looking harassed. 'Tomato juice, Alex?'

'Whisky, please.'

'Make that another large Bell's, please. So you're hooked on the stimulants now, are you?'

'God knows I need something, Charles.'

'Hmm. Look who's over there. The mother.'

'Oh Lord. I can't face her.'

'Come on.'

Reluctantly, Alex followed Charles to the table and sat down. He and Valerie looked at each other as cordially as two people who loathe each other can.

'So where's my baby?' asked Lesley-Jane's mother.

'Don't know,' said Charles. 'She said she had to rush off after rehearsal.'

Valerie looked piqued. 'Oh, from what she said, I gathered she usually came round here.'

'Quite often. Not tonight.'

'You don't know where she is, Alex?' she asked sweetly. And then, with a touch of venom, 'Or are you no longer the right person to ask?'

Alex spoke without emotion. 'As far as I know, she has gone out to dinner.'

'Oh, has she? Then we've both been stood up.'

'So it would appear.'

'Do you know who we've been stood up by?'

'The version I heard was that Lesley-Jane was going out to dinner with Michael Banks "to go through his lines".'

'Oh,' said Valerie Cass. And then, with a different intonation, 'Oh.' The news gave rise to mixed emotions in her. She was glad her daughter had stood up Alex Household. She was impressed that her daughter was out with someone of the eminence of Michael Banks. But at the same time, she was nettled that her daughter hadn't told her she was going out, and the sexual jealousy, which was so much part of their relationship, was irritated by the news. She responded by testing her own sexual magnetism on Charles. 'Had you thought about eating?'

'Me? Eating? Oh, I'm not much of an eater. Had a pie at lunch. That does me for the day.'

'Oh.'

'Tell me, Alex,' said Malcolm Harris suddenly, 'how is Micky Banks doing on the lines?'

'Well...' Alex Household pursed his lips sarcastically. And, whereas Charles had left it at that, Michael Banks's understudy proceeded to tell the author just how much of a massacre the star was making of his play.

It was just the two of them left in the pub. Valerie Cass had left rather petulantly as soon as she had finished her gin, and Malcolm Harris, breathing imprecations against Michael Banks, had gone soon after (without, of course, buying a round). Charles and Alex drank a lot, but Charles didn't feel the relaxation he normally experienced when getting quietly pissed with a fellow actor. Alex was too jumpy, too neurotic, too dangerous.

Towards the end of the evening, indiscreet with the unaccustomed alcohol, he suddenly said, 'I don't think I can take it much longer.'

'Take what?' asked Charles.

'The humiliation. The sheer bloody humiliation. You take a decision rationally. You say I'll do this or that, it'll be hell, but I know the stakes, I'll do it, I can cope. And then you do it, and it is hell, and you realise that you can't cope.'

'You mean this understudy thing?'

Alex nodded unevenly. 'That, and other things, yes. I just feel it can't go on much longer. There's got to be some resolution, something that breaks the tension.'

'What sort of thing?'

'I don't know.' Alex Household laughed suddenly. 'Someone's death, maybe.'

Thursday's rehearsals built up to a run in the afternoon. Whatever Michael Banks had done with Lesley-Jane the previous evening – and something in their manner towards each other suggested he had done something – it had not improved his grasp of the lines. In fact, he was worse than ever. It was as if his mind had a finite capacity for lines; put in more than it could hold and they would start to overflow. He would surprise everyone by getting a new speech right, but then show that it had been at the expense of other sections of dialogue. The fact could not be avoided: Michael Banks could no longer learn lines.

He was cold and hurt at the end of the run-through, knowing what was wrong and unable to admit it.

'Look, Micky,' said Peter Hickton, 'would it help if we were to go through the lines again this evening, just the two of us?'

'No, thank you,' the star replied politely. 'I'll go home and put them on tape. That sometimes helps.'

'Are you sure there's nothing that –'

'Quite sure, thank you,' came the firm reply. 'Don't worry about it. I once learned all of Iago in three days when I was in rep.'

But the old boast didn't convince anyone. Amidst subdued farewells, Michael Banks left the rehearsal room.

'Christ!' muttered Paul Lexington, momentarily losing his cool. 'What the hell do we do now?'

'I haven't a clue,' confessed Peter Hickton. 'Just run out of ideas. Unless we start pasting bits of the script all over the set. God, if only it were television. There you can use autocue and idiot boards, but in the theatre there's no technology that can help you out.'

'Oh,' said Wallas Ward, the languid Company Manager. 'I wouldn't say that.'

CHAPTER SEVEN

THE FRIDAY'S rehearsals followed the pattern of the previous day. Followed it even down to the detail of Michael Banks not knowing his lines.

The strain was beginning to tell on him. The casual bonhomie was maintained with more difficulty. There was no arrogance in the man; he was desperately aware that he was letting down all his fellow-actors, and by one of the least forgivable of professional shortcomings. Knowing the lines was the basic equipment for the job. Actors throughout history had staggered on to stages in various states of alcoholic debility, but they had almost always got through the lines, or at least an approximation of them. Michael Banks knew how much he was showing himself up, but the lines just wouldn't come. The dark circles under his eyes suggested he might well have spent the entire night going through them on a tape recorder, but it hadn't helped. Every improvement was at the cost of another speech forgotten.

And he knew fully what was at stake too. He was aware of his responsibilities as a star. One of the reasons why people in his position were paid so much money was because their presence could often ensure the survival of a production and keep the rest of the company in employment. They were responsible for the complete show, which was why stories of stars giving notes to other actors or ordering changes in sets and costumes were not just examples of megalomania, but the desire to maintain the overall standard of whatever production they put their names to.

Michael Banks knew that *The Hooded Owl* was not up to the required standard. It was due to open in less than a week. It was due to be shown to the paying public in a preview on the Monday evening. More important than either of these, it was due to be run again on the Saturday afternoon in front of Bobby Anscombe. And if it didn't live up to the investor's rigorous standards, no one had any doubt that he would make good his threat of withdrawing his backing.

Consciousness of all these pressures did not improve Michael Banks's concentration and, together with fatigue, ensured that the lines were worse than ever on the Friday afternoon run.

The rehearsal ended in apathetic silence. The actors drifted uselessly to their belongings.

'Micky, could we have a quick word?' asked Paul Lexington, and the star, with the dignity of a man mounting the scaffold, went across to join the producer, director and Company Manager.

Conscious of the straining ears of the rest of the company, Paul Lexington led the little group out into the corridor. They were out for two or three minutes, during which no one in the hall spoke.

Michael Banks led them back in, saying, 'No, I'm sorry, Paul. I couldn't think of it. I have a reputation to maintain.'

'Do you have any alternative to suggest?' asked the Producer, careless now of listening ears.

The star spread his hands in a gesture of frustration. 'Only that somehow I'll get the lines. Somehow.'

'Micky, you've said that for a fortnight, and there's no sign of it happening. We've got to do something.'

'But not what you suggest. There must be some other way.' And, to put an end to the conversation, he walked firmly off to pour himself a cup of coffee.

After a muttered colloquy with Peter Hickton and Wallas Ward, Paul Lexington announced, 'O.K., everyone. We'll break there. Ten o'clock call in the morning. There's still a lot of work to do.'

'You can say that again,' murmured Alex Household, who was standing beside Charles, 'but I fear it will all be in vain.'

'Alex,' said the producer, 'could you just stay for a quick word?'

'Of course.'

'I'm going round the pub,' said Charles. 'See you there maybe.'

'Perhaps,' Alex replied abstractedly. And looking at the glow of restrained excitement in the other actor's face, Charles knew that Alex Household thought he was about to get his part back.

It was nearly an hour before Alex appeared in the pub, and one look at his face told that his expectation had not been realised.

He no longer even mentioned his 'no stimulants' regime as he took the large Bell's from Charles.

'The nerve! The bloody nerve! I cannot believe it!'

Charles didn't bother to prompt. He knew it was all about to come out.

'Do you know what they have asked me to do? Cool as you like, Paul bloody Lexington has asked me to sit in the wings for the entire run of this play and feed Micky Banks his lines!'

'What, you mean to be a kind of private prompter, whispering at him right through the play?'

'No, it's a bit more sophisticated than that. This is a deaf-aid job.'

'I'm sorry. I don't understand.'

'Oh, haven't you heard of these things? It has been done before in similar circumstances. It's a new device, whereby, thanks to the wonders of electronics, a star can still give a performance without bothering to learn the lines.'

'Explain.'

'Very simple, really. It's a short-wave radio transmitter. Some lemon – me, if

Paul Lexington has his way – sits in the wings feeding the part line by line into the transmitter. The character on stage, for reasons which may possibly be explained by the insertion of a line or two into the script, wears a deaf-aid...'

'Which acts as a receiver?'

'Exactly.'

'But does it work?'

'It has worked in some very eminent cases. Has to be modern dress obviously, and ideally an elderly character. You can't have Romeo swarming up the balcony in doublet, hose and hearing aid. But the part Micky's playing...why not?'

'I'm amazed. I never heard of that being done.'

'Well, now you know. And if ever you see an actor on stage with a deaf-aid that is not integral to the plot – be suspicious.'

'Has Micky agreed to use it?'

'He's still blustering and saying he never will and he once learnt Iago in three days, but he'll have to come round. There's no alternative. Except for the obvious one.'

'Which is?'

'Reverting to the original casting.' Alex Household let out the words in a hiss of frustration.

'Which they won't now they've got Micky's name all over the posters.'

'No, of course they won't.'

'I agree, it's a bit of a cheek, asking you to do it.'

'Oh, you should have heard the way it was put. Paul Lexington at his greasiest. Of course, Alex old man, it could be done by an A.S.M., but you do know the part so well, you could time it properly. And of course we would raise your money for doing it.'

'By how much?' No actor could have resisted asking the question.

'Fifty quid a week.'

'That's pretty good.'

'Oh yes, Paul Lexington pays you well for totally humiliating yourself.'

'So you told him to get stuffed, did you?'

'No, I haven't yet.' A cold smile came to Alex Household's lips. 'And do you know, I'm not sure that I will.'

'You mean you'll accept it?'

'I just might.'

'Good idea,' said Charles soothingly. 'Take the money and don't think about it. That's always been my philosophy.'

'Yes.' Alex's mind was elsewhere. 'Because now I come to think about it, it could be a good job.'

'Sure, sure.'

'A position of power.'

'Power?'

'Yes. How does one gain revenge for humiliation'?'

'I've no idea.' Charles didn't like the way the conversation was going. The old light of paranoia gleamed in Alex's eye.

'Why, you humiliate someone else.'

'Maybe, but –'

'And if you're stuck in the wings feeding lines to some senile old fool who can't remember them…' he laughed harshly, '…then it's really up to you what lines you feed.'

By the Saturday morning Michael Banks had accepted the inevitable. He sat in shamefaced silence while Paul Lexington explained to the company what was going to be done and was still silent, but attentive, while Wallas Ward, who had encountered the deaf-aid on a previous production, demonstrated the apparatus.

They started rehearsing with it straight away. Alex Household sat in a chair by the wall, smugly reading the lines into a small transmitter with an aerial, while Michael Banks moved about the stage area with the deaf-aid in his ear.

'We can't really work out sound levels properly until we get into the theatre. Better just work on timing the lines,' advised Wallas Ward.

'Come the day,' asked Alex languidly, 'where will I perch? On the Prompt Side?'

'No. You'd be too near the Stage Manager's desk there, might pick up his cues on the transmitter. No, you should sit OP.' Wallas Ward used the theatrical jargon for the side opposite the Stage Manager.

'Fine,' said Alex, obtrusively cooperative.

They started. It was not easy. Michael Banks was not used to acting with a voice murmuring continuously in his ear, and Alex Household found it difficult to time the lines right. If he went at the natural pace, Michael Banks got lost and confused, unable to speak one line while hearing the next. The only way they could get any semblance of acting was for Alex to speak a whole sentence, Michael to wait for the end, and then repeat it. This method didn't work too badly in exchanges of dialogue, but again it was disastrous in the long speeches. With all the waits as the lines came in, the pace slowed to nothing. The lines were coming out as written, but the play was dying a slow death.

Michael Banks struggled on gamely for about an hour, but then snatched out his ear-piece and said, 'I'm sorry, loves. It's just not working, is it?'

'Persevere,' said Wallas Ward. 'Just persevere. It takes a long time to get used to it.'

'How long? We don't have that much time.'

'Keep trying.'

It was painfully slow, but Michael Banks kept trying. His memory might have gone, but he showed plenty of guts.

Bobby Anscombe was due at three. Then they would do a run for him. By then they had to have mastered the device. By unspoken consent they worked on through their lunch-break. Every member of the company was willing their star to succeed.

Slowly, slowly, the pace started to pick up. Alex spoke more quickly and Michael Banks lost the flow less often.

It was a cooperative effort between the two. It had to be. Alex's task of dictating the pace was quite as difficult as Michael's of delivering the lines. And Charles noted with relief how Alex was rising to the challenge. Whatever resentments he might feel, whatever threats he might have voiced against the star, the understudy was now totally caught up in his task, spacing the lines with total concentration, caught up in the communal will for the subterfuge to work.

They staggered through the second act. It was half-past two, and the minutes were ticking away till Bobby Anscombe's appearance. The tension in the room built up, the concentration of the entire company focusing on Michael Banks, living every effort with him.

He was approaching the big speech about the Hooded Owl, the speech which Malcolm Harris had rightly claimed to be the centre of his play, the speech that the star had not once got through since he had abandoned his script. All was silent in the rehearsal room, except for the actors speaking their lines.

The big speech was the climax of a scene between Michael and Lesley-Jane, playing his daughter. The dialogue which ran up to it showed good pace, and the strength of the star's performance, absent in recent days, began again to show through.

The speech was partly addressed to the Hooded Owl of the title and ended with the bird in its glass case being smashed on the floor. Though this was to happen every night in the run, the Stage Management had requested that, to save on glass cases, the action should be mimed during rehearsal.

Lesley-Jane cued the big speech, and no one breathed. 'But, Father,' she said, 'you will never be forgotten.'

'Oh yes,' said Michael Banks with new authority. 'Oh yes, I will.

'Three generations of us have lived in this house. Three generations have passed through this room, slept here, argued here, made love here, even died here. And the only marks of their passage have been obliterated by the next generation. New wallpaper, new furniture, new window frames…the past is forgotten. Gone with no record. Unless you believe in some supernatural being, taking notes on our progress. A God, maybe – or, if you'd rather, a Hooded Owl…

'Why not? This stuffed bird has always been in the room. Imagine it had perception, a memory to retain our follies. Oh God, the weakness that these walls have witnessed! And this bird has lived through it all, has seen it all, impassively, in silence.'

He picked up the glass case and looked at the bird reflectively. Then, with a sudden change of mood, he shouted, 'Well, I'm not going to be spied on any longer!' and dashed it to the ground.

They all burst into applause. Lesley-Jane threw her arms round Michael

Banks's neck. The sense of achievement was felt by every one of them. Not only had he mastered the lines, he had also delivered the speech with greater power than it had ever received, either by him in rehearsal, or by Alex in performance. And yet Alex had contributed. Something of his timing, something of his delivery had come into Michael Banks's performance, giving it new depth and stature. The applause was for the joint effort.

It was five to three. Paul Lexington held up his hands for silence. His glowing face showed that he was aware of the breakthrough. 'I think we're going to be all right. We'll stop it there. Thank you all for your hard work. Bobby'll be here in a minute, and I want you all to give him a performance that'll blast him out of his seat!'

The run was not perfect, but it was good. Occasionally the timing between Alex and Michael went and the star lost his lines, but for most of the play the flow was maintained. Bobby Anscombe, who had reacted badly when he had first heard of the deaf-aid idea, was forced to admit at the end that it might work. Like everyone else, he recognised that there was no alternative.

'O.K.,' he announced to everyone in his usual grudging style. 'We're still in business. Just. But you're all going to have to work a darned sight harder. The last week's rehearsal has been a virtual write-off, and you're meant to be facing a preview audience on Monday.'

'You think we go ahead with that?' asked Paul Lexington. Clearly cancelling the previews had been one option the producers had discussed.

'We'll go ahead. The show needs the run-in, and even if it's bad, there won't be too much word-of-mouth outside the business. And any word-of-mouth'd be better than what we've got at the moment. What the hell's happening on the publicity front?' He rounded on his co-producer as he asked the question.

'Show-Off say it's all in hand.'

'A bit late to have it in hand. It should be out of hand and all over the bloody media by now. Is *anything* happening?'

'Micky's doing *Parkinson* tonight – the Beeb's sending a car about six, Micky…'

The star acknowledged this information with an exhausted nod.

'…and then there's supposed to be an interview in Atticus in *The Sunday Times* tomorrow.'

'Better than nothing, but where are the bloody posters?'

'Apparently some delay about those. You know, the people who put them up are quite difficult to organise.'

'I know that…'

'But it's supposed to be sorted out now.'

'I should bloody well hope so. We open on Thursday and at the moment we've made about as much noise as a fart in a hurricane.' Bobby Anscombe turned to Peter Hickton. 'All set for the get-in at the Variety tonight?'

The Director nodded with relish at the prospect of a sleepless night of hard work.

'Tech. run tomorrow night and D.R. Monday afternoon?'

'That's it,' Peter Hickton confirmed.

'Hmm. Well, for God's sake see that Micky and Alex get some practice with that bloody walkie-talkie tomorrow afternoon. There's a long way to go before it sounds natural.'

'Don't worry,' said Paul Lexington diplomatically. 'We'll sort it out. This is going to be a show you'll be proud to be associated with, Bobby.'

The investor barked a short, cynical laugh. 'Bloody well better be. Don't forget, Paul, we still haven't got a contract. I can still pull out if I don't like it.'

'Yes, sorry about that. There's been so much on this week I just haven't had time to get the details of the contract finalised.'

Charles wondered whether this was true or whether Paul Lexington was once again using delaying tactics for devious reasons of his own. Distrust of the producer was now instinctive.

Bobby Anscombe gave an evil grin. 'I don't mind having no contract if you don't. Gives me the freedom to walk out at will.'

But nobody believed his threat. They all knew that *The Hooded Owl* had just survived a great crisis. For the first time that week, they all dared to feel confident that the show would open the following Thursday, as planned.

CHAPTER EIGHT

THERE'S NOTHING like a long Technical Run to dissipate any euphoria attached to a theatrical production, and that was the effect of the one held for *The Hooded Owl* on the evening of Sunday, 26th October, 1980.

As is often the case with such events, it started late. Peter Hickton had had trouble with the resident stage crew at the Variety over the Saturday night. He was used to working with crews who knew him and who, like his casts, were prepared to work round the clock to achieve the effects he desired. The staff of the Variety did not have this attitude. They had no personal loyalty to him and were too strongly unionised to accept his way of working. Peter Hickton, unaware that co-operation could be bought by payment of 'negotiated extras', responded to the crew's apparent lethargy by throwing one of his tantrums, which had only served to make them less willing to help out. Paul Lexington and Wallas Ward had had to devote much energy to smoothing ruffled feathers, nobody had got much sleep, and everything was way behind schedule.

When eventually, after ten o'clock at night, the run started, it was very slow. Apart from the unfamiliarity of the entrances and exits and the other customary problems for the cast, Peter Hickton had not had time to complete the lighting plot, so much of that was being done in the course of the run, which meant endless waits while new lighting settings were agreed. This left the cast standing around; they got bored and giggly, which set off explosions of bad temper from the technical staffs working around them. The atmosphere degenerated.

Members of the resident stage crew wandered round, looking at their watches and making dark remarks about amateurism and provincial rep. and the folly of trying to bring in a show so quickly and the unlikelihood of its being presentable in time for the Monday night preview.

Paul Lexington rushed around, also looking at his watch and working out how much overtime he was going to have to pay (or, to Charles's suspicious mind, how much overtime he was going to avoid paying).

The latest technical innovation, the deaf-aid transmitter, did not make things any easier. For a start, the resident sound engineer didn't like it, because he hadn't been consulted about its introduction and he maintained that he should be responsible for all sound equipment. This led to a circuitous discussion with Paul Lexington about whether it was sound equipment or not, which was only settled after much wrangling (and, almost definitely, money changing hands).

But even when its use had been approved, it didn't work as it should. Michael Banks, who by this time looked terminally tired, seemed to have lost the knack of timing which he had so laboriously achieved the day before, and so his lines were once again all over the place. Alex, from his position in the wings, was not concentrating as much and could not easily be kept informed about when they were stopping and starting, going back to rehearse lighting changes and so on, with the result that he was often feeding the wrong words.

Setting the transmitter's volume level was also a problem. If it was too low, Michael kept mishearing lines and producing bizarre variations, many of which would, under other circumstances, have been funny, and did in fact produce some snorts of ill-advised laughter from the overwrought cast. If the level was set too high, Michael could hear all right, but unfortunately so could the rest of the theatre, in a sort of ghostly pre-echo.

But the climax of technical disaster came, as the climax always did, with the Hooded Owl speech. Charles was out in front and saw what happened.

It was then getting on for three in the morning, but in the last quarter of an hour things had been getting better. With the end of the play in sight, everyone seemed to get a second (or possibly tenth) wind. Michael Banks, for the first time in the run, showed some signs of his real power as the Hooded Owl speech drew near.

'But, Father,' said Lesley-Jane, 'you will never be forgotten.'

'Oh yes. Oh yes, I will.

'Three generations of us have lived in this house. Three generations have passed through this room, slept here, argued here, made love here, even *picked up a passenger in Shaftesbury Avenue to take out to Neasden....*'

There was silence in the theatre. The star, suddenly aware of what he had said, looked pitifully puzzled. Charles wondered if Alex Household had carried out his threat of feeding the wrong lines. If so, he had chosen a singularly inappropriate moment for the experiment.

It was some time before the cause of the error was identified. The transmitter was on the same wave-length as a passing radio-cab.

Somehow the Technical Run ended. Somehow a Dress Rehearsal was achieved on the Monday afternoon. And somehow, not too long after eight o'clock on the Monday evening, the curtain rose for the first time on the London production of *The Hooded Owl* by Malcolm Harris.

It was just competent. To say more would have been to overstate the case, but as a first preview it got by. The West End had witnessed many worse first previews.

The house was about a third full and they were respectful if not ecstatic in their reaction. Those of the cast who remembered the euphoria of Taunton were disappointed, but they comforted themselves with the fact that they were at least *on*, something which three days previously had looked most unlikely.

Michael Banks managed his lines fairly well, with only a couple of mishearings and one awfully long thirty seconds where he totally lost the thread. Perversely, George Birkitt seemed to have lost his lines completely and had to take at least half a dozen prompts. Charles Paris was heard to remark cynically that George, having seen that the star had got a deaf-aid, thought he ought to have one too.

Though he got the lines, Michael Banks's performance was very subdued, only a vestige of what he could achieve. That was just the result of fatigue. The strains of the last fortnight were catching up with him, and he looked every one of his sixty-four years.

No one was too worried about it. After all, these were only previews. Wait till the first night they thought, and watch 'Doctor Theatre' do his work.

Two more previews to go, and then, at seven o'clock on the Thursday (early so that the critics could get their copy in), the curtain would go up on the first night proper of *The Hooded Owl*.

'Hello, it's me.'

'Charles.'

'Sorry to ring you at school, but I wanted to get hold of you and I'm in the theatre in the evenings.'

'Yes.'

'Can you talk, Frances?'

'Well, I've got someone with me, but if you're quick…'

'It's about the first night.'

'Oh yes. Of your play. When is it?'

'Thursday.'

'Ah.'

'I wondered if you could come…'

'Thursday. Hmm. I am actually meant to be going to a meeting…'

'Frances…'

'But I suppose I could…Yes, all right, Charles. After all, I don't want to miss your opening in this wonderful part you told me about.'

'Ah.'

'What?'

'Hmm. It is a long time since we spoke, isn't it?'

'What do you mean?'

'I'm afraid you won't have the pleasure of seeing me on-stage. Instead you will have the no doubt greater pleasure of sitting beside me.'

'Why? What's happened?'

'I'll explain all on Thursday. See you in the foyer of the Variety Theatre in Macklin Street at quarter to seven.'

'All right.'

'Goodbye.'

'Goodbye.'

He shivered. Was it imagination, or did she really sound colder towards him?

There was a small reception after the Tuesday night preview. This was not Paul Lexington pushing the boat out for the cast, which would have been very out of character; it was for the ticket agencies.

Charles had forgotten how important these now were to the survival of a West End show. As transport costs rose and London's reputation for violence after dark grew, business was increasingly dependent on coachloads of theatre-goers coming in from the provinces. So the ticket agencies and the people who organised the coaches were very important and managements were wise to make a fuss of them.

Hence the reception, with bottles of wine and the odd crisp provided by Paul Lexington Productions. It was typical of the outfit that before the performance, the Company Manager, Wallas Ward, had come round the dressing rooms with a message from the management. The message had been that the reception was for the ticket agencies, and the cast were requested to ration themselves to one glass of wine each. It was like the old admonition at nursery teas, F.H.B. (Family Hold Back).

Charles thought it was appalling. He wouldn't have minded the meanness of only allowing one glass each, if it hadn't been that the reception was so timed as to prevent that vital half-hour in the pub before closing time, which was so much a part of the necessary wind-down from giving of himself in performance. (The fact that, as understudy, he wasn't giving a performance did not reduce the necessity for the wind-down.)

But the cast were all very professional and knew the importance of the agencies' backing, so they presented their most charming fronts. Needless to say, the focus of the visitors' attention was Michael Banks, who, in spite of his fatigue, made himself most affable and approachable. Charles admired the skill with which the old pro conveyed an air of ease and relaxation, of the company having been one happy family, of the great fun he had had rehearsing for the show. At one point he overheard the star laughing and saying, 'Long time since I've done theatre. Even had a little trouble learning the old lines. Still, got that sorted out now.'

As an exercise in the skills of understatement and of giving the wrong impression without actually lying, Charles thought that took some beating.

He himself got landed with a boring little man from Luton, who was a great stalwart of the local amateur dramatic society there and clearly, though he didn't quite put it into words, thought *The Hooded Owl* a pale shadow of their recent production of *When We Are Married*. 'Also,' he said expanding his criticism, 'your show's too long.'

'Oh really?' said Charles mildly. 'You mean it sags?'

'No, but it finishes too late. Coach party'd be very late back to Luton, and they don't like that.'

'Oh.'

'What you want to do...' The man paused, then magnanimously decided to give the benefit of his expertise, 'What you want to do is chop ten minutes out of it. Then you may have a show.'

'Oh,' said Charles. 'Thank you very much.'

It was Paul Lexington's party, and since courting the ticket agencies was very much a management job, Charles was surprised to notice that the Producer wasn't there. Wallas Ward was filling in, exercising his rather effete charm on the guests, but it wasn't the same. Charles heard more than one question as to where Paul was. The ticket agents felt they weren't getting the full treatment.

The Producer did finally arrive about half an hour into the party, and he scurried around meeting everyone, making up for his earlier absence. He did so with his customary boyish bounce, and yet there was something strange in his manner. His face had the dead whiteness of someone in shock. Charles wondered what new disaster had hit the production, or which of the Producer's dubious deals had just blown up in his face.

He was soon to find out. The guests were eventually ushered out at about eleven forty-five. This took some doing, as they seemed prepared to stay all night. They didn't seem to share their clients' reservations about getting home late. It was only when the bottles of wine had been firmly put away and the last glass drained that they got the message. (Charles also got the message that he wasn't going to get the quick slurp of wine at the end of the evening that he had been promising himself.)

Etiquette had demanded that none of the cast should leave until the last of their guests had gone, but, as soon as the final raincoat disappeared round the door of the theatre bar, the entire company leapt for their belongings to make a quick getaway.

'Shall we go, Micky?' Charles heard Lesley-Jane Decker say to the star.

Which was in itself interesting.

But they were all stopped by Paul Lexington clapping his hands. 'Listen, everyone. I have some news. I'm afraid once again it's good news and bad news. The good news is that we've got the ticket agencies on our side. They like the show and they're going to recommend it to their clients – on one condition.'

'That condition is that we cut ten minutes out of the running time.' This was greeted by a ripple of protest. Malcolm Harris, who would have been the most vigorous protester, was not present, but Peter Hickton, acting on the author's behalf, remonstrated. 'Look, we can't do that. The play's really tight now. We'll ruin it.'

'Sorry,' said Paul. 'Got to be done. Anything'll cut down if it has to. Peter, see me in the production office at ten and we'll go through the script. Then we'll have a full cast call at two to give you the cuts. O.K., Wallas?'

The Company Manager nodded.

'We should let Malcolm know,' protested Peter Hickton. 'It is his play.'

'There isn't time. Anyway, it's not his play now. I've got the rights. I'm sorry it's necessary, but it is. We won't get the coach parties if the show ends as late as it does now.'

If anyone needed evidence of the power of the ticket agencies, there it was. Grumbling slightly, but accepting the inevitable, the cast once again made to leave, but Paul Lexington again stopped them.

'Then there's the bad news.'

They froze. They had all thought the cuts were the bad news.

'I've just come from a meeting with Bobby Anscombe. I am afraid we could not agree over certain...artistic matters. As a result, he has decided to withdraw his backing from the production.'

This hit them like a communal heart-attack. As the shock receded, Charles found himself wondering what the disagreement had really been about. He felt certain that Paul Lexington had been trying to pull a fast one on his Co-producer. Maybe the missing contract had finally appeared and Bobby Anscombe hadn't liked its provisions. It must have been something like that; Charles was beginning to understand the way Paul Lexington worked. But if he had tried to dupe the wily Bobby Anscombe as easily as the innocent Malcolm Harris, it was no wonder that he had come unstuck.

But, like the eternal Wobbly Man, the young Producer bounced back. 'Now this is a pity, but it's not a disaster. I would rather lose Bobby's backing than compromise my artistic integrity over this production.'

The fact that no one laughed out loud at this remark suggested to Charles that they didn't all share his view of the man. For most of them, his plausible exterior was still convincing.

'There are other investors, and don't worry, I've still got plenty of backing for this show. I'm not going to go bankrupt. Don't worry about a thing. *The Hooded Owl* will go on, and, what's more, it'll be a huge success!'

But, in spite of the stirring words, in spite of the cast's cheers, Charles could see panic in Paul Lexington's eyes.

And when he thought about it, it didn't surprise him He didn't know the details of the funding of the show, but he could piece a certain amount together. Paul Lexington Productions had been able to mount *The Hooded Owl* at Taunton, but had been unable to bring it into town without Bobby Anscombe's support.

And that support had been bought at the cost of considerably increasing the budget. With the Taunton cast, it remained a comparatively cheap show. But with Michael Banks's – and indeed George Birkitt's – names above the title, it was a much more expensive proposition.

And now the support, whose condition the cast changes had been, had been withdrawn.

Michael Banks was suddenly a very expensive albatross around Paul Lexington's neck.

CHAPTER NINE

THE UNDERSTUDY'S is a strange role, and never is he made more aware of its strangeness than on a first night. He is caught up in the communal excitement, without the prospect of release that performance gives. He cannot quite detach himself or even avoid nerves; he has to be eternally in readiness; only when the final curtain has fallen can he be sure he will not have to go on. During the 'half' before the curtain rises, he has his twitchiest moments. He has to watch the actor he would replace for signs of strain or imminent collapse and wonder nervously whether he *could* actually remember the lines if he had to go on. Sometimes the worst happens, and the actor does not appear for the 'half'. Then the understudy goes through agonies of indecision before the Company Manager gives him the order to get into costume and make-up. And how often, as the understudy trembles in the wings awaiting the rise of the curtain, does the real actor appear, full of apologies about a power failure on the Underground or the traffic on the Westway.

It is almost impossible for the understudy to achieve mental equilibrium. His thoughts sway constantly between the desire to go on and the desire to settle down for a relaxed evening with a book in the secure knowledge that he won't have to go on. (This at least is true of *aspiring* understudies, those who really wish they had parts. There is a breed of professional understudy, often, if female, actresses who have semi-retired to bring up families, for whom the job is all that they require. It gives them the contact with the theatre that they crave, without the total commitment which acting every night demands.)

Charles Paris was not a professional understudy. He still had dreams. And, though those dreams had taken something of a battering since the heady days of Taunton, they were resilient and survived in amended form. The image of suddenly being called in to take over from George Birkitt and astounding the critics with his unsung brilliance was one that would not go away, however hard he tried to suppress it.

He knew that that was one of the reasons why he went to see George Birkitt first on his back-stage round at the 'half'. The vulture instinct would make him acutely observant for any signs of imminent cerebral haemorrhage in the actor.

George Birkitt, however, looked remarkably fit. He was gazing into his make-up mirror, playing the same game that he always did on the monitor screens in television studios – in other words, deciding which was his best profile.

'Hello, George. Just dropped in to say all the best.'

'Oh, thanks, Charles.' He seemed completely to have forgotten that Charles had ever played the part. 'I think the director and some of the cast of *Fly-Buttons* should be out front tonight.'

He couldn't resist mentioning the television series, just in case anyone should forget he was in it.

'Oh great. I'll be out there.'

'Good. Then you could do me a favour. You know in the dinner party scene, when I'm down-stage doing my incest speech...'

'Yes.'

'Well, could you tell me what Micky's up to during that? I'm sure he makes some sort of reaction I can't see. Could you watch out for it? I mean, I know he's the star and all that, but I'm damned if I'm going to be upstaged, even by him...'

The Star Dressing Room was Charles's next port of call. Its door was guarded by Cerberus in the form of Micky Banks's dresser, Harve, a redoubtable old queen who had been with his master for years. Recognising the visitor, he said, 'O.K., just a quick word. Don't want him tired.'

'Fine.'

In spite of his dresser's cares, Michael Banks did look absolutely shattered through his heavy make-up.

'All the best, Micky.'

'Thanks, Charles old boy.' The star smiled graciously.

'Sure you'll knock 'em dead tonight.'

'Hope so, hope so.'

There was a tap at the door and Harve grudgingly admitted Lesley-Jane Decker. As at Taunton, she was bearing gifts. The shape of the parcel she put on Michael's make-up table showed that, for him at least, she had graduated to full-size bottles of champagne.

She put her arms around his neck and said, 'All you wish for yourself, darling.'

'Thank you, love. Same to you.' Michael Banks grinned indulgently. 'Is the redoubtable Valerie Cass up in your dressing room ready to give you lots of tips?'

Lesley-Jane laughed. 'She's out front where she should be. With Daddy.'

'She'll be round before the evening's out.'

Charles felt awkward, excluded from their scene. 'Well, I'll...er...' He edged towards the door, which Harve obligingly – indeed, pointedly opened for him.

Outside stood Alex Household.

'Break a leg, Micky,' he said with a rather strained intonation. 'I'll be out there supporting you.'

'Bless you.' The star turned round to his understudy. 'Couldn't do it without you, you know.'

'I know.' Alex Household gave the words perhaps too much emphasis.

Lesley-Jane could not keep her back to the door indefinitely and turned. Charles noted how pale she looked, almost ill.

'*Bonne chance*, Lesley-Jane,' pronounced Alex formally. 'See you're doing your rounds with the first night presents.'

He said it deliberately to make her feel awkward. And succeeded.

'Yes…yes. I'm…er…afraid I didn't get round to doing anything for the understudies.'

'No,' Alex Household snorted with laughter. 'No, of course not.'

And, slamming the door, he left the Star Dressing Room.

Charles caught up with him in the Green Room. Alex's strange position in the production must have been making all of the usual understudy agonies even worse. Charles wanted to say something to help, but all he could think of was 'Break a leg'.

'Oh, you think you should wish luck to people who merely feed lines, do you? People whose job could be equally well – and probably better done – by a tape recorder.'

'We all need luck,' said Charles gently.

Alex laughed. 'Yes, we do, don't we?'

Then he started trembling. His whole body shook uncontrollably. His teeth chattered and he whimpered.

'Are you all right?'

'Yes, I'm…Yes, I'm…Yes, I will be.'

And, sure enough, he soon had control of himself again. The shivering subsided.

'Sure you're O.K.? There'll be St. John Ambulance people out front.'

'No, I'm all right.' But Alex's eyes belied his words. They were wide with fear. 'This is how it started last time.'

'How what started?'

'The breakdown.' And he was seized by another spasm. The worst of it passed, but his teeth still chattered feebly.

'Are you cold or…'

'Cold? No. Or if I am now, I won't be later. I'll be roasting. Have you any idea how hot it gets in my little solitary nest on the O.P. side? Don't worry, I'll be hot enough. In fact, I'll take this off while I think.'

He hung his jacket on a hook in the Green Room. As it swung against the wall, there was a thud of something hard in the pocket.

Alex Household gave a twisted smile and announced ironically, 'Right, here we go. Tonight will be the climax of my career. Twenty-three years in the business has all been the build-up for this, as I take on my most challenging role ever – bloody prompter!'

'Come on, Alex. It's not so bad, it's –'

'Isn't it? What do you know about how bad it is?'

Charles retreated under this assault. 'I just meant…Never mind. Back to what I said first – break a leg.'

'I should think that will be the very least I will break,' said Alex

Household, and walked towards the stage.

Charles knew it would be unprofessional to use the pass-door from backstage
to the auditorium once the house had started to fill, so he went out of the
Stage Door to walk round.

The first thing he came across outside was Malcolm Harris being sick in
the gutter.

'Are you O.K.?'

'Yes, I...will be.'

'Don't worry. It's going fine. And at least Micky's deaf-aid thing
guarantees that he does actually say the lines you wrote.'

'Yes, I suppose so.' The schoolmaster looked up at him pitifully. 'I just don't
think I can sit out there and watch it all. I'm so jumpy, I'll be sick again or...'

'Then don't sit there. Stand at the back, go backstage, go out for a walk, do
whatever makes you feel most relaxed.'

'But if I don't sit in my seat, I'll be leaving my wife and my wife's mother
on their own.'

'Well, you could do that, couldn't you?'

'Yes, I suppose I *could*.' But obviously it was an idea that had never occurred
to him before, and his mind would take a little while to accommodate it.

'Frances, I'm sorry I'm late.'

'When were you ever otherwise?'

'I wasn't late for that meal in Hampstead.' Even as he said it, he wished he
hadn't. There was something about the memory of that evening that made
him uneasy. He kissed her clumsily to change the subject.

'Anyway, what is all this? Why aren't you going to be on-stage? When we
last met, you told me...'

'I'll explain. Have we got time for a drink?'

They would have had, but there was such a crush in the bar, there was no
prospect of getting served before the curtain went up. Which was annoying.

While they reconnoitred the bar and found their seats (on the aisle, so that,
if his services as an understudy were required, Charles could be quickly
extracted), he gave Frances a brief résumé of how he had lost his part.

'Well, I think that's rotten,' she said, with genuine annoyance. It cheered
Charles, to hear her angry on his behalf. He took her hand and felt the scar on
her thumb, legacy of an accident with a kitchen knife in the early days of
their marriage. Accumulated emotion made him weak, needing her.

'Charles!'

'Well, if it isn't that naughty Charles Paris...'

'With his lovely wife...'

'Frances, isn't it? Oh, it's been so long...'

'An absolute age...'

This stereo assault on them came from two men in late middle age, bizarrely costumed in matching Victorian evening dress. Instantly Charles recognised William Bartlemas and Kevin O'Rourke, a pair of indefatigable first-nighters.

'And how *are* you, Charles?' demanded Bartlemas.

'Yes, how *are* you?' echoed O'Rourke.

Neither waited for a reply as they galloped on. 'Are you still up to your naughty detective things we hear so much about?'

'Yes, *are* you?'

'No, not at the moment. I –' was all he managed to get out.

'Another first night. I don't know…'

'Not as glittering as it should be, is it, Bartlemas…?'

'No, not really *glittering*, no…'

'So few people dress up for first nights these days…'

'It is disgraceful…'

'Appalling…'

'That lot…' he gestured to a large block of seats full of people in evening dress, 'have made the effort…'

'Yes, but they're Micky Banks's chums…'

'Oh well…'

'At least that generation knows how to behave at a first night…'

'*That* generation, dear? They're *our* generation!' This witticism reduced both of them to helpless laughter. But not for long enough for Charles or Frances to say anything.

'Lot of paper in tonight, isn't there?' said Bartlemas, looking up to the Circle and Gallery.

'Lot of paper, yes…'

'Paper?' Frances managed to query.

'Free seats, love. Often happens for a first night if it's not selling…'

'Yes, blocks of tickets sent round the nurses' homes, that sort of thing…'

'Believe me, love, if you go to as many first nights as we do, you get to recognise them…'

'Recognise individual nurses even…'

'There's one with a wall-eye and a wart on her nose who I swear goes to more first nights than we do…'

This also was apparently a joke. They roared with laughter.

'Why is there so much paper?' Charles managed to ask.

'No publicity, dear…'

'And the theatres out of the way…'

'People'd flood to see Micky Banks…'

'Simply flood…'

'But they've got to know where he is…'

'As you say, no publicity…'

'*By* the way, who's Dottie with tonight?'

'Don't know, but looks such a nice young man…'

'Joy-boy?'

'Maybe...'

'Oh,' said Charles. 'You mean she and Micky don't...'

'Now you don't want us telling tales out of school, do you?'

'Oh, you naughty Charles Paris, you...'

They seemed set to continue talking forever, but the auditorium lights began to dim, so they scuttered off, giggling, to find their seats.

Charles and Frances sat down too. And with feelings too complex to itemise, he watched the curtain rise on the first official London performance of *The Hooded Owl*.

The applause at the interval was very generous. It almost always is on a first night, when the audience tends to be Mums, Dads, husbands, wives, lovers and friends-in-the-business. But, even allowing for that, Charles reckoned they were enjoying it.

Michael Banks was giving a performance of effortless authority. Some of the *cognoscenti* had recognised why he was wearing the deaf-aid, but for the majority, it just seemed to be part of the character, justified by a couple of new lines.

The performances were all up, with the possible exception of Lesley-Jane Decker, who seemed to be giving a little less than usual. Probably the result of nerves at her first West End opening.

But what also shone through was how good a play *The Hooded Owl* was. It was very conventional, even old-fashioned, but its tensions built up in just the right way, and it gripped like a strangler's hand.

Charles looked round to where he knew Malcolm Harris should be, but the seat between the ferret-faced women was empty. The author had taken his advice and was presumably prowling around somewhere. His ferret-faced women looked unamused by his absence.

Charles and Frances joined the exodus to the bar and met another couple coming towards them. The man was unfamiliar, but there was no mistaking the woman with her subsidised red hair.

'Charles, darling!'

'Oh. Valerie. I don't think you know my wife, Frances...'

'But of course I do. We met in Cheltenham.'

'Did we?' asked Frances, clueless as to whom she was addressing.

'Yes, yes, all those years ago.'

'Oh.'

'And this...' said Valerie Cass, with no attempt to disguise her contempt, 'is my husband.'

He was twenty years older than his wife and looked meek and long-suffering. As indeed he would have to be. Either that or divorced. Or dead.

'Oh God,' Valerie Cass cooed. 'I know what you must be feeling, Charles. I feel it myself. Just aching to be up there with them. Only we who have worked in the theatre can understand the ache.'

She raised one hand dramatically to her forehead. She was wearing long evening gloves, indeed seemed to be fully dressed for a ball.

'Oh, it's not so bad,' Charles offered feebly.

'And I'm so worried about Lesley-Jane,' she emoted.

'Why?'

'The performance just isn't there.'

'Oh, I wouldn't say that. She's a bit subdued, but she's –'

'No, it's more than that. I know that girl, know her as only a mother can, and I know she's not well. I think I'd better go backstage and see what's the matter.'

'Oh, I don't think you should,' her husband interposed mildly. 'Wait till the end. I'm sure you shouldn't go round in the middle of a performance. Not the thing at all.'

'And what...' she withered him with a glance, 'what do you know about it?' And she stalked off to the foyer.

Mr. Decker grinned weakly, made a vague gesture with his hand and moved off down the aisle to buy an ice-cream.

The crush in the bar was worse than before the show, but this time Charles was luckier. Lucky to the extent of meeting a friend who had had the foresight to order a bottle of champagne for the interval.

'Gerald!'

The solicitor looked immaculate as ever, in perfectly-tailored evening dress. His wife Kate also looked perfect. She and Frances fell on each other. They hadn't met for years. Used to be great friends, before Charles walked out. Used to go around as a foursome. Guilt was added to the turmoil of Charles's feelings.

Gerald fought to the bar for a couple more glasses and generously shared the bottle.

'Doing any detective work, Charles?' He had helped the actor on one or two cases and found an enthusiasm for investigation which he could never muster for his extremely lucrative solicitor's practice.

'No,' Charles replied with satisfaction. It was pleasant not to have the complexities of crime on his mind for a change.

'Pity.'

'But why are you here, Gerald? Got money in it?'

Gerald was quite a frequent 'angel', though he kept his investments very secret, and winced at Charles's question. 'No, in a sense I'm here under false pretences. I was coming because a client was involved as a backer, but he's no longer involved and...'

'Bobby Anscombe?'

'Right.'

'Yes. I gather he had an "artistic disagreement" with Paul Lexington.'

'"Artistic disagreement" – my foot! You should have seen the contract

Lexington tried to get him to sign.'

Charles was glad to have his surmise confirmed. 'Yes, I shouldn't think anyone steals a march on Bobby Anscombe.'

'Or me, Charles. Or me.'

Just as he was returning to his seat, Charles met Malcolm Harris rushing up the aisle. The author had reported in to his ferret-faced women, but was now off again.

'I should think you're pleased, aren't you?' asked Charles genially.

'Pleased?' hissed the schoolmaster. 'That bastard Banks is just making nonsense of it.'

'What do you mean?'

'I mean he's cutting great chunks. Big speeches – just because he doesn't like them, just cutting them out.'

'But, Malcolm, *he's* not making the cuts. They were made yesterday for –'

But the author was already out of earshot.

Oh dear. Another black mark for Paul Lexington's liaison and diplomacy.

The audience settled quickly after the interval and was soon once more caught up in the mounting dramatic tension of *The Hooded Owl*. Charles found himself swept along too. He realised that the cuts forced on the production had in fact helped it. By trimming down the first act, they kept the pace going, and the second act benefited.

And Michael Banks was growing in stature by the minute. Once again, Charles was aware of Alex Household's contribution to the performance. With him timing the lines, the star could concentrate just on the emotional truth of his acting, and the result was very powerful.

The Hooded Owl speech approached, and Charles felt the excitement building inside him. As ever, it would be the climax; this time the climax of one of the finest performances he had ever witnessed.

The scene of father and daughter in the bedroom began. Lesley-Jane was still low-key, but it did not seem to matter. It almost helped. The pallor of her acting threw into relief the power of Michael's.

'But, Father,' she said, 'you will never be forgotten.'

'Oh yes. Oh yes, I will.'

They stood facing each other. Maybe, over her shoulder, he could see his faithful feed in the wings. Probably not. He was too deeply into the part to see anything outside the stage.

The silence was so total that the auditorium might have been empty.

'Three generations of us have lived in this house. Three generations have passed through this room, slept here, argued here, made love here, even died here. And the only marks of their passage have been obliterated by the next generation. New wallpaper, new furniture, new window frames...the past is forgotten. Gone with no record. Unless you believe in some supernatural being, taking notes of our progress. A God, maybe – or, if you'd rather, a Hooded Owl…"

As he mentioned the bird, he turned his back on Lesley-Jane to look at it in the glass case. Every eye in the audience followed him.

'Why not? This stuffed bird has always been in the room. Imagine it had perception, a memory to retain our follies. Oh Lord!'

Something had gone wrong. The audience did not know yet, but Charles, so familiar with the script, knew.

Slowly Michael Banks wheeled round. He looked puzzled, and seemed to be looking beyond Lesley-Jane into the wings.

'No,' he said. 'No, put it down. You mustn't do that to me. You daren't. Please. Please I –'

There was a gunshot. Michael Banks clutched at his chest and slowly tottered to his knees. Lesley-Jane turned to look into the wings, and screamed.

The tableau was held for a moment, and the curtain swiftly fell.

The audience didn't know. Still they weren't sure. Was this a bizarre new twist of the plot? What had happened? The darkened auditorium was filled with muttering.

Then the house-lights came up. The curtain twitched and the Company Manager, Wallas Ward, resplendent in midnight blue dinner jacket, appeared through the centre.

'Ladies and gentlemen, I regret to have to inform you that, due to an accident to Mr. Banks, we will be unable to continue the performance.'

He did not say that the accident which had befallen Mr. Banks was death by shooting.

And he did not say that, even if they'd wished to finish the play with his understudy, they couldn't, because Alex Household had run out of the theatre immediately after the shooting.

CHAPTER TEN

CHARLES GOT round to the Stage Door as quickly as he could. Frances followed silently. One of her good qualities was the ability to keep quiet when there was nothing appropriate to say.

They were there before the rush. There were a few people milling around, but not yet the main surge of puzzled well-wishers, police, press and sensation-seekers.

Charles found the Stage Doorman, who was already regaling a little circle of cast with what he had seen. The murder had only occurred ten minutes before, but the old man already saw himself in the role of vital witness, and was polishing the phrases in a story which he would tell many times.

'I heard the shot over the loudspeaker. I knew there was something wrong. I've heard that play so many times in the past few days, I knew the lines wasn't right. Mind you, then I didn't know it was a shot. Could've been something falling over on-stage, or a light-bulb blowing but something inside me knew it was serious. I felt like a cold hand on my heart...' he paused dramatically, relishing the metaphor which he then spoiled by mixing it, '...as if someone had walked over my grave.

'Next thing I knew Mr. Household was rushing past me out of the door. It was so quick. I didn't have time to stop him,' he said, suggesting that under any other circumstances he would have downed the suspect with a flying tackle. 'Not, of course, that I realised what he'd done then. I didn't know he'd just shot Mr. Banks.'

'Are you sure he had?' asked Charles.

'Well, of course he had.'

'I mean, was the gun in his hand?'

'No,' the old man was forced to concede, 'but –'

'Was he wearing a jacket?'

'I think so. I didn't notice. It was very quick, like I said.' The old man sounded testy. Charles's questions were spoiling his narrative flow.

'Wait here a minute, Frances.' He went through to the Green Room, hoping that he'd find Alex's jacket still hanging there, with the gun still cold in its pocket, with all five shots still unfired.

Alex was a prickly person, an unbalanced person, sometimes an infuriating person, but Charles didn't want to think of him as a murderer.

Various members of the cast were lolling about the Green Room, in various stages of shell-shock. George Birkitt was looking distinctly peeved, aware that Michael Banks had upstaged him in a way that was quite unanswerable. In a corner Malcolm Harris slumped on a chair, pale and whimpering.

The coat-hook was empty. Exonerating Alex wasn't going to be that easy. And was exonerating him appropriate anyway? All the evidence so far pointed to the fact that he had done the killing.

Charles wandered through the door on to the stage, and found even more evidence. Clinching evidence.

Backstage the overhead working light gleamed on something metal that lay discarded by the door. Charles recognised it instantly.

It was the Smith and Wesson Chiefs Special revolver that he had first seen in the Number One dressing room of the Prince's Theatre, Taunton.

He knelt down and, so as to avoid leaving fingerprints, felt the barrel with the back of his hand.

It was warm.

Depression flooded through him like fatigue. He didn't quite know why he'd hoped that Alex could be cleared of the murder, but the confirmation of his friend's guilt sapped him of all energy.

He left the gun where it was. The police would find it soon enough. Back at the Stage Door, Frances looked at him and, instantly reading his emotional state, took his hand.

'Shall we go?'

'I don't know. I feel I should stay around, try and find out what's happened and...'

But the decision was made for him. The police had arrived while he had been on stage, and a uniformed constable was now clearing the growing crowd round the Stage Door.

'All right, if you could move along, please. There's nothing to see, and we've got a lot to do, so we'd be very grateful if you could just go home. Come on, move along, please.'

He came face to face with Charles and Frances. 'On your way, please. On your way. Unless you're connected with the show, could you go home, please.'

'I'm a member of the cast,' said Charles.

'Oh. Were you backstage during the show?'

'No, actually I was in the auditorium.'

'Well, in that case, could you go home, please. You'll hear anything there is to hear in the morning.'

Not only excluded from performing, the understudy was not even to be allowed to take part in the murder investigation.

'Come along,' said Frances. 'Come home with me.'

Back at the house in Muswell Hill, they went upstairs and stood on the landing. 'I think the spare room, Charles,' she said.

He nodded. She hadn't said it unkindly, and, in the state he was in, it seemed appropriate. And, in spite of it, he felt closer to her than he had for months.

The tensions of the week had taken their toll and he slept instantly. He had no dreams. But when he woke at quarter past six, his mind was full of ugly images, of Alex trembling, of the gun, and, most of all, of the expression of bewilderment and betrayal on Michael Banks's face as he clutched at his chest and sank to the ground.

To frighten off these visions, and because further sleep was out of the question, he went downstairs to make some tea. It was strange being in the kitchen of the house they had shared. He was aware of the parts of it that remained unchanged and equally of the innovations. Nothing could he view without emotion. He saw Frances had bought a dishwasher. Yes, time was precious. She was a busy lady these days.

And she wanted to sell the house. That thought disturbed him almost more than the events of the previous night.

The kettle boiled. He warmed the pot, instinctively found the tea in the caddy Frances's Auntie Pamela had given them as a wedding present, and brewed up. He arranged two mugs and a milk-bottle on a tray with the pot, and took them upstairs.

The door was ajar, and he pushed it gently open. Frances was still asleep. She lay firmly in the middle of their double bed, as he supposed she must do every night. In repose her face looked relaxed, but the fine network of wrinkles round the eyes showed her age.

He felt great warmth for her. Not desire at that moment, just warmth. He must never lose touch with her.

He put the tray down on the dressing table, and the noise woke her. She started, unaccustomed to anyone else in the house, but when she saw him, she smiled blearily.

'Charles. Good gracious. A cup of tea in bed. I can't think when you last did that for me.'

'When you were pregnant with Juliet, maybe.'

'Probably.'

He poured the tea. He felt slightly awkward, as though he were in a strange woman's room. He passed a mug to her and she propped herself up on the pillows to accept it.

'You feeling better this morning, Charles?'

'Yes, thank you.'

'You looked terrible last night.'

'Yes, I felt it. Thank you for salvaging me.'

'Any time.'

They were silent. There was still a restraint between them. Frances moved over positively to switch on the radio. 'See what's happening in the world,' she said breezily.

'Hmm.' Radio Four murmured earnestly from the speaker. 'Are you still thinking of selling the house?' Charles blurted out.

'Yes. It's with the agents.'

'Oh.'

'Mind you, they say the market's pretty slack at the moment. And the trouble is I'm only here in the evenings to show people around. So I think it may take some time.'

'Yes.' This information made Charles feel disproportionately cheerful, as though he had suddenly been reprieved from something.

He became aware that the radio was talking about Michael Banks. Someone was giving an appreciation of his career. They must have worked fast to get it together, Charles thought. A busy night for them.

And no doubt a busy night of police questioning for *The Hooded Owl* company at the Variety Theatre. A lot must have been happening while he had slept.

The appreciation of Michael Banks was made up of interviews with his friends in the business. It was remarkable how many eminent names had allowed themselves to be woken up in the middle of the night to talk about him. And remarkable with what unanimity of love they spoke.

But, as Charles knew, Michael Banks had been a person who inspired love. For the first time since the shooting, Charles felt, not shock, but a sense of the tragic waste of his death.

For Alex he felt nothing but pity. The killing had not been a rational act; when he did it, Alex Household had been mentally ill. Charles felt guilty for not having recognised the seriousness of the actor's state. Maybe he could have done something to avert the tragedy.

'*But what of the show?*' asked the radio presenter. '*Needless to say, no reviews of* The Hooded Owl *have appeared in the papers today, but from all accounts the play was being very well received when the tragedy occurred. But surely Michael Banks's death must end the run before it had even started. Apparently not, according to the show's producer, Paul Lexington.*'

Paul's familiar voice came on, tired but as confident as ever. '*No. Of course, we are all shattered by what has occurred, but we are professionals. It is our job to entertain the public and that is what we will continue to do. Don't worry, the show will go on.*'

'*How soon?*'

'*Tonight. There will be a performance of* The Hooded Owl *tonight.*'

'*Tonight? But can you replace Michael Banks at that sort of notice?*'

'*Yes, we can.*'

'*But I understood...*' The interviewer picked his way carefully around the sub judice laws. '*I understood that Mr. Banks's understudy is ...nott available.*'

'*That is true. The part will be taken by another member of the company.*'

'*May I ask his name?*'

'*Certainly. His name is Charles Paris.*'

'*Who?*' asked the interviewer.

'*WHO?*' echoed Charles Paris.

CHAPTER ELEVEN

THE NERVES on the first night at Taunton had been bad; so had the understudy nerves of the first night at the Variety; but they were nothing to the sheer blind terror that attended Charles Paris as he waited to go on stage in the role in which Michael Banks's career had been so tragically cut short the night before.

Charles had not really believed it would happen. After hearing his name on the radio, he had thought it must be just bravado on Paul Lexington's part, the young producer falling into cliché, insisting that the show must go on when all logic showed it was impossible. He must have been interviewed during the night of panic following the murder; in the rational light of dawn he would recognise that his words had been just heroics.

Charles had so convinced himself of this that he didn't ring in to the production office until ten-thirty, deliberately giving the producer time to sober up his intoxicated imagination.

'Charles!' said Paul Lexington's voice. 'Where the hell have you been? I've been ringing your number for hours.'

'Ah. Well, I didn't actually spend the night at home.'

'Well, now you have rung, get in here as quickly as you can. Where are you?'

'Muswell Hill.'

'Get a cab and charge it.'

'But what's the hurry?' asked Charles, deliberately obtuse.

'You're going on tonight playing the father.'

Charles took a deep breath, mustering the arguments he had prepared. 'Paul, I don't know if you have realised this yet, but I am not the understudy to the part of the father. I am understudying George Birkitt, who, when I last saw him, was looking as fit as a flea.'

'Charles, this is an emergency! It's not the time to argue about the small print of your contract. I'll sort out the extra money with your agent.'

'That is not what I'm arguing about. If I could play the part of the father for you tonight, I would be happy to oblige. But the point you seem to have missed is that I don't know the lines.'

'Nor did Michael Banks.'

'No, but...Good Lord, you don't mean...?'

But that was exactly what Paul Lexington *did* mean. If Michael Banks could get through the part having his lines relayed to him by radio, then so, the Producer's reasoning ran, could any other actor. And since Charles knew the production so well, he'd be able to remember the moves and...

Anyway, the show had to go on that night. Paul had given public undertakings on national radio and television that it would. His boast would also be in the later editions of the evening papers. It was a God-given publicity opportunity.

Charles was prepared to contest the definition of 'God-given' under the circumstances, but Paul didn't give him time. 'Find that cab and be here ten minutes ago!' he ordered before putting the phone down.

It was a strange day, most of which Charles walked through in a dream. What remained of the morning was to be spent acclimatising himself to the deaf-aid receiver and learning how to pace himself with the A.S.M. who was going to feed the lines.

That was agony. Charles kept remembering what Micky Banks had gone through at the same stage, and often, like his predecessor, was ready to throw in the towel and say it was impossible. His mind wasn't up to speaking one line while listening to another, and at the same time trying to remember the next move. His familiarity with his own original part didn't help either. In the scenes where the father talked to the character now played by George Birkitt, he kept hearing the father's line in his ear, mistaking it for his cue, and coming in with George's line. There seemed no prospect of his ever getting the technique.

He bashed away at it with the A.S.M. solidly from eleven-fifteen, when he arrived at the theatre, until half past two, without any break for lunch or the drink he desperately craved. The rest of the cast were called for three to do a complete rehearsal of all the scenes he was in.

And, suddenly, just as had happened to Michael Banks, at the eleventh hour the rhythm started to come. Partly it was familiarity with the lines after three hours of going through them, but also it was a kind of relaxation that came with the acceptance of disaster. This is never going to work, Charles was thinking, so what is the point of worrying about it? With that thought came relief, and with relief sufficient detachment for him to split his mind, to let one part concentrate on hearing the lines, and the other on performing. The only sensation he could equate it with was that remoteness that comes during a long run, when the lines of the play get delivered every night, but the actor's mind is miles away, thinking about anything but the performance he is giving.

The rest of the company was wonderfully supportive. They all looked shattered after the shock and lack of sleep of the night before, but they all worked for him, recognising his need as only professional actors can. The only one who was less than whole-hearted in his support was George Birkitt, whose mind seemed to be on something else (no doubt whether his billing would be affected by Michael Banks's demise, and whether it was really appropriate for him to stay in the show and play a smaller part than Charles Paris).

But all the others demonstrated the unshakeable freemasonry of actors in a crisis. They were all very sharp and attentive, prepared to go back over scenes or lines as often as was required, patient when Charles lost the line, encouraging when he got a flow of dialogue working.

Through his haze, Charles realised that it wasn't just the crisis that made them so deferential; it was the part he was now playing, too. Willy-nilly, he was now the star of *The Hooded Owl*, and the rest of the cast were giving him a taste of the treatment afforded to stars. It was something Charles Paris had never before experienced, and it felt very strange.

And so, like a grotesque dream, the hours passed. The 'half' came. Charles made himself up for the new role, and dressed in the new costume. Fortunately, the latter was really new. Apart from the fact that Michael Banks had been bigger than he was, the dead man's clothes were still being examined by the police. Which was a relief to his replacement.

As he was preparing, all the company came in with good wishes and pledges of support. Paul Lexington exhorted him to do his best. The house was full, he said. As he thought, all the publicity had paid off.

The young Producer looked buoyant. Charles wasn't too distracted to have the thought that Michael Banks's replacement must have considerably reduced the running costs of the production.

Then came the reassuringly calm voice of the Stage Manager over the loudspeaker. 'Beginners, Act One, please. All the best, everyone.'

Charles rose from his seat and walked out of the dressing room. As he closed the door, he noticed for the first time that there was a star on it. The dream continued during the performance, but its nightmare quality receded. Once the sheer terror subsided and Charles realised both that he wasn't going to pass out and that he could manage the lines, he even began to enjoy it. He had forgotten the pleasure of playing a major part in a good play in the West End. (Well, to be honest with himself, he had to admit that 'forgotten' wasn't the right word. But he did enjoy the unfamiliar experience.)

The performance was not without mishap. He did lose the lines on more than one occasion and threshed around helplessly through pauses that seemed eternal, until the A.S.M.'s quiet voice in his ear managed to get him back on to the right track. But these moments did not seem to lose the play's tension. The concentration of the cast was so strong that the mood was well maintained.

The audience kept up their concentration too. They all knew what had happened the previous night and, from Wallas Ward's announcement before the curtain rose, they knew that Charles had stepped in at very short notice. They didn't know about the device of the hearing-aid, but that was a point in Charles's favour; it made his feat of getting through the part even more remarkable. As he stood on the stage he felt pouring out from the audience that most British of reflexes: the will for the underdog to win.

He spent the interval just sitting in his dressing room, gathering his strength for the next act. People came in and out, but he didn't really notice them or their words of encouragement.

In the second act, he felt the power of Malcolm Harris's writing, and felt his own performance rise to the rhythms of the play.

The scene with Lesley-Jane started. Everyone knew the climax was approaching. Lesley-Jane looked strained and peaky and her performance was once again subdued. The audience was silent, waiting. They seemed to know when the tragedy of the previous night had occurred, and had maybe come to the theatre in such numbers in the vague hope that they might get a repeat showing.

This thought came into Charles's already overcrowded mind, and he found himself looking off into the wings, whence the fatal shot had come.

He was surprised how little he could see. The brightness of the light on stage made it difficult for him to focus, and a large spot, positioned to give the illusion of daylight from a window of the set, left the recesses of the wings in obscurity. Charles could not even see the A.S.M. who was reading his lines, though he knew the youth would be keeping him in view to watch for signs of difficulty. To be seen from the stage on the O.P. side, a person would have to stand very close to the edge of the set.

Lesley-Jane Decker had seen someone or something in the wings the previous night and it had made her scream. He felt sure of that. It wasn't the sight of Michael Banks falling that had set her off. She had looked off-stage and then screamed.

Charles decided he must talk to her when the opportunity arose.

But the thoughts of detection were fatal to his concentration. He lost the line again and, though he tried to disguise the lapse with a dramatic move, he feared he had broken the tension of the scene.

But it was a good scene and, by the time he got to the Hooded Owl speech, he was back on course. He felt very emotional, caught up in his own acting and awareness of the speech's significance from the night before. The emotion and power built through the lines.

As he turned to face the glass case, he felt every eye in the theatre on him.

'...This stuffed bird has always been in the room. Imagine it had perception, a memory to retain our follies. Oh God, the weakness that these walls have witnessed! And this bird has lived through it all, has seen it all, impassively, in silence.'

He reached for the case and took it in both hands.

'Well, I'm not going to be spied on any longer!'

He dashed the Hooded Owl down on to the middle of the stage, where it shattered satisfyingly.

In the audience no one breathed. He had them exactly where every actor who ever lived wants his public, watching his every movement, letting him dictate their lives for a little moment.

He knew the speech had worked.

Probably it was because of what had happened in the play at that point on the previous night.

But was perhaps a little part of its success, he dared to hope, because he had done it rather well?

It was only when he got back to the star dressing room after the performance that Charles fully took in its luxurious appointments. It was wallpapered in a pleasing pattern and the chairs were painted gold with red velvet seats. There was an attractive screen in one corner. On the make-up table was that incredible rarity backstage – a telephone. And, as if that wasn't enough, the dressing room turned out to be *two* rooms. Through a door was another little compartment, with a *bed* and a *fridge*.

Charles kept looking round for the room's occupant. He still couldn't believe it was him.

Members of cast rushed in and out, throwing their arms round him effusively. It wasn't what usually happened to him after a performance. To his fury, he found he was crying.

Paul Lexington came in. 'Terrific, Charles. Really bloody marvellous!' And he thrust a brown paper parcel into his hands.

It felt like a bottle. It was a bottle. And a better bottle than he had dared hope. A large bottle of Bell's whisky.

Charles realised that he had previously underestimated the young Producer's sensitivity.

'You like one now, Paul?'

'No, thanks. Look, I've booked us all into the Italian place round the corner. Sort of thank you. See you there as soon as you can make it.'

'Terrific. Thank you.' Charles poured himself a large slug of whisky and downed it. It didn't touch anything till his stomach, whence it sent out radiance.

Then he noticed that there was an envelope on his make-up table. Addressed 'Charles Paris', he was sure it hadn't been there at the interval.

He tore the envelope open, his mind full of various pleasing conjectures. The letter lived up to none of them, though its contents were not unpleasing.

The notepaper was headed with a Knightsbridge address.

Dear Charles,

I gather that you are taking over tonight from poor Micky. Just wanted to drop you a note to say break a leg and all those other theatrical clichés. You are very brave to step into the breach.

Be nice to see you some time. If you'd like to meet up for a drink or something, do give me a call on the above number.

All the best for tonight, Dottie

Try as he might, he could not read the letter without feeling sexual overtones. Just as when she had spoken to him, the invitation seemed overt. And, in the heightened mood brought on by the success of his performance, it was an invitation he felt inclined to take up.

On the other hand, it was strange…If he was reading it right, it was hardly the behaviour of a recently widowed woman, particularly one who had lost her husband in such dramatic circumstances. Even if they lived apart, surely… Perhaps he was fantasising.

He looked at it again, searching for another reading. He found one, but didn't like it, because it hinged on the word 'brave'. Micky Banks had been shot dead on stage. Might his successor be 'brave' because he was laying himself open to the same fate…?

There was a tap at the door. 'Come in.'

He saw Frances in the mirror. With an instinctive and depressingly familiar reflex, he pushed Dottie's letter under a towel and turned to greet his wife.

'Good God. Were you out front?'

She nodded. 'Charles, you were wonderful.'

Her arms were round his neck and her lips against his. Unwelcome tears threatened again to expose him for a big softie.

'Oh, Frances.'

'Charles.'

They swayed together. Very together.

'You really did it. I knew you could. I've always known you could be much better than the sort of parts you usually play. And tonight you proved it.'

'Thank you very much, Frances.' He meant it. She was a shrewd lady and not over-generous with praise, so, when it came, he appreciated it the more.

'I was really proud of you tonight, Charles.'

He felt embarrassed. 'Would you like a drink or…?'

'No, thanks.'

'We're all going out for a meal. Now I come to think of it, I haven't eaten anything all day. Nothing's passed my lips since that cup of tea this morning.'

'What about your old friend?' Frances pointed to the bottle of Bell's.

'I've only just had one slug of that. Five minutes ago.' Again his mind was clouded by the heresy that had struck him after the first night in Taunton. 'Do you realise, Frances…' he said slowly, 'I did that performance tonight without having had a single drink all day…? And it was all right. wasn't it?'

'It was wonderful.'

'Good Lord.' He had to sit down because of the shock.

'Perhaps.' But the shock stayed with him. He had to have a long swig of Bell's to shift it. 'Well, what about coming out for a meal with all of us?'

'No. Thank you, Charles. I have eaten and I've got to get back. Anyway, this'll really be a cast thing. I'll just be out of place.'

He didn't attempt to deny it. Frances had been married to an actor long enough to know what she was talking about.

'Well, look, we must meet soon.'

'I'd like that. Incidentally, I rang Juliet today.'

'Oh yes?'

'To tell her what you were doing. You know, taking on this part. She was very proud.'

'Oh.' It had never occurred to him that his daughter might be proud of him.

'She and Miles'd love to see you.'

'Oh, I'd love to see them.'

'I'm going down Sunday week. It's my half-term. I don't know if you'd like to...'

'Oh. Oh well, yes, I might. I'll give you a buzz.'

'Fine,' said Frances without excessive confidence. Charles's buzzes were not notorious for their reliability. 'And, incidentally, what I suspected is true.'

'Ah,' Charles observed knowingly. But there was no point in pretending with Frances. 'Er, what did you suspect?'

'Juliet's pregnant again.'

'Oh, is she?'

The theory that Charles Paris might be a better actor without alcohol was not put to the test any further that night. Like all good scientists, he knew that one should not rush experiments, so a great deal of Italian red wine and a good few Sambucas were consumed before he finally tottered into a taxi and gave the driver (with some difficulty) his address.

The meal had been fun. He had needed to wind down after the spiralling tensions of the day, and once again he felt the company warmth and support that had sustained him through the day. Meals after shows, with a company who all got on, Charles found, were the moments he most enjoyed of being an actor. They did not happen that often – at least the meals happened, but not often with such unanimity of good humour. But when they did they were wonderful, and some of Charles's happiest memories were of Italian or Chinese or Indian restaurants after hours in quiet provincial towns.

In spite of the alcohol and the fatigues of the day, he did not feel sleepy when he got back to his bed-sitter. His mind was too full. Every time he lay down, some new thought or memory would excite him, and he would start walking round the room.

He knew he should sleep. The next day was Saturday, which meant two performances, and he was already nearly on his knees from exhaustion. But sleep didn't come and round about half past three he realised it wasn't going to come.

So he made a cup of coffee (realising, sensibly for once, that he'd had enough alcohol) and sat down in the low upholstered chair with wooden arms that was one of the room's few comforts.

It didn't take long before he was thinking of Michael Banks's death. Something about it disturbed him – not the obvious facts of its shock and tragedy – but some discordant element, something that didn't ring true. His dormant detective instinct was stirring.

For the moment he set aside the obvious solution. Say Alex Household *hadn't* murdered the star, then who else might have had motive and opportunity to do it?

Michael Banks had been a man who inspired love, but even so Charles could produce quite a list of people who might have had a grudge against him. Whether any of the grudges was strong enough to justify murder was another consideration he put on one side for the time being.

Paul Lexington resented the money he was having to pay to Michael Banks since Bobby Anscombe had backed out of the production. His sums worked better with the star out of the way

Malcolm Harris had been furious with Michael Banks for, as he mistakenly thought, making arbitrary cuts in the author's precious speeches.

George Birkitt resented Michael Banks's precedence over himself. Dottie Banks might have resented her husband's apparent liaison with Lesley-Jane Decker and killed him out of jealousy.

Lesley-Jane Decker, if she was having an affair with Michael Banks, might have turned against him because he tried to break it off or committed one of the million other offences which men can commit against women with whom they are having affairs.

Valerie Cass might have resented Michael Banks's affair with her precious daughter, either because of his age or because she was just jealous.

That seemed to be it, as far as motives were concerned, and, even to produce that list, he'd had to scrape the barrel a bit.

And some of the people who had motives were excluded from suspicion by lack of opportunity. Lesley-Jane Decker had been on stage at the time of the shooting, so, unless she had brought in a hired killer, seemed to be in the clear.

Dottie Banks had been sitting in the auditorium, so she was exonerated, with the same proviso.

The remaining four had all been backstage at the relevant time, or could have been, but the motives Charles had managed to dredge up for them didn't survive close scrutiny.

Paul Lexington had too much at stake in the production to take the risk of being discovered as a murderer. And, although he had benefited from the publicity surrounding the death and from the cheapness of the star's replacement, he would also have benefited from Michael Banks's drawing power, had he survived. No, too fanciful to consider him in the role of murderer. He might well be guilty of swindling people, but not of shooting them.

Valerie Cass's motive seemed pretty feeble, too. She might well be capable of attacking someone who threatened Lesley-Jane or the girl's career, which she lived with such fierce vicariousness, but there was no sign that Michael Banks did represent such threat. On the contrary she seemed rather to welcome Lesley-Jane's attachment. She liked the reflected glory of her daughter's being with such a famous star, and thought it could do nothing but good for the girl's future in the theatre. Had it been Alex Household who had been shot, the situation would have been different, because she so patently disapproved of him but with Michael Banks as victim, it was difficult to cast her in the role of murderer.

And to think of George Birkitt in that light was just ridiculous. He resented

Michael Banks, but no more than he resented anyone else more famous than he was. He was far too lazy (and not bright enough) to plan a murder.

Malcolm Harris was a slightly different proposition. He was clearly not a very stable person. He was absolutely obsessed by his play, and might regard what he saw as wanton tampering with it as a threat to his whole personality. But he was also a great admirer of Michael Banks, who was his dream casting for the role, and, unless one introduced very tortuous psychopathology, for him to murder the star was utterly unlikely.

And for any of these suspects to have done it, one had to posit a very unlikely set of circumstances. They would have had to know where Alex's gun was in the Green Room, they would have had to run the risk of being observed on the O.P. side of the stage when they committed the murder…This last was not such a great risk, because most of the stage staff were needed on the Prompt Side at that point in the play for a forthcoming scene change.

But there was one witness the potential murderer could not avoid, and that was the main suspect. No one could have gone into the O.P. wings and shot Michael Banks without being seen by Alex Household.

At that point all theories of alternative murderers fell apart.

Alex Household had a history of mental instability and paranoia. He had recently had a starring part and a new girl-friend, both of which he saw as part of a new start in his life, taken away by Michael Banks.

He had voiced threats against the star, and that very evening showed signs of starting another breakdown.

He had been sitting all evening in exactly the spot from which the gun had been fired. He was still there right up until the moment of the shooting, because Michael Banks, who didn't know his lines, was still delivering them correctly and therefore still having them fed to him.

The gun that had shot the star was Alex Household's gun, on which, Charles had discovered at dinner that evening, the police had found no fingerprints but those of the owner.

And, if anyone needed further proof of guilt after that, Alex Household had run away from the scene of the crime. And, in spite of police demands that he give himself up and intensive searches, he was still at large.

Anyone who tried to prove Alex Household didn't do it, when faced with all that evidence, needed his head examined.

Oh, sod it. It was five o'clock. Charles went back on his resolution and poured himself a large Bell's. Maybe lull himself into a little sleep. All this thought of death was unsettling him.

He remembered the words of Tate Wilkinson, the eighteenth-century actor-manager. 'No actor can speak of death without a bottle in his hand.'

Charles Paris knew what he meant.

CHAPTER TWELVE

THE SATURDAY'S performances of *The Hooded Owl* were not very good. In the euphoria of getting through the first night, Charles had forgotten how much concentration that effort had taken, and found it difficult to get back the rhythm of his lines with the A.S.M.. The sleepless night and the excesses which it had incorporated did not help, either.

And the rest of the cast were less altruistically supportive. They too were suffering from exhaustion after recent events, and had less energy to carry Charles; their main concern was just to keep themselves going. They had all reached that stage following a crisis, which can often be more difficult than the crisis itself, when it is no longer a matter of one superhuman push, but husbanding resources for an indeterminately prolonged period of stress. There was huge relief when the curtain fell on the Saturday night performance. No talk of going out for meals then, the cast rushed off to their respective homes, grateful for the knowledge that they would not have to be back in the Variety Theatre until the 'half' on the Monday evening.

There was still no news of Alex Household, though police investigations were being vigorously pursued. Either he had gone to ground very effectively and was in hiding, or – and this was a rumour that spread increasingly amongst the cast – he had killed himself. The more days went by, the more likely it became that the end of the police search would be the discovery of a corpse. It was a thought that depressed Charles considerably.

He slept a lot of the Sunday and Monday and, when awake, just mooched about his bed-sitter in the gloom that inevitably followed moments of high excitement.

He thought of ringing Frances, but something deterred him. She had spoken of meeting the following weekend and going down to Juliet's. That possibly meant that she had something else on this weekend. Or would be busy sorting things out at school with the run-up to half-term. He didn't feel up to the mildest of rebuffs from her; he seemed to have got back to a relationship like an adolescent infatuation, reading rejection in the most innocent of her actions.

His mood also deterred him from ringing Dottie Banks. It was something he still intended to do, but he felt he should be at a peak of confidence to arrange such an encounter.

Still, the rest did him good, and the performance on the Monday evening was better. It was well received by a fairly small house. About a third full. The publicity of Michael Banks's death had now been replaced in the public's mind with news of fresh disasters, and the show was running on its own impetus. The Variety Theatre's position off the main West End beat, the obscurity of the play, and the (*pace* George Birkitt) lack of star names – all the elements which pessimists had predicted would work against the show – were now beginning to take their toll.

Paul Lexington seemed, as ever, undaunted by the small audience. It was Monday night, he said, and that was always bad. The following for this kind of play would build up by word-of-mouth, he insisted. The coach-parties hadn't started to come in yet. And he was going to give a rocket to Show-Off, whose performance on the publicity front had been absolutely dismal. Get another burst of publicity in the second week, and the show would be fine. Every production went through troughs.

As ever, he sounded terribly plausible, and Charles was as willing as all the rest of the cast to believe what he said. How true it all was, Charles didn't wish to investigate. And how the show was now funded, how tightly Paul Lexington was running his budget, what his break-even percentage of audience was, indeed how much of the audience was made up of paying theatre-goers and how much of free seats; all these were questions to which he knew he was unlikely to get answers.

All they could do was work from day to day, from performance to performance, and through the second week, Charles started to feel his confidence in the part building up again. The play settled down with its new cast. The size of the audience didn't increase noticeably, but the faithful few who did turn up seemed appreciative.

He even got another nice review. Obviously there had been no notices after the first night, and few of the critics of the major papers would have had time, let alone interest, to give the play a second viewing; but a North London local paper with a weekly deadline had sent along its critic on the Monday of the second week, and their review appeared on the Thursday.

The significant sentence read as follows: 'The part of the father, played by an actor unfamiliar to me, Charles Paris, grows in stature through the evening until the powerfully climactic scene of confrontation with his daughter.'

It was not, of course, unambiguous praise. Indeed, it could have been read merely as appreciation of Malcolm Harris's writing; it was the part, after all, not the acting, which was said to grow in stature. And, to the cynically analytical mind which Charles usually applied to praise, the review could be read to mean that the part grew in stature until the powerfully climactic scene of confrontation with his daughter, at which point, in the hands of this actor, it diminished considerably.

But, on the whole, he thought it was good. Like all actors with reviews, he checked through it for quotability, and decided that, with only slight injustice to the meaning, and the excision of a comma, he could come up with the very serviceable sentence, 'Charles Paris grows in stature through the evening'.

He even wondered if he ought to suggest to Paul Lexington that that sentence was put on a hoarding outside the theatre, but didn't quite have the nerve. The Producer had been satisfied with snipping out from the same review the words, 'a thoroughly solid evening's entertainment', to join the other encomiums that guarded the Variety's portals.

(These others, incidentally, demonstrated once again Paul Lexington's very personal definition of truth and his skill in the use of small print. Since he hadn't got any London press reviews, he had used the Taunton ones, and artfully disguised their provenance. Thus the passerby would observe in large letters the exhortation, 'I urge everyone to go and see *The Hooded Owl* now! – *Times*'. He would have to go very close indeed to the hoarding to read the word '*Taunton*' between 'now!' and '*Times*'.

In the same way, the *Observer*, which acclaimed 'an evening of theatrical magic', was the *Quantock Observer*; and the *Mail*, who had 'rarely been so entertained', was the *Western Mail*.

The cheekiest of the lot was actually from a London newspaper. 'One of the greatest dramas in the history of the British Theatre' was, as its by-line claimed, from *The Daily Telegraph*; it had come, however, not from the Arts page, but from the front-page description of Michael Banks's murder.

There were no flies on Paul Lexington.)

Charles cut out and kept his probably-nice review. He never kept bad ones. That was not just vanity. He always found that, while he could never exactly fix the wording of the good ones, the bad remained indelibly printed on his brain, accurate to the last comma.

Though over thirty years had passed, he could still remember how his first major role for the Oxford University Dramatic Society had been greeted by an undergraduate critic (who, incidentally, later became a particularly malevolent Minister of Health and Social Security):

'Charles Paris had a brave stab at the part, but unfortunately it did not survive his attack'.

On the Wednesday matinée, when the house was minimal and so was the cast's concentration, Charles came rather unstuck with his deaf-aid.

To be honest, it wasn't his fault. Or it wasn't *completely* his fault. He got fed the wrong line.

Inevitably, it was in the Hooded Owl speech, the play's focus for either triumph or disaster. Charles had just turned to face the glass case, having made the analogy of the Hooded Owl and God. The line he should have received next was, 'Why not? This stuffed bird has always been in the room.' But, unfortunately, what the A.S.M. read to him was, 'Why not? This bird has always been stuffed in this room.'

And, even more unfortunately, that was the line Charles repeated. The audience probably didn't notice anything wrong; their reactions were so minimal, anyway, that it hardly mattered. But Lesley-Jane certainly did, and she started to giggle. That, and the mild hysteria that a tiny audience always engenders, got Charles going too, and the pair of them were almost paralysed by laughter. It was what actors call a total 'corpse', and, although they managed to get through to the end of the play, any tension they might have built up was dissipated.

The lapse was duly noted by the Stage Manager and no one was surprised to be summoned on stage at the 'half' for the evening show, and receive a dressing-down from the Company Manager.

'You're all meant to be professionals,' Wallas Ward berated them petulantly, 'and this sort of behaviour is unforgivable. We already have our problems with this show, and we're at a very pivotal point. If we are to survive in the West End, we have to guarantee that *every* performance is up to scratch. Nothing brings a show's reputation down quicker than the rumour going round the business that the cast has started sending it up. You really should know better.'

Charles owned up, like a naughty schoolboy. 'Sorry, it was my fault. I got fed the wrong line.'

'Well, you should have been concentrating on what you were saying. You are meant to think, not just relay the lines like some glorified loudspeaker.'

'Yes, I know. I'm sorry. Lapse of concentration. Won't happen again.'

'It'd better not. I think you ought to be off the deaf-aid by now.'

'What?' Charles was very taken aback.

'Well, you are going to learn the lines at some point, aren't you?'

'Oh, I...er...I hadn't really thought about it.' He hadn't. Now he had sorted out the technique of using the deaf-aid, he found it wonderfully relaxing. The strain of remembering the lines was removed, and he could enjoy the acting. It hadn't occurred to him that at some point his life-support system would be taken away.

'*I* think you should be off the deaf-aid now,' asserted Wallas Ward righteously. 'But Paul says wait a bit, no hurry, and it's his decision.'

'Right, well, I'll wait till I hear from him.'

'And, in the meantime, let us have no repetition of this afternoon's disgusting display of amateurism.'

Very good, Wallas, yes, Wallas, certainly, Wallas, said all the cast, touching their forelocks in mock-abasement.

'Maurice Skellern Personal Management.'

'Still holding out for the twenty per cent, I see, Maurice.'

'Charles, one has to pay for personal service in this day and age. It's the same all over the board, you know.'

'Humph.'

'Well, and how's the show going?'

'Oh, thank you for asking. I take it that question is an example of your Personal Management, the individual care you lavishly bestow on your clients.'

'Exactly, Charles.'

'Listen, Maurice, we last spoke nearly a fortnight ago. Since then, not only has the show opened in the West End, but also I, your client, have taken over the leading part. And during that time, what kind of "individual care" have I received? Not even a lousy telephone call. I always have to end up ringing you.'

'I'm never sure where you are, Charles.'

'Rubbish. You could always find me if you tried.'

'I think you're being very hurtful, Charles. I spend all day beavering away on your behalf and –'

'Oh, damn it, Maurice, can't you –'

'That's very good, Charles, very good.' Wheezes of laughter wafted down the telephone line.

'What?'

'Beavering – damn it. Very good.'

'Listen, Maurice, as I say I am now playing the lead in this show, and I think it is about time you sorted out some deal on the money I get for doing it.'

'Now, Charles, if you would calm down a moment and allow me to get a word in, I would be able to inform you that I have already negotiated just such a deal for you.'

'Then why the hell didn't you tell me?'

'Because the details have only recently been finalised with Paul Lexington.'

'Well, when did you ring him?'

'He rang me, actually.'

'When?'

'Yesterday.'

'And I suppose that was the first you knew of my taking over the part?'

'It was, as it happens.'

'I don't bloody believe it. Your office must have a great pile of sand in it instead of a desk, so that you can keep your head buried all bloody day.'

'Now, Charles...An agent's job is difficult enough without his clients being offensive.'

'All right. Tell me what the deal is.'

Charles had devoted considerable thought to this subject. He knew that he wasn't the most eminent actor in the world, but he still knew that nobody played a starring part in the West End for peanuts. He had to be on three hundred and fifty a week minimum, surely? Maybe a bit more. Maybe a lot more.

'Paul Lexington was very fair on the phone, I thought, very fair.'

'Oh yes?'

'What he said was...'

'Yes?'

'...that he'd continue to pay your existing contract –'

'But that's only a hundred and fifty a week.'

'Wait, wait. But, on top of that, he was prepared to pay a supplement.'

'Oh good.'

'Because you are actually playing the part.'

'I certainly am.'

'A supplement of ten pounds for each performance you do.'

'Ten pounds! But that's nothing!'

'It's quite generous for an understudy.'

'But I'm not an understudy. This isn't the part which I was understudying, anyway. And I am actually playing the part.'

'Not according to Paul Lexington.'

'What do you mean?'

'According to him, you are acting as understudy. And, in a few weeks when he sees how business is going, he will make the decision as to whether to confirm you in the part or to recast.'

'Good God.'

'As I say, I thought it very fair. I mean, considering your stature in the business.'

'Thank you very much,' said Charles dully.

'I pushed him up, you know. He only wanted to give you eight pounds a performance, but I pushed him up.'

'Terrific, Maurice.'

But the sarcasm was wasted. 'Good, I thought you'd see it my way. And now perhaps you understand what I mean by Personal Management.'

'Oh yes, I think I do.'

'Good. Well, nice to talk to you.'

'Hmm. I don't suppose your Personal Management and "individual care" would actually extend to coming along to see the show, would it?'

'Oh now, Charles…I spend all day in the office slaving away on your behalf. Surely you don't want me to give up my evenings too. Do you…?'

Michael Banks's death niggled away at Charles like a hole in the tooth. He had done all the sums, and he knew only one answer fitted, but still something snagged. There seemed little doubt that Alex was the murderer, but Charles felt somehow he owed it to his friend to isolate the element about the case that was worrying him.

So, just before the 'half' on the Thursday night, he knocked on Lesley-Jane Decker's dressing room door.

She was dressed in a silk kimono and lying on the daybed when he went in. Her face was scoured of street make-up, prior to the application of her stage make-up. The result was pale and sickly, stress lines showing how much she would look like her mother in a few years' time. It was brought home to Charles for the first time how much of a strain the last weeks must have been for a girl of her age. To have broken off one affair and started another, then to have witnessed the shooting of her new lover by the old one, was quite a lot to take. He knew some actresses, hard-boiled as eight-minute eggs, who would have revelled in the situation, casting themselves as *femmes fatales* with enormous relish. But Lesley-Jane didn't seem the type. Her sophistication was paper-thin, and underneath she was just a very young, and probably over-protected, girl.

She made no attempt to move when he came in, just lay there looking vulnerable. Nor did she say anything beyond 'Hello, Charles.' Her champagne bubble was distinctly flat.

'Tired out?' he asked solicitously.

'Shattered.'

'Yes, it's been tough for all of us. Doing eight shows a week is enough, without all this other business.'

'Yes.' She looked at him, curious as to why he was there. But not that curious; she seemed too tired to be very interested.

'I wanted to talk about Michael's death,' he began bluntly.

'Ah.' Even this didn't animate her much.

'I'm sorry to go through it all again, but there's something about it that seems odd to me.'

'What?'

'You see I don't know. There's just something that doesn't seem right about it.'

'I don't think murder's often right,' she observed with a touch more spirit.

'No. By definition it isn't. But listen, we both witnessed that murder. I was out front, and it was pretty horrible from there. From where you were standing, it must have been...'

She gulped, forcing back nausea, and nodded.

'But what interests me, what I wanted to ask you, is about how you reacted.'

'I screamed, didn't I? I can't remember very well, but I thought I...'

'Yes, you screamed all right. It was *when* you screamed that interests me.'

'When?'

'Yes. What happened was this: Micky stopped getting the lines, turned round in confusion, then presumably saw someone in the wings pointing a gun at him. He said 'Put it down. You mustn't do that to me' or something and then he was shot.'

Lesley-Jane nodded. She wasn't enjoying the re-creation of the shock.

'But you didn't scream then.'

'Didn't I? I can't remember. It was all confused...'

'No, you didn't scream until you looked off into the wings.'

'Delayed shock, I suppose. I couldn't believe what had happened to Micky straight away, I didn't even *know* what had happened to him.'

'But when you looked into the wings you *did* know. And you also knew who had done it. And then you screamed.'

'Yes. I suppose it brought it home to me.'

'And who did you see in the wings?'

She looked at him as if he were daft. 'Well, Alex, of course.' He didn't know what he had been expecting, but he felt very disappointed. Something inside had been hoping against all logic for a different answer. He didn't know what, just anything that would settle the unease he felt about the death.

'What exactly did you see?'

'I've been through all this with the police.'

'I know. I'm sorry. It's just...I wasn't backstage for all the police inquiries, and I really would like to know,' he appealed pathetically.

'All right. I saw Alex. He was very near the edge of the set...'

Must have been. He knew how impenetrable the shadows were in the wings.

'He looked over his shoulder at me, our eyes met for a split-second, then he rushed off and I screamed. I suppose it was the expression on his face that made me scream.'

'Because it made you realise what he'd done?'

'Yes, I think he'd only just realised himself. His face was...I don't know...it was full of fear.'

'Was the gun in his hand?'

'The police asked me that, too, and honestly, I just can't remember. I didn't notice his hands.'

'Was he wearing his jacket?'

'Again I just don't know. All I seemed to see was his face – or maybe just his eyes. I can't get them out of my mind even now. Those eyes full of terror. I felt awful, as if I had hurt him. He was always very unstable, you know.'

'Yes.' Charles reckoned he could take advantage of her lethargic state to push a bit further. 'I suppose, of course, you had hurt him.'

'You mean by going off with Micky?'

Charles nodded.

'Yes. I suppose so. It didn't really seem like that at the time. I mean Micky just seemed so nice, so friendly and, in a strange way, so lonely. Going and having a few meals with him didn't seem evil or furtive in any way. Somehow it was difficult to feel anything was wrong with Micky around.'

He knew what she meant. Michael Banks's effortless charm no doubt carried through into his romantic life.

'And it was just a few meals...?

He had hoped she wouldn't notice the impertinence, but she coloured and began angrily, 'I don't see that that's any business of yours...but yes, it was.'

'Whereas with Alex...?'

'That again is no business of yours...'

'Come on, we were all in Taunton together...It certainly had the look, to the impartial observer, of a full-blown affair.'

'All right, yes. But I had wanted to break it off after Taunton. It was getting awkward, even before I met Micky.'

'Awkward?' Charles fed gently.

'Alex was so strange. The more time I spent with him, the stranger he seemed to be. All his mystical religion thing, his faddishness about food, his belief in being close to nature, following nature...all that appealed to me at first. It was so unlike anything I had come across before. He was so unlike any of the people I had met before...'

Certainly unlike the nice middle-class friends of Mr. and Mrs. Decker, Charles imagined.

'But, after a time, I began to see all his ideas as sort of odd, not charming eccentricities, but...you know, symptoms.'

'Symptoms of what?'

'Of his mental state. I knew he had had the breakdown and at first I didn't mind. I thought, oh, he just needs someone who really loves him and will look after him...'

'And you thought you could supply that want?'

She nodded. 'I thought we really would make a new start, that I would sort of...make him blossom.'

She blushed as if aware of the cliché she was using. Charles wondered how many naive young girls had got caught in messy affairs with older men from the belief that they could bring new love into their lives and 'make them blossom'.

'But,' he prompted.

'But I came to realise that it's all very well gambolling about the countryside feeling at one with nature, but people don't change completely. We couldn't go on pretending that the first forty-seven years of Alex's life hadn't happened. And, as soon as I realised that, as soon as I thought about his breakdown, I started to worry, I started to see just how unstable he still was. I started to be afraid.'

'Afraid of what?'

'Afraid he would do something...well, something like he did do last week.'

Charles nodded slowly. 'What about now? Where do you think he is now?'

Tears came to her eyes. 'I think he'll have killed himself.'

Charles nodded again. It seemed depressingly likely.

Further conversation was prevented by the door opening, unknocked, to admit Valerie Cass. She was smartly dressed in a fawn trouser suit and seemed in high spirits.

'Hello, darling, I've brought you some – oh, hello.' This last was to acknowledge Charles, whom she looked at for a moment with suspicion.

'Charles just dropped in to wish me luck,' Lesley-Jane supplied hastily.

Don't worry, Valerie, I'm not another older man sniffing round your precious daughter. Which, considering the fate of the last two, is perhaps just as well.

As a matter of fact, I don't really fancy her. I used to, I think, but since I met you and saw what she was likely to turn into, I seem to have gone off her. In spite of your excellent state of preservation, Valerie Cass, I'm afraid there's something about you that doesn't appeal to me.

Valerie cut short further interior monologue by gracing him with a smile and saying, 'I just brought Lesley-Jane some home-made soup for the interval. She doesn't eat properly. I keep saying she should eat little and often, but the young don't listen. You have a daughter, don't you, Charles?'

'Yes, I don't see her that often.'

She leapt on this, a useful confirmation of one of her pet theories. 'Yes, as usual no doubt it's the woman who's left to take care of things. Poor Frances, I do feel for her.'

'My daughter is twenty-eight, you know, quite capable of looking after herself without her parents breathing down her neck all the time.' He just managed to resist adding, 'Yours is twenty, and I would have thought the same went for her too.'

Sensing that something of the sort might be going through his mind, Lesley-Jane interposed, 'We were just talking about Micky's death.'

'Oh, what a terrible tragedy.' Valerie Cass made an elaborate gesture, reminding Charles once again what a bad actress she had been. 'It was so awful for all of us. Lesley-Jane was desolated, but desolated. I was so glad that I was up here when she came off stage. If ever there was a moment when a girl needed her mother, that was it. And to sort of protect her during all that police interrogation. I was just glad I could be of help.'

She smiled beatifically. She seemed to have new confidence in her hold over her daughter. It's an ill wind, thought Charles. Micky Banks's death and Alex Household's disappearance were tragedies, but at least they had removed possible rivals for Valerie's daughter's affections.

And Lesley-Jane didn't seem to mind her mother's renewed take-over. In her shocked lethargy, she seemed content to let Valerie run around after her and do everything for her.

But Michael Banks's memory remained sacred. Perhaps, after all, Valerie hadn't resented him, grateful for his reflected glory. That seemed to be the case from what she said next. 'Poor, dear Micky. Such a terrible tragedy. And just when he and Lesley-Jane were getting close. Oh, I know some people would say it was May and December, but I thought it was a lovely relationship. He just seemed so delighted, so *rejuvenated* to meet my little baby. What might have been...'

She sighed the sort of sigh that drama teachers spend three years eradicating from their students. Lesley-Jane, perhaps from long experience of having her mother going on about her or perhaps just from exhaustion, did not seem to be listening.

'Oh yes, I think Lesley-Jane could have mixed with some very eminent people. She is just the sort of girl to stimulate the artistic temperament. Don't you agree, Charles?'

Charles, who shared G. K. Chesterton's opinion that the artistic temperament is a disease which afflicts amateurs, grunted. He could well believe that Lesley-Jane could stimulate male lust; but he found her mother's visions of her, launched in society as a kind of professional Laura to a series of theatrical Petrarchs, a little fanciful.

'Mind you, at the same age, I myself...' she blushed, '...was not without admirers in the...world of the arts. If I hadn't been trapped by marriage so young...who knows what might have been...? Though of course I wasn't *half* as attractive as Lesley...'

This was said in a voice expecting contradiction, which Charles wilfully withheld.

CHAPTER THIRTEEN

THE CONFIDENCE to ring Dottie Banks, absent over the weekend, came after the Friday's performance. The show had gone well, and Charles felt his acting had matched it. There was even a slight swagger in his stride as he entered the star dressing room. (In spite of his enduring understudy status and certain representations that George Birkitt had made to the Company Manager, Charles was still in there.)

Once inside, he saw that great perk, the telephone, and remembered Dottie's note. He also remembered that he'd said he'd ring Frances about the possibility of going down to Miles and Juliet's on the Sunday, but decided to do that the next morning.

He dialled Dottie's number, trying not to dwell on thoughts of the times Michael Banks must have done the same from the same phone.

No, she didn't mind his ringing so late. And yes, she was glad to hear from him. And yes, she had meant what she had said in her note, that it'd be nice to get together for a chat and…things. And why didn't he drop round to her flat in Hans Crescent for a drink after the show tomorrow?

Charles conceded that he would be free, and graciously accepted the invitation.

Drinks with strange women after the show fitted well into the fantasy of himself as the big West End star that the night's performance had engendered.

Even as he thought it, he couldn't help remembering that West End stars tended to be paid a bit more than he was getting with his humble understudy-plus-supplement deal. He really must have a word with the company Equity representative about that contract. Surely Equity wouldn't approve it.

On the other hand, since his agent had accepted the terms so avidly, he thought there might be problems in getting them changed.

Still, there was plenty of time to sort that out. His main priority was Dottie Banks. When he thought of their forthcoming encounter, he felt the guilty excitement of a schoolboy sneaking into the cinema to see an 'X' Certificate movie.

The block of flats in Hans Crescent was expensive and discreet. The porter who rang up to Mrs. Banks and directed Charles to her flat was also no doubt expensive, and would have been discreet if he had refrained from accompanying his directions with a wink. Charles got the impression that perhaps he wasn't the first to have followed this particular route.

The Dottie Banks who opened the flat door was looking expensive; as to her discretion, he would no doubt soon find out. The black satin trousers, the fine black silk shirt and the black lace brassiere which was meant to show through it; they too were expensive. And just about discreet.

'Charles, how nice to see you.' She threw her arms round his neck and kissed him on the lips, enveloping him in discreetly expensive perfume. 'Come in and have a drink.'

The same adjectives which had applied to everything else applied to the flat. Charles was unused to moving in circles where interior designers were used; most of his friends just accumulated clutter and wielded emulsion brushes when things got too tatty; but he recognised the genuine article when he saw it. And he had to admit it was well done.

There was a great deal of Michael Banks memorabilia about. Photographs, framed posters, the odd award statuette. Whatever the nature of their relationship, it was clear that husband and wife had shared the same flat.

Charles was looking at a film still of Banks in one of his most famous roles as the captain of a doomed frigate, when Dottie came back from the kitchen with a bottle of champagne.

'You open this.'

'Fine.'

'There are some things I always feel men do better than women.'

Charles recognised that there would come a point when one found this relentless sexual innuendo irritating. But he knew he hadn't reached that point yet. He put down the still and took the champagne bottle.

'Yes, poor Micky.' Dotty Banks sighed. 'Poor, poor Micky.'

It was said without any sense of tragedy, but with affection.

'It must be pretty awful for you, having lost him.' The cork popped and Charles caught the spume in a tall glass.

'Yes, of course I miss him. Not as much as I would have expected, in some ways.' Dottie shrugged. 'I mean, as a marriage, it wasn't, well, it wasn't a marriage in the conventional sense. We got on well, we went around together quite a bit, we were nice to each other, but we always...had our own friends.'

She looked at him unequivocally, so Charles asked the direct question. 'You mean you both had affairs?'

'*I* did.'

'But Micky didn't?'

'He had...friendships.'

'I see.' So perhaps Lesley-Jane had been telling the truth in her description of the relationship. Just a few meals.

'What I mean, Charles, is that sex wasn't very high on Micky's list of priorities.'

'Ah...Well, some people don't have much of a sex-drive,' Charles observed fatuously, aware that his own was revving up like mad.

'In Micky's case, he didn't have any.'

'Sex-drive?'

'None at all.' She shook her head to punctuate the words. 'He couldn't do it anymore.'

'Ah.' Charles wasn't sure whether to say he was sorry or not. He didn't know the correct etiquette for replying to a lady who's just told you her recently-murdered husband was impotent.

'This made us, in certain respects, incompatible.' Dottie Banks emphasised the obvious by placing her hand on Charles's thigh.

'Ah. Well. Yes. I can see that.'

Her fingertips started to move gently up and down. He felt it would soon be the moment to make a move, and her behaviour left him in little doubt as to what sort of move it should be. Indeed, the only question seemed to be whether he should even bother to make a move, or just let her do everything for him.

But, even then, the nagging thought in his mind would not go away. 'Dottie, about Micky's death...'

'Uhuh.' She was now leaning over towards him and breathing very close to his ear. He could feel the hard outline of her breasts against his upper arm.

'Did you think there was anything odd about it?'

'Odd?' she murmured. 'Well, no odder than any other murder that takes place on stage during the first night of a new play, when the leading actor is shot dead by his understudy.'

'No, I just thought you, knowing Micky so well, might have...'

'Uhuh.' She shook her head, which wobbled the ear she was now nibbling in a way that he found extremely stimulating.

But he still sat still, puzzling, the scene of the murder running like an old movie in his mind.

'Did you come here,' mumbled Dottie, very close, 'to ask me fatuous questions the police have already been through a hundred times, or for other reasons?'

'For other reasons,' he assured her, though deep down he wasn't certain.

'Well then,' she said, 'are you paralysed?'

His hands, sliding from her hair to her neck and down inside the filmy black blouse, denied the imputation. And, after the two of them had slipped down on to the expensive and discreet rug, the rest of his body also demonstrated its unimpaired mobility.

They moved from the rug to the king-size bed for a second demonstration, after which they lay entwined.

Charles was beginning to wonder whether he actually liked Dottie or not. Her intimacy seemed completely impersonal, and he did rather like being appreciated for himself.

Also, his best efforts did not seem sufficient to her. She didn't say anything, but the way she toyed with him suggested she wanted him to be demonstrating all day like a vacuum cleaner salesman.

At last she realised that, for a little while, her ambitions were vain. She lay back.

'You know you asked if there was anything I thought odd about Micky's death.'

'Yes?'

'Well, there was one thing. One tiny thing. So tiny I've only just thought of it.'

'What?'

'Well, you know when you spend a lot of time with someone, you get used to how they speak, their mannerisms and so on...'

'Yes.'

'Just before Micky died, he said something I've never heard him say before.'

'What was that?'

'He said, "Oh Lord!" I've never heard him say that before. "Oh God," yes. "Oh Christ," many times. But not "Oh Lord".'

'Good Lord!'

'No "*Oh* Lord!"'

'No, I mean just "Good Lord!" you know, "Good Lord!"'

'Hmm?'

'Never mind. Look, Micky never said "Oh Lord!", but Alex Household was always saying it.'

'Oh, was he? Oh well, that explains it.'

'How?'

'Alex Household must have said it just before he shot the gun; Micky heard it over the deaf-aid and just repeated it.'

'Yes, I suppose so.'

Dottie's hands were once again busying themselves. 'Hmm. I don't know, Dottie. I keep wishing there was another solution to this murder.'

'How can there be? Alex Household shot Micky. That's the only possible solution.'

'Yes, I suppose so,' Charles conceded, disgruntled. 'I have to admit, it's the best I can come up with.'

'Oh, I wouldn't say that.'

But Dottie was no longer talking about the murder.

After the third demonstration, Charles said he'd better go, and Dottie, recognising that she'd had all she was getting, took a sleeping pill and let him.

In the taxi back to Hereford Road, Charles felt despicable. Sex without any element of love, or even affection, always had that effect on him.

But this time it seemed worse. It was her taking the sleeping pill that had done it. It had reduced him to the same level, just another anonymous treatment that her body had required.

CHAPTER FOURTEEN

FRANCES REPRESENTED many things for Charles, amongst them a kind of fixed moral standard in his life. To ring her the following morning seemed, therefore, not just a good, but even a right idea. Like going to confession (though he had no intention of confessing anything), a bracing moral scour-out.

'Charles. Well, are you coming or not? You've left it late enough.'

'Left what late enough?'

'Charles, you remember – Juliet and Miles invited you down for lunch.'

'Oh yes, of course.'

'You hadn't forgotten, had you?'

'Oh no,I...er...um.'

'Well, are you going to come or not?'

'Um. I hadn't really thought. I...er...'

'I will be leaving in an hour, Charles. If you're here when I go, you will be coming. If you're not, I will be going on my own.'

'Yes, well, of course I –'

'Goodbye, Charles.'

Yes, he would go. After the moral squalor of the night before, he needed the redemption of playing at being the respectable husband, father and grandfather. A nice, straight day with the family – that seemed morally appropriate. Though a day with his son-in-law, Miles, could take on certain qualities of a penance.

'Thing is, Pop, you see, that when Mums sells the house, she's going to have a bit of cash in hand.'

'Yes, I suppose so.' Good God, at what point had Frances lapsed low enough to let Miles call her 'Mums'?

'And this is where she's really going to feel the benefit of having someone in the family who knows about insurance.' Miles took his mother-in-law's hand confidently. 'Aren't you, Mums?' To Charles's amazement, she didn't flinch. 'Now, I've got a really exciting little annuity scheme worked out which I think will be just the ticket.'

Charles looked across at Miles Taylerson with his customary disbelief. Anyone who could get excited by an annuity scheme must belong to a different species from his own. And yet Miles appeared to have the same complement of arms and legs as he did, the same disposition of eyes, nose and mouth. Maybe, Charles reflected, his son-in-law was the result of some cloning experiment, by which creatures from another planet had created something that looked like a human being, but lacked the essential circuitry of humanity. Maybe one day Miles's head would flip open like a kitchen bin to reveal a tangle of wires and transistors.

'You haven't thought any more about insurance, have you, Pop?'

'No, I think I can honestly say that I haven't.' And come to that, what's this 'more'? his mind continued silently. It is one of my proudest boasts that I have never thought about insurance and I am convinced that, even under torture, I could resist the temptation.

'I was just thinking that now's a good time. Now you're getting regular money from this West End show, it'd be a good opportunity to put a little aside each week – it needn't be much, but you'd be amazed how it accumulates.'

'Thank you. I'm sure if ever the occasion arises when I want advice on insurance, you're the first person I'll come to.' Charles thought that wasn't bad. It was the nearest he had ever got to saying something to his son-in-law that was neither untrue nor offensive.

Miles seemed to appreciate it, too. He sat back with a satisfied grin and looked contentedly around the open-plan hygienic nonentity of his executive sitting room in his executive house on an executive estate in Pangbourne.

His wife seemed to recognise some signal and took up the conversational baton for the next lap. 'Incidentally, Daddy, I haven't said how delighted we all are about this West End play. We really hope to get to see it soon, but, you know, things are pretty busy, what with this and that, and the boys.'

'Of course.' He couldn't help feeling affection for Juliet whenever he looked at her. There was something about the set of her eyes which hadn't changed since she was three years old, when she had been all hugs and trust for her father. He often wondered what it was that had brought about such a change in their relationship. Maybe his walking out on Frances.

He looked across at his wife. She was unaware of his scrutiny, gazing with fondness at the two blond-headed little boys who were shovelling gravy-sodden potato into their mouths, an exercise – and apparently the only one – that kept them silent.

At such moments he knew that he loved Frances, and he could feel the seductions of a conventional marriage, of meals such as this happening every Sunday, of knowing each other's daily news, not always having to catch up on a few months' worth of events. There was a kind of peace about it.

And maybe that peace was not completely beyond his grasp. If he really made an effort, perhaps something could be salvaged.

'No,' Juliet continued, 'I mean this West End thing is something I can really tell my friends about. It was like when you had that part in *Z-Cars*. Something sort of…respectable.'

'Thank you,' he muttered. Good God, what had happened to Juliet? Her mind had set irrevocably into middle age when she was about ten. Marriage to Miles had only hardened her mental arteries further. The pair of them had just quietly fossilised together.

Julian finished his potatoes and looked gravely round the family gathering. 'My penis,' he announced, 'is as big as the Empire State Building.'

His four-year-old twin, Damian, not to be outdone, immediately responded. 'Mine penis,' he proclaimed, 'mine penis is as big as the World Trade Centre.'

In the confusion of scolding that followed, Charles reflected that maybe there was hope for the family after all.

Closer acquaintance did nothing to dispel his good impression of his grandsons. After lunch, Juliet, looking peaky and feeling grim, as she had done in the early months of her previous pregnancy, went upstairs to lie down. Frances and Miles went off to the kitchen to do the washing-up (and, no doubt, to talk annuities), leaving Charles to entertain the children.

He found that this was a two-way process. The two little boys were full of ideas for games and, even if most of them ended rather predictably in throwing the sofa cushions at their grandfather, they showed considerable powers of invention.

They were also at the stage when they still found funny voices funny, and Charles had his best audience in years for his Welsh, developed for *Under Milk Wood* ('A production which demonstrated everything the theatre can offer, except talent' – *Nottingham Evening Post*), his Cornish, as used in *Love's Labour's Lost* ('Charles Paris's Costard was about as funny as an obituary notice' – *New Statesman*) and the voice he had used as a Chinese Broker's Man in *Aladdin* ('My watch said that the show only lasted two and a half hours, so I've taken it to be repaired' – *Glasgow Herald*).

Somehow they got into a game of Prisoners. Charles would capture one of the boys and only release him if he said the magic word. The secret of the game was to keep changing the magic word, making it longer and longer and sillier and sillier, in the hope (always realised) that the prisoner would be giggling too much to repeat it. Since, while the prisoner struggled to escape, the unfettered twin would be bombarding his grandfather with cushions, the game was not without hilarity.

Charles clasped his hands round Julian.

'What's the magic word?' Julian gasped.

Woomph, went a cushion from Damian into Charles's face.

'The magic word is – Ongle-bongle-boodle-boodle-boodle.'

'Ongle-bongle-boodle-giggle-giggle,' Julian repeated, wriggling free.

Damian rushed into the imprisoning arms.

'What's the magic word?'

Woomph, went a cushion from Julian into the back of Charles's neck.

'Nick-picky-wickety-pingle-pang.'

'Nicky-picky-diddle-poo-poo.' Damian snickered at his daring.

But it wasn't good enough to secure his release.

'No, you have to repeat exactly what I say,' insisted Charles.

'No, you have to repeat exactly what I say,' repeated Julian, who was catching on. As he said it, he threw a cushion, which went woomph into the side of Charles's head.

'But it's nonsense,' objected Damian.

'Even if it's nonsense. You just repeat it like a machine.'

'Even if it's nonsense. You just repeat it like a machine,' crowed Julian.

'Even if it's nonsense. You just repeat it like a machine,' agreed Damian.

'Whatever I say, you have to repeat without thinking.'

'Whatever I say, you have to repeat without thinking.'

'Whatever I say, you have to repeat without thinking.'

Like a light switched on, Charles's mind was suddenly clear. He knew what it was that had struck him as odd about Michael Banks's death. And he knew that Alex Household had not committed the murder.

'Good God! I've got it!' he shouted.

'Good God! I've got it!' shouted Julian.

'Good God! I've got it!' shouted Damian.

He was dialling when Miles and Frances came in from the kitchen.

'Sorry. Hope you don't mind my using the phone.'

'Feel free.' But Miles didn't look very pleased.

It rang for a long time, and he thought he was going to be out of luck, but eventually the receiver was picked up the other end.

'Hello.' Her voice was rather woolly.

'Lesley-Jane, it's me – Charles.'

'Charles?'

'Charles Paris.'

'Oh.' She didn't say what on earth are you ringing for; she put it all into the oh. 'Sorry, I was asleep.'

'I was glad to find you in. I thought you might be away for the weekend.'

'Yes, I was going to my parents, but I...I decided not to.'

'Listen, I've just thought of something important.'

'Oh yes.' She sounded belligerent and slightly resentful. Was he going to give her some note on performance, some idea he'd had for a new bit of business in the play? Surely it could wait till tomorrow.

'It's about Alex.'

'Oh.'

'I've just remembered something he said to me in Taunton.'

'Oh yes?'

'He said that one should always sort out a bolt-hole for oneself.'

'Well, what does that mean?'

'I thought you might know.'

'No idea.'

'What I mean is...when you were in Taunton, you were fairly discreet about your affair…I wondered where…'

'Oh, I see.'

'You said something last week about "gambolling in the countryside". Was there somewhere…'

'There was, but…'

'Where?'

'Do you think…?'

'It's a possibility. I think it's worth investigating.'

'You?'

'Why not?'

'I don't know. It just seems vindictive. The idea of bringing him to justice. Still, I suppose you could just tell the police and –'

'I wasn't thinking of bringing him to justice. I was thinking of finding out from him what actually did happen.'

'Really?'

'Yes. Tell me where it is.'

She told him. 'But I've a nasty feeling,' she concluded dismally, 'that if you do find anything there, it'll just be Alex's body.'

He put the phone down and turned round to see the whole family looking at him, open-mouthed. Juliet stood half-way down the stairs, familiarly pale. Charles's mind was working well, making connections fast. He felt confident.

'Frances,' he asked, 'do you fancy a little trip?'

'Where to?'

'Somerset.'

'When?'

'Now.'

Miles's face contorted. 'Oh really, Pop! It's a hell of a long way. You can't just do things like that, on a whim.'

'Why not?' Charles looked at Frances. 'It's your half-term, isn't it? Be good to see some real countryside. We could stay in a nice hotel.'

'But,' objected Juliet, whose every holiday was planned at least six months in advance, 'you haven't booked anywhere!'

'What do you say, Frances?'

'All right.'

Good old Frances. She wasn't where Juliet got it from either.

It was a nice hotel. On the edge of Exmoor. There was no problem booking. Indeed, after another bad summer for British tourism, they were welcomed with open arms.

They had a drink before dinner sitting in a bay window, watching dusk creep up on Dunkery Beacon. They talked a lot during dinner and then after a couple of brandies, went up to the bedroom.

It was a family room, with one double bed and one single. They sat down on the double one. Charles's hand stroked the so-familiar contours of his wife's shoulders.

'This is another of your detective things, isn't it, Charles?'

He nodded. 'Yes. Tomorrow will, I hope, be a significant day.'

'Dangerous?'

He shrugged. 'I suppose it might be. I hadn't thought. Or it might just be nothing. Me barking up yet another wrong tree.'

Frances took his hand. 'I wish you wouldn't do it, Charles. I do worry about you, you know.'

He felt closer to her than he had for years, as he tried to explain. 'It's strange. When something like a murder happens, I just feel I have to sort out what really happened. I feel…' he struggled for the right word, '…responsible.'

Frances laughed wryly. 'Responsible for anonymous corpses, but when it comes to those close to you…'

He felt suitably chastened. 'I'm sorry, Frances.' He looked out of the window at the clear night over Exmoor. 'I was thinking about that today over lunch. About you and me, about…you know, responsibility.'

'Oh yes?' It wasn't quite cynical, but nearly.

'And whether responsibility and truth are compatible. I've always found truth a problem. That's really why I left you.'

'I thought you left me for other women.'

'In a way. But it was because I needed other women, and I needed to be truthful about it. I hated all the subterfuges, I hated lying to you. At the time it seemed more truthful to make a break; then at least the position was defined. If I had left you, then I wasn't expected to be…'

'Responsible?' Frances supplied.

'I suppose so'

After London, the quiet of the country was almost tangible. 'You know, Frances, I often wonder if we could get back together.'

'So do I, Charles.' She sighed. 'But if it did happen, there are certain things I would demand.'

'You could have truth. I've always tried to be truthful to you, Frances.'

'And what about that other recurrent word…responsible?'

'Hmm.'

'There's still the matter of other women.'

'Oh, there aren't many of those now. Never have really been many who counted.'

'No?'

'No.' He sighed. 'Hasn't been anyone for months, really, Frances. I don't seem to feel the same urge to wander that I used to.'

'All right, Charles,' asked Frances softly, 'when was the last one?'

Oh dear. He had genuinely forgotten about Dottie Banks until that moment. And he had promised Frances that he would always be truthful. 'Well, last night, actually. But she didn't mean anything.'

Charles spent the night in the single bed.

CHAPTER FIFTEEN

IT MUST have taken a while from Taunton, Charles thought, as Frances drove them in the yellow Renault S along the route Lesley-Jane had described. How they ever found time to get there during Peter Hickton's intensive rehearsals, he could not imagine.

But then he remembered that Lesley-Jane and Alex had both been in the company before work on *The Hooded Owl* began. Perhaps they had discovered and used their secret love-nest during the lazier days of the summer.

He glanced sideways at Frances. He thought it might be some time before he was looking for a love-nest again with her. His wife's face was rigidly set, not with anger, which would have been easier to manage, but with hurt, which was almost impossible.

Damn Dottie Banks. And damn all the other Dottie Bankses in his life – all the quick irrelevant lays, who had a nasty habit of suddenly becoming relevant when he was with Frances.

Still, Dottie Banks had given him more than most of the others. She had sent him on the way to solving the mystery of her husband's murder.

'Not far along here,' he said. 'The North Molton road out of Withypool.'

'What are you expecting to find, Charles?'

'I don't know. I just hope it isn't another corpse.'

They drew up beside the stone-pillared farm gate which Lesley-Jane had described. Charles got out of the car. It was very muddy underfoot. Damn, he didn't have any boots. Hardly surprising. He hadn't expected a trip down to his daughter's for lunch to end up in the middle of Exmoor.

'Do I come too?' asked Frances. She looked a little less resentful than earlier, and – dare he hope it? – even slightly anxious for him.

'No, love. Stay in the car, if you don't mind.'

'All right. I have a book.'

'What are you reading?'

'*Re*reading *Anna Karenina*.'

'Oh well, that should keep you going for a little while.'

'You bet.'

'Funny, I find I'm rereading more books now. Going through my old favourites. Must be entering the last lap.'

'Don't be morbid, Charles.'

'No.' He outlined a tussock with the toe of his shoe. Now he was so close to a possible solution, he felt the urge to linger. It wasn't exactly that he was afraid; he just didn't want to leave Frances.

'Off you go then.'

'Yes. Yes...' He turned away and started trudging through the wet grass in the direction Lesley-Jane had specified.

The landscape was very empty. Charles could see why it had appealed to Alex Household. Humankind and human structures seemed a long way away. The hills rolled and folded into each other, hiding little patches of dead ground. The tall, tough grass that covered them ruffled and flattened with the wind, like a cat's fur being stroked. Disgruntled sheep with strange dye markings cropped away at the grass, glowering at Charles as he passed. Anyone who wanted to feel at one with the earth, to shed the twentieth century and all its trappings, might think that here he had achieved his ambition.

No doubt in the summer, the area would be spotted with ardently rucksacked walkers, but it was now early November, and the recent rain and cold would have deterred all but the most perverse. Given shelter, someone might pass undetected in this landscape for some time.

But he'd need a lot of shelter to survive. The cold wind scoured Charles's face and whipped his sodden trousers against his legs. He wished he had brought his overcoat.

He looked round, but the undulations seemed to have shifted, rolled into a new formation. He could not see the distinctive yellow of Frances's car. Still, there was a little stream just beyond the mound to his left. That would give him his bearings again.

He reached the top of the mound and looked down. The stream, like the hills, had moved. He now had no idea where he was.

He looked at his watch. Eleven-twenty. He had to be at the Variety Theatre in Macklin Street at seven-thirty that night for another performance of *The Hooded Owl*. If he wasn't there, he rather feared Paul Lexington might have come to the end of his understudies.

The sky was dull, with a foreboding of rain. He set off briskly in what might be the right direction, but found it difficult to get up any speed over the snagging grass.

He changed his mind, and set off in another right direction, but this offered only more hills. Over each new brow, more hills.

He tried another way, now slightly sweating from anxiety. He didn't care what he found, the car, the stream, or the hut that was the purpose of his visit. Anything that would give him his bearings again. He listened out for the trickle of water, but the wind offered nothing but rustling grass, now very loud in his ears.

Another hill-top gave on to more hills. He turned randomly at right angles, and set off at a lolloping run. His foot caught in the grass, and he sprawled headlong.

He picked himself up and breasted another mound.

Thank God. In the crease of the hills beneath him, in a channel of rushes dark like body-hair against the brightness of the grass, was the stream.

And at the bottom of the dip stood a small stone hut with a broken-backed roof.

He followed the stream down towards it. Presumably once the building had been a shepherd's hut, even his home perhaps, but it was long derelict. The thatch of what remained of the subsided roof was streaked with the dark green of lichen.

It was a dank and unwholesome spot.

And yet he could see how different it must have looked in the summer, how it would have appealed to Alex at the beginning of his supposed new start, and to Lesley-Jane in the throes of her first grown-up affair. It had what all lovers seek, secrecy, privacy, exclusivity. Charles could picture the smugness with which Alex Household would have sat in such a sanctuary and discussed the frenetic activities of the Taunton company. It was a place that offered a kind of peace.

Along the stream pale grey rocks stood exposed. Charles picked his way between them, sometimes having to clamber up, sometimes jumping from one to the other across the water.

As he drew close to the hut, a sense of dread took hold of him. Down in this hollow the sky seemed darker, the wind colder. A fine rain was now dashing against his face.

He felt he was about to find something.

And he feared it would be his friend's body.

'Alex! Alex!' he cried out, not knowing what reply he expected.

He certainly did not expect the shock of a gunshot, cutting through the sounds of the grass.

Nor the sharp impact of the bullet that shattered into the rock a yard in front of him.

Nor the fierce pain in the shin that took his leg from under him and sent him sprawling to the ground.

CHAPTER SIXTEEN

CHARLES FELT the blood trickling down his leg into his wet sock and, still keeping low behind a rock, rolled round to look at the wound.

It was a deep graze, but nothing more. He had been hit, not by the bullet, but by a sliver of quartzy rock. He would undoubtedly survive.

He lay there and thought. If Paul Lexington were describing the situation, he would undoubtedly have said that he had some good news and some bad news. The good news was that Charles's conjecture must have been correct: Alex must be in the hut. The bad news was that Alex had a gun and was shooting at him.

Charles raised his head above the line of the rock and looked down towards the hut. Immediately another shot cracked from the doorway and ricochetted off a rock a couple of yards to his right.

He ducked back.

But after a moment's thought he popped his head up again. It was immediately answered by another shot, which hit a rock behind him.

He lay back down and squinted round. There weren't that many rocks. Certainly not enough to afford shelter for him to get nearer the hut.

But he read another significance into their scarcity. Alex had fired three shots at him from about twenty yards. Each one had missed by at least a yard. But each one had actually hit one of the few rocks scattered around.

Surely that wasn't just bad shooting. A bad shot would have sprayed bullets all over the place, hitting rocks or earth at random. Only someone who was after the maximum deterrent effect would have ensured that each shot hit a rock and caused that terrible screech of ricochet.

In other words, Alex was not shooting to hit him.

Well, it was a theory.

And Charles didn't have many others. From where he was lying, he could neither go forwards nor backwards without exposing himself as a target. So, unless he planned to lie there until nightfall, which would rule out any possibility of his getting up to town to give his evening's performance, he had to make a move.

Besides, his whole thesis, the whole reason why he was there was that he didn't believe Alex Household capable of actually shooting anyone.

He stood up.

A bullet hit a rock three yards in front of him. Confirming his theory.

'Alex, I'm coming down.' He stepped forward.

It seemed a long, long walk.

But only one more bullet was fired.

It screamed away from a rock behind him.

When he finally reached the doorway of the hut, he could see Alex Household slumped against it, the arm holding the gun limp at his side.

Had he not known who to expect, he would not have recognised his friend. Through its beard and filth, the face was sunken and ghastly. The eyes flickered feverishly like guttering candles. From the hut came the nauseating stench of human excrement.

'Alex.'

'Charles, you shouldn't have come.' Alex Household shivered and the words tumbled out unevenly.

'I'm your friend.'

'J-j-j-judas was a friend,' the filthy skeleton managed to say. 'Why not just let me take my chance? If the police find me, that's one thing. But for you to make the trip just to turn me in…'

'I haven't come to turn you in.'

'Of course you have. Don't pretend. You all think I'm a murderer.' The old light of paranoia showed in the feverish eyes.

'No,' said Charles. 'I know that you didn't shoot Michael Banks.'

'What?' Alex Household's body suddenly sagged. He slipped down the door-post to the ground. When Charles knelt to support him, he saw tears in the sick man's eyes.

'You're ill, Alex.'

The shaggy head nodded, and then was shaken by a burst of vomiting.

'When did you last eat?'

'I'd left some stuff here. From the summer. Tins and…With the gun, too. This place was always my last line of defence, when they – when they came to get me…' Again the paranoia gleamed. 'But I finished all the food…I don't know, two days ago, three. Of course, I still had water from the stream, and then…the earth's plenty…' He gestured feebly around at the hillside.

'You mean grass and…'

Alex nodded. 'Yes, but it…' He made a noise that might have been a giggle in happier circumstances '…made me ill. Ill.' He retched again.

'I must get you to a doctor. Quickly.'

Alex shook his head. 'No, Charles, please. Just let me die here. It's easier.'

'What do you mean?'

'I can't spend my life in some prison. If I'm alive, I need to be free.'

'But you will be.'

'No, Charles. Everyone thinks I killed Micky Banks. Go on, be truthful. They do, don't they?'

He couldn't help admitting it. 'But I know you didn't, Alex.'

'Clever old you.' This was accompanied by the weakest of smiles. 'What do you think happened then?'

'I'll tell you. Stop me when I'm wrong.'

'Oh, I will, Charles. I will.'

'This is what I think happened that night. I'll grant you were in a bad state, which was hardly surprising after all the business with losing your part and then Lesley-Jane going off with Micky – incidentally, there was less in that than you thought, but that's by the way. O.K., so you had all the motives, you even had the gun, but you didn't do it.

'The gun stayed in the pocket of your jacket in the Green Room until well into the second act. It was taken from there by the murderer, while you were still in the wings, in your shirt-sleeves, feeding Micky his lines through the deaf-aid. The murderer came into the wings with the gun and with the firm intention of shooting someone.

'But this is the bit that took me longest to work out. It's been screaming at me for days, but I just couldn't see it.

'The murderer had no intention of shooting Micky Banks. You were the target.'

'When you saw the gun pointing at you, you realised the murderer's intention and begged for mercy. *You* said, 'Oh Lord! No. No, put it down. You mustn't do that to me. You daren't. Please. Please…' I should have realised that from the fact that Micky said "Oh Lord" – an expression incidentally, that wasn't in the script of the play and that he had never used in his life – *before* he turned round from the Hooded Owl and looked into the wings. So it wasn't a reaction from him. He was merely relaying what he heard over his deaf-aid.

'I should have realised it earlier. I've been working with the deaf-aid for over a week, for God's sake, and I realised how much I rely on it. When you're using it, you just repeat the words you hear, regardless of the sense. I got caught last week because I got fed the wrong line. Even if it's nonsense, you still repeat it.

'Which is what Micky Banks did. He just kept repeating what you were saying. He knew there was something odd, which was why he turned round to look into the wings, hoping for some signal from you.

'By then I reckon you had your back to the stage and were facing the barrel of the gun. At the moment the murderer squeezed the trigger, you threw yourself sideways, the bullet missed you, but hit Micky Banks, who was standing directly behind you.

'You then looked round in shock to see him fall. At that moment Lesley-Jane saw your face – she told me you "looked over your shoulder at her", but I didn't at the time realise that meant you must have been facing away from the stage. Anyway, Lesley-Jane jumped to the conclusion that everyone else has since jumped to – that you shot Micky – and screamed.

'The murderer was meanwhile standing, shocked at what had happened, but still holding the gun. Rather than risk the danger of another shot, you followed your natural instinct to run. You grabbed your jacket from the Green Room and rushed out of the theatre.

'It was probably only when you got outside that you realised how much circumstances looked against you. All your recurrent fears of the world ganging up on you came to the surface, and you ran away. Somehow you got down here, where you have been since, quietly starving and poisoning yourself to death.

'After you had gone, the murderer went backstage, abandoning the gun on the way. The hue and cry started for you, but you could not be found. Rumours spread that you had committed suicide. This was all good news for the murderer. So long as you didn't reappear, or if, when you did reappear, you were dead, there was no danger of the police looking for any other killer.

'The accidental shooting of Michael Banks must have been a shock, but, as time passed, the murderer must have begun to feel very secure from the danger of discovery.'

Charles looked at Alex's haggard face, which now glowed with a new light. 'How'm I doing so far?'

'Bloody marvellous, Charles. That's exactly what happened.' A shadow passed over his face. 'But how you're ever going to convince anyone else that's what happened, I don't know...'

'If we explain to the police.'

Alex shook his head. 'Come on, Charles. The police are not notorious for their imagination. Everything is stacked against me, you have to admit. I bet the gun was even covered in my fingerprints.''

Charles had to admit that it was.

'So *I* know. And now, thanks to a very neat bit of deduction, *you* know. But I don't see that either of us could produce a shred of evidence to support our extremely unlikely thesis, so I don't see that we're much further advanced. If I give myself up, I'll be charged with murder.'

'Hmm,' said Charles. 'Then what I'll have to do is to get a confession from the real murderer.'

Alex snorted hopelessly. 'Good luck.'

'I think it may be possible. And that, of course,' said Charles, 'brings me to the identity of the real murderer.

'Very difficult to work that out at first. So long as I was looking for someone who might want to murder Michael Banks, I was getting nowhere. But once I got the right victim, finding the right murderer became easier.'

'Who do you think it was then?' asked Alex. Charles told him.

'Dead right,' said Alex.

Charles looked a mess when he got back to the car, but Frances made no comment. Nor did she mention the fact that she'd been sitting there for nearly three hours.

'How's *Anna Karenina*?'

'Fine. She is now living with Vronsky as if they were married.'

'Good for her. Mind you, it'll end in tears.'

'And how are you?'

'Fine.'

'Anything I can do for you?'

'There are three things, actually.'

'Name them and I'll see if I can help.'

'Right. First, I would like you to drive me to Taunton, so that I can catch a train back to London, in order to be at the Variety Theatre this evening for – among other things – a performance of *Th e Hooded Owl*.'

'That's possible.'

'Second, I want you to buy blankets, food, a portable heater and some sort of stomach medicine, and come back here.'

'Right here?'

'Yes. Then I want you to follow instructions I will give you to a small derelict hut, where you will find a very sick man, who needs looking after.'

'Shouldn't I get a doctor too?'

'No. Not for the moment. I promised him I wouldn't involve anyone official until I've...sorted something out for him.'

'And how long am I likely to have to play Florence Nightingale? When will you have sorted this something out for him?'

'I'll do it tonight. Then I'll let the emergency services know and someone will come out for him.'

'I see. Well, that sounds a jolly way to spend a half-term. And, if I may ask, what was the third thing?'

'To give me another chance.'

'Oh, Charles,' said Frances sadly, 'I'm not so sure about that.'

CHAPTER SEVENTEEN

THE TRAIN from Taunton was delayed. It was after the 'half' when Charles arrived at the Variety Theatre. The business of getting into costume and make-up and then giving his performance as the father in Malcolm Harris's *The Hooded Owl* meant that details like confrontations with murderers would have to wait.

He was on stage for most of the first act, and it was only when the curtain fell for the interval that he could concentrate on anything other than the play.

As soon as he walked into the Green Room, he knew that something was wrong. Actors and actresses, who spend all their professional lives creating fictional atmospheres, do not stint themselves when real opportunities come along.

'What's up?' he asked Salome Search, who was draped over a sofa doing Mrs. Siddons impressions.

'It's Lesley-Jane,' the actress breathed dramatically.

'What? What's happened to her?'

'She passed out in the wings after her last exit.'

'Good God!'

'Yes, she was in a dead faint.'

'Where is she?'

'She's been taken up to her dressing room. The St. John Ambulance man's up there with her.'

'Do you know what it is?'

'No. But...' Salome Search's three years at R.A.D.A. had taught her that the pause before a sensational line can be extended almost infinitely. 'There was blood in the wings.'

'Oh, my God!' Charles turned towards the Green Room door and the stairs to the dressing rooms.

But the doorway was blocked by the figure of Wallas Ward, holding up limp hands for attention.

'Ladies and gentlemen,' said the Company Manager, 'you may already have heard that Miss Decker was taken ill at the end of the first act. It seems that she will not be well enough to proceed with the rest of the play, and so her understudy will be taking over the role. Now it's not going to be easy for the girl, so I hope you will give her all the support you can. I will be making an announcement to the audience before the curtain rises.'

'Is she all right?' asked Charles desperately.

'Yes, she's fine. Just weak. We've rung for her mother who's going to come and take her home. The St. John Ambulance man doesn't reckon she needs to go to the hospital.'

'What's wrong with her? Do you know?'

The Company Manager looked embarrassed. 'Women's things,' he said with distaste.

'Is she on her own up there?'

'No, the St. John Ambulance man's still there. And Paul went to see what was up. Oh, and I think Malcolm Harris was one of the ones who helped her up. He may still be up there. So she's got plenty of people.'

'I think I'd better go up and see her.'

But before he could, the Company Manager stopped him with an admonitory 'Incidentally, Mr. Paris…'

'Yes?'

'I gather you were late for the "half" tonight.'

'Yes. I was in a train that got delayed.'

'Where were you coming from?'

'Taunton.'

Wallas Ward tutted, spinster-like. 'Mr. Paris, you should have left more time. While you are contracted for a West End show, it is very irresponsible to go such a long way. In fact, I wouldn't be surprised if there were a clause in your contract forbidding that kind of journey on a performance day. Remember, you are under contract to Scenario Productions and –'

'I thought I was under contract to Paul Lexington Productions.'

'No, Paul is now working through a new company.'

'Why?'

'That is not at the moment relevant,' reprimanded the Company Manager. 'I am talking about your lateness for the "half".'

'Yes, all right. Well, I'm very sorry. Won't do it again. Now if you'd -'

'And another thing,' Wallas Ward continued inexorably. 'The lines in the first act were very sloppy this evening. I had a note from Malcolm Harris who was out front and was very annoyed about it. You got badly lost in the dinner party scene.'

'Yes, that was because Lesley-Jane was giving me the wrong cues. Her lines were all over the place tonight.'

'Yes, Malcolm Harris mentioned that, too. Presumably that was because she was unwell. But in your case, when you have every line being repeated in your ear, it's unforgivable.'

'But if you get the wrong cues, you have to adjust the lines to make sense of the dialogue.'

'That's as may be, but Malcolm Harris said –'

'Look, come on. Every author is obsessed about his lines. You don't have to –'

'It is my job as Company Manager,' said Wallas Ward primly, 'to listen to points from everyone in the company and the author is just as important as –'

'I would have thought it was also important for you to keep the author informed of everything that's going on. Do you know, on the first night, Malcolm Harris didn't know about the cuts we'd had to make for time. He thought Micky Banks was just randomly slashing great chunks out of his script.'

'I agree. He should have been told. And he was extremely annoyed that evening when he came round at the interval. But I pointed out to him that Mr. Banks was not making cuts himself – he was merely repeating the lines he heard in his earphone.'

'And you said that Alex was reading from a cut script?'

'I didn't have time to do that. Mr. Harris rushed off in something of a paddy.'

'I've got to get upstairs and see Lesley-Jane!' hissed Charles.

Wallas Ward stepped aside with mock-deference.

But as soon as his foot was on the first step of the stairs, Charles heard the fatal summons over the loudspeaker.

'Beginners, Act Two, please.'

He froze. It was rarely that he felt such a direct clash between his twin roles as actor and detective.

But there was no doubt which triumphed. Thirty-two years of professional conditioning left him no alternative.

He turned round and walked towards the stage.

The father was on for the whole of the second act of *The Hooded Owl* and never had that part of the play passed as slowly as it did that evening. Mechanically going through the motions, repeating his words, hardly aware of the small Monday night audience, hardly aware of the new girl hesitantly feeding him Lesley-Jane's lines, he was in an agony of apprehension throughout the performance.

But he had to play his part through to the end.

The end of the play, one curtain-call, and then, sod it, he'd risk another slap on the wrist from the arch Mr. Ward. He rushed offstage and up to Lesley-Jane's dressing room.

He tapped on the door and entered.

There were four people inside.

And one of them was Michael Banks's murderer.

Lesley-Jane lay on the daybed in her kimono. She was drained of all colour and animation, but alive.

Her mother, Valerie Cass, was busying herself, packing things into a small overnight case.

Paul Lexington (now of Scenario Productions) was looking at Lesley-Jane anxiously and asking if he should arrange an ambulance.

Malcolm Harris sat disconsolately in a chair, chewing his fingernails.

'No, for the last time, she'll be quite all right,' said Valerie Cass, in reply to Paul. She looked round to see Charles. 'Oh, not another man. Really. Just leave us alone, will you, all of you? Lesley-Jane's quite all right now I'm here. Only a woman can understand what's wrong, and there's nothing any of you could do. So thank you for your concern, but will you now please go.'

'Look, we're worried about her,' grumbled Malcolm Harris.

'If you don't want me to call an ambulance, I'll drive her to the hospital, if you like,' offered Paul Lexington.

'No, thank you very much. We needn't involve hospitals.'

'I think she should be seen by a doctor,' the Producer insisted. 'Look, I'm employing her. I have to know how long she's likely to be out of commission.'

'Oh, I should think she'd be all right,' said Charles. And then, deciding that it was time to start dropping bombshells, 'Some actresses have continued acting well into the eighth month of pregnancy.'

He should have realised it before, but it was only when he had seen Juliet that the obvious had appeared in all its blatancy. The same strained paleness. Even the detail of needing a sleep in the afternoon.

Lesley-Jane herself was the only one who didn't react. The two men looked at him open-mouthed. But Valerie Cass's response was the most interesting. She turned to Charles with an almost beatific expression and said, 'Well done. Yes, the little secret is out. I am to become a grandmother.'

To say 'Congratulations' somehow seemed inappropriate. Instead, he asked cautiously, 'Even after tonight?'

'Oh yes,' replied Valerie with breezy gynaecological certainty. 'That was just a little "show". Lesley-Jane will be fine if she just rests up for a few days. Exactly the same thing happened to me at the same stage when I was pregnant.'

'I...um...think I'd better be off,' said Malcolm Harris awkwardly.

Charles stood aside, and let him go.

Paul Lexington also looked embarrassed. 'Well, of course, this will affect her availability for the show.'

'As I say, only for a few days. Then she'll be fine. It'll be a good three months before she shows, and, with skilful dressing, she could go on a lot longer.'

'But,' said Charles, 'It's going to curtail her theatrical career a bit, isn't it?'

'Oh no.' Valerie Cass looked at him radiantly. 'I've got it all worked out. I will be able to look after the baby. Lesley-Jane's career will be hardly interrupted. No, no, my little girl's talent will still take her right to the top.'

The prospect realised Valerie Cass's most exotic dreams. Her daughter would be perpetually in her debt, perpetually chained to her, and she would have the new stimulus of another baby to bring up. Best of all, there would be no father around to challenge her supremacy over either her child or her grandchild.

'Hmm,' grunted Paul Lexington. 'I still think she should see a doctor.'

'I'll get our family doctor to take a look at her in the morning. There – will that satisfy you?'

'I suppose it'll have to. Let me know what the prospects are.'

'I will.'

Paul Lexington moved towards the door.

Charles stood aside, and let him go.

'Well, now, Charles. As you see, everything is fine. I'm now going to take my little baby home. So there's nothing to keep you here.'

'Oh, but there is,' said Charles. 'I want to talk about Alex Household.'

'I can't think what relevance he has to anything.'

'Can't you? He's the child's father.'

'As I say, I can't think what relevance he has to anything.' In those words Valerie Cass expressed everything she felt about the relationship between the sexes.

'You think the father is irrelevant?'

'Yes. It's the woman who carries the child, the woman who does the work, the man does nothing.'

Charles restrained his anger, and started on a new tack. 'It was on the first night that Lesley-Jane told you she was pregnant.'

Valerie Cass was silent, surprised by the change of direction. 'She told you Alex was the father, and suddenly you saw the awful vision of history repeating itself. You saw Lesley-Jane's career being cut short by pregnancy, just as yours had been. And all your hatred of men, all the anger you have used to make your own husband's life a misery, it all became focused on Alex Household. Not only did he threaten your daughter's career, he also threatened to take her away from you.'

Valerie Cass now looked as pale as her daughter. 'I don't know what you're talking about.'

'I'm talking about the death of Michael Banks. I'm talking about the taking of human life. I'm talking about murder.'

There was a wail from the bed and, for the first time since Charles had entered the room, Lesley-Jane spoke. 'I have taken human life,' she cried. 'I am the murderer!'

They both looked at her in amazement. Tears were running freely down the girl's face. She clutched at herself to claw away a sudden pain.

Charles understood. He hadn't known until that moment, but now he understood. 'But the life you have taken,' he said gently, 'was not that of Michael Banks. Was it?'

The girl shook her head tearfully.

'No, the life you have taken is the life of your baby. You had an abortion today, didn't you?'

She nodded.

'Which is why you passed out. Why you are in this state now.'

'No!' screamed Valerie Cass. 'No, you didn't!' Lesley-Jane looked at her mother. The tears were receding and there was a hardness in her eyes.

But Valerie refused to believe their message. 'It's a woman's sacred duty to bear children. That's what we were put here for.'

'Listen, Mummy.' Lesley-Jane had control of herself again and spoke evenly. 'The child effectively had no father.'

'But it would have had you. And me.'

'I didn't want it. I got pregnant because you spent all my life filling my head with romantic ideas rather than giving me any practical advice. If I had had the baby, I would never have been able to pick up my career again.'

'But as I said, I would have looked after it.'

'What?' hissed Lesley-Jane. 'And turned it into another confused, neurotic mess like me?'

'But, darling, suppose I had done the same when I was expecting you? Suppose I had had an abortion?'

Lesley-Jane looked at her mother without any trace of affection. 'It would have been the best thing you could ever have done for me. Someone like you is not qualified to bring up children.'

Valerie Cass sank back into a chair as if she had been slapped. There was no resistance left in her, just a void of pain.

Charles said what he had to say, softly but firmly.

'What you did after you heard about your daughter's pregnancy was hardly rational. You went down towards the stage, vowing revenge on her...her what?...seducer? You looked for him in the Green Room, but found only his jacket. In its pocket you found the gun.

'You went into the wings on the O.P. side of the stage to shoot Alex Household. He saw you coming and begged for mercy, not realising that his words were being transmitted and repeated by Michael Banks on stage. At the moment you fired the gun, Alex dodged, and Michael was killed.

'Alex rushed off. You left the stage, abandoning the gun as you went. Then I should think you came up here, and that was probably the first time you realised what had happened. Also the first time you realised how unlikely your crime was ever to be discovered. No one had seen you, you were wearing gloves so there were no fingerprints on the gun, and Alex Household's flight looked like an admission of guilt.

'If he had never been found, you'd have got away with it. But I spoke to Alex today, and he confirmed what I've just described to you.'

'He's alive?' asked Lesley-Jane softly.

'Yes, he's alive.'

There was a long silence. Then Valerie Cass looked at Charles. There was a new glow of resolution in her eyes, and he feared she was about to deny everything. If she did, he didn't know what he would do; he had not a shred of evidence.

But no.

'Very well,' she announced. 'I admit it. I killed Michael Banks.' She spoke boldly, like Charlotte Corday, like Joan of Arc. Charles understood what had caused her new surge of spirit.

Valerie Cass had found a new role to play. It was the one she had been rehearsing for all her life – that of martyr.

CHAPTER EIGHTEEN

DURING THE ensuing week, *The Hooded Owl* seemed to be gaining momentum. The audiences were growing almost imperceptibly, and the word-of-mouth was good. One or two of the national papers, feeling guilty about the show's first night, sent second-string critics along for a second look, and their reports were, on the whole, favourable.

The performances gained in strength. On the Thursday, Lesley-Jane Decker came back into the cast. After the abortion and her mother's arrest, she seemed to have matured. She approached her work with a new single-mindedness, and acted better than ever.

Charles Paris got better, too. On the Tuesday night, as an experiment, without telling anyone (least of all Wallas Ward), he had a word with the A.S.M. before the show, and asked him not to feed the lines until absolutely necessary. To Charles's amazement, he managed to get through the whole show without a single prompt. The constant repetition had fixed the lines indelibly in his mind.

The loss of this crutch did not, as he had feared, diminish his confidence. Instead, it made him feel more relaxed, stronger, more in control. And he knew this improvement was reflected in his acting.

He also came to rely less on drink. He had proved he could give a performance without it, and, though it frightened him to remove another support, he dared another night without his customary stimulus. To his surprise, he found his head was clearer, his concentration better, and his nerves no worse. He repeated the experiment on subsequent nights, and felt better for it. He'd still wind down with a couple of large Bell's, but he got out of the habit of drinking before the show.

He also spoke to his agent, and the company Equity representative, and finally to Paul Lexington direct, about his unsatisfactory status in the play, acting the part regularly and being paid only as an understudy. The producer, probably already under pressure from Equity, and unwilling to take on the expense of another star, agreed that he would regularise the position as soon as possible.

So, for a couple of weeks, *The Hooded Owl* soldiered on in the West End. Everyone knew the early weeks would be tense. Like a sick baby, a show has to be carefully nursed until it can build up its own strength.

But *The Hooded Owl* seemed to be winning the fight for survival. The audiences in the second week after Valerie Cass's arrest were definitely getting bigger, and their reaction more positively approving. At this rate the production should soon reach the break-even point its budget required.

A few coach parties started to come. Soon the show would be an established signpost in the Entertainments columns of the newspapers, and begin to run on its own momentum.

When the company was summoned to a meeting on stage at the 'half' on the Friday of that week, they expected some sort of announcement of how near they were to their break-even. The signs were good. They had been running for nearly a month and were gaining strength daily.

They were in for a disappointment.

Wallas Ward clapped his limp hands for silence, and began without Paul Lexington's ambivalent opening.

'Ladies and gentlemen, I am afraid I have some bad news.

'As you know, today is the day you should be paid. Since the money goes to your agents in most cases, you won't yet have noticed anything wrong. But I'm afraid I have to tell you that no money has been sent to your agents.'

He raised his hands again to still the outcry which this provoked.

'Ladies and gentlemen, I am sorry, but it appears that there is no money anywhere in this show. The production company has gone bankrupt.'

The screams of fury which greeted this finally resolved themselves into one question: Where was Paul Lexington?

'I am sorry, ladies and gentlemen, but I cannot answer that. Not for any reason of discretion or protecting him; the fact is, I do not know where Paul Lexington is. He hasn't been seen round the theatre for two days and, when I spoke to his landlord this afternoon, I discovered that he had left his flat yesterday, taking all his belongings and owing three months' rent.'

In fact, not to put too fine a point on it, Paul Lexington had done a bunk. Living up to another stereotype of the theatrical producer, though not usually the sort of producer who reached the heights of the West End.

So that was it.

'As a result, ladies and gentlemen,' the Company Manager concluded unctuously, 'I regret to inform you that the notices will go up tonight. We will do the two performances tomorrow, because of advance bookings, but I'm afraid otherwise, that is the end.'

So it was that, after three and a half weeks at the Variety Theatre, *The Hooded Owl* by Malcolm Harris closed.

'Could I speak to Gerald Venables, please? It's Charles Paris speaking.'

'I'll put you through.'

'Charles! Sorry to hear about the show. I'm afraid that Paul Lexington was a bad lot.'

'To put it mildly.'

'Indeed. As you know, I'm trying to sort out Bobby Anscombe's end, and it's only now I'm beginning to see the full extent of the mess. Lexington owed money everywhere. God knows how he got as far as he did. So far as I can see, once Bobby was out, he was running the production on sheer cheek.'

'That was one thing he didn't lack.'

'No. He seems to have kept going for a while by constantly starting up new companies and borrowing on them, but quite honestly it's going to be some time before everything's crawled out of the woodwork and I can get a clear picture.'

'What'll happen to him?'

'I don't know. I doubt if he'll get prosecuted unless one of his creditors decides to make the effort. He hasn't got any assets – apart from the fact that he's vanished off the face of the earth – so there's not a lot of point in suing him. That's what I'm going to advise Bobby.'

'He seemed so plausible.'

'Of course he did. To all of you in the company. He always said what you wanted to hear. He painted in your dreams for you.'

'Yes.'

'Trouble is, he was really out of his league. Trying to tangle with the big boys like Bobby. And Denis Thornton was ripping him off, too.'

'Was he?'

'Oh yes. Lanthorn Productions only took on the show because they didn't want the Variety Theatre dark.'

'Really?'

'Yes. They just wanted a show in there, because they'd acquired the lease and wanted to demonstrate that it could still work as a theatre.'

'But I thought *The Hooded Owl* was going to be their big opening.'

'No, no. That's going to be a revival of *Flower Drum Song* in March. Been planned for months.'

'But if *The Hooded Owl* had run, we'd still have been there in March.'

'Denis Thornton knew it wouldn't run. He's a wily old bird. Best thing that happened for him when Paul agreed to let Show-Off do the publicity. Since they're part of Lanthorn, Denis could control how much coverage your show got.'

'You mean he deliberately limited our publicity?'

'Ooh, mustn't say that. Might be slander. Let's just say that most of Show-Off's energies during the week of your opening went into Lanthorn Productions' new musical at the King's.'

'But surely that's criminal?'

'Tut, tut, you mustn't use words like that, Charles. When you've been dealing with theatre managements as long as I have, you come to realise that there's a very thin dividing line between skilful dealing and what you choose to call crime. Paul Lexington wasn't sufficiently experienced, so he ended up the wrong side of that line.'

'Hmm. I wonder what'll happen to him.'

'Well, I think it'll be a long time before he surfaces in the West End again. The Society of West End Theatre Managers'll see to that.'

'Yes, but I've somehow a feeling he'll pop up again somewhere. That sort always finds someone new to believe them.'

'True. Incidentally, Charles, Kate was saying the other day what a long time it is since we've seen you, and wouldn't it be nice if you could come over for dinner one of these evenings. I said it'd be difficult because you d got the show, but now of course...'

'Yes. Sounds great.'

'With Frances, of course. I mean, I gathered at that first night that you were back together again. You are, aren't you?'

'Well...er...not exactly.'

So what happened to them all in the weeks running up to Christmas?

Valerie Cass was convicted of killing Michael Banks, but the charge, to which she readily confessed, was manslaughter, and she was sentenced to three years in prison.

Lesley-Jane Decker landed a very good part in a television series about the Bloomsbury Group, which guaranteed her six months' work and national recognition when the show hit the screens. She also, in her mother's absence, got to know her father for the first time, and found she got on with him very well.

Alex Household spent two weeks in hospital and, when he came out, decided to give up acting and join a monastery dedicated to a pantheistic view of the universe.

Peter Hickton kept his cast up most nights rehearsing for the Prince's Theatre, Taunton's, annual pantomime, *Babes in the Wood*, in which Salome Search played a somewhat gnarled principal boy.

Paul Lexington, from his new base in Hull, set up a company called Pierre Productions, whose aim was to put Northern club comics into end-of-the-pier summer seasons.

Malcolm Harris, who had received no money from the production of *The Hooded Owl* except for the pittance of the long-lapsed option, went back to his school teaching. In his evenings he worked on a play about Mary, Queen of Scots, because his wife's mother had read somewhere that costume drama was coming back.

Dottie Banks continued to entertain a stream of men in Hans Crescent. Then, to everyone's surprise, she died of a drug overdose on Christmas Eve. She must have missed her husband more than she showed.

George Birkitt received the first scripts for a new series of *Fly-Buttons* and sent them back to the producer, complaining that his character hadn't got enough lines. He also opened two supermarkets, which pleased him greatly, suggesting as it did that people were starting to think of him as a star.

Wallas Ward met a very nice black dancer at a party and settled down with him in Pimlico.

Frances Paris had an offer on the house in Muswell Hill. It was two thousand less than the asking price, but, because the housing market was depressed, and on the advice of her son-in-law, she accepted it.

And Charles Paris? He got drunk.

Lightning Source UK Ltd.
Milton Keynes UK
UKOW041126031212

203110UK00001B/183/A